Etched in Granite

A Historical Novel

Mj Pettengill

I dedicate this book to my children, Miles, Shelby, and Anna.

~ Perfectus Quidem Amor ~

Acknowledgements

THIS BOOK WOULD not have been possible without the paupers buried anonymously beneath 298 numbered granite stones. They beckoned me to look beyond the numbers. At the beginning of this journey, their names were absent and lost to future generations. The identities of many of the transients, laborers, and farmers have finally been restored. The sum and substance of their lives is an integral part of the fabric of our complex social history. We can learn from them.

I am grateful for Mrs. Lewis, grave number 140, listed in the town records as a pauper, a 100-year-old "Indian" woman. In this story her birth name is Nanatasis, and her Christian name is Nellie Baldwin, after my own great-grandmother, another old "Indian" woman of the same era. Her memories were brought to life through the stories told to us by my Aunt Irene.

Thank you, Nellie and my Abenaki ancestors. I honor the fallen and those who were able to preserve sacred traditions and maintain the integrity of our indigenous roots, while surviving the intended systematic elimination of their people and customs. Not only did researching and writing this book present the opportunity to strengthen my connection to our family roots, it was also the beginning of reclaiming ancient healing practices.

I have many people to thank. First, I would like to thank my editor, Mariel Brewster, for her expertise and insight. For the powerful image on the front cover and for my portrait, photographer and friend, Brenda Ladd; Brian Height for his technical assistance in formatting the cover; the clerks in the Ossipee Town Hall for permitting access to the records in the vault; Alan Richardson and Shelby Trevor for their valued feedback; and DW Cooper for his reliability and ongoing support.

Finally, I express my deepest gratitude to my mentor and professor, Richard O. Hathaway. Under his guidance, I completed the academic research of *Etched in Granite* – my culminating study at Vermont College. He encouraged me to think broadly and deeply about this study, which he fondly referred to as a "monster project." He inspired me to reach beyond what was expected. He didn't simply believe that I could do this – he knew I could. I honor him for this.

Preface

ON A DREARY March afternoon in the quiet town of Ossipee, New Hampshire, I encountered a place that would forever change me. Sprawled out in long, meandering rows on a snow-covered hillside, were 298 numbered gravestones. When I learned that this was a county pauper cemetery, I was inspired to discover who lie in the earth beneath the shadowy graves. I decided that this would be the subject of my culminating study at Vermont College.

Initially, I was advised by several people not to bother with my research because the records burned in a fire. Although I have lived in Carroll County and in other parts of the state for most of my life, I faced resistance. I was new to the Ossipee region and was considered to be an outsider. My questions raised suspicion, and many others had little or no interest in the paupers. Meeting with these obstacles fueled my own fires. I had no choice but to follow my instincts and unveil a somber truth.

My research led to a comprehensive, painstaking account of life in rural New Hampshire in the late 19th century, which carries with it dramatic lessons about a nation torn by the devastation of a civil war and economic depression. I quickly realized that this significant part of our past was essentially omitted from traditional history books.

Some of us may have heard references made to the *Poor Farm* in jest, but we do not comprehend the depth of its meaning. I believe that it's worth knowing what it meant to be a pauper in the late 19th century and what it means today. It's a part of our story.

Following the days of auctioning off the poor to the lowest bidder (yes, the lowest bidder), came the 19ᵗʰ century county poor farm. Sometimes known as almshouses or poorhouses, these farms were large complexes intended for people of all ages, character, and circumstances, to be housed together, resulting in wretched conditions.

Contrary to what we may have heard, a poorhouse was not a debtor's prison. A person with debt, but able to meet his needs and the needs of his family, would not be required to go to the poorhouse. The plight of the paupers was affected by the unsustainability of a rural, post war society. When they became a burden on the community, it was the county poor farm that offered relief. Their crimes were that of poverty, old age, vagrancy, mental and physical disabilities, being orphaned, or being pregnant and unwed.

I focused primarily on the life and death of the paupers, also referred to as inmates. The question that continued to motivate me was, "What did it mean to be a pauper?" However, in order to fully comprehend the complex nature of the county poor farm, it was necessary to expand my investigation to include a cross section of others associated with the institution, such as overseers, workers, townspeople, the religious community, and those who found relief at the facility by checking in voluntarily during hard times. From their multi-faceted perspectives, I was afforded a glimpse into the foundation of America's current welfare system.

Ongoing societal change, reform, and local and state laws brought about many changes within the county farm complex. Separate institutions such as hospitals, correctional facilities, orphanages, nursing homes, and agricultural extensions emerged. The roles of charitable and religious organizations regarding the poor and disadvantaged were redefined, bringing about the field of social work, which was and has continued to be invaluable in promoting quality care, adequate placement, and the protection of human rights.

In New England, many of the aforementioned facilities are situated on the very same grounds as the original county farms and are somewhat, if not completely, operational. Some of the historic buildings currently standing are partially or fully renovated, and they serve a variety of functions, while other buildings are crumbling. In many cases the land is used for local agriculture, community action programs, and working farms in connection with correctional facilities.

When you see a sign marked "County Farm Road," it is certain to lead to a current or past site of a county farm dating back to the 19th century. We do not deny the existence of these farms, but what we know about them are merely remnants of information scribbled in handwritten records, yellowed newspaper articles, fragments of dwindling stories passed down from our elders, or what we have read in popular Victorian literature. The paupers themselves are no longer visible.

After careful thought and deliberation, I decided that *Etched in Granite* would be a work of historical fiction. The personal narratives of three individuals with diverse backgrounds and connections to the Poor Farm are woven together to tell a story of tragedy, courage, and lost love. Any resemblance to real people is coincidental.

The narrators are: Abigail Hodgdon, a young woman who through unexpected events becomes an inmate at the Poor Farm; Nellie Baldwin, an Abenaki Elder and healer who shares her rich story of immigration from Northern Vermont to New Hampshire during a time of racial intolerance; and Silas Putnam, a young farm boss and the object of Abigail's affection. He offers a male perspective, illuminating the administrative or "other" side and how being in a position of authority often brings conflict.

The aftermath of the Civil War is clearly defined in this story, as both Abigail's and Silas's fathers served together in the 6th New Hampshire Volunteer Infantry. Like so many others, Abigail's family endured the loss of the male head of the household when her father was killed, and Silas's father returned home with a wooden leg, an affinity for whiskey, and Post-Traumatic Stress Disorder.

Although veterans received pensions and had access to rest homes, the casualties of war left many orphaned and widowed. A substantial number of those who survived returned home with physical and emotion wounds, unable to sustain a healthy, functioning family unit. These conditions resulted in insurmountable stress on the family structure, leaving it both economically and emotionally unstable for generations, adding to the ongoing burden of pauperism and general dysfunction.

My experience as a Civil War Music Historian was of great worth. The research required to ensure a historically correct performance, sifting through archives and participating in living historical events, broadened my comprehension of the era, providing insight into details that may not have been included.

The process of gathering information, opening a dialogue, and sharing the names of the paupers, is a story in itself. I became keenly aware of the collective fear and shame regarding the secrets of our past. I believe that acknowledgment and acceptance bring healing.

To preserve the integrity of native language and dialect, a handful of Abenaki terms are used throughout the narrative. A glossary is provided.

It is my mission to give voices to those silenced, to evoke images where they have been erased, and to replace numbers with names. During the early stage of exploration, I discovered the identities of more than 260 souls. They are listed at the end of this book.

CHAPTER 1

Abigail Elizabeth Hodgdon – June 30, 1872 Ossipee, New Hampshire

THE THICK, GREY stones hid like timid children in the field beyond Papa's grave and the splintered fence. Quite void of spirit and life, they went almost unnoticed, yet they begged for attention.

I pressed up against the giant white pine, grippin' the rough, swirly bark with my red stained fingertips. My mouth went dry as I peered through the tight curl that encircled my eye like a monocle. I strained to hear a man's voice over the gravedigger's shovel as it kept time with my moist, throbbin' temples.

"Dig a little more." Ben Wallace, a thickset man from Water Village, grunted and spat a brown, sticky wad of tobacco from the side of his mouth. Mother said that while most other folks were puttin' in a good days work, he swilled down hard cider behind the feed store with the likes of Liam McDonald.

"I'll keep on diggin', but he ain't goin' nowhere." Charles Spencer rolled his eyes and squealed like a sow at feedin' time. He always wore a crumpled, brown hat and a simple half smile on his long, thin face. Some folks said he wasn't right in the head and that he beat his children in public. I never trusted a man who hated children or animals.

I turned to catch sight of a figure that I would never mistake. I swallowed. *Why was he not down at the County Farm?* Silas Putnam stood tall. His sandy, blonde curls tumbled onto his shoulders.

I ran my tongue over my parched lips, tastin' sweet remnants of nature's merries and blushin' at the mere thought of kissin' him. I resisted the urge to run, unsure of which direction I would flee. I bit my lip and watched as he whistled that song he learned from the men in the Sixth.

He paused, jammed his hands into the pockets of his trousers, and glanced towards me. I ducked behind the tree. I couldn't swallow and struggled to breathe. Droplets of sweat trickled between my breasts. I clenched my apron and squeezed my eyes shut, wobbly at the thought of his limitless blue eyes and dimple set perfectly in the middle of his chin. Nothin' compared to his musky scent and the feel of his strappin' arms wrapped around me. Surely, under those circumstances, my heart would be overwhelmed.

My cheeks burned in the afternoon sun, bringin' my thoughts to Mother, who never missed a thing. She'd notice the fresh crop of freckles on my nose and ask me what was a doin'. She always had a word. She said Silas's folks were no good and he wasn't the marryin' kind. She didn't take into account that at nearly sixteen years of age, I could tend to the affairs of my own heart.

The whistlin' started in again, blendin' with the afternoon bird chorus. The chickadees' song persisted over and above all else. I stared at the vivid dandelions by my earth-blackened toes. They seemed to be lookin' at me, wantin' to exclaim my presence, but remained loyal.

Silas turned away. I could barely see him as he ran his dirt-caked hands through his hair. Finally able to exhale, I slid down, scrapin' the tiny pearl buttons on my blue and white checked dress against the jagged bark.

The wheels on the rickety cart squeaked when the immense horse stirred. His leather harnesses flapped, and his muscles twitched as he swished his tail at the relentless flies.

"Simmah down." Silas's voice sliced into the muggy stillness.

The downy carpet of brownish-green moss felt cool against my skin. I turned and watched the three men grapple with the crude pine box that had a gap in the side from poor workmanship. It wasn't too awful big. *A child? Where are his folks?* Again, I wanted to flee.

They perched the box onto the edge of the freshly dug hole. Silas looked my way. I whipped around, pressin' my back into the wide trunk with my heart poundin' in my ears.

Finally, I peeked out from behind the tall pine. My curl trembled, framin' the trio perfectly. My spirit almost fainted within me when the shovel struck a rock as if it collided with my own heart.

Ben Wallace spat again, displayin' a brown-toothed grin with foul, stringy liquid seepin' onto his whiskers. They lowered the box into the ground. I dabbed my brow with the only handkerchief that I ever sewed myself, seein' I would rather manage untamed colts than do needlework.

Silas and Charles Spencer shoveled dirt back into the hole while Ben unbuttoned his shirt, revealin' a hairy belly that extended over his trousers from consumin' too much salt pork and liquor. He grinned and leaned on his shovel as the earth swallowed the pine box.

Their obscene laughter came in short bursts, echoin' off the stones. The berries churned inside of me. *Would they never leave?* At last, Ben and Silas climbed onto the cart. Charles Spencer rushed along beside them, takin' long strides with his skinny legs, and his head bobbin' like a dim-witted rooster.

I waited until the whistlin' and the jangle of chains and harnesses faded into the road dust before headin' down the grassy hill. The deep yellow sun hesitated over Brown's Ridge. The trees cast wiry shadows on the small granite stones. The smell of dirt choked my airways, and the familiar giant hand pressed down on my chest. The delicate roots of the buttercups were in a heap beside a granite stone etched with the number 46. I walked down the long row of stones readin' the numbers – 47, 48, 49…

I wandered back to the child's restin' place. "I suppose you are number 50." My voice cracked. I knelt down and dug a shallow hole with my hands, quickly foldin' the wilted flowers into the earth by the head of the fresh grave. I wiped my hands on my apron, bowed my head, and tried to ignore the agitatin' mosquitoes that swarmed around me.

"Heavenly Father, I come before You, meek and lowly in heart, to ask earnestly that You accept the soul of this innocent child to be safe in Your arms.

Without faith, it is impossible to take comfort in these times. I pray for his or her folks and that You will bless them in their hour of need. And I pray for life everlastin' and all that is good. A-men."

The song of the hermit thrush spiraled down from the trees as salty tears mixed with a tinge of strawberries and fresh earth. A twig snapped. I heard rustlin' in the trees as a creature scampered towards the river at the bottom of the hill.

The sun lingered long enough for hope, leavin' the day and all its secrets inside of a patient, violet cloud. I took one last look at the spindly flowers layin' face down on the soil, tucked my wayward curl into my bonnet, and set out for home.

⋅⋗▭◉ ◉▭⋖⋅

The usual scent of baked beans and salt pork drifted out from the kitchen window and hung in the dense ochre twilight. I dipped the ladle into the rain barrel, hastily bringin' it to my dry lips. The cool water splashed down my chin.

"Is that you, Abigail?" Mother always asked, even though she knew.

"Yes, I'm home." I wiped the water from my chin onto the sleeve of my dress, bent over, and yanked a few chives from the herb garden, somethin' particularly irritatin' to her.

"Where have you been?" She stepped onto the back porch. Considerin' she was no thicker than a birch saplin' standin' less than five feet – her resonant voice alarmed me. One would not expect such a response from a seemingly gentle woman like Mother. Before the war she was quite pleasin', a blushin' rose, indeed. Like all else, her smile faded along with her red hair that she wore in a braid twisted into a bun at the nape of her neck.

"Out pickin' berries." My reaction disappointed me as I trembled like a child caught stealin' from the cake box. It didn't matter if I was innocent or not; it was our way.

"Never mind." She folded her arms and looked up as though she might pluck the next word from the sky. "We've already had supper. Couldn't wait for you all night, young lady." I waned in her shadow as it lengthened in the last light of day.

"I'm sorry." The words stung my throat like a bite of fresh rhubarb.

"Why can't you be more like your sister and stay close to home?"

My cheeks reddened as if she had slapped them. It was true. I wasn't Sarah. We were sixteen months apart, with Sarah bein' the eldest. I had my share of freckles and an abundance of rebellious mahogany curls, impossible to stuff into a snood. Sarah's skin was milk-white, and her silky hair was like Papa's, as black as a starless night.

Sarah was disciplined; she did her schoolwork; practiced her cornet every day; and managed to play beautiful melodies on the skeleton of a piano in the barn. I was the one who pricked her finger and stained the fine linen with her blood; who rode too fast on Old Gray Mare with her skirts flyin' about; and who laughed aloud in church. Papa liked me that way and never wanted me to change. I could have been dull and proper, but I preferred boyish games.

As different as we were, nothin' would ever divide us. We were bound together like bees to clover.

I went into the kitchen, leaned over his chair, and ran my fingers over the smooth, worn wood, tryin' to conjure his spirit. Although some years had passed, I still longed to hear his voice. He would have spoken on my behalf, for this I was certain. The room wavered through tears that threatened to trickle. That vivid November day in 1861 seemed far away.

I remembered gatherin' at the train station. The wind blew the last of the brittle, orange leaves from the unbendin' trees, and the sky spat icy rain. God Himself was furious. Papa mustered with the men of the Sixth New Hampshire Volunteer Infantry, all puffed up with pride and filled with the fightin' spirit. It was oddly festive for such an unfortunate event.

I watched the short, plump man in the brass band. The dimpled bell of his peculiar long horn rested on his shoulder – a perfect fit. His crimson cheeks bulged out like the shiny frogs in the pond behind the feed store. He swayed from side to side while they played "Yankee Doodle." As always, the sound of a brass band sent Sarah's spirit flyin' and was possibly the reason that she became a fine cornetist a few years later. Some folks sang along. Not me; I didn't feel much like singin'.

I took notice of the men folk when they returned, lookin' straight past me with their hollow eyes and drooped shoulders. Mother said that their bodies came back, but their spirits were left behind with their fallen brothers. Amos Weeks lost an eye durin' a battle at a place called Bull Run, while Hiram Putnam came home with his leg missin', of course he got a wooden one. Silas said he took to the jug, never to be the same.

I squeezed Papa's rough, beefy hand with all my strength, unwillin' to let go. He dabbed my tears with the one handkerchief that I embroidered myself. "Don't you cry. I will be home," he promised.

The band played "Red, White, and Blue." A chorus of men sang out as Papa placed a partin' kiss on my forehead and then Sarah's before takin' Mother into his arms. How were we to know that this farewell kiss would be the last?

Sarah and I locked our gloved hands together and watched as he joined the other men on the train car. I craned my neck to see through the thick forest of blue frock coats, kepis, muskets, swayin' hoop skirts, and carriages that lined the rutty road. We stood by and waved our handkerchiefs until the train was out of sight, 'til the light and life of our beloved Papa vanished with a regretful train whistle.

We returned home, and I dashed to my bed, embracin' the doll that Papa gave me our last Christmas together. She was made of such tidbits as cornstalks, cattails, and beads. I thought it queer that she had no face but was intrigued with her jest the same. I had begged Papa, "I must have her. Please?"

"Abigail, we are here for necessities and then off to the feed store." He did not waver. He was a man of his word.

When we left the store, I looked over my shoulder at the doll upon the shelf, knowin' that she was not to be my own. On Christmas day but a few months later, I was delighted when I saw her on our table amongst the Farm Sweet apples, mittens, and merries. I named her Hope.

Durin' the war, we worked all day and into night, always waitin' for Papa to return. I believed I heard him callin' me from the hayfield, and I would run towards his voice. I finally owned up to the truth. My own will and desire created him in the wind.

It was not until early April that we would receive news of Papa. The stench of thawin' rot and earth burned my nostrils as it always did that time of year. I held tight to the egg basket and stood starin' at my footprint in the last patch of brown, speckled snow in front of the barn door. Rattlin' metal and beatin' hooves interrupted the lament of the cardinal and the rush of the swollen stream out back. I slipped into the shadows of the barn and watched George Wood descend slowly from his carriage and mosey up the path. His gnarled hand wrapped around a shiny oaken stick fashioned into a cane, makin' it impossible to know where his hand began and the stick ended.

I found it difficult to breathe. George Wood wasn't a family friend. He was the official type, a man about town. Even though he couldn't stand upright, he had an air about him. He wore a fancy black hat and a long frock coat with polished brass buttons. He flipped his pocket watch about so that it glimmered in the sunlight.

Filled with dread, I leaned against the door while Mother greeted him with an edgy, unnatural voice, like someone other than our mother. Sarah, her face flushed and braids comin' undone, rushed towards me holdin' two fuzzy black kittens. I put my finger to my lips.

The kittens fell to the floor with a thud and frolicked about her ankles as she stood motionless. I wrapped my warm hand around her icy, pink fingers. The sun slipped behind the ridge. The chickens cooed and murmured, settlin' in to roost. The day we feared had finally arrived.

I could feel my heart throb over the hushed tones comin' from the kitchen. We strained to hear from the back porch, but couldn't make out the words. I will never forget Mother's anguished cry. It was a cry that could only be born of the pain of losin' one's other self.

Although we knew that Papa was gone, we were afraid that if we approached Mother, somehow it would be real. After several hours passed, we finally gathered the courage to go to her and face the dreadful news. Papa was dead. He was shot straight in the heart while breakin' up a rebel camp at a faraway place called Roanoke Island.

Mother didn't speak of him often. She kept his chair at the table and his boots set inside the barn door. Was it possible that Papa occupied the vacant chair? I believed it to be so.

Sarah and I entered into the efforts of the farm with all possible strength. Grampa Wills helped until his death jest one year after losin' Papa. Fences needed mendin', and the roof needed patchin', but we did a fine job keepin' up with it.

Mother kept us in line. "You girls get out here and help. You don't want to end up like them folks at the County Farm, do you?" In rain, snow, and in the heat of summer, we collected eggs, milked the cows, fed the pigs, cows, and chickens, and we even stacked wood.

We knew that the County Farm was a place to fear, but we didn't know for certain why. Silas wouldn't speak of the goin's on. Rosie Wiggins told us that they beat the women and children and chained up the men like animals. Some folks who went there never returned, while others went for the winter and came back in the spring like nothin' happened. It was a wicked place meant for the weak minded and sinful. We would not end up there, not if we could help it.

Mother stormed into the room, stopped in front of me, and glared. My breath reeked from the silky, green chives. I stood very still with my eyes fixed on Papa's chair.

"Look at you!" She grabbed a hold of my hands and inspected them. "Go inside and clean up, and then get some suppah for goodness sakes." She shook her head, plopped down in Grampa Wills's old rocker, and she started in rockin'.

The smell of beans gnawed at my stomach. Beads of sweat burst out on my forehead and over my top lip. Mother squinted her green eyes, emphasizin' the deep creases at the corners. "Girl, you better not have been down by the County Farm again. It ain't no place for a young lady."

"No, ma'am." My eyes rested on the spider web that spanned between the bookcase and the ceilin'. "Like I said, I was out pickin' berries." The spider scurried to the center of the web.

Her look softened in the amber glow of the lantern. She started in rockin' again. Her small feet dangled jest above the floor. The chair creaked harmoniously with the banjo frogs from outside the window. "There's nothin' but trouble down there. Now go eat." She jabbed the needle through the garment that she was mendin'.

"Yes, Mother." I went into the kitchen and wiped the back of my neck with her faded blue dress that was draped over the chair. I pressed it to my face and inhaled her unique, peppery scent. The crock on the back of the cook stove was barely warm. I picked up a spoon and poked at the beans. I was hungry, but not for that.

I gripped the chair until the urge to heave passed. I sat down at the rickety maple table. The image of numbered stones invaded my thoughts. *Who are they?*

I pushed the beans around in the dark, almost black liquid. Silas knew. I dropped the spoon, walked over to the brick mantle and fetched the lantern. My distorted shadow flickered on the wall. I looked away to avoid feelin' faint and then tiptoed across the wooden planks, hopin' that Mother wouldn't hear me. I stood in front of the stove and listened to her hum in unison with the frogs and her creakin' chair.

The juice spattered onto my apron when I dumped the beans back into the crock. I peeked under the frayed, green cloth that covered the basket in the middle of the table. My mouth watered when I set my eyes on fresh cornbread. I broke off a rather large end-piece and smothered it with butter. I admit, I fussed when I had to do the churnin', but it was quite merry on cornbread. I took another crumbly piece and devoured each speck, not wantin' to waste and not wantin' to hear Mother accuse me of mussin'.

The soothin' breeze intermingled affectionately with the night chorus. Shadows of pointed oak fingers trembled on the wall, as the timid moon gazed through the openin' of the heavy winter curtains that hung despite Mother's constant fussin'.

Sarah slept soundly. Her dark hair spilled onto the tattered, gray pillow and her cornet was on the floor beside her with a rag stuffed inside of the bell to keep Mother from complainin'. I sneaked across the room. The floorboards protested noisily with each step. She stirred. I held my breath until she muttered and rolled onto her side with her back to me. I fiddled with the buttons on my dress.

"Abby?" She sat up and rubbed her eyes.

"Sorry. I tried to be quiet." I pulled my nightdress over my head, secretly hopin' that she wouldn't invite me to talkin'.

"Where were you? I was lookin' for you to help in the garden." She yawned and fell back onto her pillow.

"Sorry, time simply escaped. I found the most pleasin' strawberry patch down by the County Farm." Images of granite stones emerged.

"You must have been in the chives again." She pinched her nose and sat up, drawin' her knees to her chest. "Did you go lookin' for Silas?"

"It's no secret that I love chives," I said. "And no, I wasn't lookin' for Silas. I was jest out walkin'." We both knew that I was lyin'.

"But why were you way down there? We have plenty of berries here."

Her eyes pierced right into my thoughts like she had a way of doin'.

"What are all of these questions?" I yanked my thick braid over my shoulder and started untanglin'.

"Everyone knows that you fancy Silas. You don't hide it well."

"That's not true. I do hide it. And what business is it of anyone's?" I wound my hair ribbon around my finger. "I confess that I have given him my whole heart. We have affection for each other and know that it must be kept within bounds."

"Well, we can't have folks talkin'. No good ever comes of it," she whispered. "It is high time for you to get married."

I sighed. "He hasn't spoken of marriage yet. I—"

"And at the dance, you were away with him for some time." She smiled, knowin' that I would try to wiggle away from the truth.

"That is nonsense." My eyes watered when I tugged the brush through my snarls. "Well, I don't mind. Let them wag their tongues."

The curtains flapped. I waited for her to push more, to probe for the answers that were locked up inside. I vowed not to give in to her. Not yet.

"Abby?"

"What?" I continued brushin'.

"I heard Rebecca and Mercy Porter talkin'." She always cleared her throat when she was about to say somethin' unpleasant. "They're leavin' for Fall River – Fall River, Massachusetts. They're goin' to work at the mill."

"Shhh. You must whisper or Mother will stir. Now... what? Why are they doin' that?" I welcomed the change in our conversation.

"Because, they're leavin' Ossipee. They're goin' to work, earn their own wages, and live away from home. Isn't it excitin'?" The moon appeared, makin' the room almost as light as day.

"Why?" I nestled into the soft part of my bed that sagged a little.

"Don't you understand? No more farm. No more chores. It will be a new life, away from here. A chance to see the world."

"I don't think that I would want to go there. I heard that Massachusetts is a dreadful place..." A barred owl from the edge of the woods interrupted with throaty confidence.

"Abby, you jest don't want to be away from Silas." She tucked her blanket under her chin. "I think it's a good idea."

"Don't get any notions. We're quite fine here. You, Mother, and I... we're fine." The thought of bein' alone with Mother was unacceptable.

"I always have notions. You know that." Her voice trailed off.

I closed my eyes only to see thick, small stones lined up with an occasional cluster of buttercups. Sleep was impossible. I squeezed my eyes shut tighter. When the white spots on the inside of my eyelids cleared, I saw him standin' near the pine box in the cart with his hands jammed in his trouser pockets, whistlin' that old, sad song like he always did.

CHAPTER 2

Nellie May Baldwin – June 30th, 1872 Carroll County Farm, Ossipee, New Hampshire

I WALKED TO where tall grasses meet the garden. I rejoiced with bare feet upon the breast of Our Mother. The voices of men and beasts flowed quiet with the wind. I plucked a strand of grass and chewed; sweetness brought a smile.

I was at the edge of the day, a place of truth. I moved swiftly into the shelter of the trees. The white men's laughter came from the road behind me. They carried the dead and planted them in the stone garden. I held tight to the handle of my sweetgrass and black ash basket. Because it was Nokahigas, the berries were plentiful.

I blended with light, leaves, and ferns. I watched. A young white woman was at the burial ground, away from the safety of the pine grove.

She crouched on the earth and talked to her god. Her hair was the color of maple. I saw her on the footpath with the kind, young boss.

I closed my eyes to see the faces of my ancestors and the mask of the good dance. The small black and white birds searched and took me to the highest part of the tree, where I could hold the world in my eyes. Crooked River called. I longed for her. I soared on the wings of the red-tail to her banks.

A branch snapped sending birds in flight. I followed the sloped land until it reached the broad, familiar river bottom.

⋅→═◉ ◉═←⋅

My thick, black braids – no longer white and silver – fell from my hat. From the Other World, I heard the spirit of my mother, Kchi alakws, call out to me. *See how fast you can run, Nanatasis!*

I lifted my skirt and ran. Laughter rose from my heart, releasing the over-flowing spirits and the fire that burned within.

Crooked River sang. I was safe in her current, flowing over smooth, gray rocks and yellow sand. Crickets chanted, always heard, never seen.

I shed my clothes and my hat. The wind caressed my skin. I sat on the warm rock and slipped my feet into the waiting water, quenching the dry earth of my spirit until the bite of cold surrendered.

I remembered my mother at Bitawbagok in summer. I went with her to draw water three times each day. She was sad and silent.

When I asked of her sadness, she looked without blinking. *You mustn't ask of my tears. Now, let us fetch water.* She motioned for help.

The sun struck her lined face. Her brown eyes were round and wise.

When I asked if I could play, she hushed me. *Now there is work to do.*

After we filled the jugs she spoke. Her sadness lifted. *Take off your clothes. Bitawbagok invites us to bathe in her spirit.*

I opened my eyes under the water, like a fish, like my father's brother, Wnegigw. He was strong; he could swim from one shore of Bitawbagok to the other. He did this as an elder. Grandfather told me that our fathers before us were happy with the Creator. When rivers were born, they jumped into their currents and transformed into fish. I would not be a fish, but instead, kasko, the great blue heron.

I turned onto my back and swam away from the Other World and my people. Clouds flew swiftly across Father Sky.

I swam over to the steep bank and climbed onto her shores. I took the pouch from my belt and found the juniper oil.

After bathing, I gave thanks and ate red berries from my basket. Mother taught us to make baskets with black ash and sweetgrass. Father prepared the black ash. Her baskets were of many, and she sold them to the white man. I did this too. I liked making dolls more.

I climbed upon the flat rock to rest. The cry of my friend the crow aroused me. The sun moved. It was time to depart before the song of the night bird filled the inner sky. I would bring my hook and line the next day. The fireflies had arrived.

The wind changed.

I walked until a thunderbolt fell upon me. Again, my braids fell from my hat, hurrying from black to silvery white.

◦‣▶ ◀◈◦

Sadness in dark brown eyes looked towards the white woman's stick. The powerful beasts, once far away, were close. Sweat covered bronze.

The stick hit, first soft and then hard. "Move along, old woman." She smiled... not a smile to warm, but a smile to make cold in my spirit.

I swallowed the remains of grass that grew bitter on my tongue. I walked away from where the truth lay in waiting, leaving Nanatasis's laughter at the banks of Crooked River.

She pointed to the other side of the field. "Git over there with the other idiots. Go on." She pushed against my back with the stick. "Ain't you ever got nothin' to say?"

I looked to Father Sky. The small black and white birds searched. All hushed as the red-tail made great circles. I waited for him to depart.

I walked to the gathering place of the elders, women in yellow, and those with words that had no meaning. One laughed and the other wept. At nightfall, I slept on the banks of Crooked River under the shelter of stars.

Chapter 3

Silas Putnam – June 30, 1872 Carroll County Farm – Ossipee, New Hampshire

When I picked up the coffin, I got a good sized sliver in my thumb. I licked the blood to keep it from drippin' but figured there weren't no sense in fussin'. I'd be diggin' dirt before too long.

I took to whistlin' quite loud, so to drown out Mahitable's wailin' comin' from the house. I thought 'bout her clingin' to her boy. She hollered and carried on. It took three of us to pull her away. I wish she'd simmah down. Listenin' to her made the fist in my chest clench up tight.

I turned away from Benjamin Wallace, Big Ben, so to avoid his stench. He was a hefty sot and didn't take to bathin'. And Charles was a scrapper by Jesus, a wisp of a man whose shirt sleeves wasn't long enough to cover his scrawny arms. He groaned and his face turned redder than a tomato when we hoisted the small coffin onto the cart. He 'bout keeled over when we lugged a full grown man.

It weren't even noon, and my shirt was soaked. We had a hot spell that week, and some folks still burnt up with the fever. Luckily, we had plenty of coffins stacked up.

I pictured Josiah all wound up in the cloth inside of the box. Ayuh, Daddy was right; dyin' was jest a part of livin'. My goat died when I was 'bout ten. I cried somethin' wicked. He told me, "son, if you have a farm, there's gonna' be livestock, and there's gonna' be deadstock." I took the shovel and buried my goat behind the barn and never cried at the likes of deadstock again.

Josiah weren't much older than eight. I knew he was gonna' die. The fever struck him hard, and he had it longer than most, but he put up a good fight. He was a damn good boy, and he never tried to hide from his chores, always wantin' to do men's work.

From the first day, he watched out for his mamma. He spoke with a deep voice, makin' like he was a rouser, ready to take on the best of us. He even stood up to Moses Blake, the big boss, the superintendent of the Carroll County Farm. Everybody laughed, even me. But inside I respected him for tryin' to be a man. He raised his fists and used fightin' words while hangin' on to the leather pouch that held his daddy's chisels. We put it in the barn with the other snippets they bring with 'em, in case they strike out on their own. There was no use fussin'.

Mahitable refused to cooperate with Polly and Miss Noyes. Josiah fought em, cussin' and wailin' his arms. Miss Noyes didn't spare either of 'em from her sharpened oak stick. They was in lock-up for a day with no food, jest water.

I carried no guilt. I done no wrong. I'd been takin' care of my own folks for a good six years. It was a dark day when Daddy come home from the war. I wanted to go with him and fight them Rebs… course I was too young and promised to tend to Mamma. Then he came home with jest one leg, so I tended to him too. Only problem was he took to the jug. It didn't matter what was in it; he drank himself into a stupor without missin' a day.

Moses Blake got me workin' on his own farm; he lived down the road apiece over to Brown's Ridge. After provin' my worth, he took me on at the County Farm to oversee the poor folks. Most of 'em were from right here in Ossipee, but there was folks from other towns too like Effin'ham, Wolfeboro, and Wakefield.

The feeble-minded was sent to the County Farm along with old folks who couldn't take care of themselves. Others fell on hard times after the war, 'tho the veterans got a pension and such; it hit us all in some way or another. There was plenty who wound up there durin' the long winter months and a few folks like Gil Smith after he lost his arm at the mill.

Girls who wasn't married went there to have their babies if a man didn't own up to bein' the daddy. They was a disgrace to their families, church, and town. They was the ones who wore yellow dresses. They could keep their babies there 'til a family stepped in and took 'em into a good home. Seein' a babe ripped away from its mother was an awful sight. Nothin' like a mother protectin' her young. There weren't too many children there over three years old, but like all rules there was exceptions.

Then there was the old Indian woman, Nellie, who didn't talk. Some said she was deaf too, but I thought she could hear fine, and it was her own choosin' to keep quiet. She took to wanderin' about. She picked berries and plants and used 'em to make potions for folks who was sick. They said she was a witch. I didn't think so.

Nellie tended to the old and feeble folks too. They stayed together all slumped in the Great Room day after day, starin' straight ahead, waitin' to die. There weren't nobody to cling to 'em when it was time for the pine coffin, like poor Josiah.

Sweat stung my eyes, and the flies tormented us. Usually when we went to dig graves, Big Ben and Charles rode on the cart, and I walked along beside 'em. Movin' around helped me when I got all jittery. It was quiet 'cept for the steady thumpin' hooves, cussin', and occasional spittin' into the dust. I whistled to keep from catchin' the habit of cussin'.

I took a gander down Brown's Ridge Road and thought of my pretty Abigail. Well, she weren't mine really. I used to meet her in the field behind the Blake's farm. I weren't a church goin' man, but Abigail liked to talk 'bout God and nature. I tried to tell her that she didn't need the likes of no preacher to talk to God, but she never missed so much as one church meetin'.

She was a proper girl, but it kept gettin' harder to resist her. Her touch got my heart to poundin', and I nearly lost my wits. We came close many a time, 'til them fires inside got burnin' too hot, and there was no turnin' back.

Goin' up to the hayloft invited temptation. Then after, down at the river, she was tearful and claimin' to be a sinner. I was a man of honor, not sin. I promised myself that I would not get familiar with her, but I lost my way, somethin' that altered our lives in unthinkable ways.

I weren't ready to have all them troubles that came with a woman and her folk. Abigail was from a good family, but I needed to keep workin' on the farm a spell longer. Then I could get us a nice home with all the fixin's.

Once the cart was settled, Charles and I got to diggin'. The ground was still soft from the week before when we buried Hattie Perkins. That ole lady weren't right in the head, and she never spoke a word that made any sense. Heck, she had more whiskers than both me and Charles put together. She showed off her toothless grin while she laughed and rocked back and forth on the stump by the barn. Poor thing was grinnin' when I found her cold stiff body fixed on the stump leaned up against the barn. Moses said he thought that woman would live to be a hundred.

We lowered the box into the hole. I removed my hat and stood 'til the bugs got too thick. I whistled a song I heard at the train station. Somethin' 'bout "Comin' Home to Die." Abigail thought it to be morbid. Daddy sang it nearly every night after the cider set in. Charles took his sweet time, but I rushed to throw the dirt back into the hole. I started whistlin' again so I could leave my feelin's behind. Moses said I needed to get hardened to be a good farm boss.

CHAPTER 4

Abigail – July 21, 1872

I HESITATED ON the stairs while Mother and Sarah bustled into the store. I pretended not to notice Silas watchin' me from across the way. He helped Mrs. Cobb load a sack into her carriage. Our eyes met. He nodded and then turned away. I secretly hoped for him to speak with me.

I ran my hands over the new calico skirt that Mother worked so hard to sew. When she was fixin' the last touches, she fussed and jest about pricked me with the needle. "Abigail, you must stop eatin' so much corn bread. By the time I finish your skirt you'll have outgrown it."

I admit that I wiggled as I had a mind to do, and I tried to hold my breath to avoid hearin' her complaints. I was not one to suffer in the likes of a corset, like Sarah, who relished wearin' hers. She begged me to tie it so that her waist all but disappeared. Surely a man came up with the idea. A woman would never create such a thing.

I twisted my mitt, coverin' the hole by my thumb. *Why is he takin' so long?* Mother stood by the door. "Hurry up and come help your sister." Her green eyes darted across the way to Silas and then back at me. I followed her into the store, where Sarah counted lemon drops one at a time. She fancied sweets, while I preferred to eat straight from the garden, yet that day my mouth watered for lemon drops.

I heard his footsteps above the chatter. *Should I turn around? Do I dare look into his eyes?* My cheeks burned as I struggled to open my fan. Sarah tied it together where a piece was missin'.

Since Papa died, Mr. Tibbetts showed a great deal of affection for my mother. Every time we went into the store he invited her to talkin'. I could tell by the way she laughed that she was quite fond of his fussin', but she said that he was nothin' more than an annoyance. He was an agreeable fellow, but no one would replace Papa.

The three of them stood beside the cheese wheel discussin' the weather. No one really cared about the weather, but around here it seemed to be the topic of discussion, a way to avoid the things that really mattered.

I broke a sweat at the sound of footsteps behind me.

"Aft'noon Abigail."

I whipped around, knockin' a jar of honey off the shelf. I watched it roll towards my feet and disappear under my skirt. "You startled me." The chatter about the weather stopped, and all eyes fell upon me.

We both bent over to fetch the honey. I snatched the jar away from him. "You shouldn't do that. The next time it might break, and we'd have quite a mess," I said as a curl fell from my bonnet.

It was the most unpleasant scene. I knew Mother was frownin', jest as I knew that Sarah was holdin' in laughter. I placed the jar on the shelf.

"Never mind." I straightened my skirt as my heart withered.

"I was hopin' to see you in town," he whispered, coverin' his mouth with his hand while lookin' over his shoulder.

The words scattered about my head in graceful confusion. "I must go help Mother." I stumbled across the room precisely when Mr. Tibbetts lifted the cheese cover. The scent washed over me. I pinched my nose and weakened. I waited for Silas to reach the front door before I ran to the back room, threw open the door, and vomited.

I could not recall feelin' as poorly as I did that day. I emptied the contents of my stomach, and continued heavin' 'til there was nothin' left.

"Abigail?" Mother came out with Sarah and Mr. Tibbetts close behind her. She rubbed my back. "Oh dear! Come on. Let's get you home." Her fingers pierced into my elbow.

Mr. Tibbetts fumbled as he wrapped the cheese and handed it to Sarah. "Don't worry. You can pay me next time."

I climbed into the back of the cart, relieved that Silas was nowhere in sight. I held my head in my hands as we swayed from side to side, tryin' to ignore the smelly cheese. I hung over the side and heaved once more. I reached into the crumpled sack and took out a lemon drop. At the first pucker I thought it to be a mistake, but as my mouth watered I felt better.

I jumped off the carriage and winced at the sight of my soiled skirt. Washin' clothes was a chore that I detested. Mother often complained that I did not scrub hard enough, while she scrubbed down to the bare threads.

"Come here now," Mother ordered in her edgy, yet carin' manner. "I'll make some ginger tea, and then you lie down."

"It was the heat. I'm fine." I watched a blue jay flicker from branch to branch while she pressed her small, cool hand on my forehead.

"You don't feel warm, yet you're flushed. You need to rest." She spun around and marched into the house with her burgundy dress draggin' across the grass.

"What is wrong with you?" Sarah stood before me holdin' a sack of coffee. "I'm worried." Her black eyebrows curved in question.

"Don't fret. It was the heat and excitement. Perhaps when I see Silas my stomach flutters." I dipped the ladle in the rain barrel and took a long drink.

"That is such foolishness." She rolled her eyes. "You ate somethin' disagreeable."

"I had the same as you and Mother – eggs, salt pork, and beans. You're both fine. It's a passin' illness." I shook my head. "I must wash my skirt." I walked away, leavin' Sarah by the rain barrel.

Mother sang out from the kitchen, paintin' a picture of the false angel who I sought endlessly, even though I knew she had long since disappeared, never to be the same after Papa died. I stood behind the weedy barn clad in my pantaloons and camisole, shiverin' in spite of the heat. *Why did I react in such a way? I have given him my whole heart for some time, but to become ill?*

Mother stopped singin'. The porch door creaked. "Abigail? Your tea is ready."

I didn't care for tea, but Mother had a mind to peck. "After I fill the wash tub." Gray clouds rushed over the top of Brown's Ridge, posin' a threat to the boastful blue sky.

"Don't dilly-dally around," she said.

I had dilly-dallied all my life accordin' to her, and I could never quite put my finger on exactly what happened when one dilly-dallied. It must be good, or I wouldn't have bothered with it. To her it was awful, and of course, Sarah never had a mind to dilly-dally.

The thunder in the distance closed in, rumblin' right on down to my feet. I had hoped that it might rain.

CHAPTER 5

Nellie – July 21, 1872

I CARRIED THE sorrow of men, women, and young ones upon my shoulders to where the shadows of trees divided the light. I looked to the spirit of the mountain for calm.

A red-tail soared above in the inner sky, making circles and hunting for small creatures. Soon the tall white man with much hair would come. He carried his stick to move me to the gathering place of the elders and those with no wisdom.

I found my place to rest, closed my eyes, and faced the north wind. Seasoned fingers caressed soft moss that became fur. Day became night. Old became young.

⊶⊷ ⊶⊷

I clawed at the fur beneath. Mother looked into my brown eyes with hers. *Nanatasis, do not fight. Be calm.* She stroked my face.

Pain struck like the claw of the black bear. I did not hear the words of my mother. My screams filled my ears. I looked at the circle of women around me. When I closed my eyes, I saw the face of the one who hunted me, the white man with blue eyes and corn silk hair. His spirituous liquor burned my skin. It was a dark, moonless night when he thrust himself inside, bringing shame upon my spirit, bringing life where there was none.

The flow of water and blood came, and the rising and falling of harsh pain brought forth the child. My screams stopped when her cries began. Then silence. In the stillness of twilight, the one from my womb looked upon me. The violet flame from the Other World flickered in her eyes. Mother held her. *You have a daughter. You will not be the same.*

First, I feared her. Mother pushed her closer to me. I took her into my arms, pressing her warm body against mine. She was wet with our blood – a baby bird, searching. She found my breast. When she turned her head, I saw on her neck the mark of Mamijôla, the butterfly.

She is Mamijôla, my daughter with a mother and no father. I will protect her. She will not know how she came to be.

⋅⊱═◉ ◉═⊰⋅

Tears became the rain that washed away Mamijôla and the spirits of my ancestors. I gave thanks to the great white pine for medicine.

The soft orange pine needles upon the forest floor gave way to grass in the open field. I walked with no shoes. The weight grew as I neared the place where many were without hope.

The long shadow of the white man and his stick moved towards me. I looked to Father Sky. My friend the crow watched from the leafy limb as thunder fell from the gray clouds, silencing the crying child.

CHAPTER 6

Silas – July 21, 1872

HIS SHOCKIN' RED comb flapped each time he jerked his head. He scuttled down the path with his wings drawn back. His pace quickened. I glared, ready to take on the ornery bastard – the Rhode Island Red that we got from Leavitt's farm as a fuzzy yellow chick. It was the last time he would screech outside my window, invitin' me to scrap.

Every damn time I went to fetch the eggs, he come runnin' after me with them spurs, achin' to fight. This mornin' was no different. It weren't a problem for me; I could kick him, but Mamma didn't have the nerve, and chances are she'd get hurt.

My fingers slipped over the smooth walnut stock of Daddy's rifle. I pressed it into my chest. Red took to flutterin' about in the yard gettin' all the hens in a tizzy. I closed one eye and looked down the barrel tryin' to predict his next erratic move. I took a shot. Rusty brown and white feathers burst from the center of the flock, followed by a hush. Then they all got to scurryin' around him. His pupil damn near disappeared into that yellow eye of his when he jerked his head above the crowd, mockin' me, and thinkin' I wouldn't spare a hen. I blasted him. He got what he was fixin' to get.

I propped the gun in the corner by Daddy's old, cracked saddlebag and wiped my hand on the leg of my trousers. Damn chicken blood was sticky. With his nostrils flarin', Major pushed his head out of the stall and stomped into the dirt. I stroked the white patch on his nose.

"Damn it, boy... help me out!" Daddy wailed as he clomped out from the kitchen draggin' his bad leg across the floor. "Where's my chair? Goddamned thing ain't where I left it." He banged his cane on his wooden leg, supposin' that his chair would appear, or worse, to make me run to him.

"Comin' Daddy." I punched my hand on the bar post, shreddin' the skin on my knuckles. He weren't tryin' to git me mad. He jest didn't wanna' wait is all. The hens clucked and scattered away from my feet when I passed 'em on my way to the house. I lugged the chair out from the kitchen, resistin' the urge to heave it down the steps.

Daddy watched closely as Mamma teetered out with coffee spillin' out of the cup. He squirmed, his eyes flittin' here and there, thinkin' of somethin' nasty to say. They rested on me. "What was all that ruckus this mornin'? Ya didn't shoot Old Red did ya?" He jammed his stubby thumb into the bowl of his pipe. His nose made a whistlin' sound with each slow breath. His wispy, gray beard nearly hung down to his trousers.

I stumbled on the steps and ran to the barn. A handful of red feathers drifted past my boots when I snatched the dead bird by his golden feet and swung around. "Ayuh, I shot him by Jesus, no more battles. Damn thing won't be crowin' outside my window no more neither." I dropped him on the ground. His dead, yellow eye looked up at me.

Daddy's wiry eyebrows merged into one. He gurgled and struggled with a match.

I went to my workshop in the back of the barn. I liked workin' with wood. I eyed the box that I was fixin' to give to Abigail for her birthday. It took two weeks jest to carve the box into the shape of a heart and another week to make the cover fit perfect. I steadied my hand and carved the bottom – *A.E.H. + S.J.P. Nov 10 1872.*

I blew the wood shavin's onto the floor and smiled. I had the most pleasin' hopes to fashion a ring from a horseshoe nail.

I decided to ride to the store for a swig of cider. I hoped to catch Abigail and her folks when they stopped in after church, and if Old Lady Cobb was there she'd give me somethin' for loadin' up her cart.

The dust kicked up, and Major jerked his head away from the hitchin' post. "Simmah down." I tugged on the reins and watched Old Lady Cobb wag her tongue at poor Mr. Tibbetts.

"Can I help you with them sacks, Mrs. Cobb?" I paused when I tasted blood under my fingernails. Tibbetts, hunched over and fretful, escaped into the store.

"That would be fine, young man." She waddled to the back of the cart with her puffy eyes dartin' about. She wasn't one to look me in the eye.

I loaded the sacks and heard laughter that had a way of ticklin' inside my chest. Although her voice was joyful and childlike, she also spoke soft like a woman. I turned, removed my hat, and wiped the sweat line from my brow. I helped myself to the sight of Abigail sittin' in the back of the cart, danglin' her legs, smilin', and lookin' at me with them brown eyes.

I couldn't stop the grin. Damn if she didn't look away, actin' like she didn't see me. Like every woman I knew, she changed with the weather.

They kept chattin' and carryin' on while Mr. Tibbetts hitched 'em up to the post. Old Lady Cobb glared from behind them little, round glasses pinched on the end of her long nose. "You stop down for some strawberry rhubarb pie. I'm fixin' to do some bakin' this afternoon." She gripped my hand and hoisted herself onto the wagon. She didn't quite reach my chin, but she weighed as much as a small cow.

I turned in time to see the last of Abigail disappear into the store. I cleared my throat and slowly walked up the front steps and into the store. She stood with her back to me. I tried to think of somethin' to say. I figured there weren't no harm in talkin'. I stepped towards her, touchin' the rim of my hat. "Abigail?"

She twirled around and knocked over a jar. Everyone quit talkin' and stared. We scrambled to pick it up, nearly bumpin' heads.

I started to apologize in front of her mamma, who I knew would be fitful, and her sister was holdin' back laughter. Abigail slammed the jar on the shelf. I flinched.

"Never mind." Her face was red as an apple. She was pretty, even when she was mad.

"Well, I hoped to see you in town." I squeezed my hat and ignored 'em watchin' me.

"I must help Mother." She cinched the sides of her skirt and stormed over to the cheese wheel.

I waited for a bit. I had a notion to get some sugar for Mamma but thought otherwise when I caught sight of the clouds. Major got spooked when it thundered.

CHAPTER 7

Nellie – July 22, 1872

MOTHER CAME TO me. *When the time of fishing has passed, we will prepare for the hunt.* The light of the new day showed lines of knowing on her face.

I know this. I bent down towards Bitawbagok to drink.

We must make ready for winter snow and winds. Brown eyes to brown eyes shared sacred wisdom.

My breath hurried from coldness.

Mamijôla was three winters. Her hair was black, and her blue eyes held questions to be asked. She was quiet within the remains of the dream world.

The others awoke. The boats on the shores would go to deeper waters for fishing. The women prepared food, made clothing, and some would make baskets to sell to the white man. I went into the woods to gather pine, roots, and plants for many medicines. I no longer carried the cradleboard. Mamijôla walked by my side.

⇥⟡ ⟡⇤

Sharp pain struck. The large woman with hair the color of a fox stood above my bed sack. "Git up, Old Squaw. Come git your gruel 'fore it's all gone, then you'll go without." Mamijôla and Mother returned to the spirit world. My feet were not cold from Bitawbagok but from being with age.

I was slow to rise. Another day was before me. I did not hear the cries, laughter, or senseless words of the others. When it was time, I would go to the banks of Crooked River.

"Don't you ever say nothin'?" She jabbed me with the stick. "Git up."

She left my room to follow the scream. It was Bella. It was not like other days. It was the cry of birth.

The woman with hair the color of a fox spoke with anger. "Stop yer damn hollerin'!"

Bella screamed more.

I pulled the board from the floor – my medicine place – to get hemlock needles, raspberry leaf, and yarrow.

Silence followed the mother's birth cries. I looked to Father Sky. *Great Spirit let us hear the cry of the child.* The stillness brought darkness.

The first cry was weak. My eyes were wet. *A mother's love is joy. A mother's love is strong.* The woman with the hair the color of a fox spoke. I waited for cries of the child while cups and spoons from down below drummed with the falling rain.

The first cry was the last. The woman with hair the color of a fox carried the dead child.

"William!" Bella called for her husband. He worked in the fields with the great beasts. He was strong, his ways quiet, and his hair was black like my people.

We saw the young men from afar. Only elders could live as husband and wife. Those who spoke words with no meaning were amongst us as well.

I entered Bella's room. She looked but a child herself upon the straw bed. Her face was pale with shadows beneath her eyes. Her yellow hair was wet and pressed against her face. The pile of cloth beside her was red with blood.

"My baby is dead." She pulled the blanket to her face. She moaned like the sorrowful wind. "I had a son." She shook with tears.

I placed my hand on her heated face as Mother did to me upon the birth of my daughter. I held her close to my breast while her blood flowed. It was time for nourishment of body and spirit. I released her. Healing must begin.

I went down below, where people waited for food. Polly was not there. The strong, young one named Silas spooned the heavy gruel into my bowl. I pointed at the steaming kettle.

"What do you want?" He questioned.

Again, I pointed at the kettle and then to the only tin cup on the shelf.

"Speak up." He frowned and looked past me to the next one.

I beat my spoon on my bowl and pointed once more.

"I ain't used to the kitchen." He poured the water.

He did not see my smile. He tried to be like the others, but his spirit was good.

I went swiftly to Bella as she cried softly. I packed the hemlock, raspberry leaf, and yarrow into my pouch, crushing them to release medicine into the water. It would slow the blood and bring about calm. Medicine would not completely heal the loss of her son. It would remain with her until their reunion in the Other World.

I took away the cloth that was wet with their blood, and I washed her with a clean linen. I stayed with her while the light moved across the room, holding her small hand in mine, a merging of white birch and oak.

First she turned away. Then she took the offering of cold gruel. I brought the tea to her lips. She drank.

When she slept, I went to the yard. Three men stood beside the open box. Inside was the elder, Emery. The child, wrapped in a blood spotted cloth, rested on his chest. It was time for planting in the stone garden. The sound of the hammer striking the pine box beat heavy inside.

Chapter 8

Silas – July 22, 1872

THERE HAD BEEN too much deadstock. Moses and Asa was jawin' and lookin' in the box settin' in the back of the cart. I swallowed and got to thinkin' about Emery. He talked nonsense and all, but he sure worked hard crushin' bone meal and carryin' wood even when he was weak. The fever claimed him like all the others. Of course, Nellie gave him bits of bark and oddities like she had a mind to do.

Asa turned away. He took charge of the barn and didn't take kindly to me. He was a mean sort, taller than most, with arms as sturdy as an ox. Matter of fact, he handled the oxen almost as good as William Quimby.

"Fine mornin'," I said, hopin' to soften him.

He grunted. I walked my horse to the pasture and leaned against the slanted fence post.

"Silas!" Moses shouted. Sweat trickled down his face, and his eyes was saggy even though the day had jest begun. "I need you in the kitchen. Polly ain't here."

I set my sights on the coffin. My temples pounded. *By God, it's Emery.* His face looked frozen, as if he was surprised, or somethin' gave him a scare.

"Damn, Emery went and died." I jammed my hands into my pockets and looked away hopin' to conjure up a picture of the way I wanted to remember him.

"You and the boys will be takin' 'im over to be buried after you finish in the kitchen." He tugged at the sheet coverin' Emery's scared face.

"Yes, sir." I turned and watched Major graze on clover. I waited 'til Moses went into the stone shed, into the puffs of thick black smoke and the ringin' anvil, before I went up to the big house. *Damn, Polly.*

I scraped the dirt from my boots and then stepped into the kitchen. I stopped when I heard awful screams comin' from upstairs. It had to be Bella. Accordin' to her husband, William, she'd been ready to have the baby for 'bout a week.

William was a good man. He didn't have a lot to say. He had a look of longin' when he watched his wife from afar. He worked with the horses, oxen, and steer. Whether plowin' or drawin' logs on the sled, he drove 'em hard. He didn't holler. He guided 'em easy with a slight twig.

My stomach gurgled along with the sticky brown gruel that simmered in the pot. I was pleased that I didn't have to eat it. If given a chance, even the pigs might walk away from the swill that them folks ate each mornin'.

At night we gave 'em potatoes and a few carrots or turnips in a boiled meat stew. It weren't nothin' like Mamma's. Hers was all thick with gravy, and we had it with fine meal bread. But the folks here didn't seem to mind the watery slop. After workin' all day, they wasn't too fussy.

There was a clatter. Miss Noyes hollered to Bella to hush, but she kept right on screamin'. I glanced out the window and caught sight of William lookin' up at the house.

I s'posed I should tend to the folks who was in line, hangin' on tight to their bowls and starin' at me with fear in their eyes. We all tried ignorin' the screams and poor William, who didn't know what was a doin'.

Mrs. Kennison was first in line. She held out her bowl with her shaky hand. I smiled at her when I spooned out her gruel. She looked down at her feet. They weren't used to the bosses smilin'. Sometimes I forgot all about bein' mean, 'til the others scolded me, but I saw no harm in bein' pleasant from time to time.

The shoutin' stopped. I looked towards the stairs and strained to hear a single soft cry. It was quiet. All you could hear was the scrapin' of spoons on metal and the scuffin' of feet. Mrs. Kennison looked up at the stairs. I knew that somethin' weren't right.

Bella's cry was sort of like a fisher cat deep in the woods on a dark night. I rushed, and in an attempt to keep my wits about me, splattered the gruel from the pot into the empty bowls.

Miss Noyes hurried into the kitchen. Her sweaty, pink face was 'bout to burst, and a clump of orange hair hung over her eye. She snorted and pressed her ample backside against me, squeezin' her way through the door.

I stopped with the spoon in midair and stared at the bundle that she had tucked under her arm. There was no mistaken what it was.

She shifted the bloody linen. "What are you folks lookin' at? Mind your P's and Q's." She bustled through the door and out into the yard.

The old Indian woman, Nellie, stood still lookin' up towards the ceilin'. She was always thinkin'. She pointed at the old crumpled kettle and cup on the shelf. *What was she doin' that for?* I looked away.

She came closer. Beads of sweat rolled over my top lip. She weren't makin' no sense. "What do you want?" I needed to go outside.

She pointed again. Her face grew redder.

I poured water from the kettle into the cup. "Take it and move along."

She bowed her head and left.

Miss Noyes returned to the kitchen, took off her apron, and threw it on the floor. "What a mess. I'll have to take this to the launderin' room."

"What about Bella?"

"What about Bella?" She reached behind and tied the fresh apron around her fat belly.

"How's she doin?" My mouth was dry. Bella was about my age. She had a kind heart and a pleasin' face.

"You never mind. You shake them thoughts from your head and tend to your work." She took a deep breath. "You're too soft."

We worked in silence. I watched over the women as they scrubbed the crusted, brown pots. I ordered 'em to sweep the floors and then go out to the garden. All the while I kept thinkin' 'bout Emery's face all twisted up, and I wondered what scared him.

"Silas!" Moses hollered from the yard.

I went out to the barn, where he stood by the cart. I looked at the box and the small blood covered linen bundled in with Emery. "Ayuh?" I turned away. In the distance I could see the sun shinin' behind Nellie as she knelt by the pond lookin' up at the sky. She was a curious one.

"Bury 'em." Moses held a match over his pipe and took a long toke.

Charles was fixin' up the brown horse. Big Ben came over carryin' the cover to the coffin. He bent down, picked up some nails from the bench, and stuck 'em in his pocket. I watched William outta' the corner of my eye as he worked in the field.

I put my hands in my pockets. "Was it a boy or girl?"

"What good comes from knowin'?" Moses spat.

"I was jest…"

"If you have ta know, it was a boy. Now go."

Charles hopped onto the seat. "Let's go. I wanna git home."

The horse spooked, causin' the pine box to slide. "Goddamn!" Ben started in cussin' as he slid the box back in place.

We walked down the road towards the cemetery. I had that ole feelin' 'bout seein' Abigail. I wanted to see her, but not with the coffin. So, it was jest as well that I didn't.

The horse hauled the cart up the hill at the cemetery and came to a halt. I got the shovel and started diggin'. The sun beat down on my back, so I took off my shirt. Damn flies buzzed around as the sweat rolled off me. Ben was chewin' and spittin' while Charles tapped the nails on the cover of the coffin.

Finally, a breeze rustled through the tall pine trees, dryin' the sweat and scatterin' the flies. I climbed out from the hole. It was up to Big Ben and Charles to lower the box. I crouched down and wiped my face with my shirt. The buttercups by my boot caught my eye and invited me to thinkin'. I looked over to Brown's Ridge Road.

The sound of dirt hittin' the coffin brung me to my feet. The thought of William and Bella made my throat itch. I gagged and coughed a spell. I didn't like it because I was s'posed to be different. I wanted to please Moses. I pressed my shirt on my eyes and remembered jest like Daddy said, "Livestock, dead-stock – can't have one without the other."

Dependin' on the person and the time of year, there might have been a service, but Emery had no folks. Although he belonged to someone at some time, nobody claimed him. I swatted at a fly on my arm. Baby Quimby was in Emery's arms. He would see to it that they both got to Heaven. The clenched fist in my chest let go, makin' it easier to breathe.

CHAPTER 9

Abigail – August 22, 1872

THE DANGER OF namin' a baby chick too soon is that you're apt to mistake a rooster for a hen. My favorite rooster, Pearl, was pure white with a bright red comb and wattle. He was a high-spirited creature, and he crowed each day for at least an hour before sun up.

We had our share of roosters. Of course, their fate was to end up on our table with turnips, potatoes, and fine meal bread. I simply could not imagine Pearl comin' to that end, and I knew that complainin' would invite Mother to throwin' him in the pot.

I rolled onto my side and buried my head under the pillow. He continued crowin'. In fact, he crowed louder. I gazed at the blanket of apricot clouds hoverin' over the ridge. The cool mornin' breeze felt good on my skin.

Sarah stirred. Pearl did not wake her. She could sleep through a train whistle if it were in the yard. The room swirled about when I rose to my feet. My face reddened, and moist curls clung to the back of my neck. I looked frantically for a place to heave. I spotted the chamber pot, dashed to the corner of the room, and lifted the cover. There was little in my stomach. I wanted to expel that which made me ill as I continued to heave the foul stench of nothingness.

"Abby?" Sarah rushed over, puttin' her hand on my back. "Oh dear."

I choked and covered my mouth with my hand.

"I must get Mother."

"No!" I gagged at the sight of the brownish, watery bile circlin' in the pot. "I'll be fine." I wiped a string of saliva from my chin with the corner of my nightdress and sat on the edge of the bed.

"You were ill last week too. Perhaps Mother should call Doctor Moulton?" She stroked my damp, knotted hair.

I pulled away from her. "I'll be fine." The smell of bacon filled the room. "Mother is makin' breakfast. We should go."

My mouth watered. I stumbled back to the chamber pot. *Lord, please make this peculiar illness stop.*

"I am havin' dreadful thoughts." Sarah leaned over beside me and looked into my eyes.

"This is not the time for dreadful thoughts. Now hush." I hung my head over the chamber pot and clutched my nightdress while heavin' up nothin'.

"Girls! Come now before the heat of the day sets in!" Mother hollered from the kitchen as she did each mornin'.

Sarah hurried to the top of the stairs. "We're gettin' dressed, Mother."

"Today we'll go to Clark's for grain." She rattled off the list of chores in a sort of melodic way.

My fingers shook when I buttoned my blouse, and it was cool where the sweat dried on my skin. When the room stopped spinnin', I opened the window and dumped the chamber pot.

"Listen," Sarah said. "Did you know that Patience Cook was ill in the mornin's when she was with child?"

"Do my ears deceive me?" The room blurred through my tears. "Would my own dear sister think this of me?" I yanked my snood over a mass of thick curls.

"It is not usual for one to vomit in the mornin' and then set out for the day as if it never happened," she said. "Were you intimate with Silas?"

I closed my eyes. "God help me."

Sarah took me into her arms.

"Young ladies! The animals must be fed and eggs collected!" Mother yelled.

"We'll be there!" Sarah dabbed her eyes with the corner of her skirt.

"It's true," I said. "I was intimate with Silas at the barn dance. Passion consumed us. I fear this is my fate. More than two months have passed since I have had bleedin'. Sarah, I'm afraid. Please don't speak of this to a soul."

"What will we do?"

"I don't know."

"Will you speak to Silas?"

"I have no answers. I will pray and God will provide answers." I drew in a deep breath and walked towards the stairs. *I have to be brave.*

"Now your breakfast is cold. You mustn't dilly dally around in the mornin'. Get up and tend to your chores," Mother said while water trickled onto her skirt, jest missin' the washbasin.

"Yes, Mother." Sarah had a way of dismissin' her.

I slid my bacon onto her plate and reached for the fine meal bread. "We'll go about our chores with haste." I started to stand. "Did you say that we'd be goin' into town?" *Silas, Silas, always thinkin' of Silas.*

"Yes, we'll go to Clark's for grain and stop at Tibbetts' for molasses if you get to your chores before the heat sets in." She crossed her arms.

The chicken coop was in the back corner of the barn, where the roof sagged from the weight of ice and snow. I went from nest to nest, gatherin' eggs, and placin' them in the hay-lined basket.

Once in the cow barn, I set the egg basket on the floor and pulled the stool up to our beloved cow, Lizzie. She lowed, ready for milkin' with her udders full and swollen. As her milk streamed into the pail, I recalled the fiddler at the barn dance playin' a familiar reel. Silas held me close. I could taste him and feel his warm breath on my neck, which brought about an unexpected, urgent tinglin' throughout. Everybody was tappin' their feet and laughin' and twirlin'. Even Mother was flittin' about with Mr. Tibbetts.

Silas helped build Moses's barn, so he knew of a secret way to the hayloft. When Mother was not takin' notice, Silas took my hand and led me out behind the stables.

"Silas, we should get back. What if Mother sees that I'm missin'?"

He leaned real close, pressin' his nose up against mine. "Shhh. It's a secret. Your mamma is busy with Mr. Tibbetts. She ain't gonna' notice."

I thought that my heart might leap from my chest.

"Follow me." He squeezed my hand and led me into the shadows. The wrought iron bar on the oak door creaked when he lifted it. We walked until we came to a wide ladder. "You go first," he said.

"I can't." I looked back thinkin' that Mother would burst through the door.

He grinned. "Well then take them boots off."

I looked to see if he was makin' merry. He was not. I untied the laces and yanked my worn, black boots off my feet.

He took them from me one at a time and dropped them on the floor. "After you." He extended his arm.

I gathered my skirt and placed my foot on the first step.

He tugged at my elbow and smiled. "Leave the petticoat here too."

I patted my new sack cloth petticoat that Mother made. It was true; I would struggle on the ladder. As God was my witness, I do not know why, but I stepped out of my skirt and petticoat and stood there shiverin' in my corset, pantaloons, and stockin's. I knew that it was a sin. It seemed like someone else was climbin' that ladder, not Abigail Elizabeth Hodgdon.

The light of the full moon streamed into the loft and onto the golden hay mounds piled around us. Silas shook a bundle onto the floor, took off his sack coat, and placed it over the hay. He took me in his arms. "I have missed you." He kissed me.

Before I met Silas, I only knew of kissin' upon closed lips. He taught me to kiss with my lips slightly parted and then caress our tongues. I thought it odd, but within moments, I appreciated the sensitivity of his way of kissin'.

On that night, he kissed me with more passion than I ever remembered. I could only hold back for an instant before completely surrenderin' myself to him. He carefully lay me down onto his coat and pressed his body on top of mine. I could feel his hardness pushin' into my thighs. He reached for my hand and placed it on him. My breath quickened at the feel of his silky skin. I had never seen a naked man, nor touched one intimately. I once saw photographs of statues in a book and found them to be perplexin' at best.

He pulled his shirt over his head, stepped out of his trousers, and stood naked before me. He looked jest like one of those statues, only with his arms intact. His golden curls rested on his broad shoulders. He pulled me to my feet and untied my pantaloons; they dropped to the floor. He then reached behind me and fumbled with my corset ties. I rarely wore one, but gave in to Sarah. She believed in keepin' a small waist as required for high fashion. So silly for a farm girl. He finally pulled it away and placed his hands on my breasts. I quivered, feelin' hot and cold at the same time.

Mother didn't matter. Mr. Tibbetts didn't matter. Nothin' mattered. The music from below pulsed in me, and the laughter came in swells. He pulled me down onto the floor and knelt over me. He started kissin' my neck and then brushed his lips over my skin and onto my breasts. I had never felt such a sensation. I arched my back, wantin' more. He pulled me closer to him as he kissed my stomach, lingerin' jest above the softness of my femininity. He gently parted my legs and touched me. Moist from desire, I ached for him. He pushed himself inside of me.

The pain was sudden, sharp. Tears rolled down my cheeks. He stopped the rhythm. "It's alright." He leaned over and kissed me tenderly and pushed himself deeper inside of me.

I held my breath. My insides were bein' torn to shreds. *I should get away. What am I doin'?* I tensed my legs and started to sit up. "You're hurtin' me," I cried.

He kissed my neck and ran his hand lightly over my breasts. "I'll be easy."

I threw my head back and stared at the beams and Silas above me. The moon framed his curly hair. His eyes were closed. He moved faster and with more strength. My back scraped against the prickly hay and hard wood floor. I bit down on my finger to stifle a scream.

"Oh my God… my sweet Abigail." He shuddered and then hunched over and lay on top of me in a sweaty heap.

His weight crushed me. I took short breaths and whimpered. "I need to get up. I need to leave." Tears and sweat trickled down my face and glistened on my nakedness. *Where can I hide?*

It was hot and wet between my legs, a mixture of his fluids and my blood. I gasped for air. I could not help myself. The loss of my innocence was immeasurable. I was no longer pure. I gave in to lust.

Thick, gray clouds swallowed the moon, makin' the barn dark. I sobbed quietly while I felt around on the floor for my undergarments. Mother must have been lookin' for me.

"Abigail, I've wanted you for so long." He cupped my face in his hands. "Are you cryin'? Aw… don't cry. It ain't gonna' hurt next time." He pulled me to his chest.

I rolled out from under him. "We should have waited 'til we got married. I'm from a good Christian family." I untangled my pantaloons and stepped into them and stumbled towards the ladder. Folks carried on with their clappin', dancin', and merriment. I reached the bottom step and pulled on my boots and laced them before slippin' into my petticoat and skirt. I tugged at my frayed corset. "Silas, tie this. Would you?" My face was ablaze and I fought for air, expectin' Mother to appear.

He yanked the ties much too tightly, to Sarah's standards. "Is this good?"

"It's fine, thank you." I combed my fingers through my hair and headed for the music.

Jest as I was about to open the door, Silas took my hand in his. "Abigail, you're the most pretty girl in all of Ossipee. This was truly a special night." He kissed my hand.

"Do you really think so?" I searched his eyes. I didn't know for what, but I searched. Maybe bein' the prettiest girl jest wasn't enough anymore. Besides, there weren't too many to choose from on a good day.

"I sure do."

"I need to get back." I walked through the door and into the crowd.

Mother was pourin' lemonade for Mr. Tibbetts. She saw me and waved.

My legs wobbled as I approached her. "Could I please have some lemonade?" I forced a smile. She knew.

"Certainly." She examined me.

My hair is mussed. Is my skirt soiled? "Thank you." I took the glass with my shaky hand.

She scanned the room with her eyes. "Where's Silas? I saw you leave together."

I fixed my sights on Sarah as she whirled around in James Moulton's arms. "I'm not his keeper. We went out for some fresh air. I don't know where he is now." Shame burned in my cheeks.

She brought her face close to mine. Her eyes sparkled. "Good. You mustn't stray too far with that young man on such a night. Moonlight breeds temptation."

⚬►═◉ ◉═◄⚬

I sat up straight on the milkin' stool. The pail was close to full. Lizzy was relieved 'til the next mornin', and we would do it all again. I waited a bit before makin' my way to the vile, filthy pigs. Unlike my sister, I had lost the ability to tolerate their stench, but the piglets were delightful.

Sarah was throwin' grain into the trough and singin' to Mabel, our prize winnin' sow that won a blue ribbon at the fair last year. They had reached about fifty pounds, jest startin' to get big. Boars frightened me. Thankfully, we didn't keep any. We took the sows to Moses's farm to breed.

After finishin' the chores, I secured the curls that escaped from my snood and splashed my face with cool water from the rain barrel. Feelin' somewhat refreshed, I plucked a red clover for my buttonhole.

I took my usual place in the back of the cart. Sarah sat beside Mother in the front. I lay back and watched the golden flecks of dust kick up from the road as we rolled along. The sun slipped in and out of cloud puffs while I started in singin' a song that kept time with the horse's hooves. Sarah giggled and then joined in.

For a short spell, I nearly forgot about Silas and my troubles, that is until I heard some men shoutin' off in the distance. I turned my head in time to see the back end of a horse and cart roundin' the corner. My heart thumped wildly at the sight of Silas walkin' alongside that cart from the County Farm.

I sat up and craned my neck to see. Yes, it was him. He had his hand restin' on one of those pine boxes.

I leaned back in the cart and looked up at the sky as I had a mind to do. A well-defined, golden rim outlined the clouds over the Ossipee Mountain Range.

Sarah turned to me. "Are you not goin' to sing? I fancy it when we sing together." She crossed her arms and frowned.

"What shall we sing?"

"'Come Dearest the Daylight is Gone.' I learned to play it on my cornet last week." She rushed the words.

"Start and I will join you."

She started singin', and I joined in as promised. The glowin', celestial clouds merged with new, thick clouds that rose up over the ridge becomin' the color of a ripe pumpkin.

Chapter 10

Abigail – August 25, 1872

A FLY INCHED its way from the bottom of the window to the top, only to buzz back down and start all over again. In an attempt to clear her throat, Mother chirped and glared at the Bible that lay closed on my lap. She ran her finger along the page, mouthin' the words from Corinthians along with Pastor Leighton. Sarah looked beyond him, unblinkin'.

Mr. and Mrs. Cook were in the pew in front of us. Mr. Cook had a habit of noddin' off. His head dropped further and further to the side with each raspy breath, 'til he got an elbow from his wife.

I often wondered what happened to their daughter, Patience. Some folks said that she went to Boston to become a teacher, while others claimed to see her down at the County Farm. It was no secret that she was with child. The way the poor Cooks carried on, one would think that she never existed. No one had the courage to mention Patience in front of them, but tongues wagged when they turned their backs.

I had a pleasin' hope to see Silas and his folks. It was a rare occasion for them to visit the house of the Lord. When I asked, he shrugged his shoulders. *He ain't got no time for that. Besides, you don't hafta' be inside a meetin' house to talk to God.* He said that he talked to God whenever he pleased and without the help of a pastor.

I felt the thwack in my chest when the pastor closed his Bible. "And that ends our readin' from the Old Testament. Let us pray."

His bushy eyebrows gathered like rain clouds over his beady eyes, and he glared at me. My mouth went dry. I closed my eyes while Sarah rested her head on Mother's shoulder.

"...sinners shall repent, O Lord thy Father..."

I willed Pastor Leighton away, and in my head I shouted louder than him. *Heavenly Father, I have sinned. I gave in to temptation. I beg for forgiveness and pray for my illness to be of a different sort and not because a child grows in me. I do solemnly promise to be forever in Your service, as I am now quite void of spirit...*

"...We gather together this morning to pray for our souls, so that we shall not be damned to Hell. We pray to Thee Father our souls to take..." His deep voice wavered.

I squeezed my eyes shut tighter and rested my chin on my hands and continued. *If it is my fate to have a child, God, please let it be when I am Silas's lawful wife. I shall be an obedient and willin' servant. I will never question my faith or the Word of God...*

"...In the Lord's name we pray..."

...Amen... Mother nudged me.

I leaned forward with my head barely touchin' the pew before me, secretly dabbin' away my tears. Mother cleared her throat and squirmed in preparation to stand up and sing.

"Let us open our hymnals to number 258." Pastor Leighton raised his hands as if he were partin' the Red Sea. The congregation scrambled to their feet.

Mrs. Leighton began pullin' out organ stops and pumped the foot pedal with both feet. Her plump body rocked from side to side as her fingers danced over the yellowed keys. The familiar strains of "Abide with Me" blared into the airless room.

Mother's voice rose over and above the rest of the folks, and her cheeks turned as red as Pearl's comb. Everyone knew that she had the best singin' voice in town, and she sang quite loud lest anyone forget.

Sarah stifled a giggle behind her mitted hand when her eyes rested on Mr. Tibbetts. There was no mystery surroundin' the fact that he was smitten with Mother. He stood shamefully with his mouth hangin' open while he stared. I pulled my cracked sandalwood fan from my reticule and covered my glowin' cheeks.

We hadn't reached the end of the hymn and Mr. and Mrs. Cook were out the door to avoid talkin'. Mother fussed with the well-worn feather that hung from her hat and tucked her Bible under her arm. I waited and watched as a fly plummeted from the top of the window down to the corner of the sill, desperate for a way out.

Trapped in between pews, I fanned my chest and turned. I caught sight of a man, woman, and girl who looked to be of my age. All the folks were eyein' them, payin' special attention to the girl. You could tell that she was proper and led a charmed life by the way she stood erect in her fancy emerald dress, which boasted frilly lace, ruffles, and flounces, an uncommon sight in this town. My cheeks burned at the thought of my sack-cloth under my meek skirt.

Her tiny straw bonnet was adorned with silk flowers, pleated cotton lace, and a long velvet ribbon tied at the side of her jawbone, matchin' her corn silk curls. The cameo fastened upon the collar of her dress rested against her slender, white neck. She caught me lookin' and smiled and fiddled with the parasol in her dainty gloved hands.

I nodded quickly and turned towards Sarah. "Don't be lookin' now, but there's new folks up near the front."

Sarah glanced. "I saw them at Mr. Tibbetts' on Wednesday." She held her hand in front of her mouth. "There's talk that they moved to Water Village and that he's a physician."

We stood in line until it was our turn to greet the pastor. I stared at his limp, white hand that had never seen the likes of a hard day's work as he extended it to Mother. "Fine day, ladies, so nice to see you. I trust that all is well?" He always stood erect and leaned to one side. I was certain that he had a troublesome kink in his neck. He was taller than most with a full head of thick, white hair. His wife stood next to him bobbin' her head, barely reachin' his chest. She didn't talk much and she always scrunched her nose and squinted her eyes like she was strugglin' to see.

Jest as Mother was about to speak, Effie Morrill reached in front of her and grabbed his hand. "Hello, Pastor... fine sermon." She pushed Mother aside with her ample hips.

Mrs. Leighton blushed as her husband stammered.

"C'mon, girls." Mother marched down the grassy hill towards the cart, stompin' right past Mr. Tibbetts, who was by his horse watchin' and waitin'. "Effie Morrill has no manners at all. Every time I see that woman, she gets me madder than a hornet. If I had the sense, I would have told her right there in front of all those folks to hold her tongue, but I have proper manners, and I am the one who holds my own tongue." She snapped the reins, and Old Gray mare trotted with a bit more spirit than usual. She rattled on for the whole ride home and into the better part of the afternoon.

Sarah had a curious look about her that day, and she only played her cornet for a short spell, which was quite uncommon for her. After dinner, we retired to our rickety chairs on the porch.

"I have somethin' to say," Sarah said, breakin' the silence.

"What is it?" Mother picked up her needlework from her basket.

"Well." She looked down at her feet. "Mrs. Porter invited me to talkin', and she says that Mercy and Rebecca find workin' at the mill to be quite pleasin'." Suddenly it became too quiet, too muggy, and too dark for that time of day.

"And what might that have to do with us?" Mother jabbed the needle through the cloth.

My chair creaked; my breath quickened. I had hoped that Sarah would get rid of the notion of leavin' home for the mills.

"I have made my decision to go to the mills in Fall River and join them." The lines on her forehead went away as she exhaled.

"Sarah Jane Hodgdon. That is nonsense. You will stay here with your sister and me." Mother dropped her needlework on her lap.

"Sarah, is this wise?" I asked.

"I have thought about this long and hard. I am of age and able to make this decision. I want to go to Fall River to see the world, to have an adventure, to work and earn wages." She sat up straight as though each word helped to support her delicate frame.

"I wouldn't know what to do if you left. Please... don't," I said, tryin' to remain unruffled.

"I know that this is difficult, but I'll be leavin' on the train Saturday mornin'." She would not look at us.

There was a stirrin' in the barn. Lizzy stomped and Pearl's crow cut off midway. Thunder clouds rumbled from afar, and the wind blew the underside of the leaves on the silver birches, a sure sign of an impendin' storm.

The afternoon heat ached for relief. I walked around to the front of the house, dipped the ladle into the rain barrel and drank. *She will not leave me. Not now. I cannot be here with Mother. I need her.* I choked on the water, gaspin' and carryin' on so.

"Abby, don't." She took me in her arms. "I will not be gone forever. I promise." Her voice cracked. "You could come with me, but it is best for you to stay with Mother. Do you agree?"

We shared the moment with words unspoken. What she meant was that I could not go with her because I was with child. She could not stay. She had made plans for nearly a year to move to Fall River, to free herself from the farm, from Ossipee, and to become an independent woman.

Mother's needlework fell to the ground with a clatter, and she dashed into the house. Her cries followed as she fled to her room. It was best for her to be alone. Sarah and I walked hand in hand to our favorite childhood spot, the sittin' rock by the brook, which was but a trickle in late August.

The wind blew hard, and the sky was a blush of pinkish yellow hue. The warm rain started out softly and soon pelted down hard on the roof, drownin' out the cries of our mother. We sat together until our clothes were soaked and clingin' to our skin. We cried for Papa, and we cried for Mother. We cried for each other and for the child that grew inside of me.

CHAPTER 11

Nellie – August 25, 1872

IT WAS THE sugar-making month. The north winds blew hard. I held Mamijôla inside of my fur, close to my breast. She viewed the world with curious eyes as we rode on the horse of my father's brother. We followed the season of the fish to the other shore.

The last snow of winter clung to the breast of Our Mother and hid in the shadows of the great pines. My people went before me, deep in the woods. There was no rain.

My mother's face shined in the new day. *Nanatasis, what is it that makes your journey slow?* She did not smile.

Mamijôla's hair touched my face. *There is new life and offerings for Mamijôla.* I parted the low branches.

Ride fast Nanatasis, or you will be lost. She circled around us.

I will find my way. I know these woods.

So be it. We will gather around the fire at sunset. She departed with great speed.

The icy winds came from Bitawbagok. I took the path of the fox towards the inner circle of the trees, where there was warmth. White River swelled with melting snow and spring rain.

Mamijôla reached for the small flower that shivered in snow. I took her hand. *You must never take a plant without purpose. For then it will die. We gather for medicine and food, leaving some for those who follow. This brave flower stands tall in snow, rain, and wind. Like you, she is a warrior.*

Mamijôla looked with round blue eyes. She held my leg and pointed. *The tree touches Father Sky.*

It holds many secrets. Her small hand was warm in mine. *We must follow the path to where three rivers cross, and then meet the others.* We rode to the river crossing.

The moaning chased Mamijôla into the dark corners of the dream world.

⋯⊱═◉ ◉═⊰⋯

From the other side of the room the cries grew. Mahitable mourned her son. She shed many tears.

I closed my eyes to bring Mamijôla back. The cries grew stronger. I sat up. I pulled the board from the floor and searched for bark and needles of white pine. The one with hair the color of a fox would give me water.

I carried the pine inside of my belt. The floor was cold. Many people stood quiet in the room where people waited.

The lady with hair the color of a fox was by the stove. "What are you doin' here so early?"

I raised my cup.

"You'll be wantin' some hot water again, I s'pose."

She poured the water.

"I ain't givin' you no more today, so don't ask me agin."

I snapped the needles and bark into pieces and added them to the hot water to make medicine. I went to Mahitable.

"Why do you come?" She sat on the floor. Her dress fell away from her white skin.

I joined in sitting.

"I hope you don't think I'm gonna' drink that."

It was not time. I looked to where the men were with the animals. The roosters called.

"I don't feel right."

I stirred with a pine stick and looked long at her.

"You want me to drink this?"

I nodded.

"It's hot." She did not smile.

I brought it to her lips.

"I'll drink it," she said.

I watched her drink it all. I rose up to leave.

"Nellie? Thank you. It tastes like Christmas."

Mahitable would be strong and join with the others to get food.

I carried my bowl and stood behind the elder who could not see or hear. I would help him.

CHAPTER 12

Silas – August 25, 1872

"SILAS!" HER VOICE rose above the squealin' and snortin' of hungry sows.

The empty feed bucket clattered when it rolled on the ground. "Comin' Mamma." I kicked it clear across the yard before latchin' the gate.

"We've got folks stoppin' in for dinner." Golden dust sparkled around her as she wailed the floor with the broom's remainin' brittle strands, matchin' her own wiry, gray hair. She leaned on the splintered handle and wagged her finger. "So don't be makin' no plans to leave."

"I was gonna' go play checkers with Eb." Truth be known, I was fixin' to see if I could catch a glimpse of Abigail up at Tibbetts'.

"Well you can do that another time." She started in thrashin' the broom. "We met the new doctor and his family over to Clark's. They come down from Parsonsfield."

"Ayuh." I thought of Daddy talkin' nonsense with foamy brown cider drippin' off his whiskers. "I'll stick to home and see Eb next week."

"And see to the wood, will ya?" She took a good swipe at each step, makin' her way to the bottom.

"Ayuh." I stared at the woodpile thinkin' that I would have to hunt down Abigail durin' the week, which was no easy task with me at the farm and her mother perched over her like a broody hen.

My stomach grumbled when I smelled blueberry pie. Mamma was a fine cook when she weren't fussin' over Daddy. When we had company, she cooked all the merries that was abound.

I picked some pretty flowers out in the pasture. My favorites bein' the red and yellow ones that Abigail called Indian Paintbrushes. I was settin' 'em into a crock of water when I heard a squeaky carriage.

"Silas, go help them." Mamma uncurled the frayed doily onto the table, tuckin' the corner in so you couldn't see the stain.

"Ayuh." I set my eyes on the finest pleasure carriage I had ever seen in Ossipee. It was shiny black and had them fancy seats. The doctor was wearin' his Sunday best — a tall, black hat and a fancy watch with a chain that flashed in the sunlight. We was able to see eye to eye. He was nearly as tall as me. He gawked at me over his gold spectacles and raised an eyebrow. His big waxed moustache wiggled like the whiskers of a giant rabbit when he spoke to his wife, a plain, slight woman wearin' a dark red dress and matchin' hat.

The daughter? Well, I ain't never seen one like her before. She had pleasin' green eyes, milky white skin, and her full lips was like ripe strawberries beggin' to be picked. A row of tight yellow curls bounced with each step.

I caught sight of my muddy boots while makin' my way over to 'em. I looked away, laughed a little, and wiped the sweat from under my nose.

The doctor helped his wife down from the carriage while I offered my hand to the girl. "Fine day, Miss." I nodded. "I'm Silas, uh, Silas Putnam."

The scabs and calluses on my hand made a scratchin' noise against her white glove.

"Thank you. I'm Jessie." Her voice was easy on the ear, makin' my legs a bit shaky. She held tight to me and seemed to float like she had wings or somethin'.

I released her and stiffened when I heard Daddy's leg draggin' on the ground behind me, leavin' a distinct trail in the dirt. I squeezed my hand into a tight fist inside my pocket. Mamma's skirt brushed against my leg as she stood beside me with her words all tangled up inside.

Mr. Gilman reached out. "Hello, Silas. I'm Dr. Gilman and this is my wife, Betsey."

I pulled away from his soft clammy grip and wiped my hand on my trousers.

I nodded at Mrs. Gilman. "Pleased to meet you." A flowery scent washed over me, makin' it hard to swallow and concentrate. I sort of laughed again.

"This is quite a farm, Hiram," the doctor said as he fiddled with his moustache.

"Well, my boy does most of the work. I get around as good as can be 'spected." He tapped his wooden leg and laughed hard and too loud.

"Betsey, come on inside." Mamma finally spoke. She smiled and put her arm 'round Mrs. Gilman's waist, and they walked towards the house.

Jessie went to the pasture, and Major trotted right up to her. My feet might as well have been growin' roots. I couldn't move to save myself, so I jest watched. She plucked one of them little purple flowers by the fence, and she put it in her buttonhole.

"Let's join the ladies," Daddy said rather clearly. He was at his best. Each time he spoke he opened his eyes real wide. He hadn't taken to his jug and was almost makin' sense.

"Come now, Jessie," Dr. Gilman called out.

She walked gracefully, as though she was swayin' to a waltz. The sides of her skirt were pulled up, revealin' a ruffled petticoat. Mamma served tea while we sat politely and listened to Daddy and Dr. Gilman talk about taxes and affairs of the town. Daddy agreed with jest about everything the doctor was sayin' and kept wipin' his forehead and glancin' at the jug in the corner.

Their words blended with the bees that buzzed in and out of the flowers. Every so often, I caught Jessie lookin' right at me. When I tried to speak, my words got mixed up, and I blushed like a girl. I bit my nails right down to the quick, hopin' for them folks to leave.

Finally, after a good part of the afternoon passed, I stood watchin' 'em through a cloud of mosquitoes as they sauntered down to their fancy carriage. I fought the urge to follow.

CHAPTER 13

Abigail – August 30, 1872

WHEN I IMAGINED how an angel might look, I saw the face of my sister. I stared at her as she slept beside me. It was impossible to believe that she would not be there the next night. She was always there. Each time I went over this in my head, I struggled for air while a great invisible hand pressed down on my chest. I finally fell asleep only to awaken with a start from a wave of sickness that passed as quickly as it came.

Sarah was up with Pearl's crowin', packin' the last of her belongin's. Her silky black hair fell over her shoulders as she folded her camisole and packed her beloved cornet in its case. I would miss hearin' her playin' every day as she had for the past several years. Tears hurried down my cheeks.

"Where's my tortoise shell comb?" She rummaged through our pine trinket box.

"I don't know." I rushed to the chamber pot, removed the cover, and heaved, but nothin' came.

She patted my back. "Oh dear. I fear leavin' you, but I've dreamed of this day for at least two years. The time has come, but it doesn't look promisin' for you." She sat on the edge of the bed.

"You mustn't change your plans on the account of me. I have gotten myself into such a way." I sat beside her. The heavin' stopped. "I will find a way out."

"I promise to write. When your illness passes, you can join me," she said.

I lay back on the pillow. "We must be truthful now. I am with child. This is not a passin' illness. Tonight at the barn dance I'll tell Silas, and he'll do right by me." I wrapped a springy curl around my finger. "I'll never work in the mills. I may never leave Ossipee because I will be Mrs. Silas Putnam." I peered through the curl and smiled. "We will have a house full of children and be merry."

She clasped her hands to her breast. "Dear God."

"After you have worked in the mills and have a husband, you will return and live in a farm beside us, and we'll raise our families together. Mother will be proud."

"I promise to return." She wrapped her arms around me and squeezed. "I will work feverishly and tell you of my adventures."

"Your comb is on my dressin' table... I will miss it," I said and laughed quietly.

"Mother is not pleased about me partin' this way, but she has you, and before long she will have Silas and a grandchild," she said.

"She will fret and fuss as she has a mind to do, but I will remain her loyal servant." I rolled my eyes. "You are her favorite, but she'll have to settle for me for the time bein'."

"Nonsense. She favors us both." We both knew it was a fib, but far be it for either one of us to muck through it.

"Well, we have a lot to do for the harvest. You're leavin' jest in time. Winter is harsh as you well know." I tugged on the drawstring of my pantaloons.

"I'll be in a new world, but Fall River isn't too far away. I'll miss you somethin' awful."

Mother served up a hearty breakfast of eggs, beans, and corn bread before we took to the dusty road. No one uttered a word, leavin' so much unsaid.

When we arrived at the train depot, Eb Burrows came straight over to the cart. He was a friendly sort who shuffled about as if he was doin' a peculiar dance. "Good mornin', ladies." He flashed a brown checkerboard smile, unable to contain his pride in holdin' a position of such high rank for the likes of him.

"Mornin'." Mother brushed past him with her chin up. "Can you get these bags?"

"That's what I'm fixin' to do." He glanced at Sarah. "You're the one travelin'?"

"That's right. Here's my ticket." She rooted around in her reticule.

"Hold on." He spat a thick gob of tobacco before scoopin' up her bags.

I reached out to her as my heart withered. "Well… this is farewell."

"This is jest for a time." She nodded, tryin' to make herself believe it to be true. "I will write often." She flung her arms around my neck.

"I know." I choked back the tears. "Be safe." I stumbled backwards.

Mother wailed pitifully. "Oh Sarah, what will I do without you?" She covered her mouth with her soakin' wet handkerchief. She looked small and defeated, lettin' go of her favorite child and no doubt thinkin' of Papa and the drab day that he left on the train.

I watched as they clung together. The daughter — afraid yet determined — comforted the mother, a wilted remnant of what once blossomed. My chest heaved as I kept my tears prisoner inside of my own thick walls. I wanted to run. Instead, I looked at her squarely. "Do you have your cornet?"

"Of course." She blushed and her eyes filled with tears. "I would not go anywhere without it."

The train let out two short whistles and chugged to the platform. A few unfamiliar folks boarded before Sarah slipped through the door almost unnoticed. I watched her willowy shadow pass by each window before she took a seat near the back. She turned towards us and pressed her hand on the glass, always the brave one.

We waved our handkerchiefs as we did for Papa, only there were no crowds, no flags, and no brass band. Unlike Papa, Sarah would return.

Mother and I rode in silence amongst the rattlin' wheels and the clip cloppin' of Old Gray Mare while the cart rocked gently. I stared numbly as we passed beneath trees that sprawled against an infinite sky. Some leaves already showed hints of yellow and red, a sure sign of a bitter winter to follow.

My thoughts turned to the barn dance. Silas would want to take me to the secret loft. I would go, but not to give in to passion, as we were in much want of it. No, I would tell him about our child. He would gather me in his arms and ask me to be his wife. First, we would tell our folks and then plan a splendid weddin'.

Jest as we approached Brown's Ridge, we passed a fancy, black pleasure carriage. I whipped my head around to catch a good look. Such a carriage was an unusual sight here. It was certain to be a person of importance.

I felt a curious shiver. It was the new folks we had seen at church. The man and woman sat tall and proud in the front, while their lovely daughter was perched in back like a porcelain doll. She tossed her golden curls and looked away. The man tipped his hat, and the woman smiled rather shyly. Trapped in her own misery, Mother did not take notice and said not a single word.

When we arrived home, she wasted no time goin' to her room and throwin' herself down on her bed. After I got Old Gray Mare settled in her stall, I went to comfort Mother.

"Go away. I do not need anything now," she muttered into the pillow.

With all the fuss, the chores remained undone. "I'll collect the eggs, tend to the feedin', and see to the garden." I spoke with a child's voice. I willed her to call me, to hold me close enough so that I could smell the lavender oil in her hair, and for her to stroke my face and tell me that we would carry on and that all would be well.

"Do what you wish." I tried, but failed to conjure up the heavenly voice that filled the church earlier. What a dismal condition she was in.

My cheeks burned. I preferred her to strike me with her hand, rather than sting me with words. I walked down the path to the chicken coop, plucked a red clover, and sat on a rock by the fence nibblin' the sweet nectar.

⋅⇥⊨◉ ◉⊨⇤⋅

Mother finally got up from her bed, her eyes red and swollen. "I will not be at Moses's barn dance tonight. There is no need to celebrate." She collapsed into her rockin' chair.

"Perhaps you would feel more cheerful if you went dancin'." I placed a heavy yellow squash on the table.

"No, and it is not wise for you to go unaccompanied."

"Mother, I look forward to these dances." My mouth went dry.

"There will be no disagreement. You will stay home." She picked up a garment and poked the needle through the cloth aimlessly.

"I cannot—"

"Abigail, you will respect my wishes, and there will be no discussion." The rhythm of the creaky chair quickened as she suddenly transformed from a wounded sparrow into a vicious rooster.

I fled, takin' the stairs two at a time, and fell on my own bed and wailed. *What will happen if I don't see Silas? I must see him... he must know... this is unjust!* I stared at Sarah's bed. She was truly gone. The tears came from a place deep inside and continued until I was sure that the well of my soul had run dry.

I awoke some hours later all clammy and with my damp curls clingin' to my skin. The sun left a layer of dense, pink clouds over the ridge, makin' way for the coolness of the evenin'. I stood still in the doorway. There was no sound comin' from below.

I tiptoed downstairs and entered the dark sittin' room, where she slept in her chair with her sewin' beside her in a tangled heap. Her eyes fluttered and then opened wide causin' my heart to leap.

"Mother, you were asleep," I whispered.

"Yes, I was sewin' one moment and asleep the next." She gathered her needlework.

"I'm not hungry. I'll take a bath and then go to bed. It has been a long day." I started for the water pump.

"There is no fire to heat the water. It would be wise to wait 'til tomorrow." She lit the lantern and smiled weakly. "Nothin' much to dance about." The light flickered in her green eyes.

"True. I feel dreadful from the dust and heat of the day. I will take a splash of cool water from the pump."

The night chorus quickly swallowed the words that she uttered behind me. With fresh undergarments in hand, I walked to the pump, dropped my clothes, and stood in the sultry August night in all of my nakedness, shiverin' as the air dried the sweat on my breasts.

The icy water splashed over me in bursts, stealin' my breath. I had the most pleasin' hopes to be fresh for Silas. I dried myself hastily, not wantin' to raise Mother's suspicions. Wearin' only pantaloons, I entered the sittin' room. "Good night." I kissed her soft cheek. "Tomorrow is a new day."

"Good night. Sleep well." She leaned back into the chair and started in hummin' "Rock of Ages." Her voice, rather quiet at first, rallied with each note.

I sat on the bed and watched the stars appear. I focused on the first one that came into sight, for it is only the first star that one sees that will grant a wish. *My wish is for Silas to rejoice when I tell him that I carry his child.* I counted on my fingers as I always did. *The birth will take place in the latter part of March. I must tell him.*

All was quiet 'cept for a slight rustlin' of leaves. The lantern by Mother's chair cast enough light for me to see. I leaned out the window and dropped my sackcloth petticoat and skirt to the ground.

I stretched one leg out the window, felt for a branch with my foot, and stepped on it. Then I bent down and brought my other leg around 'til I was sittin' right in the heart of the tree. *Lord, please don't let me fall.* I climbed carefully, feelin' my way along the rough bark with my hands and feet until a branch beneath my foot snapped with a loud crack and plummeted to the ground. I gasped and clutched the nearest branch. I searched with my foot for a stronger, thicker branch. I finally reached the ground and stood in silence.

I peered into the window. Mother slept soundly in her chair; the lantern flickered on the table beside her. Old Gray Mare walked towards the fence and snorted.

"Shhh. Go back," I whispered.

She kept on comin'. I went behind the barn and stepped into my petticoat and skirt. I sighed and ran my fingers through a mass of damp, unruly curls. I had forgotten my snood.

The rusted gate moaned when I touched it. I paused. There were no signs of Mother awakenin'.

Old Gray Mare followed me 'til we got down the road apiece. I grabbed a hank of mane and mounted up. With no one to scold me, I took the liberty to go fast. I leaned forward and kicked into her sides, nearly forgettin' my woes.

It had been some years since Sarah and I climbed down the tree to frolic in the night.

-»⊨◉ ◉⊨«-

Laughter mingled with the fiddle and concertina as they hammered out "Turkey in the Straw." The barn was all lit up. Folks were dancin' and makin' merry. I stood in the darkness catchin' my breath while my horse blissfully chomped clover.

Even though I was late, I did not rush. I forced myself to take small, un-hurried steps. I stopped in the doorway and scanned the barn to catch sight of him.

I spun around when I heard his voice above the commotion. Folks were clappin' and dancin' in a circle. He was in the middle with his arm around the girl in the fancy carriage. He held her close.

She wore a lush, plum taffeta dress cinched tightly around her tiny waist and a black plume feather cascadin' down from the curls piled atop her head.

I tried to swallow. I thought that I might vomit. *Gather yourself, Abigail.* I held my head up high and walked to the refreshment table. Noah Jones and his portly wife, Mariah, were pourin' drinks. "Abigail, want some lemonade?" She forced a smile.

I had no tolerance for the likes of insincere folks. I wanted to scream but responded almost too quietly to hear. "No, thank you."

The dance ended and Silas approached with the girl. He noticed me and dropped her hand while she continued laughin' and carryin' on. She stopped, glanced at me, and then looked away.

"Abigail, what a surprise. I didn't think you was comin' to the dance... not at this hour," he said with his cheeks ablaze.

"I am fond of surprises, didn't you know that?" I turned towards Mariah. "I will have that lemonade now, please."

"Did you meet Jessie?" He touched my shoulder.

"I have not had the pleasure." *How could I detest someone I had never met?*

Her green eyes did not waver. She wore a string of pearls around her neck and the beads on her dress could only be from the finest dressmaker. I searched her face for a flaw, but there was none. She was possibly the most beautiful girl I had ever seen. I gripped the table.

"Abigail Hodgdon, this is Jessie Gilman," he said quickly.

"Such a pleasure meeting you." She curtsied.

"The pleasure is mine. Now, if you will excuse me." I spun around nearly fallin' flat as the room whirled about. I stumbled towards the musicians.

The fiddler lifted his bow and started up a jig. Weston Jones, an agreeable fellow with an uncertain voice and apologetic look, approached me. "May I have this dance?"

Limp, shaken, and without an excuse, I managed to speak. "I would be honored."

Uncommonly tall and lanky, Weston wore his black hair slicked tight to his small head. Sarah fancied him, but he was not to my likin'. He bowed and removed his hat in one broad sweep. I managed to grasp his hand and go out with him to join in a square.

I watched Silas over my shoulder. He appeared to be attentive to that horrid girl as she bobbed her head and flirted with her fan. When his eyes rested upon me, I pressed close to Weston and smiled, as my heart was grieved and my soul done in.

We twirled and twirled. I tried to fix my eyes on somethin' to keep from faintin'. We turned to do-si-do, and I saw the bottom corner of the plum taffeta dress disappear through the back door. The dance that seemed like it would not end, finally did. I dashed outside with Weston close behind. "Are you alright?"

"Oh, I am fine. I simply needed some fresh air." My chest rose and fell sharply with each breath. I thought that I might be ill.

"I'll get us some lemonade. Wait right here."

"No, thank you. Uh… it's late and I must be leavin' now." I worked up a smile. "And thank you for the dance."

I watched his mouth move but didn't hear a word. I ran to my horse, mounted up, and fled into the darkness.

An orange glow appeared on the knoll. Old Gray Mare reared and pranced sideways. As I got closer, an explosion of sparks surged into the night sky. I gripped her mane as we halted. I could barely see through the thick cloud of smoke. I tried to accept what I saw as true.

I kicked the mare hard, passin' through a wall of heat. "Mother! Mother!" I cried and ran towards the house, only to stop when the heat scorched my skin, throat, and nose. A sheet of flames licked the eaves and hurried onto the barn roof as heavy beams toppled inside. "Mother! Where are you?" My screams were consumed by the cracklin' roar.

The chickens flapped about, and Pearl crowed sporadically. Lizzy stomped and shrieked along with the pigs. I ran to the side of the barn and yanked on the door of the coop. The chickens flushed out, squawkin' and beatin' me with their wings as they took flight.

I touched the latch on Lizzy's stall, gaspin' as the flesh sizzled on my hand. She backed up against the wall with the whites of her eyes showin'. "Go on!" I swatted her hindquarters. She scrambled out, almost losin' her balance.

The pigs charged the gate. I pulled at the door, causin' it to swing open and jam against my ankle. A stabbin' pain ripped across my leg when the pigs trampled over me. I jerked my ankle out from under the wooden slat and escaped, trippin' over my skirt, which I tore off of me and threw to the floor.

The treasure chest! I limped past the flames as they raced along the beams to the pottin' shed in the back. I grabbed the old wooden box from the bottom shelf. The fire spread to the hay bundles jest as I fled from the barn. Somehow, I managed to mount my horse. We galloped down the road towards Moses's place. I clutched the treasure chest under my arm and gulped the fresh, crisp air. I rode straight to the barn and toppled to the ground.

"Help! Help me! My house is on fire! I can't find Mother!"

Weston scooped me into his arms. "Abigail!"

"Help me!" My voice sounded far away.

"Fire at Hodgdon Farm!" He hollered over his shoulder.

The men folk shouted and mounted their horses and disappeared into the darkness.

Silas rushed up to us. "Abigail!"

I lifted my head from Weston's shoulder and looked at him standin' before me with Jessie by his side. I wiggled free and staggered towards my horse.

Weston rode beside me amidst a flurry of speedin' horses.

The orange glow had diminished, givin' way to thick, black, angry clouds. Whitish yellow flames illuminated the figures of shoutin' men, while the ravenous fire devoured the barn. The house was still burnin', but not as fiercely as before.

I ran, favorin' my ankle that swelled up twice the size it should have been. "Where is Mother? Did you find her?" I strained to see her inside the frame of scorchin' embers.

"Come here, child." Moses hugged me, pressin' my face into his smoky shirt. "I don't know how to say this other than straight out." He coughed. "Your Ma perished. She's gone to the good Lord. There ain't no sign of no one here." He stroked my head while the barn crackled and sizzled behind us. "It's a good thing you let them animals out."

I could not speak, nor believe what was before me. *This is because of me.* I stared, unblinkin' at the glowin' coals. *Oh dear Sarah, how I need you now.* The tears were too deep to rise up from within me.

"You can stay with us. Miriam will take care of you." Moses patted my shoulder.

The sound of thunderin' hooves were fast approachin'. Silas hopped down from his horse and ran to me. "Are you hurt?" He embraced me. I wanted to fall into him, to be safe. The faint scent of flowers on his shirt conjured an image of the plum taffeta skirt. I pulled away.

CHAPTER 14

Silas – August 30, 1872

I WAS APT to sort things out when I worked. I hadn't seen Abigail for nearly a week. There was talk that Sarah left for Fall River, which wouldn't be too easy. Then there was Jessie. I met up with her 'round every corner. She sure was a temptation, but Abigail was in my heart.

The sun beat down on the men, makin' work slow. Some was old, and some was simple, but it didn't matter when the garden needed tendin'. We tried to keep the women on one end of the field and the men on the other.

The anvil rang out from behind Moses as he headed in my direction. I knew that he was goin' to ask me to do a chore that wasn't to my likin'. He had that look about him.

"Silas." He chewed on the end of his pipe. "Go work with him." He nodded towards the far edge of the field where William Quimby worked a team of oxen.

"Yes, sir." I was pleased to see William.

"One more thing." He spit.

"Ayuh?"

"Make sure you come to my place tonight for the dance!" He slapped me hard on the back and laughed from deep in his gut before breakin' into a fitful cough.

"You ain't gotta' ask me twice." I wiped the sweat from under the rim of my hat and watched Nellie sittin' down by the pond. She musta' been at least a hundred years old, but she didn't make no fuss. She jest asked for hot water for her tea. Sometimes I barked at her if Miss Noyes or Polly was watchin', to show 'em that I weren't soft, but I sure as hell weren't gonna' use no stick.

I was pleased that Mamma and Daddy chose not to go dancin'. All eyes would be on Daddy if he took to stumblin' and hootin' and hollerin'. He would spoil everything, tuggin' on his jug and all, and I would have to carry him home.

⋄⟞◉ ◉⟝⋄

I hurried with the buttons on my fancy brown vest that I always wore for somethin' special. I figured I'd better get a move on, even though it was well before sundown. The way Daddy was singin' and tappin' on his leg, I thought he might change his mind.

I was there in a jiff and was still on my horse when Miriam Blake started shoutin' out orders. "Silas! Come up here and help with the chairs!" She was a hefty woman, a pleasin' sort with a round pumpkin face.

I happily obliged seein' I was jest waitin' around. I stopped in the doorway when I caught a whiff of pine and hay. There weren't nothin' like a fresh barn. I puffed up with pride at the sight of the perfect timbers.

A family of musicians showed up one by one. Sheldon — well known in these parts — always had his fiddle under his chin. He was a string bean with long, lean arms and wiry legs. I s'posed the women took to him cause he wooed 'em with his fiddle. His brother Myles followed close behind with his concertina strapped on his back. The girls had a hankerin' for him too. He was a strappin' fellow and could even beat Moses at arm wrestlin'. Their fiery sister Anna arrived last carryin' her banjo and with her loyal black dog by her side. She was easy on the eye with her wild curls flyin' free. She wore her dress off her shoulders and had a gypsy air about her. She had a singin' voice like none other. I sat and watched the three of 'em get tuned up while I waited for my pretty girl.

Folks wandered in bit-by-bit 'til the place was nearly full. The chatter hushed when the Gilmans' carriage approached. Jessie was peerin' out from behind her fan. I jerked my head around when the music started with a sharp sour chord that quickly came in tune. I watched Jessie outta' the corner of my eye. She was walkin' my way, wearin' a dark purple dress. I never saw nothin' like it. It was a kind of special material, silk or somethin', with jewels on it. Her hair was all fancy with a big black feather stickin' out. I leaned back into the chair.

"Good evening." She was all a flutter with her fan.

"Evenin'." The chair clattered when I stood up and removed my hat.

"I shall think it finer after I have had the pleasure to dance." She fanned. She laughed.

I scanned the room for Abigail.

"Will you accompany me to fetch some lemonade? It's dreadfully hot in here." A cloud of flowery perfume stung the insides of my nostrils.

"Ayuh." I was a bit unhinged when I took note of folks gawkin' and whisperin'. She placed her small gloved hand in the crook of my elbow, and we walked over to the refreshment table where Noah and Mariah Jones served up lemonade and hard cider for the men folk.

Noah raised a thick black eyebrow. "Hello, Silas. I don't believe we've met the young lady." His face shined with sweat.

"Noah and Mariah Jones? Miss Jessie Gilman."

"You're the doctor's daughter?" Mariah asked and smiled.

Jessie blushed. "Yes."

Noah grabbed her hand in both of his, shakin' too hard. "It's a pleasure meetin' you, young lady. Would you like a glass of lemonade?"

She wiggled her hand free. "Yes, please." Her smile caused a sort of peculiar feelin' that was good and bad all mixed up together.

Every time a new dance started, Jessie peeked out from behind the fan and giggled. I kept my eyes fixed on the door waitin' for Abigail. My stomach stirred thinkin' about askin' Jessie to dance. She moved a little closer and pressed her arm against mine. Her fair skin was soft.

Before I knew it I was talkin'. "You wanna dance?"

"I would love to." She slapped her fan shut.

People parted to let us through to the middle of the floor, where a new square was formin'. I undid the top button of my shirt on the account of the heat. She knew all the calls and was quick as a deer. I set my eyes on her and pretty much forgot about everything else.

The musicians started in playin' "Turkey in the Straw" and the caller shouted, "Swing your partner round and round!" My hand fit perfectly around the curve of her waist. I felt her firm breasts when I pulled her against me. She glistened with sweat. I could taste her.

We carried on, pressin' closer and closer with each dance. I had a mind to look up. Abigail was lookin' straight at me. *Oh hell! What am I doin?*

The music stopped. Pretty near all the folks stopped talkin' and took notice. "Jessie, I need a drink."

"I would like that." She muckled onto my hand and ran towards Abigail. I tried to pull away, but she held on tight.

"Abigail... uh... I didn't think you was comin' to the dance at this hour." I finally freed my hand.

Her face was pink. "I'm fond of surprises."

Folks hollered over the blarin' music, and I had trouble gettin' a good breath. I put my hands in my pockets. "Abigail, did you meet Jessie?" I talked at her backside.

"No, I have not." She turned and glared at me.

The two women bore their teeth in what some would consider a smile, but I knew better. Abigail lifted her chin as she had a mind to do. Jessie giggled and flipped her fan in front of her face. I looked out the door at the invitin' darkness.

"Uh– Abigail Hodgdon, Jessie Gilman." I forced a laugh that was more like a snort.

"Such a pleasure meeting you," Jessie said.

"Likewise. Now, if you'll excuse me." Abigail marched over to Weston Jones. He weren't a bad fellow. We used to go fishin' together. I heard that Sarah was sweet on him. He shot me a look and shuffled his feet, sort of holdin' back while Abigail pulled him towards a cluster of folks in the middle of the floor.

"She seems nice. She looks like one of the girls I saw down by the County Farm last week." Jessie sipped her lemonade.

"Oh no, she ain't one of them. She lives down the road a piece." I watched Weston and Abigail promenade.

"I could swear that I saw her." Her eyes darted about. "I am dreadfully uncomfortable in this corset. I need to loosen it. Do you know of a private place?"

"Well, I s'pose I could take you out back. Follow me."

We wound our way through the crowd to the back of the barn. The closed door muffled the music and chatter. She grabbed the back of my shirt. "It's dark."

We walked by the stalls and ladder. "What's up there?" She stepped on the bottom rung.

"The hayloft. I helped build this barn." The pride seeped in.

"I would love to go up there. Will you take me?" She leaned close. Her lips quivered, and her breath was warm on my face.

"Not tonight. It's too dangerous with no lantern. You might take a fall, and that would spoil everything." I thought of Abigail. Weston. My head pounded.

"So be it. But you must take me there someday." She reached behind her and loosened her corset. Will you tie this for me?"

I fumbled with the laces. "Like this?"

She whipped around and placed my hands on her waist. "No, like this." She wove her fingers into my hair; her corset fell away, exposin' the creamy white skin of her breasts, beggin' for my touch. She ran her tongue over her full ripe lips, her breath comin' in short, raspy puffs. She pulled my head down. My mouth covered hers. Apparently she knew well and good how to kiss. I ran my hands down the soft skin of her arms as she opened her mouth for more. She arched against me quiverin' and kissin' and pantin' like an animal. I didn't care about nothin'. She tugged at the corset more, invitin' and teasin'. She threw her head back. I kissed her salty, sweet neck.

"Are you alright?" It was Weston talkin' outside the barn. A pang shot from my chest to my stomach. I jerked my head around.

"I'm fine. I need some fresh air." Abigail's voice barely sounded.

I leaned closer to the wall.

"I'll get us some lemonade; wait here," Weston said.

I got a lump in my throat and strained to hear. Jessie started whimperin' and tuggin' at her laces. She reached for me, but not as the hot-blooded woman she was before but more like a child needin' comfort. My hands got all clammy. "We should go back now."

She pouted. "You don't find me desirable?" She sat before me with a lock of silky hair fallin' off to the side and her corset busted wide open, exposin' a sweet round breast. Like any man's dream, she was willin' and eager. Unlike most, I was walkin' away.

"Yes, I do. I mean, I did." I folded my arms. "It was real temptin', but it ain't right. Not here. Not now. We best go back before your folks come lookin' for you."

"I don't want you to think that I'm improper," she said.

"I don't think nothin' bad." I looked away.

"I have never done anything like this before." She twiddled with her hair.

"I'm sure you haven't."

She was quiet for a moment. "I must say, I was completely overcome with passion," she said. "I'm terribly ashamed. Will you forgive me?"

"Forgive you?" I paused when I detected her perfume on my sleeve. "There ain't nothin' to forgive."

"I acted like a harlot. And I'm not," she said. "I gave you the wrong idea."

"No… you didn't. Had it not been for folks talkin' outside, I would have had my way with you." I shook my head. "It jest ain't right."

I led her back to the barn; the folks was dancin' and carryin' on. No one saw us 'cept for Moses's wife, whose eyes turned to narrow slits. Lord only knew what she thought.

"Silas, we must have one more dance before the night ends." Jessie no longer used the fan or giggled.

"Of course, one more."

She skipped out to join in the square. We danced, and all I could think of was Abigail. I didn't know how she was able to come to the dance without her mamma, but she did.

It was gettin' late. The gatherin' was thinnin' out, and I was thinkin' of headin' home. Jessie's parents were meanderin' towards the carriage. I cleared my throat. "It's time to be gettin' along."

"I know. I wish the night didn't have to end, but I had a wonderful time." She mussed with the feather in her hair.

I was searchin' for a word when I heard a ruckus. It looked like Old Gray Mare in a full gallop. It was Abigail! She raced into the crowd and fell from her horse. Weston picked her up.

"Help me! My house is burnin'... I can't find Mother!"

I elbowed my way through the folks. "Abigail!" I wanted to rip her out of his arms.

She pulled away from Weston and headed for her horse. "Hurry!"

Moses hollered, "To the Hodgdon Farm!" The men mounted up while the women gathered in small circles.

Jessie joined her parents, who was waitin' by their carriage. I mounted Major and followed the men towards Abigail's house. The smell of smoke stung my airways. When I arrived, the barn was ablaze, and the house was a pile of pulsin' red coals. The pigs squealed and charged towards the road. Moses was with Abigail.

I rushed over and held her close. "Are ya hurt?" I buried my face in her thick, smoky curls. She stiffened and turned away.

CHAPTER 15

Nellie – August 30, 1872

THE SPIRIT OF my daughter came when the ripe Corn Making Moon revealed images in clouds. Dreams were abundant. The men worked in the field to the east, the women in the field to the west. Yellow and green squash filled my basket. I gave thanks.

The orange butterfly danced upon the milkweed and called to me. I followed. The departed spirits of those before us return on the wings of the butterfly. The sun was past the middle of the inner sky, when the truth would make itself known.

The masters shouted at the elder who walked with the help of a stick. He could not hear, but they did not take time to know this. Their voices grew like howling winds that fell upon deaf ears. He had fear in his eyes, and he bowed to the earth.

I followed the butterfly to the pond, and I sat upon the soft grass. The stillness of the pond reflected Father Sky. I no longer heard the men, just the quiet song of the oxen chains in the open field.

The butterfly rested upon my knee. I watched the wings open and close.

⤖ ⬱

The rhythm of the horse beat in unison with the movement of the great white pines. Mamijôla pressed her head into my chest. *Where is Kmitôgwes?* Blue eyes searched.

Mamijôla, Kmitôgwes left us for a greater place when I was a child. There was a time when many of our people were sick. I embraced her. Speaking of my father brought warmth.

When will we see him? Will we go to that place?

I guided the horse close to the river. *When the time is right, we will see him. Until then, remember that the spirit of those who have departed, come to us on the wings of a butterfly.*

When I see a butterfly it is Kmitôgwes?

You will know. Our ancestors come to us in dreams, sharing spirit wisdom of plants, birds, and animals.

It was the season of restless wind. The sound of rushing water grew strong as we neared the crossing where three rivers flowed into one. We would reach the others before nightfall.

Great white teeth and the fury of winter past stirred the three rivers. The wind changed. There was much white water. We traveled carefully upon the land trail to reach the other side. The water rushed above the ground. The howling river filled my ears, and the wind carried a spray, making us wet. The earth fell away. The horse cried out and fell away too. I held Mamijôla as a mother would.

The river swallowed us. The water was with ice and fury as it tore my daughter from my arms. The great rush silenced my screams. I reached for her as the currents pushed me below. The rushing sounded no more in the deep rocky place, where the river shakes. I faced the death struggle.

I arose from the depths into the flow amongst rocks, thick tree roots, and branches. Ice struck me until I was surrounded by whiteness. The wind blew cold. Mamijôla was not in my sight. Each time I cried for her, the river took me back in her rage. I fought White River until I could fight no more. The darkness came. I fell into peaceful slumber.

Nanatasis! The angry waters of White River returned. I opened my eyes. The outstretched arms of the giant pines waved against gray clouds. Mother held my head. Pain was great. To move took strength I did not have.

Mamijôla! Where is Mamijôla? My spirit shook.

Nanatasis, Mamijôla is not here. There is no sign of her. Tell us of your path taken. I feared her fear. *You are hurt.*

Wnegigw and the others searched the banks of the river. My head was warm with blood. *We were at the crossing of three rivers. There were many great winds and white water. The earth fell, swallowed by the river, and swept us away. I fought. White River defeated me, and I lost Mamijôla.* I moved. The pain made me still. *I must find her. She is in danger and may perish.*

Wnegigw approached and wrapped a match coat around me. He spoke quiet. *Darkness will be upon us. It grows late. We must take Nanatasis to warm by the fire. We will look for Mamijôla into the night.*

A thunderbolt pierced my back when he lifted me onto his shoulder. I returned to darkness under a blanket of shadows, where the river was silent.

Nanatasis, you must drink. Mother offered medicine: tea of red clover, white pine needles, and mullein root. She covered my wounds with fresh yarrow flower and leaf.

I looked long into the fire. She pressed the feathered yarrow leaf onto my arm. I closed my eyes to see Mamijôla slip under the fierce waters of White River. Until she returned, I would not speak.

->=@ @=<-

The dragging of the oxen plow entered into my dream. I watched the tip of the orange wing depart into the reeds. I rose to my feet while the sun neared the end of day. I tasted the salt of sorrow upon my lips.

"Come on, Old Lady! Git inside now!" The woman with hair the color of a fox called to me. My steps to the big house were slow. I looked at the stew of carrots, potato, and warm brown broth. The spirit that came on orange wings took hunger away.

Sleep came with rushing, white water. I fought the river's rage with that of my own. I cried into the cold wind for Mamijôla. I awoke in sorrow. I looked out of the small window, at the other side of the ridge. Father Sky was red with fire. The owl messenger sang the death song.

CHAPTER 16

Abigail – August 31, 1872
– Blake Farm

THE LIGHT FROM the lamp danced fitfully on the beams overhead. When I closed my eyes, visions of hot white sparks peppered the dark corners of my mind. I held my breath and stared at the bright yellow flames that licked around the window, framin' my mother in death. *Her rockin' chair was right there by the window. Why didn't she escape? Maybe she was off in the woods hidin'.* I sprung from the bed. "Mrs. Blake! Come quickly!" I yelped when I stepped onto the cold floor. A severe pain spiked through my ankle, forcin' me back onto the bed.

"I'm right here, child." Her glowin' lantern swung wildly in the dark.

"I think that Mother is hidin' in the woods. We must find her and tell her it's safe to come out." *There are always possibilities in the woods.* I examined my blistered fingers and then pressed my other hand against my warm, swollen ankle.

She sat on the edge of the bed and wove her fingers, red and irritated from lye, through my sooty curls. "Abigail, I know this is painful. Your mother is not in the woods. I fear that she has perished, gone to be with the Lord." She cradled my head to her breast and held me close, rockin' back and forth. "She is with your Papa now." Her nightdress smelled of perspiration.

When I closed my eyes, I saw Papa in his blue sack coat with the shiny brass buttons, wearin' his kepi perched on his thick black hair, smilin' and wavin' from that train bound for Hell. A good number of the men who went off to war met with a bloody, violent end. The ones who came back were no more than dead men walkin'.

I shook my head to make the train go away, but it stopped on the tracks as Mother peeked out from behind Papa, wavin' her handkerchief. She was wearin' her favorite Sunday dress, only it was blackened and smolderin'. She could not go where he was. It simply wasn't possible.

I pulled away from Mrs. Blake. "No! Mother would not leave us. She must have leapt from the window. She would not die without tryin' to escape." The giant invisible hand that tended to press down on my chest had ripped it open.

"The ways of the Lord are mysterious. But we must pray and give thanks for our blessin's." She folded her hands in her lap. "I'm so sorry."

I wanted the tears to escape, but they pressed against my insides, where they remained for some time. *Thank the Lord?* I pounded the bed with my fists. "No! I need Sarah! She must come home!"

"The men are siftin' through the remains of the fire and bringin' the animals here. Eb's goin' to send a telegraph to Fall River, and she'll most likely be on the next train. It'll be a long ride for that poor child." She stood in front of the window, starin' out into the night. "You can stay here for the time bein'."

"I got no one, only Sarah."

"Does your mother have kin?"

"No, she's an only child. Papa's brother died of the fever before the war. It's jest Sarah and me." The wretchedness started buildin' up inside. "No grandparents."

"We have time to make plans. Get some rest now." She sat down on the bed and fiddled with the buttons on her nightdress. The soft light from the lantern illuminated the roundness of her cheeks. "We should have Doc Gilman take a look at your ankle."

"Do you have a chamber pot? I feel ill." I gripped my stomach.

She scurried down the hallway. "You jest wait..." Her voice disappeared with her into another room.

Overcome by the smell of smoke and the flickerin' lantern, the room whirled about. I started sweatin' and cupped my hand over my mouth.

She burst into the room with the chamber pot and set it on the bed. "Now, now." She pulled my hair back when I started in heavin'. "You're distraught. You'll feel better in time."

I choked and sobbed and vomited into the pot, and then I tried to stand again. The pain was worse than before and brought me back down. I clutched the blanket. "Where are you, Mother? Oh, God. I need Sarah."

I rolled onto my back and started spewin' out whatever came to mind. "When Papa died it was like a peculiar dream. He's been gone for so long. Oh, God... this is real. I'm afraid." I pulled the blanket up under my chin.

"Abigail, the Lord will see you through. In time, your grief will fade, and you will have your Mother with you in memories. I was nine years old when my mother passed on. I cried every night for a year or more. A day doesn't go by when I don't think of her in some way." She stood in the middle of the room holdin' on to the chamber pot.

It was impossible to keep my eyelids from closin' as the monotonous tone of her voice melted away the hard edges of that which unfolded. Each time the flames burned into my thoughts, I forced myself to think of the sittin' rock by the brook. It was a war between the tricklin' brook and the cracklin' fire. The fire always won.

Her voice seemed to be far away when she sang "Holy, Holy, Holy," one of my favorites. Mother had a finer voice, but I liked Mrs. Blake for tryin'.

I was about to fall asleep when I heard the sound of horses. I opened my eyes and sat up. "They found Mother! I'm sure of it!"

Mrs. Blake didn't move. She looked towards the window and then at me. "Lay down, child. I'll go talk to Moses." She struggled to her feet, showin' her age.

"No disrespect intended, Mrs. Blake. I must hear what they have to say." I limped out into the hallway.

She took a deep breath. "Let me help you on the stairs." With lantern in hand, she positioned herself in front of me. "Hold onto my shoulder."

The steps creaked under her heavy footsteps as we shuffled down the stairs and into the kitchen. She pointed to a chair. "Now sit."

The door burst open. Moses came in followed by Silas, Weston, and the smell of smoke. Silas stared at me. I looked away.

Weston rounded the table and stood before me. "I'm so sorry about your Ma." He got on his knees and started in wailin'. "We looked for her outside, all around I mean." A tear cleared a path down his blackened cheek. "But she weren't nowhere to be found." He covered his face with his hands. "Then we found her... what was left to her... in the ashes," he sobbed. "It ain't right."

"Yes, but did you look in the woods?" I asked. "It simply can't be..."

"Yes, we searched everywhere around the house first." Moses cleared his throat. "Then we found her."

Silas stuffed his hands inside his pockets. "I'm sorry. It ain't gonna' be easy. I know you loved your mamma." His voice was unfamiliar – quiet and unsure.

"You were brave to get the animals out, and you did it jest in time or they'd been lost too. There's plenty a room for 'em in my barn." Moses glanced at his wife, who seemed to be in prayer with her head bowed and hands locked together.

The kitchen was dreamlike as the amber light of day poured in through the windows. I leaned over the lantern and blew at the dancin' flame. It skipped away then kept right on burnin'. I took a deep breath and blew again. I watched until the orange ember faded and a wisp of gray smoke swirled around my face.

CHAPTER 17

Silas – August 31, 1872

MY EYES WATERED. The wild blaze weren't gonna' settle down 'til it ravaged every last bit of the Hodgdon farm. I managed to hold back the tears lest anyone got to thinkin' I was soft.

I started headin' in closer and stopped right quick. The red-hot coals pulsated in the wind, scorchin' my face. I hadn't seen a fire like that since Ian McDowell's barn burned flat to the ground. He lost all twelve of his cows and a whole flock of layin' hens.

I took another step back as tall yellow flames roared and clawed their way up to the sky, while sparks tumbled into the field, landin' on cornstalks jest long enough to singe 'em.

The cow, spooked and unwillin', was a ways into the woods when I found her.

"Simmah down, girl." I rubbed her singed nose and led her out to the lower pasture, where Weston herded most of the pigs. The chickens were scattered in trees and on fence posts, and one was even roostin' on the handle of the water pump, flickin' its head back and forth.

Moses hollered from out back, "Annie! Are ya out there?" Twigs snapped as he and the other men rummaged through the debris. We all knew that she most likely died in the fire.

Even though there weren't nothin' left to save, I joined the bucket brigade, a group of seasoned men, and we passed buckets from hand to hand to extinguish the fire. The agonizin' heat and heavy black smoke caused me to choke, so I buried my face in my shirtsleeve. After about a dozen trips with the water bucket, I left the brigade in search of a thick, long stick.

Weston and Moses approached with a few stray pigs followin' behind. Moses stopped. "Whatcha' doin', boy?"

"I'm lookin' for Mrs. Hodgdon is what I'm doin'." I knew if there was somethin' left to her that I needed to find it for burial. Abigail's face haunted me as I poked the stick into the sizzlin' hot coals. I wanted to find her and not find her at the same time. I returned to the pump; this time I hung my head under the gushin' water and gulped it down.

"It's still burnin'. You ain't gonna' find her." Moses crossed his arms over his chest like he was usin' fightin' words.

"I'm lookin' for her. I ain't gonna' leave 'til I know." I set the stick down and started in pumpin'. Water splashed into the bucket and over the sides.

Weston found a milk pail by the lower pasture and headed for the brook. Together, we poured water over the coals and stirred what had become steamin', grayish-black mud.

Suddenly, Weston's cries broke the silence. "I found somethin'! I found her!" He bent over, holdin' his stomach like he might vomit.

I scrambled through the black muck to where he was standin'. There in the ashes was the charred body of Mrs. Hodgdon, still smolderin'. I stepped back and closed my eyes, conjurin' up an image of the woman who despised the likes of me. She was nothin' but a pile of chunky ashes. I leaned on the stick and cocked my head to the side tryin' to make out her shape. A white leghorn clucked from high in a tree, sort of warnin' me that even in death this woman could read my mind. Moses trudged his way through the mess to join us. We stood real quiet amidst the smoky steam and stared at what was once Annie Hodgdon.

Weston coughed. "We should say a prayer or somethin'."

"Go on then," Moses said.

Weston pushed up his sleeves and cleared his throat. "Dear Lord, bless Mrs. Hodgdon here and take her soul up to Heaven. She was a good woman. We remember her with kindness and pray that You keep her, as Your will be done. A-men."

It was silent 'cept for the last part of the cracklin' fire finishin' off the back of the barn.

"A-men," I said while Moses stood beside me lookin' up at the sky.

Someone galloped in our direction. I tried, but couldn't see nothin'. Eb Burrows rode up to us and jest sat there on his horse, starin' at the ruins.

"Eb, send a telegram to Sarah Hodgdon down in Fall River. Her mother perished in the fire." Moses paused and toked on his pipe. "Tibbetts knows the particulars on how to reach her."

"Ayuh, it's a darn shame. Wonder why she didn't git out. S'pose she fell asleep," he said and spat.

"Abigail had the good sense to let the animals out, but it was too late for her mamma. Poor girl," Weston said.

Not wantin' to see her blackened body no more, I went to the water pump. After discussin' the heroic deeds of the evenin', Eb and the others left.

"C'mon, boys," Moses said. He mounted his horse. We followed him to his house. A single light flickered in the upstairs window.

We stepped into the kitchen. With the help of Mrs. Blake, Abigail was jest sittin' down. She had a troubled look about her, almost like it weren't even her. We had to tell her. I know she didn't want to believe it and would try to find reasons why it weren't true. I wanted to put my arms around her and tell her it was jest a dream. She looked straight ahead when we told her that her mamma weren't in the woods and that she died. She tried to blow out the lamp, but she was tuckered out. She smiled a crooked half smile, like when she knew somethin' that other folks didn't. The flame gleamed perfectly in them soft, chocolate brown eyes.

Chapter 18

Abigail – September 3, 1872

Becomin' an orphan left a sort of hole that could only be filled by mergin' with someone who shared the same hole or at least knew what the hole was all about. Like before – the only other time we occupied the first pew – we sat with our black mitted hands laced tightly together. She fixed her eyes on the pine coffin settin' on the sawhorses, and I fixed my eyes on her. I couldn't stand the sight of the pine box or the horrible thought of our mother's burnt body. I knew it to be morbid, but I was tempted to look inside to make sure it was true.

Mrs. Blake offered me a fine black dress to wear for proper mournin'. It needed mendin', so she took to sewin' it for me. Sarah borrowed her mournin' dress from Mrs. Porter, who had three daughters. Her husband passed away two years before.

We wore our perfectly matched wool felt bonnets – black, cotton trimmed, with long wide ribbons so that we could tie an enormous bow if so desired. When we milled about in Mr. Tibbetts' store, he insisted that we take them. We offered to pay him later, even though we didn't have access to Papa's pension or know how it would come about. Bein' a decent sort and knowin' how he felt about Mother, he refused any and all payment.

The flies, usually buzzin' about noisily, lay dead in random clusters upon the sills. It was quiet 'cept for the rain peltin' against the windows, roof, and into anxious puddles, threatenin' to wash out the road. There were more folks in the church than I can ever remember. Eb Burrows huffed and clattered while settin' up chairs alongside the pews. Mrs. Leighton swayed more and plunked harder than usual on the organ keys. Sarah squeezed my hand and released, squeezed and released, as if playin' a concertina.

Pastor Leighton cleared his throat. "See, the home of God is among mortals. He will dwell with them; they will be His peoples, and God Himself will be with them. He will wipe every tear from their eyes. Death will be no more; mourning and crying and pain will be no more, for the first things have passed away. Revelation 21. 1-7."

Effie Morrill's weepin' became uncontrollable as the pastor continued. "Let us join together in song. Turn to page 282 in the hymnal." Mrs. Leighton started in on the foot pedal and the sounds of the organ filled the room.

"Please stand." He raised his hand upwards, and we shuffled to our feet. I winced when the pain in my ankle struck with the force of a double barrel shotgun. Doctor Gilman stopped by and fixed me up with a bandage. He said it would take time to heal and to avoid walkin' on it as much as possible. He offered me a crutch. I said no at first, but Mrs. Blake insisted that I take it.

Mrs. Morrill's voice rose in pitch. Mother would have disapproved of her behavior and would have clucked all the way home. She didn't take kindly to that woman on basic principles. The last time we were at church Mother was whipped into a fine frenzy. I smiled at the thought.

Sarah's voice wavered as she looked upwards, searchin' the timbers and tryin' to ignore the wailin' woman in the pew behind us as we sang "My Faith Looks up to Thee." I wasn't much for singin' aloud in church. I had a receptive audience at home with Lizzy and Pearl, and it was then that I sang my best.

I felt an ache uprisin' in my chest. The music vibrated in my stomach as I thought of home. *What does that mean? There was no home. Lizzy and Pearl are now at Moses's Farm.* I squeezed my eyes shut to stop the tears, but it did not help. Soon I cried right along with Effie Morrill while the other folks stared and continued singin'.

The weather had been unkind in the early part of the day. However, the drivin' rain finally let up on our way to the cemetery. The sun emerged, causin' large droplets on the leaves to glitter like jewels. I sat in the carriage with Moses, Mrs. Blake, and Sarah. No one spoke as we rattled along behind the cart that carried Mother.

The carriage turned up the hill and stopped with a jolt beside the next to last row of stones. I hadn't been there since I secretly watched Silas and the others buryin' the child on the other side of the fence. It went straight down the middle, dividin' the poor folks from everyone else. *I don't suppose there's much to fuss 'bout. It isn't like the poor folks are goin' to get across to the other side once they're buried.*

We stood around the hole in the ground – next to Papa and Grandfather Wills. I leaned on my crutch, focusin' on the brown, rotted floral wreaths that Sarah and I worked so hard to make, but never bothered to remove or replace. My cheeks reddened with the flame of regret as I made a pledge never to neglect my duties of remembrance again.

I recalled the day we buried Papa. Some folks said that we were fortunate to have brought him home. Many others were laid to rest where they fell dead. We were supposed to be filled with pride because he was a veteran, and he lost his life in the Great War of the Rebellion. None of that mattered to me. I wished that he had returned as I remembered him – a strong man – not a secret hidden inside of a box nailed shut.

Creakin' carriages and jinglin' harnesses blended with the low murmur of voices. We waited for all the folks to make their way up to the waitin' hole. Sarah whispered, "I cannot bear to think of Mother in that box or to be buried in the ground. I simply cannot bear it." She quickly brought her handkerchief up to her mouth.

"It's awful. What will we do without her?" I wept openly. Weston patted my shoulder from behind. Folks pressed in close, makin' a circle around Pastor Leighton. Mrs. Blake came between Sarah and me and cradled us in her arms. I glanced across the way at Silas standin' tall, holdin' his hat and lookin' at the coffin. Jessie Gilman and her parents were right there beside him. Our eyes met, and she slipped her hand into the crook of Silas's arm. I folded my hands together, coverin' my mid-section and lookin' down at my creased, muddy shoes.

The wind picked up and pushed the remnants of the short-tempered clouds from above, makin' way for blue skies. The hermit thrush's sweet song tumbled from atop the hill near the dividin' fence. My monocle curl fell from my bonnet and onto my forehead. I stood up straight, pressed the wrinkles from my skirt, and listened carefully to Pastor Leighton.

"The Lord is my shepherd; I shall not want. He maketh me to lie down in green pastures: He leadeth me beside the still waters. He restoreth my soul: He leadeth me in the paths of righteousness for his name's sake. Yea, though I walk through the valley of the shadow of death, I will fear no evil: for thou art with me; thy rod and thy staff they comfort me. Thou preparest a table before me in the presence of mine enemies: thou anointest my head with oil; my cup runneth over. Surely goodness and mercy shall follow me all the days of my life: and I will dwell in the house of the Lord forever. A-men. Psalms 23. 1-6."

The moment had come when my Mother would be returned to the earth. The bird chorus fell silent. My heart throbbed in my ears while the world around me slowed down, almost stoppin' completely. Sarah and I found each other's hands and held tightly.

Relief washed over me when I caught sight of a monarch butterfly that flickered atop the dividin' fence. It flew over into the poor folks' section. I leaned forward to keep it in my view. It rested upon the stone with its orange and black wings openin' and closin', keepin' time with the shovel as it struck the pile of fresh earth, and then thumped onto the pine box. I focused hard 'til the black and orange blurred with my sorrow.

The wings stopped, the shovel stopped, my breathin' stopped. Slowly the folks walked away, breakin' the circle. Sarah and I stood alone together in front of where our mother lay cradled in the earth's womb.

The butterfly left the granite stone and perched on a nearby yellow prim-rose. The lament of a cardinal spilled into the air, weavin' through the tall pines.

Mrs. Blake tapped my shoulder. "Come now. Folks are gatherin' at our home."

My feet were rooted into the ground. My ankle throbbed, and it was tender where the crutch rubbed under my arm. I couldn't take my eyes away from the moist brown dirt, smellin' it, and tastin' it, and imaginin' it squished between my toes like after tillin' in the fresh rain.

Sarah put her arm around me not takin' her eyes away from the grave. "We should go," she said, tryin' to convince herself more than me.

"Not yet." I mustered enough strength to speak.

"Folks are gatherin' at the Blake's farm. We mustn't keep them waitin'," she said.

"I appreciate their kindness, but I cannot leave her. Not yet." I bit my lower lip.

Sarah turned towards the Blake's and shrugged and smiled weakly. She usually cared what others thought, but it was a different day.

⊷⊶⊷ ⊷⊶⊷

The air was crisp as we neared the foggy ridge. All the other carts left the cemetery in a long meanderin' line. Moses waited alone on the crest of the hill. He looked like he was asleep, sittin' on the carriage with his head hangin' down while holdin' the reins. His horse rustled a bit, causin' him to stir.

Mrs. Blake afforded us more time before leadin' us to the carriage. We left prints where our feet sunk into the soggy earth, drenchin' my shoes, makin' them all shiny, and bringin' them back to life.

After ridin' a spell, we approached what was left of our farm. The clouds – ribbons of red, orange, and purple hues – streamed across the horizon, forgettin' about the earlier rain. A slice of the orange sun appeared, formin' a brilliant golden rim around the edge of one perfect cloud. "Sarah, look." I pointed. "That's Heaven... a sign from Mother. What do you think?" I whispered, wantin' it to be our secret.

Sarah had been hummin' with her head bumpin' against the side of the carriage. She sat up, wide eyed like when she used to watch for shootin' stars and other little miracles. "I s'pose you're right, Abby. It's a sign." She squinted, not commentin' or even lookin' at the crumbled remains of our life as we passed by.

The house, a silhouette of what once was, emerged with its tall, bony chimney restin' against the dark blue curtain about to fall, bringin' an end to the day. There was one wall of the barn still standin' next to the water pump. I caught sight of the gate swingin' in the wind, bangin' against the post. Pieces of charred fence sat in a heap next to the sittin' rock and little brook. I turned to watch it vanish from sight while Sarah continued to stare up at Heaven.

No one uttered a word as we rounded the corner to the Blake's farm. There were carriages lined up in front of the barn and people millin' about. Dread swept over me at the thought of engagin' in polite conversation.

I tried not to stare at Silas as he towered over his mother on the front porch. I expected to see Jessie clingin' onto him like a mornin' glory wraps itself around a fence. It took me by surprise when she was nowhere in sight. The carriage halted. We remained rigid in our seats with our hands folded on our laps preparin' for what would come next. Like slow curious cows, folks moseyed over to greet us.

Moses assisted his wife and then Sarah down from the carriage. Weston Jones edged in front of him and offered me his hand. I met him warmly. His slight smile felt safe, and his eyes were kind, though they looked somewhat sad. I reached for him and he suddenly whisked me to the ground. My face was all ablush and I wobbled a bit. Silas watched closely.

"How are you holdin' up?" Weston asked. "It's been a tryin' day."

"I have never known such sadness. When Papa died, I was a child, not aware of the finality of death. I know that we'll be together again, Mother and I, but at this moment I'm filled with deep sorrow." I leaned on the crutch and limped towards the house.

Sarah scurried to my side. "Abby, wait. We must be alone for a spell before greetin' all of these folks. I'm weary. Can we go to our room?"

I paused to take in the essence of manure and freshly cut hay. "Yes, I feel the same. Weston, thank you for your kindness. We'll return shortly." We slipped quietly into the barn and through the door that led to the kitchen.

He returned to the crowded porch. Folks carried on as if it were a church picnic, cluckin' about the fire while their eyes lit up with wicked curiosity. We sneaked behind the kitchen stove, fetched a lantern, and walked up the creaky stairs. I sat on the bed that still carried a slight trace of smoke and slanted noticeably to one side. Sarah lay down on the other bed with her clothin' strewn about in an unfamiliar way. We lay wordless amongst the hum of voices that drifted up from below.

Sarah glanced down at the floor and gasped. "The treasure chest!" She scrambled over and picked it up. "Oh Dear Lord, how did this come about? It's a miracle!" She dropped it on her bed and opened it.

"Jest when the sparks were spreadin' to the barn, I ran to free the animals. I thought to get it in that instant. I ran into the pottin' shed and grabbed it," I said and smiled.

"We haven't had an opportunity to speak of that dreadful night. Do tell me the particulars. I must know." She picked up an embroidered handkerchief that she made when she was quite young and held it up to the light.

"I fear that this is all my doin'." I rubbed my ankle. "Mother was beside herself after you left. She forbade me to go to the dance. As you know, it was urgent that I see Silas."

She placed the handkerchief back into the chest and pulled out another, one that Mother found displeasin'. She was quite hard on herself when it came to her needlework. Sarah and I hid it in our treasure chest because we fancied the delicate purple pansies and could not find a flaw. Mother wanted to use it for practical purposes, but we did not want it spoiled. Sarah pressed it to her cheek and closed her eyes. "What took place next?"

"Mother was in her rockin' chair goin' at her needlework. I retired to our room and waited until she was asleep." The achin' began to hammer inside my chest, makin' it difficult to breathe. "I climbed out the window and down the tree like we used to do."

She didn't move. "Go on."

"I looked in the window and Mother was sound asleep in the chair." I swallowed hard. "Then I hurried off to the barn dance... Oh, Sarah. I shouldn't have left her!" Anguish surged from the depths of my chest and into every part of my bein'. "It's my fault. It's because of me that our mother lies dead in the ground." I buried my face into the quilt.

Sarah rushed to my side and rubbed my back. "Now, now. If you stayed at home, perhaps you would have perished as well. You mustn't blame yourself."

"I cannot change what happened that night. If I had stayed at home, Mother might have lived. I would have gotten her out of the fire."

"Abby, I love our mother and am filled with grief, but you must make a promise to me," she said.

"What is it?"

"You must forgive yourself and never take blame. It will take residence in your soul and crush you. You must stop now. Do you hear?"

"I cannot promise you that. In my heart, I know that my leavin' was a wrongdoin'." I sat up and faced her. "Mother perished because of my careless and selfish ways. I will think of that until my dyin' day."

"Pray to God and ask for forgiveness, or that dark cloud will hang over you always."

"I will. I will pray for mercy. I have spoiled all that is. I am fearful for my life and of what will become of me and this child." I searched her face. "Surely you'll tell Silas, and he'll do right by you. You did see him."

"Yes. Silas was at the dance. My heart ripped apart when I saw him with Jessie Gilman in his arms." I took to cryin' again. "It's worse. He brought her to our secret place. I witnessed it myself."

"That fancy tart at church?" She rolled her eyes. "And what secret place?"

"The hayloft in the back. He knows of it because he helped Moses build the barn. It's where my virtue was lost and where this child was conceived." I had turned the corner from possibility to certainty.

"Are you positive?" She knew the answer.

"I saw them with my own eyes. And then I have seen them all about town together. Even at the church and the cemetery, as a bee is to clover.

"You have to tell him. Jessie Gilman will not stand in your way. You will summon your courage. Assure me that." She stood before me with her hands on her hips, stickin' her chin out like Mother had a mind to do.

"I will make an attempt," I said quietly.

"You'll do better than that. You will succeed."

"I must tell you about the night of the fire," I continued. "When I returned home and saw the house on fire, of course, I called for Mother. The fire was burnin' so brightly; I've never seen such a sight. I ran to the barn to free the animals. That's when I injured my ankle. It was jammed under the gate of the pig pen, and they trampled over it."

"I returned back here to the farm, as fast as Old Gray Mare would gallop. Moses and the men responded swiftly. There was not a thing that could be done to save the house, the barn and worse... our mother."

Mrs. Blake knocked on the door. "Girls, come and greet the guests. Many folks are askin' for you." The dim light from the hallway illuminated the tiny sprigs of hair that quivered around her face.

"Yes, we would be actin' poorly if we stayed up here," Sarah said. She quickly tucked the handkerchief back into the treasure chest.

Mrs. Blake lumbered down the hallway, scuffin' her thick feet, soundin' more like a sizable man than a pleasingly plump woman.

We stood still for a moment, disrupted by the chatter of folks that came in swells from down below. Sarah closed the chest and lifted the lantern.

A chillin' silence prevailed when we entered the kitchen. All eyes were upon us. Mrs. Putnam was the first to speak. "Girls, I'm so sorry for the loss of your mother." She bowed her head slightly, seemin' like she might simply vanish into the dense air.

"Thank you," Sarah replied.

I nodded. I wasn't much for words at that time and feared that I might come unhinged. Tears should fall in the privacy of my room and in the company of Sarah, not in a busy kitchen.

"It's most upsettin' to think that your dear mother is gone," Mrs. Morrill said in a shrill voice. "We don't always understand the Lord's ways."

"Have some food, girls. It's been a long day." Mrs. Blake cut in, savin' us from more rigid discussion.

Food was not my desire, but it was proper to accept her generous offer. She motioned for us to sit and eat dinner at the table, which was crowded with several plates of food brought by the guests. Sarah ate well, but I did not, for I felt ill and generally worn out.

Folks spoke in hushed tones, as if Sarah and I would somehow shatter. We held courteous conversations and secretly wished that the ordeal would end. Weston was by my side for a good part of the evenin'. Silas watched, however, the opportunity to converse did not present itself. We had not spoken for some time. Under the circumstances, I decided that tellin' him of my news was not appropriate. I admit that I was quite relieved that Jessie was not in attendance.

When the last of the visitors departed, Sarah and I offered to help tidy up the kitchen, but Mrs. Blake would not hear of it, so we gladly retired.

Tucked snugly into bed, I watched Sarah as she carefully packed her travel bag. "Please don't go to Fall River." I was hopeful but knew that she would go.

"I must return. I have a room and a station at Granite Mill." She climbed into her bed. "I had jest gotten settled, when I had to come back. Things happened so quickly. It's hard to think clearly." She swiftly unbraided her hair. "Workin' will keep my thoughts occupied, and bein' away will bring no painful reminders."

"I'm sentenced here. I must pass our farm each time I go to town, and I must face my quandary. I cannot go to the mill in this state, or I would join you."

"You must remember your promise and tell Silas," she said. "Time does not stand still. Soon all of the world will see that you are with child."

"I'm aware of that. Mother will never know of my fate." I fought the impulse to cry. "It's so confusin'. She would have been ashamed. Perhaps that is why God spared her of this. So it is my doin' in that light as well."

"Abby, you must put an end to those horrid thoughts. You will marry Silas, and Mother would have been a happy, dotin' grandmother."

"She did know her arithmetic. She would have been aware of my sinful ways."

"You are her daughter, and she'll look down on you with love. You mustn't forget."

The pain finally surfaced. I buried my face in the quilt and cried.

Sarah got into my bed, curled up behind me, and pressed her cold toes against my leg like she always did.

"I'm here," she said. "Mother will always love us."

We cried together, finally surrenderin' to sleep jest before the break of day. It wasn't until Pearl's third crow that I opened my swollen eyes. Sarah stirred and snuggled in closer behind me. I closed my eyes and returned to the safety of slumber.

CHAPTER 19

Silas – September 3, 1872

IT WAS A shame that no sooner had Sarah arrived in Fall River, she had to come back home to bury her mamma. She returned to the mills after the funeral, and Abigail stayed with the Blakes until things settled. With all the commotion, I had no chance of gettin' in a word.

We was one of them tarnished families that only stepped foot inside a church for funerals and weddin's. Mamma roped us into goin' to Easter service a few times, but Daddy changed all that when he tried to hoist himself up them impossible stairs and took to cussin'. Her face was every color of red when he started hollerin', finally tumblin' to the ground and then drivin' off, leavin' her to get a ride with the Cooks, while I went on and walked home.

The rain pounded hard on the roof, quickly fillin' the bucket under the leak. I harnessed Major to the carriage and was wipin' the dampness off the seats when Daddy came out. He took a tug on his whiskey. "What's takin' so long, boy?"

"I'm ready." I looked past him towards the house. It didn't matter if we was goin' to Tibbetts' or to a funeral, he always had his whiskey. I could take it, 'til he got out of hand.

I helped Mamma onto the carriage and put the crate down for Daddy to step on. He had some trouble with that wooden leg of his. He set the jug on the seat. "You never mind; I can do it." He kicked the crate aside, splinterin' the gray, wooden slats.

I stood back. Arguin' would make things worse. I watched as he tried to pull himself onto the carriage. He lost his balance and landed hard on the barn floor. "Goddamn!" He scowled and rolled onto his back.

"Let me help you." I reached for him.

"You never mind! I ain't no Christly invalid." Covered with a good bit of mud, he stood up, wobbled, and then leaned against the carriage. He snatched the jug and took a few good swigs.

"Hiram! You've had enough! We have a funeral to attend!" She took it from him and handed it to me.

"I ain't done with that, woman!" he shouted.

I set the nearly empty jug on a shelf and watched him stagger out the door. The steady rain streamed down his head and onto his beard.

"Are you comin, Daddy?"

It was then that he took me by surprise and lunged at me. He grabbed me by the shirt and hit my face with his closed fist causin' me to see white spots. I whipped my fist back, ready to strike. I stood still with my hand raised, lookin' him in the eye. The glint that was there when he hit me had disappeared.

We switched it all around; he became the scared boy and I the violent man. Without takin' my eyes off him, I leaned over, plucked my hat out of the puddle, and shook it off good. I ain't never hit my daddy. I feared that if I did, I'd hurt him.

The blood trickled from my nose and into my mouth, mixin' with the rain that spilled onto my shirt. I stared him down 'til he finally looked away.

Mamma leaned out the side of the carriage. "Hiram! Look what you've done!" She was holdin' the sides of her dress so that you could see the ruffles of her tattered petticoat.

"Never mind, Mamma. I'm fine." I went into the barn and wiped the blood from my nose on to my shirt sleeve. "He can't hurt me." I climbed onto the carriage. "Daddy, are you comin' with us or not?"

He stumbled into the house and he started in hollerin'. "I ain't goin' with you! I'll walk there by myself!" Other than the rain, all I heard was the sound of his wooden leg draggin' across the floor.

I yanked on the reins, and we splashed through the rutted road. He yelled and cussed from the porch steps. Mamma looked back at him all fearful, 'til his shoutin' faded behind us. I paid him no mind. There was more important things besides Daddy and his whiskey drinkin' ways. Abigail needed me.

The church brimmed with folks standin' in the aisles and outside the doors. We found a spot to stand near the organ, where I had a perfect view of Abigail and Sarah. They was both wearin' black dresses and bonnets. Abigail rested her head on Sarah's shoulder. Weston Jones sat behind 'em with his eyes fixed on Abigail.

I took off my hat and ran my hands through my hair. I tried to hide my blood stained cuff, so I shoved my hand in my trouser pocket. A familiar flowery smell invited me to turn jest in time to see Jessie squeezin' past people with layers of ruffles, lace, and a pretty skirt revealin' her fancy petticoat. She smiled as she finally edged Mamma out of the way and stood beside me.

"Silas, it's such a tragedy that brings us all here and so dreadful for the Hodgdon girls to lose their mother." Her eyes sparkled.

Eb motioned for me to step back while he set up more chairs. Most of the women were able to sit. I offered a chair to Jessie but she insisted on standin' next to me holdin' the crook of my arm.

Pastor Leighton started speakin'. He walked from the pulpit to the coffin that was set upon three sawhorses. The rain raged and the wind howled. I knew that Abigail's heart was broken. It was my intention to speak with her at the earliest opportunity.

The long line of carriages headin' to the cemetery moved slowly. Charles, Big Ben, and I went to the cemetery often but always on the other side of the fence. I knew every stone on the poor folks' side. We used numbers; it weren't practical to have names etched in granite. When I asked Moses 'bout it, he told me to mind my business. I weren't much for bickerin', but I wondered how anyone would be able to find their folks if there weren't no names.

I drove the carriage off to the side and draped the harness over the hitchin' post. I helped Mamma up the hill to where the folks gathered in a circle. The sun peered through the clouds, and there was a slight wind.

Once we got close to the grave, I could see Abigail real good. Mrs. Blake was comfortin' her and Sarah. We was about to start a prayer when I felt a tug on my shirtsleeve. Her scent drifted in as her slender hand found my elbow.

I closed my eyes and listened to Pastor Leighton. All of a sudden, the birds started in singin'. I s'posed they was happy to see the rain go away. I looked up from prayin', and Weston was starin' straight at me.

The sound of Big Ben and Charles throwin' the dirt onto the grave caught my attention. I bowed my head and prayed one last time for the soul of Annie Hodgdon.

I helped Mamma onto the carriage and waited for all the folks to go 'round the back side of the cemetery and down the hill. Abigail and Sarah lingered at the grave. There weren't no use in hurryin'.

Doctor and Mrs. Gilman nodded when they passed. Jessie followed close behind. She came around to the front of my carriage, where I stood waitin'. "It's such a misfortune." She stared at Abigail and Sarah. "Those poor girls will be without most everything now that they've lost the farm." She shook her head. "I s'pose the one girl will join the other at the mills now that she has no place to go."

"You mean Abigail?" I crossed my arms. "Ain't no way Abigail will go to the mills. She's a farm girl. She wouldn't take kindly to bein' locked up inside and takin' orders."

"You seem to know so much about her."

"I've known Abigail since we was children. Our daddies went off together to fight the Rebs. Only hers came back in a pine box, and mine came back without a leg and full of trouble." I fiddled with my hat, thinkin' I said too much and invited her to talkin'.

"That's quite a story. I think that your daddy is charming and amusing."

"I ain't so sure about that. He's a bit of a handful sometimes."

"In fact, I think that you're quite charming too." She brushed a perfect curl away from her shoulder. "I have always thought…"

The Leighton's carriage squeaked and started movin'. Mamma leaned forward. "Silas, time to move on."

"I'm right here and ready." I gave Major a handful of clover. "We'll be goin' to the Blake's for dinner. Will you be there?"

"I regret that we'll be returning home. I'll try to persuade Father," she said. "Until we meet again."

You would never have known the sadness of the event; her smile coulda' lit up an entire barn. She slipped gracefully into the carriage. I couldn't help but notice what a fine lookin' woman she was with all them fanciful things that most women here only dreamt about. I snapped the reins, and we rolled into the line. The girls was still standin' at the grave.

My stomach rumbled when we passed the Hodgdon farm. The skeleton of the house hovered like a beast over the lifeless earth – nothin' but a pile of burnt timbers with the chimney standin' proud. Abigail was brave to get them animals from out of the barn before the fire took to it.

I waited on Moses's porch for a spell before he and his wife returned with the girls. I headed down to greet 'em when I spotted Weston. He seemed to come out of nowhere. He reached for Abigail and whirled her to the ground. I wanted to throttle him. I stuffed my hands in my pockets.

I trailed behind Abigail, who leaned on her crutch and worked her way to the barn. She and Sarah slipped inside. I s'posed they wanted to avoid all them folks who was cluckin' and waitin'.

It was some time before Abigail and Sarah came down to the kitchen. You could tell that they'd been awful upset, for their eyes was all red. Weston wasted no time gettin' to Abigail. I was itchin' to be alone with her, but we only managed to speak across the room in a polite manner.

Finally, it was time for Mamma and me to get home. There was no doubt that we would find Daddy asleep on the kitchen floor.

CHAPTER 20

Nellie – September 15, 1872

AFTER THE SUGAR-MAKING month, the ice melted away from the lower, quiet stretch of Crooked River, signaling the time for boat making. Four winters passed since Mamijôla perished in White River. I traveled with my people along the shores of Bitawbagok. With uplifted voices, they danced around the fire. Mother asked me to join the circle. I danced no more.

The men fished, hunted, and made things such as snowshoes and canoes. The women made baskets to sell to the white man. We planted, harvested, cared for the children, and kept warm fires. The women sewed bark for canoe making. I looked beyond the laughter and children who played by my feet. I searched for Mamijôla. The warm wind carried her to me on the wings of the orange butterfly.

Many times, a strong white man came to trade with my people. Unlike the others, he respected Our Mother. The day he spoke to me, I made a doll with cattails and scraps of deer hide. He waited for the men to accept his offer of spirituous liquor to trade for baskets and snowshoes. *May I join you?* He had a good face, blue eyes, and hair the color of corn.

I watched the fire.

Don't be afraid.

White Flower came forward. *Nanatasis does not speak.*

He spoke. *Can she hear me?*

The wind blew gentle. *She hears but has not spoken since the waters of White River took her daughter, Mamijôla. From that day, she is with great sorrow.*

He rubbed his hands over the fire and looked upon me. *It is heartbreaking to lose a child. I don't know from experience, but I would like to say that I'm sorry.*

His gaze warmed me on the new day. He stood in his truth.

The men came. Running Bear spoke. *We will talk. Come. Sit.*

He went with the others. I wished for him to stay.

He returned and bid farewell. *I will see you again, Nanatasis.*

To the others he was Elijah Baldwin. He wandered much and spoke wisely. To me he was Searching Owl.

⇥⊚ ⊚⇤

The shadow of my friend the crow flew overhead, shaking wings and calling. The wind changed with the passing of time. I sat with the others in the silent garden. The young woman who sat near me wore a dress of yellow, the color worn by one who gives birth without a husband. Her child would come within the passing of two moons.

Her eyes beamed while she husked corn. She spoke with a small voice for one so brave. "Hello. I'm Patience. Who are you?" She touched the pain in her back.

I smiled.

She tried to stand. "You are a peculiar woman. Is it true that you're a witch? Folks in town say so."

I smiled again. I knew the white men thought of me as a witch. They are without clarity. I did not think of it.

"You don't look like a witch. Perhaps you are jest an old Indian squaw, and nobody knows better." She took rainwater from the barrel. "I don't ever remember it bein' this hot."

The boss called Polly had much anger. "Get back to work."

"I'm jest gettin' some water." She turned away from Polly.

Polly struck the girl's face. "Don't talk back to me. You ain't nobody special here."

The girl hid behind her small hands. With tears, she sat at my side. I watched Polly with stone eyes. She did not share the bonds of Our Mother and treated living creatures with hate.

She touched my face with her stick. "What ya lookin' at? Better tend to your own self, and don't be mindin' others' business." She beat my foot two times. "Git to work."

I looked ahead and saw nothing. The girl beside me cried secret tears. Polly left. After giving thanks to it, I plucked a pink yarrow flower that grew nearby and shaped it for her wound. I went to the girl and pressed it onto her face. First, she backed away. Her heart changed. She placed her shaking hand on mine.

It was silent except for the old man who sat on the stone wall. He sang a sad song and did not look upon us. The iron bell rang. I pushed the flower into her hand, and we walked to the house. Those who laughed without reason and whose words had no meaning went before us. She placed the flower in the pocket of her yellow dress before we sat together with a bowl of scalded milk, a piece of boiled potato, and a brown crust.

The sun went down. Hunger grew inside of me. From my place in the floor, I counted berries for two and went to where the girl awaited slumber. I held out my hand. She accepted my offering. I ate my berries. She did the same. I returned to my bed. The next day she would need more.

The moon smiled. I listened for the night song. I closed my eyes, and soon Mahitable shed the tears of a mother who lost her child. Her grief kept the butterfly away.

The darkness brought many cries. Coldness crept in. The spider in the window spun a web to catch dreams of yellow burning fires and animal skins. I called for Mamijôla to sleep in my arms.

CHAPTER 21

Abigail – October 5, 1872

WITHOUT SARAH AND Mother, life simply wasn't worth livin'. I often lay awake at night, consumed with thoughts, finally to fall asleep jest before Pearl and the others started in crowin'. Then, Mrs. Blake would rouse me from deep slumber.

The sickness that came over me each mornin' started to subside. For that I was grateful. My thoughts always returned to Silas and how I once believed that he loved me best on earth. I tried to summon the courage to speak with him, but when he wasn't totin' Jessie around on his arm, I found myself wordless or annoyed.

One particular mornin', I awoke from a dreamless sleep. I forced myself out of bed without Mrs. Blake havin' to shake me. I sat on the porch baskin' in the sun. The leaves on the trees were ablaze with hues of red, yellow, and orange. Autumn pleased me, even though it signaled the onset of winter.

A crisp wind blew across the field. There would be at least one more hayin' before the first frost. I hoped that Silas would work with Moses, as he often did, and that I would speak with him.

"Abigail?" Mrs. Blake stood before me with her flour speckled apron.

"Yes?" I turned to meet her frown.

"I will need your help in the kitchen. We're havin' folks over for dinner." She rolled up her sleeves.

"Of course I will help. Isn't that what we agreed upon?" I tried to hold my tongue, but I was weary of my work obligations since my arrival.

"After you tend to the animals, I'll tell you what needs to be done." The wind caught the door, closin' it with a thump.

I went to my room to fetch my shawl. My thoughts raced about wickedly. I did chores for a good part of the day. I didn't mind earnin' my keep, but I gave the Blake's a flock of layin' hens plus Pearl. Lizzy was a good milker, and there were the pigs to boot. All of that was worth a respectable sum.

I reached under my bed and pulled out the treasure chest. I grabbed Hope and held her to my breast, rememberin' the joy of findin' her on Christmas day. I placed her upon my pillow and returned to the barn.

After feedin' the animals, milkin' two cows besides Lizzy, and collectin' a basketful of eggs, I washed and readied myself for a day of cookin'.

Mrs. Blake was in the kitchen hummin' and soundin' like a moose in the rut. "It's about time you finished with the barn." She wiped her hands on her apron.

"We'll be needin' apples for bakin'. Take the basket here and fill it to the brim. Remember to pick the ones from the ground; they're good for pies. Bring in a pumpkin for a pie too. Make sure it's big enough but not too big." She smoothed her hair. "We're havin' roast duck with all the fixin's. Have you roasted a duck before, Abigail?"

"Indeed, I have. Mr. Tibbetts brought us more than one duck for Christmas dinner." The thought of Mother wrappin' the duck in bacon and fixin' special puddin' and biscuits made me smile.

I resisted the temptation to ask her who was comin' to dinner. I thought it rude, since I was now the likes of a hired hand. She was fussin' so. I could only imagine it to be someone of great importance.

"I hope you don't mind if I ask you to serve us." She poked at a log in the stove.

I stopped in the middle of choppin' a carrot. "Serve you?" I had never served anyone before. Well, only when Sarah and I played with our dolls, and then it was tea. "No, I think not." I wailed hard on the carrot, causin' her to flinch.

"It won't be difficult. I'll have you bring out the food and set it on the table. We will serve ourselves, I s'pose. Then you can collect the dishes after we eat and bring out the sweets."

"I... I..." My face heated.

"Good afternoon, ladies." Moses burst into the room. "It smells so darn good in here... makes my mouth water."

He stared at the plate of warm biscuits on the table. "I sure am hankerin' for a buttered biscuit. Jest one Miriam?" he asked, soundin' like a child.

"You never mind. You have to wait like the others." She pressed a stack of plates to her chest. "Abigail, get the silver. Most likely it needs polishin'."

"You don't s'pose the Gilmans would notice do you?" He smirked.

I thought that my soul might depart from within. The Gilmans? I became an observer watchin' from afar as I spread the silver onto the table with hands that didn't feel like my own.

"You're amusin'. Of course, they'll notice all the particulars." She examined a brass candlestick holder. "It looks like this needs polishin' too."

"Yes, ma'am." I kept my head down and continued sortin' the silver.

"She keeps ya busy, don't she?" He looked at me curiously.

"You never mind. You said that if she stayed, I could put her to work. So that's jest what I'm doin'." She untied her apron. "Abigail don't mind. After all, if we didn't let her stay, she'd be over at the County Farm. As I see it, she's quite fortunate."

Moses ran his hands through his hair. The crease between his eyebrows deepened.

"You jest wear one of those dresses that I fixed for you. The blue one will do fine." She dropped a pie plate causin' a rattlin' within the walls of my heart.

⋅→═◉ ◉═←⋅

I smoothed the sides of the blue dress with my hands, in search of a good feelin'. From years of fadin', it was almost gray in color, not blue. It lacked any and all appeal – no lace, no details. It wasn't even fit for scraps. I would look like a servant jest as Mrs. Blake desired. *Thank God no one will see me servin' the likes of Jessie Gilman wearin' this dreadful dress.*

I clutched Hope. "You won't tell Silas that I am servin' Jessie. Will you?"

The one thing I liked best about Hope was that she was always the same. Without a face, there was no judgment. I could tell her anything.

"Abigail! What's takin' you so long?" Mrs. Blake shouted.

"I'll be there shortly!" I wrinkled my nose and stuck out my tongue. Mother would approve if she witnessed her behavior. Sarah would ask, "What will become of you if you don't escape from this impossible situation?"

I ripped the brush through my hair and re-read the note that Sarah had tucked under my pillow.

Dearest Sister,

Althogh it pains me that we are not together, I shall think upon you with each passing day. I leave with a heavy heart, knowing that oure dear mother is with the angels and not here with us as she shuld be. As it is not understood by us, the Lord does have a plan, and we are to pray for the strenth to carry on without question. We must strive for Heaven, Abby.

It isn't much, but I have left the tortise combe for you to enjoy. I know that you fancy it, and it is my hope that you will keep me in your thoghts when you wear it.

Affectionately,

Your Sister, Sarah Hodgdon

I had no lookin' glass, so it was a matter of trust when I twisted my curls tightly to the back of my head and positioned the comb.

Each step was heavier than the previous one. My ankle had not healed and throbbed from standin' all day. I gripped the railin' and made my way downstairs.

The final rays of the sun cast golden light on Mrs. Blake as she stood in the center of the sittin' room. Her dress was quite elaborate. It was made of emerald green taffeta with several layers of black lace adornin' the sleeves. She was wearin' a flounced hoop of at least three bones. Although she was squat, somehow it flattered her.

"How do I look?" She curtsied.

"You look splendid." Seein' her smile again made me laugh.

"Thank you. I have waited for an occasion to wear this."

Moses entered the room lookin' a bit smart after a bath. He wore a fresh muslin shirt, and his light blue trousers were without wrinkles or farm dirt. He glanced out the window. "When will they be gettin' here?"

"I told them three o'clock. Silas said that his father had trouble gettin' places, but that he was gonna' try to be on time." She inspected a fork on the table. "Abigail, you must wear a snood to keep those curls in place. That comb will never do."

I wilted. *Did my ears deceive me? Silas? Please, God... This is a dream. Why is he comin' to dinner here with the Gilmans? I cannot serve them. I cannot.*

I felt it impossible to refrain from cryin' aloud. "Excuse me."

I bolted to my room, collapsed on the bed, and screamed into the pillow.

I rocked from side to side with my face still buried, knowin' that I could not carry on. "Heavenly Father, what is the purpose of this? Am I not tortured enough? I acknowledge my unworthiness. I have become a servant. I have nothin' on which to hope."

I ripped the comb from my hair and held it to my lips. "Sarah. Sarah. Sarah. Is God punishin' me? Will He have no mercy?"

"Abigail! You vanished again!"

I dabbed my tears with my handkerchief and took a deep breath. There was no way out. I put the comb in the treasure chest under my bed. She was right. *I must look like a servant and wear a snood instead of a fancy comb.* I wrapped the snood around my curls. I would no longer permit so much as one tear to fall from my eyes.

"Now you must not disappear. I will spoil my dress in the kitchen, so you must do the tendin'. It is up to you to do as I say." Her scowl returned to its rightful place.

I wondered how Mother could have cared for this woman. Did she not comprehend her wickedness? I knew that God would require me to forget my woes and remember that she had given me shelter.

She pressed a clean apron into my chest. "Wear this."

I took the apron from her and tied it around my waist. "What is it that you want me to do?" It took great effort to speak above a whisper. I was parched. I was prepared for the consequences of my sin.

"See to the pie crusts." She stood erect with her hands neatly folded at her midsection.

As ordered, I put on the oven glove and checked the pies. The apple pie was golden, a perfect pie by Mother's standards. I set it on the table. Careful not to get scorched, I took the pumpkin pie out of the oven as well. It was seepin' on one side and overcooked on the other. I got it out in time. "They are golden."

She went to the sittin' room to fetch Moses, who was busy packin' his pipe. They came into the kitchen quarrelin' about whether he would carve the duck in the kitchen or in front of them at the table. Moses crossed his arms. "It's better to carve the duck beforehand so folks don't have to wait."

"But bringin' the duck with all the fixin's to the table is a sight to behold." She planted her hands on her wide hips.

I lit the lanterns in the dinin' room. Their voices carried, and it was plain that they weren't resolvin' the dilemma. They stopped hollerin' when a carriage sounded in the yard. I peeked out the window. It was the Gilmans. I turned away quickly. The room started to spin. I gripped the back of the chair and swallowed hard. *Lord, give me strength.* I closed my eyes and slowed my breathin'. Jessie's laughter tinkled.

"Abigail! Go and greet the guests." Mrs. Blake pointed at the door.

"Yes." I rushed across the room. I hesitated and then pressed my ear against the door. Only a series of short raps separated them from me. I cringed and stepped back.

"Are you gonna' let 'em in?" Mrs. Blake stood behind me wringin' her hands.

I was desperately stuck in one place. I thought about movin', but I jest stood there with my heart thobbin' in my temples. The rappin' came again, only louder.

"For God's sakes." Mrs. Blake pushed me aside and opened the door. "Hello and welcome. Please come in." I stood motionless while she gave me the evil eye.

Moses helped Jessie with her cape. Once again, she was wearin' perhaps the finest dress that I had ever seen: deep blue with a large bow that streamed down her back. It was made of fancy material and set off her shoulders. She wore a thin blue velvet ribbon tied stylishly around her neck. Tiny pearls decorated her ivory lace mitts.

She dashed over to me. "Good evenin', Maribel. No one told me that you would be here."

"It's Abigail." Her flowery aroma sickened me.

"Oh dear, forgive me," she said. "I cannot keep names sorted." She laughed and turned to Mrs. Blake. "It smells delightful in here, and I'm famished."

"Thank you. I'm sure you'll be pleased." Mrs. Blake nodded.

Moses took Mr. and Mrs. Gilman's coats. "Please go into the sittin' room and make yourselves at home."

Mrs. Blake watched and waited. "Come with me into the kitchen now," she whispered out of the side of her mouth.

I looked down at my dress. *Oh how I would like to rip it from my body. It's fit for a peasant doin' a day's work. This is my lot?*

A carriage rattled in the yard. "Whoa!"

I froze at the sound of his voice. I thought of runnin' away, to never look back. I could not permit him to see me as a servant. How would I compare to Jessie with her elegant dress, flawless hair, and fancy words? I looked at Mrs. Blake, unable to comprehend her chatterin' about.

"Abigail! What is the trouble? Are you listenin' to me? For God's sakes go to the door!" She banged a silver servin' spoon on the kitchen table.

"Yes, ma'am. I mean, well… w-what is it that you wish for me to do?"

"Go to the door. The Putnams are waitin'." She shook her head.

I walked to the door, steppin' lightly on my ankle. Each rap on the wood thumped inside of my stomach. The door squealed when it opened. I stared down at my mud-caked boots and blushed.

"Hello, Abigail. So nice to see you." Mrs. Putnam's kind voice made me want to embrace her as I would my own mother. She put her hand on my shoulder, keepin' me at a distance.

I forced a smile.

Silas looked me in the eye. He was wearin' the same shirt that he always wore to the barn dances. His eyes were dark underneath. "How are you?" He fidgeted. His voice was particularly low pitched.

"I am well. Do come in." I gritted my teeth and walked gracefully.

"Please excuse Daddy. He ain't feelin' well, and he's takin' a nap in the carriage. He won't be joinin' us any time soon." He removed his hat.

"I hope that he will be well soon." Droplets of sweat trickled down the small of my back when his eyes swept over me. He had not seen me dressed in such a way before. I admit that I was not as fancy as Jessie Gilman, but I did take pride in myself and dressed as handsomely as seemed practical. Mother and Sarah were fine seamstresses and did not skimp on makin' clothin' for me. My shame was not easy to hide. I looked at Mrs. Putnam. "Please give me your cape." Silas continued to stare.

Mrs. Blake burst into the room with her face aglow. "Silas, Sally, so good to see you."

She didn't bother to wait for a response. "Abigail, tend to their hats and coats."

I started to move when she continued with her anxious peckin'. "Where is Hiram?"

Silas was wordless and ablush when I snatched his hat and sack coat away from him. Although Mother's cape was of higher quality, I was flooded with memories when Mrs. Putnam thrust her gray bonnet and cape upon me in a careless manner.

"Hiram has taken sick with a cold and is sleepin' in the carriage. I asked him to stay at home, but he insisted on comin' here." She couldn't get rid of the words fast enough. "He may waken and join us."

Moses invited Silas and Mrs. Putnam to join them. Silas did not take his eyes away from me.

I returned to the kitchen with Mrs. Blake. "Put the carrots here, the potatoes there, the biscuits here." Her head jerked from side to side, and her hair jiggled in front of her face. *If I imagine that I am someone else, perhaps I will be able to endure this.*

"And Moses is goin' to carve the duck after you bring it to the table." She grinned and took a ladle from the iron hook. "This is for the gravy."

"Yes."

"When we have finished eatin', I will have you take away the plates and then bring in the small plates. Then you will bring in the two pies. We'll cut them right there at the table." She clucked. Her hair flopped to one side of her face like the comb of a proud leghorn.

"Yes."

"Now I will go visit for a spell. I will tell you when we go to the dinin' room." She raised an eyebrow and peeked through her unruly comb before leavin' the room.

I stood in front of the stove. It wasn't roarin' like before, jest keepin' things nice and warm. Mother always kept the bread and corn muffins on the warmin' shelf, but the Blakes didn't have such a fancy stove.

Laughter trickled in from the other room. I stood nearby and listened.

"I know that Silas has learnt everything that I could teach him. He's a good worker, that boy," Moses said.

"That is quite an honor and a worthy position to have. It takes a certain kind of man to fill such a position at his age." Dr. Gilman's voice was quiet compared to Moses's.

Moses laughed. "Like I said, he ain't got no worries. He knows all 'bout farmin', and he works them folks the way they need to be worked. He's ripe for the job, but I ain't goin' away jest yet. Probably in a few more years."

"I think it is exceptional to have such status," Jessie said.

"I'll say! Lord, he'd be the farm boss of the whole entire county. It ain't jest Ossipee," Moses said, while eyein' his pipe.

Silas spoke up. "I always wanted to follow in Moses's footsteps, but it ain't been easy. Sometimes he's tougher 'an nails."

"With Hiram bein' injured in the war, it's been a hardship for him to teach Silas all that a boy should know. Moses has been like a father to Silas." Mrs. Putnam seemed apologetic.

"Yes, Silas is like the son we never had..." Mrs. Blake's voice trailed off.

"Well, like I said, that's a fine piece of land that I plan to clear." Dr. Gilman paused. "There are hardwood trees and a nice brook that runs through the property."

"And it's so close," Mrs. Gilman said.

I heard a scufflin' and hobbled to the kitchen with haste. I grasped the ladle. Tears started to spill from my eyes, but I would not permit it.

Mrs. Blake approached me. "We're goin' to the dinin' room. Now is a good time to start bringin' in the food."

"Yes." I could not call her ma'am.

She returned to the sittin' room. Voices mingled with footsteps. I paused. Weakness was settin' in from lack of nourishment. I busied myself with preparations for the evenin' and did not eat but a few apple peels.

I waited for the sound of scrapin' chairs to cease. I swallowed. With a plate of carrots in one hand and potatoes in the other, I entered the dinin' room. Jessie whispered somethin' to Silas. I was tempted to drop the carrots on the lap of her luxurious dress. My hands trembled wildly. I held back the tears on my way to fetch the biscuits and butter.

I stood over the woodpile and thought that I might heave. The back of my dress was soaked. *I cannot be ill now. No one must wonder.* I dabbed my forehead with my sleeve.

Moses watched me from the other room. "Excuse me, folks." He left the table and approached me. "Abigail, would you like me to carry the duck? You look tuckered out."

"Please do. Thank you." I leaned against the table. Moses carried the roasted duck while I gathered the courage to serve biscuits and butter. I set them on the table and then dashed off to the rain barrel. I dipped my cup into the cool water and poured it down my parched throat. It dribbled down the front of the hideous dress.

I stood on the back porch as the edge of the crisp night air cut through the heat that radiated from within. The evenin' star sparkled on the horizon. Papa told us that if we make a wish, we mustn't tell a soul, or it would not come true. I squeezed my eyes shut. I knew that I could not wish Mother back or for Sarah to come home. So, I wished that I was not with child and that I was ill instead.

"What the hell is goin' on?" A man bellowed from outside.

I hurried into the house. *Oh dear, there goes my wish.* Even though we were allowed one wish upon one star, it was important to elaborate.

Chairs were all a clatter as Silas and his mother ran out to help Mr. Putnam. He was quite liquored up, staggerin' and cussin'. I looked out the window and watched the three of them strugglin' against each other.

Suddenly Jessie was beside me. "You don't suppose Mr. Putnam is drunk do you?"

"I don't know." We stood together and watched.

"Well, it will be such a relief for Silas to be away from that man. I know that he fought in the war and all, but it has been difficult. I'm sure."

"It's his father, and he does as he sees fit," I said.

"Father is making arrangements for a parcel of land to be cleared for Silas to build a house. It is a lovely spot next to where we live in Water Village." She smiled with her lips, yet her green eyes stared like a barn cat about to pounce on a mouse.

"Water Village?" My voice sounded distant and odd. The heat burnt my neck and face.

"My parents are quite fond of Silas and think that he suits me."

"I must get the pies ready." I turned away from her and leaned against the table.

Mr. Putnam thrashed about in the dinin' room and snorted as he ate the duck. It dropped from his mouth onto the plate and floor. He weaved back and forth and sputtered utter nonsense.

Mrs. Blake burst into the kitchen. "Come out and collect the plates."

I reached in front of Silas to take his plate. He looked at me, afraid and searchin' for answers to questions that we never knew existed. I didn't care who watched. I was terrifyin'ly close as I looked right back into his eyes. Jessie cleared her throat. I continued to stare and scream in my head as though he could somehow hear. *I'm carryin' your child! I gave myself to you, and you cast me aside for this? Surely her beauty will fade and leave you bitter. Yes, we did it wrong, but who are you to break apart my spirit?*

"Abigail!" Mrs. Blake snapped me out of it.

I grabbed a plate. "What now?" It was the loudest I spoke all the night.

"Get the rest of the dishes so that you can serve dessert."

In silence, I fetched all the dishes 'cept for Mr. Putnam's. He continued to eat like he hadn't seen a good hot meal for days. Then I returned with the fresh baked pies and small plates. I turned towards Mrs. Blake.

"Mrs. Blake?" I shouted.

She whipped her head around.

"I am retirin' for the evenin'. Good night, folks." I curtsied, almost losin' my balance. I paused. Silas sat still with his fork in mid-air; pumpkin pie fell onto his plate. Jessie smiled a most endearin' smile. It was likely less than a moment, yet it seemed like a long time before I finally left the room.

When I got to the top step, I reached down and clenched a handful of the horrid dress and pulled with all of my strength. "God, will you have no mercy?" I continued to walk towards my room. My heart pounded as I tore the hooks apart. The dress fell to the floor.

"Am I not reapin' the fruits of my own rebellion?" I seized the servant's dress and ripped madly. I continued to tear it to shreds until it was but a heap on the floor. I threw myself down on the bed and cried until the well inside of me was dry.

CHAPTER 22

Silas – October 5, 1872

ALVIN TAYLOR CREAKED like an old apple tree as he lugged the last hay bundle into the loft. Never really warmin' to a day's work, he was one of the quiet ones who didn't question orders and stared at ya out of the corner of his eye. He suffered great torment when his wife and boys died of the fever. With younger men on the farm, I didn't get why Asa had Alvin doin' hay.

"I'm sendin' Alvin in for the rest of the day," I said to Asa, who stood with his back to me.

Bein' a bit ornery and uncommonly cold, he walked away without utterin' a word.

"Alvin, go on. Get outta' here." I waved towards the big house.

Crooked and silent, he wove his way up the path, not even stoppin' to take a drink.

Moses came up and gave me a good clout on the back. "You ain't got much time to get ready, son. Why dontcha' go and get all spiffy for the Gilman girl. You know she's sweet on you."

I watched Alvin stumble into the house, leavin' the door wide open. "I'm gonna' see that the stalls is done and the vegetables sorted, and then I'm headin' home."

"You don't sound too eager." Moses crossed his arms, invitin' me to talkin'.

"Course I am. I mean, the Gilmans is good folk, but I ain't known Jessie for long. I jest ain't sure I'm ready for what she's got in store for me."

"Doc Gilman has a good parcel of land that he wants to give to you. He'll see to it that you have lumber and hands to build a fine house right next to his place. Course, he has his sights on you marryin' his girl. I told him you was a good man and that you're likely to be the big farm boss one day. The superintendent."

"Well, that's generous."

"Generous? The man is offerin' his fine daughter and a home– probably a barn too. You'd be a fool if you didn't accept the offer, son." He turned to leave and then stopped. "Go home and tend to your folks. Miriam's preparin' roast duck with all the fixin's. She and Abigail is makin' pies too, if we can get Weston to leave."

"Weston?"

"Yep. A few weeks back he came around lookin' for work. I gave him some chores to do since we got so much a doin' here at the farm. Trouble is he's more interested in Abigail than work. I have Miriam keepin' an eye on 'em." He picked at the dirt under his fingernails. "Never mind."

"Ayuh." I jest wanted to run, but like impossible stumps, my feet was deeply rooted. It seemed like a few minutes passed before I made it to the pasture and mounted my horse. My chest tightened. I wound the cracked leather reins around my hand and gave an unintended jerk at the thought of sittin' at a table with both Abigail and Jessie.

Major's ears flicked back. I 'spected he was aware of all them thoughts thrashin' about in my head. I kicked into his sides to break into a gallop, not to hurry, but to feel the cool wind.

I finally got home to face Daddy. He staggered about, tuggin' on his whiskey. "Damn! I thought you was never comin' home." He glared with his one eye while leanin' against the door frame, holdin' the jug up to his chest.

I walked past him and stood before Mamma while she laced up her boots. "Silas, there ain't a lot of time. We'd better leave soon. The Blakes are expectin' us before long."

"I know. We ain't bringin' him are we?" I wiped my brow. The sweat from workin' all day made my skin gritty, and I smelled from bein' in with the pigs.

"I know it ain't the best situation, but he's your daddy, and we must make allowances."

"He won't know the difference. We oughta' leave him right here and spare ourselves the discomfort." I picked up the hot water kettle only to find it was nearly empty.

Daddy's jug toppled onto the floor, rolled over, and rested by his feet. Mamma hurried over like a trained dog fetchin' a stick. He opened one eye and then only half way. His smile drooped down on one side, wantin' to escape from the cruel trenches of his face and the stench of the rotten air that he breathed. It was jest a matter of time before he started singin' his favorite drinkin' song.

"Instead of spa, we'll drink brown ale
And pay the reckonin' on the nail;
No man for debt shall go to jail
From Garryowen in glory."

He took another swig and slammed the jug on the table. He started swayin' from side to side, holdin' his head in his hands. His beard straggled across his lap.

"I ain't sure if he'll take notice if we leave him here." I hung my head over the wash basin as if the grayish water might reply.

"He can sleep in the carriage. If we leave him and he stirs, he may come out lookin' for us. So let's load him up and pray for the best," Mamma said, convincin' herself that it would be fine.

"Goddamn you. Leave me be!" He fought us with that murky eye of his half open and draggin' his wooden leg behind him in the muck.

"You stay here and keep him from fallin', and I'll get up where I can yank him." If he didn't fight, I could land him square into the carriage.

I got him in. Before long, he was out cold and suckin' wind with his good leg danglin' out the side. Now it was time to face Abigail and Jessie. It was not only Jessie who had her sights on me, but her folks did as well.

"It's awful kind of Moses and Miriam to invite us for dinner," Mamma whispered, fearin' that she might wake Daddy.

"They're good folks." I looked over my shoulder at the unmovin', shadowy heap. "We worked wicked hard today bringin' in hay. I'm hungry."

"You know, the Gilmans was over to see us yesterday," Mamma said. "Seems they've taken a likin' to you." She drew her cape tightly around her shoulders.

"Moses told me. He hinted that they want me to marry Jessie, and they'll build a home right next to 'em in Water Village."

"It's true. He told me about it himself right there with Jessie and Mrs. Gilman lookin' on." Her head bobbled in time with the bumpy road.

An owl flew in front of us, spookin' Major. The carriage jerked, and Daddy stirred. "Where's my damn whiskey?" He started to sit up. "Oh never mind. You ain't got no whiskey…" He bumped his head when he fell back.

"She's a fine girl. I jest don't know." I squinted into the huge orange sun that was about to drop behind Brown's Ridge.

"What more is there to know? She's a pleasin' sort, comes from a fine family, and they want to build you a home." She gave me a stern look.

"I've only known her for a short spell is all."

"It isn't Abigail that's makin' this hard for you, is it?" She stared straight ahead. "If that is the case, I frown upon it."

"You frown upon it?" I snapped the reins. "Because her daddy ain't no doctor?"

"No, no, son. Because she ain't ready for marriage and you are. Jessie is ripe for the pickin', and things is jest fallin' into place. Besides, Abigail is sweet on the Jones boy. "

"How do you know that?" I tightened my grip on the reins.

"I got my ways of knowin'." She looked away.

We rode up next to the Gilmans' carriage. Daddy was snorin', so we was able to leave him in the carriage without a ruckus. I helped Mamma get down, and we headed for the house. I'd jest as soon been anywhere else but walkin' up them steps.

I stopped and looked down at the manure and hay stuck to my boots.

"Go on." Mamma poked me with her stiff, crooked finger. "Knock."

I knocked once and paused. I heard women's voices. I knocked a bit louder, still no answer. I kept on knockin' 'til the door opened. There she stood like a doe starin' down the barrel of my shotgun, a strikin' creature, paralyzed with fear, knowin' that life was about to end. I always wavered before the kill. It was them eyes, them soft brown eyes.

Mamma rushed in. "Hello, Abigail." She put her hand on Abigail's shoulder. I s'posed her sickenin' sweetness was 'cause she was glad that Weston was savin' me from a life of strugglin'.

Abigail smiled and looked past me without so much as a word.

"Abigail, how are you?" I tried to catch my breath.

"I am well. Please, do come in." She stumbled ahead of us.

Her cheeks reddened when she turned towards Mamma. "I will take your cape."

I was tryin' hard to stop myself from starin'. I hadn't seen her since the funeral. Mrs. Blake strolled into the room with her head held high and her giant green dress swishin' about her child-sized feet. She greeted us warmly, but her voice changed when she looked at Abigail. "Tend to their hats and coats."

Abigail took a deep breath. "Yes, ma'am."

Yes, ma'am? Clearly, she was not well.

With Mamma's bonnet and cape in hand, she left the room.

"Come on in." Moses puffed up his chest and nodded at Mamma. "Good to see you, Sally."

I went into the sittin' room, where Jessie was perched in a chair by the window wearin' a blue dress with ruffles on the bottom and a big bow trailin' down the back. She smiled.

Doctor Gilman stood up. "Good evening." He shook my hand quite hard. His wife sat perfectly still with her steady, tired smile.

"Sit." Moses pointed at the two empty chairs. Mamma, somewhat shaky, scrambled to the chair by the fireplace, leavin' the one next to Jessie for me.

My eyes watered from her flowery perfume, which was stronger than before, or maybe it was because we was confined.

"Today we finished the last of the hayin'. If I didn't send Silas home, he'd still be workin'." Moses looked my way and laughed. "Now I gotta' hay my own field."

I strained to hear Abigail and Mrs. Blake talkin'. I tried to catch a glimpse, but they was too far away.

"Isn't that right, Silas?" Mamma nudged me with her elbow.

"What?" I sank into the chair.

"I said, Daddy has a cold and don't need tendin'. The doctor offered to take a look." She cleared her throat. "The fresh air will do him good."

"Ayuh... jest a cold. He'll be fine after he sleeps it off. No need to fuss."

"Silas, Moses tells me that one day you'll be the superintendent." The doctor drummed his fingers on the arm of the chair.

"And a good one," Moses said and chuckled.

"I'm hopin' so. It takes time and goin' through the proper channels and all." I crossed my arms over my chest. "Moses has showed me a lot these past years."

"Well, that's a prominent position – Overseer of the County Farm." The doctor rubbed his chin and searched the ceilin' for the next thing to say. "It would be good for you to have a place of your own, do you agree?"

"Well..." I watched Jessie twist the corners of her handkerchief.

"I have a parcel of land that I am offering to you. I'll have it cleared for a house to be built for you and Jessie, if you take her hand in marriage." He hurried the words.

Mrs. Gilman stiffened and fixed her smile. Moses looked proud, Mamma squirmed, and Jessie started in wringin' her handkerchief again. Mrs. Blake was complainin' at Abigail in the kitchen. I rubbed the palms of my hot, moist hands on my trousers and looked at the door.

I felt a pang at the thought of Weston and what Mamma and Moses told me. "It's awful generous of you." I swallowed. "Jessie's a fine girl. I'd like to think on it if you don't mind." At first the words was jest there, then like a strong-willed mule I hauled 'em out.

"Well, don't take too long, young man. A lot of men in town would gladly accept this offer." His voice was quieter than usual.

"He's jest a little timid sometimes, ain't ya Silas?" Moses gave me one of them stern looks.

Jessie stared out the window. *She's beautiful. She fancies me, and she ain't afraid to show all that wild passion.* My stomach churned loud enough for all to hear. *If Abigail was fixin' to be with Weston…*

My words burst into the air, blottin' out my real thoughts. "Yep, I'm afraid Moses is right. I can handle them oxen, bundles of hay and wood stacks, but I ain't so strong when it comes to the likes of a woman."

The laughter – henhouse cluckin' – that filled the room, pounded in my head. Jessie reached over and placed her dainty hand on mine.

"It's settled then." Doctor Gilman crossed his arms.

"This is so exciting," Mrs. Gilman said. Her tired smile came to life.

Mrs. Blake poked her head in. "Shall we go to the dinin' room?"

We settled into our chairs. Abigail came out of the kitchen carryin' steamin' carrots and potatoes. I shivered when she looked past me. Her dark eyes were no longer warm. Her face had lost its glow.

Jessie's lips grazed my ear. "They have servants here. What a surprise."

I whispered, "That ain't no servant. It's Abigail."

"It's Abigail the servant," she said, gigglin'.

Moses watched Abigail leave the room. "Excuse me."

I fumbled with my fork. *Why ain't she sittin' down with us?*

Moses returned carryin' a plate with a roast duck and placed it in the middle of the table. Abigail followed with fresh biscuits. She set 'em down and hobbled away quickly.

"Silas, hand me your plate," Moses said. He heaped more meat than I wanted onto my plate. It was curious that after all the work I had done, I wasn't hungry no more. Every bite became a chore, but I managed to eat it all while Moses and Doc Gilman went on about taxes and the price of livestock. I concentrated on chewin' and keepin' Jessie's hand from creepin' up my leg.

"Here, help yourself to more duck." Moses reached for my plate.

"No, thank you."

"What the hell is goin' on?" Daddy roared from outside.

Mamma and I rushed out to see if we could keep Daddy from makin' a fuss and spoilin' the evenin'. He had a deep crease runnin' down his cheek from sleepin' face down on the floor of the cart. I caught his arm when he fell back.

He stumbled. "What the hell are we doin' here? Jesus Christ! Let's go home!"

The lines on Mamma's face returned. "We're havin' dinner with the Blakes and Gilmans." She jabbed her finger into his chest. "You got into the whiskey, so we let you sleep it off."

"Jest stand here for a spell, Daddy. Take in some fresh air." I glanced up at the house.

The doctor opened the door. "Do you need assistance?" he asked.

"No, we're fine." Mamma answered in her best, almost musical voice.

We are not fine. "Are you ready to come in and eat?" I shook Daddy a little, hopin' that both of his eyes would open.

"Yeah." His head hung down. "I can walk." He brushed me off like a pesky fly.

The three of us walked to the house. We took him straight to the dinin' room, where Moses had set up another place. Mamma was overly sweet. "Do you want some duck, dear?"

"Of course I want some duck, woman!" He gave her a mean look, fightin' to keep his other eye open as he pulled his chair up to the table.

Moses laughed and piled food atop Daddy's plate. "Here, Hiram. Food always helps me when I get all liquored up."

Jessie came in from the kitchen. She sat down and watched Daddy eat. "Your father is somewhat amusing."

"There ain't nothin' amusin' 'bout him." I pushed her hand away from my leg.

"Best damn duck I had in a long time." Meat fell from Daddy's mouth when he tried to talk. The cloth that he had tucked into his shirt was soon covered with gravy.

Mrs. Blake and Abigail carried pies and sweets to the table. I sat up with a start when Abigail reached in front of me and snatched my plate. She stood motionless. My mouth went dry, and my shirt was damp with sweat.

"Abigail!" Mrs. Blake yelled from the kitchen. She looked away from me, picked up all the plates 'cept for Daddy's, and stormed off.

After a few moments, she followed Mrs. Blake into the dinin' room. "Mrs. Blake?" she shouted.

Mrs. Blake's eyes widened. Everyone stopped and stared at Abigail.

"I'm retirin' for the evenin'. Good night, folks." She curtsied. I worried that she might tip over.

"G'night, Abigail," Moses mumbled with a mouthful a pumpkin pie. Everyone said good night 'cept for Mrs. Blake and Jessie.

"Good night." I weren't sure if I spoke or jest thought the words.

By the time Daddy finished eatin' his pie, he was pretty well sober. My stomach was full. I only wanted to sleep and wake up as if it was nothin' but a dream. Moses and the doctor talked about land and taxes again while Mamma bluffed her way through church matters. Jessie stared openly at me, runnin' her tongue over her bottom lip. It weren't soon enough when the night finally ended.

We followed behind the Gilmans' carriage. Their lanterns swayed from side to side, spillin' light on the autumn leaves. I was quiet and disturbed in mind. The raw wind whipped my face. I buttoned my sack coat all the way up to my chin.

Chapter 23

Abigail – October 6, 1872

PEARL CROWED. I pulled the quilt over my poundin' head. The crowin' continued for a spell before sleep reclaimed me.

"What did you do to this dress?" Mrs. Blake shrieked. "You destroyed it! What made you do such a thing?" Her foul breath washed over me when she leaned close to my face.

"That dress is not fit for a servant," I said.

"This is unforgivable! Do you not have gratitude for what we have given you?" Her true nature, that of pure deviltry, could no longer be contained. Inside my head, I sang a silly song that Mother taught us when we were young. Mrs. Blake continued, but I was no longer there.

She shook me. "Why did you do this?" Her eyes were wide in disbelief as she rifled through the blue scraps of material in the pile. "Do you realize that we saved you from the County Farm?"

"Thank you for takin' me in." I raised my chin. "I do not regret rippin' the dress."

"No regrets?" Thick purple veins crawled across her temples like the sightless bait worms that we used for fishin'.

"I am not accustomed to bein' nothin' better than a slave to others' wants. It was cruel to treat me as you did, requirin' me to please folks who I have been familiar with all of my days." I crossed my arms.

She pointed her finger at my nose. "You have no kin. You would be at the County Farm if it were not for the likes of us."

O Lord, I pray for the patience to endure and for the strength to have faith that You will walk with me. "If it is my lot to be at the County Farm, then so be it. Am I not but a servant?" I struggled for air.

"We are goin' to church. Find a suitable dress and do not destroy it." She dropped a piece of the blue dress on the floor and stomped down the hall.

I imagined sayin' words I only heard and never uttered. I would not make use of such hard and wicked words, though I was tempted. I s'posed the devil had a hold on me. I even thought about grabbin' her by the collar, and who knew what I would do then. I had never struck anything or anyone before. I was a patient sort and always kept my anger bubblin' inside.

I held my tongue and prepared for church meetin'. It was my duty to accept that I had become poor and needy. I was at the mercy of Mrs. Blake.

I was grateful for the time to share with those who thought well of us, especially dear Mr. Tibbetts; the main bent of his heart was to please Mother. My sinful disobedience brought much spiritual poverty upon me in recent months past. I longed for the time when God shined His candle about my head as in the days of my youth. I looked forward to goin' to church. I was in want of spiritual refreshment and needed to escape from the humiliation caused by Mrs. Blake. She was kind in the presence of the folks at church, foolin' everyone with her smile and plump, rosy cheeks. I was fooled myself until I saw what was inside of that doughy head of hers, and it was no sweet berries or sliced apples with cinnamon. Behind all that thick crust was pure evil.

I held Mother's straw bonnet up to the window. The edges rolled up from bein' stuffed in the treasure chest, and the blue ribbon was quite faded. I pressed it with my hands, but it still held a crease and was hopelessly tattered. I finally chose a brown and tan dress. I struggled with the hooks. Soon it would be difficult to hide the evidence of a growin' child within.

"Abigail! We're waitin' on you!" Mrs. Blake hollered from the kitchen. Moses was silent durin' these tryin' times. It was wise to avoid conflict.

I slipped on the brown bolero jacket with black trim. It was my desire to conceal my slightly growin' midsection. I thought of Mother as I tied the ribbon under my chin. *I am unworthy to wear her hat upon my head. The good Lord spared her from knowin' of my sin. Would she have turned from me in this hour of darkness?*

Other than an occasional peck from Mrs. Blake, the ride to church was without conversation. I did not utter a word. The deep blue sky was cloudless, and the smell of wood fires turned my thoughts to Papa splittin' wood. The chill of autumn tingled on my face, while the sun shone brightly in my swollen eyes. When we drew near our farm, I pulled my bonnet down and looked away. The towerin' chimney called to me, but I squeezed my eyes shut, fightin' the urge to look.

There was no fear of seein' Silas or his folks at church. Jessie would be there dressed in her fine garments. She would be proud and primped. She was fancier than any folks from Ossipee or Water Village. She looked like one of the women from Boston who came in on the train to spend a holiday in Wolfeboro.

Oh the awfulness of knowin' that she has taken the truest love from my heart as her own. I was lost in my unworthiness. Tears blurred my vision. I was wrong, bein' in church was not the medicine I needed.

Moses and Mrs. Blake pressed against me on each side, makin' the struggle to breathe even more difficult. I stared at the vacant pew, where I sat with Mother and Sarah for as far back as I could recall. I longed to flee from the Blakes, to climb over the pews, and maybe even spew out a cuss or two. I had fallen from grace. What harm would it have done?

Mrs. Leighton swayed back and forth as she played the organ; her short, fleshy fingers rolled about gracefully, like they had a mind of their own and operated without direction or thought. The foot pedal, barely within her reach, clicked with each pump.

The pungent aroma of flowers brought a sense of desertion and sorrow. I closed my eyes as Jessie and her folks sat behind us. Her dress swept across the back of our pew. A slender white-gloved hand reached beside me and tapped Mrs. Blake on the shoulder. "Good day," she whispered. I could hear her smile.

Mrs. Blake patted her hand while Moses turned and nodded. I concentrated on Mrs. Leighton, playin' and swayin' so much that I feared that she might topple over. I sang softly.

"*Blest be the tie that binds,*
Our hearts in Christian love,

The fellowship, of kindred minds,
Is like to that above."

Pastor Leighton made the call to worship. His eyes rested upon me as he spoke. I supposed that there was a thin veil between the truth and me. Perhaps he could see that I had sinned. Oh how I longed to be restored to a state of favor and acceptance!

Hard as I tried, I could not concentrate on the sermon. I so desired to blot out the image of Jessie and Silas sittin' at the table tellin' secrets. I was hearin' the words over and over again; *the Gilmans were givin' Silas land and lumber to build a home.* In the bitterness of my spirit, I concluded that it would be better for me to die than to live.

I looked outside. The sun danced lightly upon the leaves. The flies that used to buzz around the windows were dead and scattered along the sill.

CHAPTER 24

Abigail – October 7, 1872

I SAT ON the rickety stool beside Lizzy. Things seemed so different in the light of day. The rhythm of her milk streamin' into the bucket reminded me of a silly song. I drew a deep breath.

"O, how I wish that I could find
A green, green frog to kiss.
He would be my long lost prince
For this, I cannot miss."

My spirit bowed in despair. My song was no longer amusin' without the melodic echo of Sarah's laughter. I tugged on Lizzy's udders. I have to tell him that his child grows in me. I sang quietly and somewhat out of tune.

"I kissed him once;
I kissed him twice.
He looked at me
With large round eyes."

I jumped, almost tumblin' off the stool when Lizzy stomped and lowed in protest. "Oh, you fancy my singin'?"

The light brown eggs rattled in my apron pocket, threatenin' to break as I lugged the heavy bucket. *I will write him a letter and ask him to meet me.* Milk sloshed up to the rim, almost spillin' onto the table.

I wrapped my fingers around the eggs in my pockets and dashed to the house. My breath came in short puffs, and my hands shook while I rummaged through the desk in search of a pencil. A gust of wind thrashed the door. I caught sight of Mrs. Blake pickin' apples.

I found a quill pen, but the inkwell was dry. I recalled seein' a short stub of a pencil somewhere. *The shed. I saw it in the shed.* I hurried down the narrow pathway favorin' my sore ankle. The door squeaked when I pried it open. I stood before every imaginable tool mounted on the walls in straight, neat lines, and I couldn't help but laugh aloud when I saw the pencil that happened to be sittin' right before me on the top shelf.

I sat at the table in my room. The sun danced on the leaves makin' shadows on the wall. *I must concentrate and write the best letter ever.* I pressed out the wrinkles on the soiled paper, the bottom half page of Sarah's spellin' book.

Dear Silas,

I do find that it is nessesarie for me to speake with you, so I am penning you this letter. This is an importint mater. I have not had the oportuntie to see you privatlie since the death of my beloved mother. It is with a heavy heart that I write to you. I am in such a way that time is of the esensse. Please meet me at our spot in the field behind the barn. I will arrive at 3:00 on Saterday and I will wait there after meeting on Sunday if Saterday is not goode. If you cannot meete me, please send a reply note and leeve it under the bench in the stall beside Lizzy. I left a small box for your use. I will waite for you and know that if you do not arrive, that it is true, you have given your heart to Jesy. I pray that this is not so, as it is you who I profess my love to.

Faithfully Youres,

Abigail

I wrapped the letter inside of an old paper marked *taxes* written in Mother's graceful hand. I drew a line through it and wrote *Silas* with the short, thick pencil. At that moment, I regretted bein' more interested in boyish games and not carin' for school. Had I been mindful like Sarah, perhaps I would have had fine penmanship.

I poked around in the treasure chest. I had to come up with somethin' to make the letter look special, somethin' other than a scribbled mess. I found a frayed white ribbon, tied it around the parcel, and held it to my chest.

Mrs. Blake was nowhere in sight. I called for Old Gray Mare. She didn't respond at first, but soon she trotted my way. We were both quite happy to see one another. I climbed up onto her back and wrapped my arms around her neck. She whinnied softly before breakin' into a slow trot. I nuzzled into her straw-like, black mane, imprintin' her unique scent.

The sun warmed my shoulders. The crisp north wind kept away idle daydreams – a product of the devil – and whipped through the trees, linin' the road with brittle red, yellow, and orange leaves. The nights were cold and threatened frost.

The heavy hand pressed down on my chest as I approached our farm. I tried, but I couldn't avoid lookin' at the old chimney that stood tall and proud. I recalled the cold nights when we sat by the fire. Sarah would play a collection of songs on her cornet, Papa shared stories about his childhood, and Mother taught us all the hymns before any of the other children learnt them. She sang like a songbird. Everyone knew this to be true. By the time I was seven years old, I already understood harmonies. Sarah and Mother sang soprano, and I sang the alto part. Sometimes Papa had a tear in his eye, but he looked away hopin' that no one noticed.

Old Gray Mare slowed down and then stopped. I stared at the charred remnants without blinkin'. My heart was overwhelmed as I did only what I thought I could do. I sang.

"Nearer, my God, to Thee, nearer to Thee
E'en though it be a cross that raiseth me."

It sounded odd without the melody, alto without soprano, me without Mother and Sarah. My voice quivered. I closed my eyes and conjured them up. I could hear them singin' high above me, above the trees and clouds, right there with the angels. Tears mixed with rain.

"Still all my song would be, nearer my God, to Thee,
Nearer, my God, to Thee, nearer to Thee."

Infuriated, dark clouds hovered. The Lord had departed. He answered me no more. I looked at the black, twisted heap and tried to piece together the house and barn. Finally, I rested my head on Old Gray Mare's neck, my arms dangled against her warm body as I viewed the ridge through black strands of horsehair, leavin' the remains behind. We swayed together along the road in stillness interrupted by an occasional chatter of a bird or red squirrel. I sat upright, pulled my hood up over my damp hair and held my cape tightly to my chest. *My child needs a father. I need a husband, the man I love. What has perished has perished.*

The clouds parted quickly, and the sun's rays illuminated the top of Brown's Ridge. *It's a sign, a sign that Silas will be home and we can talk. I won't need this letter.* I tapped the letter inside my reticule.

I dismounted Old Gray Mare and walked towards the house. I didn't see Major, the other horse, or the carriage. *Oh, Lord, please see to it that Silas is here. I promise that I will be in Your service for all my days, if...*

"Well, well. If it ain't Abigail Hodgdon." Mr. Putnam burst through the door lookin' somewhat startled, as if he were confrontin' a big black bear instead of me.

"Hello, Mr. Putnam. How are you on this fine day?" I stopped.

"I ain't got no complaints, 'cept for Silas ain't here to help me with the wood." He tapped his pipe against his wooden leg. "We got all this wood to stack before winter sets in."

"Yes, it's important to gather wood." I felt for the letter. "Will Silas be home soon?"

"He ain't never home soon. Not with the last hayin' and what needs to be done down at the farm. So I don't 'spect to see 'im 'til after sunset."

"I see." I cleared my throat. "Would Mrs. Putnam be at home?"

"She went to Wakefield for a spell. She's helpin' her sister who has the fever." He chewed on the end of his pipe and looked at me with one clouded eye.

"Would you be so kind as to see that Silas gets this?" I extended my shaky hand with the letter. "It's an important matter."

"Of course." He grabbed it from me. "Somethin' you wrote?"

"Ahh... Y-yes." I looked square at him. "Please see that he receives it. I appreciate it."

"Don't worry. Now you better git on that horse and go before it gets dark." He stumbled when he reached for the door.

"Yes, thank you." I mounted my horse.

"I'm gonna' put it on the table, where he'll catch sight of it," he muttered.

The wind snatched my breath away when Old Gray Mare broke into a steady gallop. Without a glance, I passed by the wretched ash pile.

He cannot be drunk at this hour. It is his wooden leg that makes him stagger. I am certain.

CHAPTER 25

Abigail – October 12, 1872

THE THICK FOG wrapped around the mornin' like a tight fittin' glove. Sleep did not come easily to me. I endured another week of tiresome house chores. Sweat dripped off the end of my nose as I scrubbed the floor in the summer kitchen and prepared my words for Silas.

"You worked hard. After you pick a basket of apples, you may take a rest this afternoon." Mrs. Blake hovered over me.

"You are too kind." I looked up at her through my monocle curl and returned to scrubbin'.

The crows cackled and pecked at the bits and pieces left scattered in the cornfield. I stood up slowly, ignorin' the sharp pain in my lower back. I tried to imagine which dress would be the most becomin' for my meetin' with Silas. I thought of the red dress that Mother sewed. She made a blue one like it for Sarah. We bubbled with pride when we wore them to the church picnic. Mother sewed all of our garments, and we were the better for it.

The muted sun worked its way through the endurin' mist. I walked down the path and spotted a bright red maple leaf far away from the cluster of trees across the field. I picked it up and tucked it into my apron pocket to add to my collection of pressed flowers.

I froze. *I no longer have the family Bible.* I envisioned a multitude of perfectly pressed violets, daisies, periwinkle, and others carefully placed within pages that contained family names scrawled throughout on marriage, birth, and death certificates. I pulled the leaf from my pocket and stared at it. The redness seemed to match my lye irritated hands. I took a deep breath and crumpled the leaf into crispy, dry flakes that fluttered gracefully in the wind, and I continued down the path.

I stopped at a gnarly tree in the middle of the orchard and twisted the stem of an oval, red apple 'til it was free. I couldn't resist the Farm Sweets and ate two while fillin' the basket. They were much tastier than the bitter Durgin apples, which were only fit for bakin'.

Jest before my bath, I dashed to the herb shed and sneaked a pinch of lavender from a cracked clay jar. I sprinkled it in the lukewarm water and bathed quickly so not to invite questions.

The green skirt was indeed the best choice. The pleats flattened my stomach. My hands shook when I pulled my hair back and tied it with the washed out blue ribbon from Mother's straw bonnet. *What if he doesn't show?*

I peered out the window. It was the last hayin' of the season. Moses was with his team of oxen in the field workin' with Weston, who was present almost every day, even when there was no work. I knew he had taken a fancy to me. He was an agreeable fellow, but I had given my whole heart to Silas. After all that had taken place, I admit that I did look forward to our conversations.

I did not see or hear Mrs. Blake around. I carried my barn boots and walked as quietly as possible on the creaky stairs. I had fifteen minutes until I would meet Silas at our secret spot behind the barn. I gasped at the sight of Mrs. Blake headin' for the pottin' shed. When I realized that she did not see me, my breathin' returned to normal.

The wind picked up as I neared our spot – an old oak tree with a big rock beneath it at the edge of the field. We discovered this place a few years before when he was showin' me the progress of the barn.

I sat on the rock, leaned against the tree, and wiggled my toes in the silky grass. The song of a chick-a-dee alternated with jinglin' oxen chains. My mouth was dry, and my stomach overwrought with anticipation.

The fog gave way to a vivid blue sky with not a cloud in sight. At least one hour passed, and Silas did not arrive. I imagined that he must have been workin' hard at the County Farm. I continued to wait and think of reasons to remain composed.

I waited until the sun started closin' in on the ridge before I accepted that he would not come. I surrendered to an abundance of tears. I had barely moved durin' my wait, and the chill had set deeply into my bones. I walked away from our spot. All strength was gone.

The field was empty 'cept for a few crows that had returned. I entered the barn and went to Lizzy's stall. She looked at me with affectionate brown eyes. I sat on the edge of the trough and stared at my dirty pink toes. "Oh Lizzy, the fault is all my own. What will become of us?" She moved closer to me and licked my arm.

I got to my room without bein' seen. I fell onto the bed and held Hope to my chest. *There is tomorrow. He will meet me after church.* I blotted out my worst thoughts and denied my tears.

After a supper of salt pork, potatoes, and baked apples, I washed the plates and silverware. Mrs. Blake and Moses sat and talked. I had no strength to partake in frivolous conversation. I excused myself, claimin' that I had a headache.

I rummaged through the treasure chest until I found Papa's small leather Bible. I quickly turned to the inside cover, where his named was written in his own hand. I closed my eyes and opened the Bible, knowin' that I would find a scripture that offered comfort in my hour of need. I ran my finger along the smooth page, stopped, and read:

Come unto me, all ye that labor and are heavy laden, and I will give you rest. Take my yoke upon you, and learn from me; for I am meek and lowly in heart and ye shall find rest unto your souls. For my yoke is easy, and my burden is light.   Matthew 11:28-30

CHAPTER 26

Abigail – October 13, 1872

PEARL CROWED PRECISELY when the sun burst through my window. The birds chirped urgently, and the trees blushed in the peak of autumn. The heavy hand had lifted. I was ready for the day. I dressed in the green skirt with black trim and the Garibaldi blouse. My hair was still soft and shiny and carried the light scent of lavender from the day before. I tucked it into my snood and threaded the thin blue ribbon into Mother's straw bonnet. My cheeks reddened. *Silas and I will proclaim our undyin' love for one another, plan a simple weddin', have this child and many more. Thank you, Lord.*

The carriage rattled down the tree lined road. "It's a lovely day." I felt an unanticipated uprisin' in my chest.

Mrs. Blake glared. "You're in high spirits. What's so special about today?"

"Ain't nothin' wrong with bein' happy now is there?" Moses asked.

"Of course not," she said. "She's been distressed since her mother passed on. Maybe she's not mournin'. Is that so?"

"Although my mournin' is confined to my heart, I will always mourn my dear mother," I said. We passed a cluster of several white birches with brilliant yellow leaves, encouragin' my cheeriness. "I am pleased that it is a splendorous day. There is no motive other than my happiness with the nature that surrounds us."

"Hmm. There must be a different reason." She stiffened.

I chuckled. "You will think as you do. I will be happy in spite of it."

Moses threw his head back and laughed. "You do that, girl. You have been through much more than you asked for. I say, be happy."

We continued in silence, Moses and I with smiles and Mrs. Blake with pursed lips and a knitted brow, starin' ahead, unwillin' to surrender.

I wedged myself in between the Blakes in the pew. When I detected a trace of flowery perfume, I pushed away the sense of fear and betrayal and stared into her green eyes. "Good mornin', Jessie."

Strains of an unfamiliar tune spilled out from the organ. Jessie paused, searchin' for the right words. I didn't wait. I turned back, smiled, and waited for the sermon to begin.

When we returned home, Mrs. Blake was all aflutter in the kitchen. I stood in the doorway. "I'll be out this afternoon and will not join you for dinner."

She dabbed her brow with the blue calico apron. "Where are you goin' off to?"

"It's such a fine day. I will enjoy a long ride on Old Gray Mare before winter sets in."

"You'll be hungry when you return, and we will have eaten all that I have prepared."

"I'll take an apple or two."

"You'll be hungry," she said. "Please yourself."

Indeed, I will please myself, and it pleases me to be away from you and your cruel tongue and to reunite with my love. I took two Farm Sweets from the basket and dropped them into my bonnet.

Old Gray Mare was delighted when I entered her stall. "We're takin' a wonderful journey." I kissed her speckled nose and led her outside. We started easy but soon galloped in the face of the brisk wind. We circled the field. I didn't want to wander too far and miss him.

We stopped by the oak tree and rock. Old Gray Mare grazed while I leaned against the tree and bit into an apple. I pulled the snood from my head, and shook my curls free. The warmth of the sun felt good.

⤙⬤ ⬤⤚

I tried to imagine the white puffy clouds as animals and birds until they blanketed the entire sky. The gladness that filled my heart had slipped away.

In my silent waitin', I had to accept that Silas had made his decision and that sadness would be the language of my heart. I sinned against the Lord, and He had indeed turned His back on me. I started to return to the barn. Old Gray Mare lifted her head – reluctant to leave the faded clover patch. I did not climb on her to ride; once again, all strength was gone.

CHAPTER 27

Silas – October 13, 1872

DADDY WAS RIGHT when he said that firewood heated you again and again – when you cut it, split it, stack it, and finally, when you burn it.

William and I loaded the sled with trees that were felled in June and left to dry. The branches was lopped earlier, makin' 'em easier to handle. "I think this'll do." I went around to the side of the oxen and tugged on the yoke. Their tales swished. They was ready.

"Yep. She's full loaded." He wiped his brow and squinted at the sun.

William led the team forward with his long, thin stick. The beasts responded to his quiet voice with a snort. Their muscles twitched and shined with sweat. We walked back to the field behind the woodshed in comfortable silence.

I went 'round to the gardens first, the horse stalls, and then to the pigsty to round up some men to unload the logs. George Brackett, a slight man in his thirties, came outta' one of the stalls totin' a shovel. His thick, red hair fell sloppily over one eye, and he flashed his toothless grin, always tryin' to please us farm bosses. He kicked at the manure, which was caked on his over-sized boots. "Ayuh?"

"George, go unload the logs from the sled. William's waitin' by the woodshed." I looked towards the garden. Miss Noyes was hollerin' and cussin' at Hannah Foss, the old lady who came here 'bout two weeks before. She couldn't manage after her husband died. She had a son somewhere, a scoundrel from the sounds of it. No one knew of his where'bouts. Last time I heard, he was in Cornish. He didn't come 'round to help his mamma or even claim the house.

"Ayuh." George tossed the shovel up against the side of the barn.

"Put that shovel back where it belongs inside the barn!" I hollered after him. We was always havin' to keep after 'em to return things to their rightful place.

"Ayuh" He bobbed his head and ran into the barn with the shovel.

"And after you unload the logs, you can finish muckin'. Ya hear?" I shouted into the dark barn. Bein' in charge of the likes of George Brackett was good practice for me.

"Ayuh." He appeared in the doorway with his crooked grin, gazin' and weavin' a little.

"Well, get movin'." I shook my head.

"Ayuh." He yanked his trousers high above his waist and then tightened the thick rope that he used to hold 'em up.

Isaac stopped in front of me hangin' on to a pail of water sloshin' out one side. Ever since his wife Lillian died a few months earlier, he leaned a bit to the left when he walked. Moses said it was on account of his heart.

"Isaac, after you tend to them pigs, go sit for a spell. Ya hear old man?" I was thinkin' that he would be better off takin' a rest.

He walked right past me. I knew he weren't hearin' so good. I touched his arm. He spun around, almost droppin' the pail. "Isaac! Give me the pail and go rest." I pointed to where the old folks and simpletons was sittin'.

He gave me the pail, which was only half-full because he spilt most of the water on the ground. I watched him. I weren't sure if he'd make it, so I walked along beside him, ready to catch him if he fell.

The old Indian woman, Nellie, held her hand out to Asa, who was sittin' on a stump. "What the hell do you want?" He pretended not to see me.

She pointed at his pouch.

"I ain't givin' you no tobacco. Leave me alone, Ol' Squaw."

She reached inside of her dress and pulled out somethin' made with colored beads.

"What do I want that for?" He coughed and looked away.

She reached in agin', pulled out a wooden whistle, and blew into it.

"What have you got here?" He took it from her and eyed it real close.

"I can take this home to my boy. He'd like this. I s'pose I could give you a pinch." He grabbed for the whistle.

She held tight, shakin' her head, before reachin' into his pouch and takin' at least three good pinches.

"Hold on, Ol' Squaw."

She pressed her finger to her lips. He hushed. She handed him the whistle and bowed her head. Then, she wrapped the tobacco in thin birch bark paper, tucked it inside her dress, and walked over to us. She helped Isaac sit down. After he was steady, she went to the rain barrel, filled her cup with water, and gave him a drink.

I needed at least two more strong men to haul trees. I went into the back part of the barn, where Jeremiah Hubbard and Cyrus Trask was sawin' lumber to fix a door in the big house. They was happy to go unload the logs. Both of the men was strappin' and able, but they was not willin' to stay away from whiskey and fightin' long enough to keep a job.

"Silas!" Miss Noyes burst out at me with her red face matchin' her hair. "Help me get this old woman into the house." She kicked at Hannah, who was layin' in a heap on the ground, coverin' her head, and cryin'. "She ain't cooperatin'. She's stubborn."

"Excuse me, Miss Noyes, but she's probably jest scared is all. Maybe you should talk nice to her. She ain't been here too long ya know."

"Who do you think you are, tellin' me to be nice to these folks? They're filthy and most of 'em are here because they ain't no good and looked away from the Lord. They git what's comin' to 'em." She poked at Hannah with the toe of her boot.

"Well, that ain't true. They're poor folk who came across bad times is all," I said, unable to hold my tongue.

"You keep actin' soft and you won't never be a real farm boss." She tugged at the old woman's arm. "Come on."

I kneeled beside Hannah and looked into her light blue eyes. She must have been all of ninety years old. She was jest a small thing, with a round face and a pure white braid coiled around her head. "Hannah, it'll be fine if you jest do as you're told. Now stand up." She held on to my arm, and we walked slowly towards the house.

"Old crow… I ain't goin' through this every time I take her out to the garden." Miss Noyes pushed by and went to the kitchen, where the women were cannin' and picklin'.

I avoided starin' at Patience Cook's swollen belly as she rifled through the last green beans of the season. We was at the schoolhouse together 'til I was eleven years old, and then Daddy said I was better off doin' a man's work rather than spendin' time learnin' foolishness from books.

She grinned and wiped her hands on her yellow dress. "Hello, Silas." She snapped a green bean and tossed half of it into her mouth and the other half into the basket.

I nodded and headed for the door. Moses told me it weren't good practice to converse with the female inmates.

"Silas, remember to stack some wood down by the other side of the shed for me," Miss Noyes called out.

"And same for Henry and me, although I don't think we had near enough last year," Polly said with a grunt as she lifted a heavy pot.

"Clear that with Moses. I got work to do." I turned and left. The women bosses were often harder than the men bosses. I jest weren't comfortable with the likes of Miss Noyes.

By the time I got to the woodshed, there was only two trees left on the sled. The sun was high in the sky, so we could haul one more load. I sent the men back to doin' their chores and took to the woods with William.

I thought 'bout Abigail. I didn't hear a word from her. I used to see her at Clark's Grain Store, Tibbetts', or jest out for a ride. She didn't leave Moses's farm, and when I mentioned it to him, he told me that she was occupied with Weston. I weren't much of a fightin' man, but I got all riled up at the thought of it.

It was odd seein' her at Moses's. It seemed as if Mrs. Blake had Abigail servin' all her needs. Knowin' Abigail, she didn't like bein' a slave to others' wants. She was quite happy before Sarah left town, before her mamma died.

Then she didn't even spare a word for me. This made the Gilmans' offer look dandy. I mighta' never had an opportunity like it again.

William brung the oxen to a halt. We took our time draggin' one tree after another and pilin' 'em on the sled 'til we had a full load. We walked alongside the team; he guided 'em gently.

"I don't s'pose it's easy havin' Bella right near ya but not gettin' to talkin' and such," I said.

He put his hands on his hips and looked up at the big house. "Ain't nothin' I can do 'bout it now. Things will change."

We stood in silence under the fast movin' orange clouds that nestled atop the ridge. A strong gust of wind scattered dead leaves across the earth, promptin' the oxen to stir, and for us to move along.

CHAPTER 28

Nellie – October 15, 1872

THERE WAS A different joy in the woods when the world was in slumber. I departed before the rising sun, for the journey would be long. It was the Corn Making Moon – days grow shorter and darkness exceeds light. It was time for gathering bark, pine needles, plants, and roots for many medicines to heal the body and feed the spirit.

Crisp leaves swished beneath my feet in the quiet of morning. I filled my basket with acorns for making soup in the deepest part of winter. I stopped to rest on the cool moss. The sugar maple sheltered me from the north winds. Soon I would reach Cold River.

·→≡◉ ◉≡‹·

Searching Owl – a white man trader – hunted, fished, trapped, and farmed. He visited many times and sat long by the fire sharing stories with my people. He spoke of a place with many lakes, one much like Bitawbagok, called Wiwininebesaki, the great smiling spirit. He lived in a village called Asepihtegw, River Alongside. It was in the land of the great White Mountains – Wawôbadenik – that reached past Father Sky.

My heart filled with joyful song when White Flower told me that Searching Owl was to meet with Standing Bear and the elders to ask permission for me to be his wife. He brought many offerings.

Six winters passed when my father's spirit departed. He and others were sick with the white man's fever. Before the marriage, he appeared in my dream. *Nanatasis, Searching Owl is good. He will honor you. You will live far away from Bitawbagok. Go. Be fruitful.*

The tears came. I wanted to see him longer. The vision was clear. I went to my mother and lay beside her. She opened her eyes. *Nanatasis.*

We slept in embrace until the break of day. Her heartbeat gave comfort. Searching Owl talked long with Standing Bear and the elders. We filled baskets with offerings and prepared for the celebration. I had not danced since the river took Mamijôla. At our wedding, I danced.

The child of Searching Owl grew in me. Soon I would leave my people. I looked long at my mother and the yellow flames that danced in her eyes. Her skin was soft, and her thick black hair had silver strands. She was wise, graceful, and strong. How could I leave all that I knew?

The last night came. She stood tall. *Nanatasis, come.*

I followed her into the shadows, away from the light of fire. Who would help with the birth of our child? Who would comfort me? Who would guide me?

You must not be afraid. Elijah is a good husband. He is strong and knows the ways of Our Mother. He will care for you and the child. Welcome this journey. She placed her hand on my stomach and smiled. You will know the great smiling spirit of Wiwininebesaki. The Wawôbadenik hold many secrets. Be strong, my daughter.

Searching Owl stirred before sunrise. *Nanatasis, we should go before the others awaken. You said farewell. This is best.*

I took the doll that I made and left it beside my mother while she dreamed. With great sorrow, I looked upon her face for the last time.

After four days of travel, we arrived at a place called Water Village. Searching Owl's house was on the banks of Cold River. It was not a large house, but it was good. It withstood winter winds and spring rains.

Searching Owl took me to his church to hear a man like the black robes. It was then that I received my Christian name – Nellie Baldwin. I did not want to be inside of walls to pray to their dead king. I was pleased that my husband did not make me go with him. I honored the Great Spirit, Father Sky, Earth Mother, the mountains, lakes, and rivers. I honored animals and birds. They offered ways of knowing.

After the passing of three moons, I gave birth to our son, Benjamin. He did not take a breath. To me he was White Bear. His birth was difficult and with much blood. He was a small flower that came before the blossom. With sorrow, we returned him to the womb of Our Mother. We buried him on the bluff near the banks of Cold River. There were no more children born to us.

Searching Owl carved things from trees. He made a flute. I played many songs. He carved a whistle from the thick branch of a white pine. With this, I would not be lost from him.

When Searching Owl travelled no more, he worked with the other white men at the gristmill. We lived in abundance with chickens and pigs and a white man's garden. I continued to harvest from Our Mother.

Many seasons passed. Searching Owl prepared the black ash for the baskets that I made to sell to the white man. I made dolls for trading at the store in the village. In the sugar-making months, we tapped the maples and prepared seed for the Planting Moon. We worked in the garden, gathered groundnut, berries, plants, and we fished.

During the Corn Making Moon, we harvested and hunted, and we cut and split wood for winter. Our clothes and bedding of fur pelts kept us warm, and we made snowshoes for travelling in deep snow. We cut a hole in the ice to fish. We ate dried meat, berries, herbs, roots, and butternut and acorn squash.

Some people from the village spit on me and called me a witch because I would not pray inside of their walls, and I harvested on Sundays. All days are equal. I gave thanks for the gifts of the Great Spirit.

White men came to me when their doctor had no medicine for healing. Doctor Bennett, a kind man, came often, asking many questions. We walked amongst trees, rivers, and fields. I showed him where healing grows.

After eight winters, the fever came to Water Village. I had many good medicines: white maple bark, white pine tea, ground hemlock tea, and elder, mullein, and juniper berries. I cared for the sick and did not sleep. Many died from what white men call pneumonia.

My friend the crow called from above. The sun of the new day warmed my face. It was time to take flight, to continue my journey to Cold River.

The house before me was without life. The roof crumbled and emptiness stared where windows once were. A red squirrel came out from under the stone hearth with an acorn. He was wise to prepare for winter. I put my sack and basket on the ground and walked to the back of the house. The small black and white birds called out. *Chick-a-dee-dee-dee.* Cold River sang a hurried song. I crossed the field. The sun cast light on two granite rock piles pressed close to Our Mother's breast. The wooden crosses were no more.

I reached inside of my belt for the folded birch paper. I opened it and pinched the fresh tobacco in my fingers, thankful that the farm boss accepted the whistle in trade. I spread it over the rocks and earth as an offering. Facing the sun, I sat before their graves. *Another winter shall pass.* I closed my eyes and listened and waited for the departed ones.

When the sun was high, I began my journey back to the farm with my basket, sack, and heart filled with the strength to face the bitterness of the winter yet to come.

CHAPTER 29

Abigail – October 15, 1872

I FINISHED WITH the barn early. I decided to busy my thoughts and try my hand at embroidery. I had never succeeded before, but with everything bein' as it were, I tried again. I sat on the porch and relished the quiet. Mrs. Blake went into town, and Moses was at work.

"Hello, young lady." Weston hurried up the stairs and sat beside me in the weatherworn rocker. He smiled.

"Hello." I poked my finger with the needle, causin' a tiny spot of blood to appear. "I will never be as good as Mother or Sarah." I licked my finger and dropped the cloth and needle onto the floor.

"It makes no difference. You're good at other things."

"What would those things be?" I asked.

"Well, you're awful good with animals. And you sing real fine." He leaned back in the chair.

"I'm good with animals; that much is true. But what do you know about me singin'?"

"I hear ya in church." He removed his tired, old hat.

"You cannot tell me from the others."

"Yes. Yes I can."

"That is not possible. I sing quietly."

"Well, I hear ya in church. I do. And I hear ya sing in the barn and in the field," he said.

I cleared my throat. "How is that?"

"Well, sometimes when I'm workin' 'round, I hear ya singin'."

"I'll have to take notice of who's lurkin' in the shadows."

"Don't be offended. I think highly of you. Silas is a fool to have taken up with Jessie."

"How do you know this?" My stomach churned.

"It's no secret. Doc Gilman is givin' them a parcel of land. So one can only figure that they're gettin' married. I jest don't know when."

"Of course, I heard that. I didn't know it was truly goin' to happen." My thoughts turned to that tart flittin' about in her fancy dress and Silas starin' at us both, stumblin' over his words.

"I don't fault ya for bein' angry. After all, it appeared that you had a special spot for him." He chewed on a long blade of grass.

"That was long ago. Silas is boyish, and he was becomin' a bother."

"Aw, don't feel bad. He's the one who's not up to scratch." He spit out the grass. "I would fancy courtin' you."

"Weston, I've had many long days of nothin' but work and horrid thoughts of my mother in the fire, my sister bein' away and all." I paused. "I'm not able to think about courtin' anyone at present."

His smile vanished as we both looked towards the sound of an approachin' horse.

"Oh, please don't get me wrong. You're a fine man. I am simply done in from all that's happened." I put my arms around him and kissed his cheek in friendship. "Now, we can remain friends. Agreed?"

His face was quite red. He looked away. "Of course."

Mrs. Blake came into sight. I pulled away. "I must go." I bolted into the house leavin' him standin' alone.

My heart thumped as I dashed to my room. *I thought that she was gone for the day.* I sat on my bed lookin' out the window while she and Weston exchanged words. Her footsteps were heavy and deliberate. She wailed the door shut.

I waited, but she did not call for me. My breathin' finally slowed. I dragged the treasure chest out from under the bed. I rummaged through it 'til I found some scraps of paper. *I must write to Silas once more.*

I didn't know of Mrs. Blake's whereabouts when I sneaked to the shed to fetch the pencil. I returned to my room and sat at the table for what seemed like an hour before findin' the appropriate words.

Dear Silas,

I write to you in despiration. I waited for you Saturday & Sunday last & you did not show. Peple talk about you and Jesy Gilman getting maried. Surely that canot be true. For if it is true, I shall lament for the rest of my days.

What it is that I must talk to you aboute is an urgent matter. Remember when we were intimat in the hayloft? There is a conseqense for our behavore. I am not free to write it in a letter and would prefer to tell you in persone.

I remain in anguish here conserning the sad feelins that are resting upon me. My life has becom lonely & filled with drugery and tiresom work. I miss our talks and genrally being close. What I have to tell you is without questhion the most important thing in our lifes.

Come to our spot when it pleases you. Place a letter in the stall beside Lizzy under the bench to tell me when we shuld meet. I will check it evry day. I do not beleve it to be true that you love any other than myself.

I waite faithfully.
Abigail

I tied the letter with a string that I found in the barn, tucked it inside of my apron pocket, and headed to the barn to fetch Old Gray Mare.

"Abigail?" Mrs. Blake bellowed from inside the pottin' shed.

"Yes?" *That woman has the ears of a cottontail.* I stopped. Two red hens scattered by my feet with Pearl chasin' behind them.

"Come here." She stood on a chair placin' a fruit jar on the shelf.

"Yes?" I leaned against the door frame. I had that old feelin' like bein' caught eatin' an extra slice of apple pie. I could never lie, and Mother knew that I had trouble resistin' the temptation of her bakin'.

"I tried to look the other way, but I can't help but noticin' that you are familiar with Weston. I don't take kindly to you actin' inappropriately here."

Her face looked like an overripe tomato about to burst as she climbed down from the wobbly chair.

"Weston and I are simply friends. What you saw was friendship and nothin' more." I looked at her through my monocle curl.

"Call it what you like, but I ain't puttin' up with it," she said. "Moses and I are good folks. I know that you had a good upbringin', and your mother would agree with me."

"Do not speak of my mother." I clenched my fists inside of my apron pockets. "She would believe me."

"I warn you, don't sass me back. You seem to forget 'bout the County Farm." She squinted her eyes 'til they nearly disappeared.

"Forgive me. I miss Mother, and what I say about Weston is true." I fiddled with the letter in my pocket.

"I accept your apology. If Moses sees you carryin' on, he might not be so forgivin'." She brushed past me through the door and stopped. "Where are you off to?"

"I'm takin' an afternoon ride."

"With no place in mind?"

"Yes, that's right."

"I don't do such things, goin' about with no purpose." She continued walkin'.

"Perhaps you should try," I said. "Jest set out and enjoy the day and ride where you may."

"Don't fritter away the day. You need to do some mendin'." She slammed the door.

I mimicked her words and her twisted face. "Don't fritter away the day."

Old Gray Mare was grazin' by the gate. She lifted her head and stared at me while chewin'. "You were listenin', weren't you?" I leaned over and plucked a handful of grass and held it out to her. Her warm, pinkish nose rubbed against the palm of my hand. Her breath was hot.

The sun mingled with the brisk autumn air. After a short trot, normal breathin' resumed. Optimism slowly emerged as we meandered along the dusty road. I learned to force my eyes away from our farm when I passed.

However, on this day, Old Gray Mare galloped straight towards the ruins of our barn. "Whoa!" I pulled hard on the reins before she finally halted.

I froze as if I were dead. I could no longer escape the ghosts that I wished to forget, for they forced me to remember. I denied my own weepin' as I was faced again with all that brought me sorrow.

I dismounted Old Gray Mare and approached the charred fence. My foot struck somethin'. I bent down to examine it and recognized the iron latch that Grandfather made. I held it up and blew off the soot. What a prize. Grandfather was a fine blacksmith. He made all of the ironware in and about the house. *I'll put this in the treasure chest.*

Without givin' it much thought, I walked to the sittin' rock by the brook. The water was barely a trickle, enough to wash the blackness from my hands. "C'mon Old Gray. C'mon!" In an effort to stay away and avoid the temptation to search for more remnants, I beckoned her.

She tossed her mane and snorted. I stormed over to her. "You win... stubborn horse." I mounted up and gave a squeeze with my legs. We trotted at a fast pace until we came upon Mr. Putnam sittin' on a stump near the garden in front of his house.

He spun 'round, almost takin' a spill. "Who goes there?"

I laughed. "It is me, Abigail." I dismounted.

"I don't see nothin' funny 'bout scarin' an old man." He took a good swig from his brown and tan jug.

"Oh, please forgive me. I didn't mean to cause you a fright." I twiddled with the letter in my pocket.

"Never mind, girl. What do ya want?" He swayed.

"I was lookin' to see if Silas was home," I said, beginnin' to wilt.

"Of course he ain't home." He took another tug and wiped his mouth on his sleeve. "He's at the County Farm. He don't get home 'til after sundown. You's jest wastin' your time. He's got that fancy doctor's daughter all worked up."

"Is Mrs. Putnam at home?" I asked, tryin' to appear unshaken.

"Speak up. I'm 'bout deaf from them damn howitzer's." He looked past me.

"Is Mrs. Putnam at home?" I thought it to be a shout.

"Of course she's home." He turned away.

I took Old Gray Mare's reins and walked towards the house.

Mrs. Putnam came out onto the porch. "Abigail, what a surprise." She wiped her hands on her faded green apron. "What brings you here today?"

My knees shook hard. "I uh... I have somethin' for Silas. Please see that he gets it." I thrust the letter into her hand. "It's a private matter." I gathered my wits about me. "Please, Mrs. Putnam."

She took the letter and tucked it into her apron pocket. "Ayuh... I will see that he gets it." Her eyes were big and round and scared.

"Thank you." I hoped that she would invite me in for tea or a kind word.

"You're welcome." Her eyes darted about. "How's things goin'?" Her fear made me uneasy. She wasn't the Mrs. Putnam I was accustomed to.

"Well, I miss Mother and Sarah." *And your son.* "And it's been hard bein' somewhere different than what I know to be home."

"Have you heard a word from Sarah?" she asked.

"I have received one letter. It's my turn to write to her."

"You may want to be joinin' her at the mills. Might be what's best for you." She looked down.

"Perhaps... I shall ride out the winter, and in the spring I might go to the mills." I leaned against a nearby tree for fear of collapse.

"You'll decide what's best, ayuh." She shuffled towards the door and then turned around. "Goodbye."

"Good—" I flinched when she slammed the door. With a heart full to overflowin', I walked past Mr. Putnam. He was half off the stump, almost on the ground. He didn't even seem to see Old Gray Mare and me when we passed by him, leavin' dust from the road behind us.

How soon had anguish followed upon the heels of gladness. I knew not whether I was in my body or out of it, for all that had transpired was merciless in consequence. I trusted my horse for my safe return. I had lost the will to do so on my own.

CHAPTER 30

Silas – October 15, 1872

WE SHARED MOST of what we harvested at the farm with the farm bosses, includin' firewood. It was jest 'bout sunset when I finished stackin' the last of the wood on the sled for Polly. I was fixin' to leave for the day.

I looked real hard but couldn't make out who was walkin' across the corn field. As the figure got closer, I saw that it was Nellie. I stepped outside to wait for her.

I approached her. "What are ya doin' outside this time of day? You ain't s'posed to be out here." I brushed the sawdust from my shirt.

She kept her sights on the house and continued on. She carried a cloth sack and a basket, and she dragged her feet when she walked.

"I'm talkin' to you, Nellie." I raised my voice, even though she hadn't spoken a word in all the time I'd known her. She jest lumbered up the stairs like I wasn't there. I shook my head and went to the pasture.

Ridin' home always invited me to thinkin'. I hadn't heard from Abigail. The only thing I knew to be true was that she was sweet on Weston. I thought of takin' a ride over to Moses's to see if I could talk to her. She was sore at me about the dinner and the Gilmans. I couldn't say that I blamed her, but it weren't of my doin'.

The sun was down. The dim glow in the windows was off in the distance. I took my sweet time gettin' home. It would be fine by me if I had my own house.

Once Major was in his stall, I gave him two handfuls of grain and filled the bin. "Good night, boy." He quickly munched them sweet oats. I dug my hands into the sack and gave some grain to Babe, the old white mare that Mamma got from Eb Burrows. She was a gentle creature.

A mouse darted 'round my feet when I went to the hayloft. We needed a cat. The black one disappeared more 'n three months before. I climbed up the ladder and pulled a bundle forward and loosened four flakes.

I set out to check the cows and saw that they needed water. All Daddy needed to do was check on the barn from time to time. It would help us all and give him somethin' to do other than drink.

The chickens murmured and settled onto the roosts. I filled up their feed boxes. Of course, there was two brown eggs in one of the nests. I put one in each pocket of my trousers and latched the door. We hadn't lost a chicken for three weeks, since I put on the new latch that Elijah made. No critter would get one more of my chickens if I could help it.

I whistled on my way to the house, wishin' that I didn't have to talk to no one. Daddy slept in his chair with his head cocked to the side and his jug on the floor beside him.

Mamma sat beside him, patchin' his garments and hummin' one of them church songs. She looked up. "Good evenin', son."

"Ayuh." I set the eggs in the basket on the table.

"How is everything at the farm?" She smiled a little.

"It was a day for cuttin', splittin', and stackin'." I poured fresh apple cider into my cup. "Was your day pleasant?"

Daddy snorted. A dark spot appeared on his pants, and a puddle formed beneath the chair. Mamma dropped her sewin', grabbed a cloth, and knelt before him.

"Mamma, you ain't gotta' do that."

"Never mind. As I see it, I ain't got a choice." She wiped up his urine.

"It ain't right." I set a log on the fire.

"It's my lot to take care of him. I don't want to hear no complaints." Her voice trailed off as she left the room.

The fire picked up, castin' a glow on Daddy's face. I s'posed that it was time to carry him to bed. I reached down, stopped, and tried to think of a way to lift him without touchin' his soiled pants.

Mamma came back into the room. "It's still early now."

"I don't see that it makes a difference, Mamma. I'd jest as soon not have to look at him any longer or listen to his snorin'." I propped him up on his good leg. *Let the old bugger walk.*

He swayed a bit and grabbed a hold of my shoulder. He stared at me with that left eye of his. "What ya doin'? Leave me be, ya son of a bitch." He fell against the wall.

"It's time for bed." I resisted raisin' my fist. I entertained that thought often but never acted on it. "C'mon, let's go." I muckled onto his elbow.

He jerked away from me. "I can walk on my own, damn you." He teetered towards the kitchen. "I don't know why the Hodgdon girl is so sweet on you."

"What?" I walked over to him. "Are you talkin' 'bout Abigail?"

"Sure, I'm talkin' 'bout Abigail. She come by today when you was at the farm. Ain't that right, Sally?" He tugged on his beard.

Mamma glared and put her finger to her lips. "Hush now, Hiram. I'll talk to Silas. You get into your night clothes." She looked over his shoulder and gave me a nod as he mumbled in his spittle.

My cheeks got hot. I rubbed my hands over the fire while they carried on. My mouth was parched, so I got me another cup of cider.

"Such an ornery soul when he's liquored up." She burst into the room wipin' her hands on her apron.

"Is it true?" I swallowed a mouthful of cider. "Abigail came callin'?"

"You know Daddy. He ain't always right in the head, 'specially when he's been drinkin'. In fact, it's gettin' worse, I'd say." She picked up her sewin' and nestled into her chair.

"So he was jest conjurin' up a story?"

"Yes, son. Maybe in his mind he had some sorta' dream is all. But we ain't had no visitors here for some time." The fire crackled and the light flickered on her face.

"Yes, I s'pose you're right."

"You ain't disappointed are you?" she asked.

"No, I jest want to know what's a doin' is all."

"Well, from what Miriam tells me, you ain't got to worry 'bout Abigail callin' on you. She's been intimate with the Jones boy."

I felt a rumblin' inside of me that I weren't so sure of. Every time I thought of him it struck, sort of makin' me ill.

She squinted and pulled at the needle. "Annie would be beside herself." She set her sewin' on her lap. "Miriam and Moses got more than they bargained for with that one."

I stared into the flames. I had never picked a fight. *It was time I hit him.*

"You jest keep your sights on workin' hard down at the County Farm. And don't get no ideas about brawlin' with Weston. That'll spoil everything. You know that Jessie's a nice girl, and her folks'll take care of you." She started in sewin'. "Abigail ain't nothin' but trouble, son."

"Abigail ain't trouble, Mamma. She's–"

"Never mind, Silas. Keep yourself in line and pay her no mind."

I blew out the lamp and took the last swig of cider. I swished it 'round in my mouth. It was bittersweet and brung tears to my eyes.

CHAPTER 31

Abigail – October 30, 1872

THE TAN ENVELOPE stood out against the dark oak table. I walked closer to see my name penned in Sarah's familiar writin'. *Oh dear Lord, she has written to me.* Tears threatened. *I must tear it open at once.* I turned and looked at Mrs. Blake hunched over and bitin' her lip as she peeled potatoes. *No, I will bring it to the barn and read it to Lizzy.*

My boots crunched on the hardened hoof prints embedded into the earth. Kickin' dried, curled up leaves, I blazed a path to the barn. I shivered as the wind whisked them into a frenzy, and they circled about my head. We had a killin' frost the previous night. It was simply a matter of time before the first snowfall.

I rushed to the empty stall to see if Silas had responded. My hope dimmed with each passin' day, as I found not a trace of a letter from him. I stopped. *Not now.* I took hold of the milk bucket and approached Lizzy. "Good mornin', girl." I rubbed my hand on her black and white nose. "I have a surprise." I waved the letter in front of her. "A letter from Sarah."

I dragged the milkin' stool beside her and carefully opened the envelope.

Dearest Sister,

I apologize that is has taken me so long to write a word to you. My health is very good and I am well contented with my work. I want to give you the perticulers. I have been working very hard and have little time to take such plesures as penning a letter. I do find the time to play my cornet. We are much confined in our living quarters, so I have found a suitable hiding place.

I made the aquantans of a girl from Conway and her name is Wealthy Norton. She invited me to go with her to the freewill babtist church. I wuld like to, but I cannot leave the methodist church now. I must confide in you, sister. It is not as pleasing as our dear church in Ossipee, but I will not be in favore of the other girls here if I attend another church. They will become cold and indifferent if I do not acompanie them.

I have another good friend here in Fall River that is a mother to me as it were. For that, I pray to God to bless her for her caring wayes.

You ocupy my thoughts. I hope to hear a word of what came about from your talk with Silas. I have much to write, but time does not permit.

I think fondly of you and Mother. I awaite your response.

Affectionately,

Your Sister, Sarah Hodgdon

I sat in stillness. Fragments of hay dust shimmered in the long, straight lines of sunlight that poured in through the cracks of the hayloft. In harmony with my own uncertainty, Pearl crowed a half a crow. I tucked the letter inside of my apron pocket.

I took small, tentative steps to the empty stall beside Lizzy and reached under the bench. Nothin'. I sat down. My chest tightened. I came perilously close to crumblin'. His silence had spoken. I vowed never to return to that stall. I would not speak to him again. He would not know that I carried his child. He deserved Jessie Gilman.

Anger begged to reside in me, but I refused to welcome it. I gulped the frigid air and struggled to swallow. *I have sinned and for this I will pay. I will hold up my head and take what is delivered to me. Silas will get what comes his way. I must never look back.* I pulled the stool closer to Lizzy and held the milk bucket under her. I mustered up the strength to sing.

"Jesus loves me! This I know,
For the Bible tells me so.
Little ones to Him belong;
They are weak, but He is strong."

"You see? I told you that you could sing." Weston's voice stopped me cold.

I whipped around nearly fallin' off the stool. "Good Lord!" I went back to milkin'. "Don't you think you should warn a girl when you come up behind her like that?"

"Sorry. I got somethin' to tell you." He smiled showin' nearly all his teeth.

"What are you all wiggly about? Do tell." I let go of Lizzy and wiped my hands on my apron.

"My brother-in-law, John Garland, invited me to move up to Bangor, Maine to work at the lumber mill. You remember him don't ya? He married my sister Clara."

"Well, I remember Clara." She was a bit older, a soft-spoken girl with thick black hair, and a pretty face. "I was unaware that she was married or in Bangor."

"She's been there for a few years now. She and John got two children and they live close to the mill."

"There are mills here in Ossipee. Why don't you work at a mill here?"

"I want to see the world. I ain't been any farther than Concord or Portland. Besides, with Jonathan bein' a man of importance and all, he could see to it that I get treated right."

"I s'pose that's true." I reached for Lizzy's utters to finish milkin'.

"Abigail." He cleared his throat.

"Let me finish milkin' this cow, and we can go for a walk." The milk streamed into the bucket. I exhaled. The ache in my chest lessened with each squeeze.

"Did you collect the eggs yet?" He started walkin' away.

"Not yet, the basket is on the bench." I licked a droplet of milk from my finger. "You don't have to do that. It's my chore," I called after him.

"I don't mind helpin'. I'll get the eggs, and then we can go for a walk." He went away hummin' the tune that I was singin' when he came in.

Soon we were out in the mid-mornin' sun. We strolled through the orchard, careful to step around the rotten apples that were surrounded by yellow jackets. "I don't s'pose I could convince you to stay?" It was a peculiar thought, but my misery and heartache seemed to bring us together. Besides Lizzy, Pearl, Old Gray Mare, and Miss Emily, he was all that I had.

"I'm s'prised to hear you talk like that," he said.

"You and I have become friends."

He took my hand, and we walked over to a cluster of trees. He placed his coat on the ground and motioned for me to sit. "I must confess somethin' to you."

The earth was cool beneath me, and there was a slight snap comin' down from the north. I rested my head on his shoulder. I knew that he would profess his love for me, but I could not allow it. In five months' time, I would give birth to Silas's child. Besides, I did not love him. It would have been unfair of me to benefit from his good nature. I ran my finger along a crease in my skirt. "Go on."

He cupped my face tenderly in his hands. "You must know that I love you." He stared straight into my eyes.

"I did suspect it." I looked down even though he continued to hold my face. "I care deeply for you in friendship."

He released me and turned away. I grasped his warm, rough hand and drew a deep breath. "You are a very dear friend… my heart has been broken. There hasn't been time for it to mend."

"I know 'bout your woes. I'd take you with me to Maine. You can be my wife, and in time you would forget Silas and learn to love me. I jest know it to be true." He looked towards the sound of an approachin' horse.

"I can't do that to you. It's regrettable that my heart belongs to another. But you'll find a girl who is right for you."

"I ain't so sure of that, and I ain't ashamed of askin' you to come with me to start anew."

"I'm sorry things aren't different." I pulled my knees up to my chest. "I will miss you."

"Well, I'll be leavin' this comin' week." His expression changed from the innocence of a boy to the confidence of a man.

"Why are things so difficult?" I buried my face in his shirt. When he put his arms around me, I wished that it was his child in me. I knew that it wasn't right to place such a weight upon him.

We sat quietly for at least an hour. It was hard to hold on and hard to let go. The quiet was interrupted again by the sound of a horse. It must have been Moses decidin' to go to the farm.

I thought of Mrs. Blake and her spiteful tongue and stiffened. "I must get some things done." I brushed the decayed leaves from my skirt. "We best part for now."

"Alright." He got to his feet. "This ain't it. I'll say goodbye before I leave." He pulled me up close to him.

"Perhaps we should say goodbye now. It won't be any easier later. In fact, it'll be more difficult," I said.

"I can't say goodbye jest yet," he said.

"You must... We must." I turned to face him. "Travel safely." A rush of heat flushed my cheeks.

"Abigail, don't leave." He reached for me.

I paused. "I have to. You will write?" I turned to look one last time.

He had an awful look about him. "I don't write much."

"Then it is time to learn. I'll wait for a letter from you." I tucked my monocle curl into my bonnet.

"I'll try." He embraced me. "I love you." He pressed his lips against mine. The kiss was hard and unexpected, almost causin' me to faint. I opened my eyes wide and pushed him away.

He stormed off, mounted his horse, and galloped down Brown's Ridge Road. I watched until he disappeared. Miss Emily purred and rubbed against my ankles. I stood motionless, starin' at the empty road.

Mrs. Blake burst through the door with a bright red face and hair flyin' about. She crossed her arms over her ample bosom. "You ain't bringin' that cat in the house." She grabbed Miss Emily and threw her out the door, causin' her to land on the ground with a rather loud thud.

CHAPTER 32

Silas – October 30, 1872

THERE WEREN'T TOO many days when Moses stayed away from the farm. He coughed and hacked and complained of a fever for a few days. He thought it best to stay home. Once a person took sick, it didn't take long for it to spread.

I was inspectin' the new nestin' boxes when Asa barreled his way through the coop. "Where the hell are them keys?" A handful of chicks scattered when he did his usual shoutin'.

"Which keys?" I asked.

"We got bushels of potatoes that gotta' be put into the root cellar. Moses has the keys. All of them keys is here 'cept the keys to the root cellar." He kicked at the hens that gathered 'round his feet.

"I don't s'pose they have 'em in the kitchen do they?" I asked, runnin' my hand along the fresh-cut pine boxes in search of a flaw.

"Nope. Polly says that Moses has 'em on that big key ring that he carries around. It ain't like anyone's gonna' break in for Chrissakes."

"Well, I don't know why you can't wait 'til tomorrow. Them potatoes ain't goin' nowhere," I said.

"How can he 'spect us to get things done if we can't get into the damn root cellar?" He shook his head.

"I'll ride over to Moses's and get 'em." Nothin' pleased the bastard, but I kept on tryin'.

"You do that," he said.

I went to the pasture and mounted my horse. *Someday he's gonna' 'preciate me.* I rode hard thinkin' 'bout the chance of seein' Abigail. Mamma told me that if I was smart, I'd marry Jessie that winter and get to buildin' my house in the spring. I weren't ready to strike Abigail from my heart.

I neared Moses's farm and saw somethin' move in the apple orchard. At first I thought it was a deer. I slowed down. It weren't no deer. I dismounted my horse and walked around the side of the barn. I stopped when I saw Abigail and Weston. The two of 'em was leanin' against a tree, and he had his arm around her.

I coulda' gone over and cold cocked him right there. I clenched my fist. The blood rushed to my face, and my ears was hot. He was too close to her. I couldn't take it no more. I bit my knuckle as hard as I could. I paced back and forth thinkin' that I might kill the bastard. Then what?

I pictured Moses's face wrinkled in disgust while watchin' me bein' hauled off and charged with murder. He would hate me. I would be like them pathetic folks who weren't even fit for the County Farm – them vagrants, them foreigners who came through like that Irishman who shot Billy Dawes. He killed him right in front of the mill over a whiskey jug. Mamma would cry and carry on, and Abigail would turn her back on me, refusin' to talk to someone who committed such a horrible act. I leaned on the rough sawn boards, catchin' my breath 'til my face was cool and the gnawin' inside went away. I walked up to the door of the house and stopped short of hittin' it with my fist. I tapped gently.

"Hold on, hold on." Mrs. Blake opened the door a crack and peeked out. "Oh Silas, it's you. Come in." She covered her mouth with the corner of her apron. "You don't look good, you sick too?"

"No, ma'am. Jest been ridin' in the cold is all." I wiped my runny nose with my shirt sleeve.

She stepped away, bobbin' her head like an anxious pheasant avoidin' the stew pot. "Should I fetch Moses?" She called from the kitchen.

"That ain't necessary. We ain't got a key for the root cellar, and we have bushels of potatoes to put away." I looked over my shoulder at the pair.

She stood in the safety of the kitchen door. "I know." She nodded towards Abigail and Weston. "Those two jest can't get enough of each other. I talked to her about bein' intimate and such. I don't know what'll become of her. It's awful unsettlin'. Annie would have a fit if she knew how Abigail was carryin' on."

I squeezed my hands into tight fists inside my pockets. "Yes, ma'am. I need them keys, if you don't mind."

"Of course, you wait right here." She closed the door.

I whistled somethin' that didn't resemble any song as I paced in front of the dyin' fire. My heart pounded wicked hard. I wanted to kill him. I never felt that way before. I worked up a sweat and couldn't think straight.

When the door swung open I spun around, ready to fight.

Mrs. Blake looked at me like I wasn't right in the head. "I didn't mean to scare you. You should see about gettin' home after you deliver these keys," she said.

"Things is fine now that we can get into the root cellar." I grabbed the thick ring from her pudgy little hand. "Give Moses my best."

"Stubborn old fool, he'll be there in the mornin' I s'pose." She wrinkled up her nose and looked past me to the orchard.

"Good day." I touched the rim of my hat and ran down the steps to my horse. As I rode off, I stole one more look at the two of them sittin' cozy under the tree. I slapped the reins on Major and dug in my heels. He sprinted down Brown's Ridge Road. I weren't never gonna' be the big farm boss if I gave in to tears, bein' all sentimental.

"Heeyah!" My voice echoed through the silent hills. Major broke into a good clip as bright red and orange leaves waved on the tree-lined road, rootin' us on. I got to thinkin'. Ayuh, a festive Christmas weddin' like Mamma said would be nice indeed.

CHAPTER 33

Abigail – November 10, 1872

I KEPT MY birthday a secret. I figured that mentionin' such things would jest stir up Mrs. Blake's pot of bubblin' troubles. I would miss Mother's nice cornmeal cake and Sarah's usual surprise of a delightful trinket that she sewed from scraps and ribbons.

Other than a random peck, there had been few words between Mrs. Blake and me since the day of Weston's departure. I secretly hoped that he would come callin' again, but he left as he said he would. I got up each day, did my chores, and found ways to keep from havin' idle hands.

Mrs. Blake came across some yellow cloth in the steamer trunk in the shed, and she gave it to me with her sewin' basket, so I made myself a skirt. It wasn't as nice as somethin' that Mother or Sarah would fashion, but it was new and fit me well. I stayed up late at night and sewed the last of it so that I could wear it to church.

Although I pressed on the sides of Mother's straw bonnet, they sprang back up, hopelessly defiant and determined to show signs of bein' tucked away in a box too long. I shrugged. It wasn't the bonnet; it was the head in it that mattered. I smiled as I tied the pale yellow ribbon loosely under my chin. I imagined Mother's face turnin' various shades of pink. *Abigail, you aren't wearin' that shabby, old thing to church are you?*

The sound of icy rain strikin' the roof quickened my pulse. I tugged at the ribbon and hesitated as water rushed down the window pane in a steady stream. When I started to remove the bonnet, an untamed piece of straw snagged a curl, causin' a tangled mess. I yanked the stubborn bonnet off my head, tossed it aside, and went off to join the Blakes.

"That's a pretty dress you have there," Moses said, gulpin' his coffee.

"Thank you." I blushed, feelin' a peculiar mix of both guilt and pride.

"You did a fine job." Mrs. Blake pulled the hood of her cape over her head. "I didn't know you were a skilled seamstress."

"I pale in comparison to my sister and mother." I inched closer to the stove.

"We must go now, ladies, or we ain't gonna' be on time." Moses stepped in front of me. "Winter's comin' quick." He stirred the coals with a poker.

The sudden warmth smacked my face. I stared at the small flames lickin' the edges of the oak log. "Soon we will take the sleigh?"

"Yep." He buttoned his frock coat and stepped out into the frigid muddle.

The insides of my nose froze up as I paused to look out over the barren fields. *So, this is my birthday.* Freezin' rain needles pricked my face, and my skirt flapped in a sudden gust of wind. Lifeless tree limbs reached towards livid, gray skies, searchin' for somethin', anythin' other than the impendin' doom of winter.

We rocked perilously from side to side as the wheels of the carriage carved deep tracks through half frozen ruts. The only sounds were harnesses, hooves, and the steady white clouds that chugged from the horses' flared nostrils like a steam engine. When we approached the knoll, I shivered and looked away. I had become accustomed to seein' the remains of our farm and was able to look from time to time, but I preferred to close my eyes.

Jest before we reached the village, the rain surrendered to the spittin' snow. We entered the church as the folks were singin'. In the winter, it was better to sit near the back of the church by the stove. We were a bit late and had to sit in the usual pew near the front.

I followed Moses and Mrs. Blake and squeezed past the folks as they stood singin'. Effie Morrill sang quite loudly with her head tilted upwards, hopin' that the heavens might open up.

After we settled in, Pastor Leighton asked us to pray for the Burleigh family because their daughter Huldah fell through the ice at Duncan Lake and drowned. She was jest a child. It was an awful tragedy. I still wake up in fright when I dream about Sarah fallin' through the ice when we were playin' by the river. God was watchin' over us because it wasn't so deep that she couldn't climb out.

I looked up durin' a moment of silence as a man coughed and carried on like he might die. My heart ran cold when my eyes rested on Silas's golden curls all slicked down to his head like I had never seen before. His mother sat with a fixed smile and her hands folded neatly on her lap, while his red-faced father thrashed about chokin' and payin' the pastor no mind.

What on earth are Silas and his folks doin' at church? Mrs. Blake gave me an unfriendly stare. I looked down at my creased boots. My toes were deceptively warm, tingly, and about to go dead. The wind shrieked through the cracks in the windows, rustlin' through the dead, paper-like flies scattered on the sill.

Pastor Leighton stood in the back of the church and gave the benediction while Mrs. Leighton began pumpin' away on the organ. Everyone stood up and gathered their belongin's. We waited in line to leave. The Gilmans were waitin' in the pew beside us. Jessie leaned towards me with her eyes all a sparkle. "Good morning, Agatha."

"Abigail." I didn't attempt to force a smile.

"Oh dear," she said. "I can't seem to remember your name."

"It is of no concern." I turned away. Silas watched.

"That is such a pretty skirt. You must have sewn it yourself." Her voice was musical.

"Thank you. Yes, I did." I was grateful when the line moved.

"Well, time and experience will yield positive results. Keep working hard." She looked past me at Silas and fluttered her eyelashes.

Appearin' quite flushed, Silas struggled with his father. Every time Mr. Putnam almost got to standin', he wobbled and stumbled back into the pew. Mrs. Putnam chatted with Mrs. Weeks as if attendin' church was a regular occurrence and her husband wasn't fallin' down and cursin' under his breath loud enough for all to hear.

Folks generally took their merry time, which invited that giant hand to press down on my chest. Finally, our line merged into the center aisle. I stood behind Moses as he patted Silas on the shoulder. "Good to see you in church, son."

"Well, it was a long time comin'." He held his hat in one hand and his father's elbow with the other. "I suspect we ain't gonna' be usin' the carriage much more. It's time to prepare the sled before we git too much snow on the ground."

"Ayuh." Moses walked towards the door leavin' me face to face with Silas.

"Good mornin', Abigail."

"Silas." I gripped the back of the pew.

"It sure is cold, ain't it?" His blue eyes made me weep inside.

"It is. I'm afraid that winter is upon us." *In Heaven's name, why does the opportunity to speak have to present itself now? Why here?*

He started to say somethin' when a small white-gloved hand threaded through the crook of his elbow. "Good morning." Jessie slipped in front of me and nestled into Silas.

He looked over his shoulder. "Uh, it was nice seein' you."

They walked away. Her perfect ringlets bounced with each step. Her laughter was shrill, edgier than any hen. It echoed and escalated, drownin' out all other sounds.

I felt Pastor Leighton's eyes on me before I reached him in line. I tried to stop watchin' as Silas helped Jessie into the carriage. *Is it possible to flee?*

"How nice to see you." The pastor wrapped his warm, clammy hands around mine.

"It's my pleasure, Pastor." My toes were entirely numb.

"I trust that all is well at the Blake farm?" He held tight.

I attempted to pull away gently, still fightin' the urge to run. "Yes, they've been kind."

He held tighter. "Have you heard a word from your sister?"

"Yes." I broke free. "I do hear from her. She is well. Workin' at the mill suits her. Good day." His words dribbled behind me as I escaped to the safety of the carriage and the unavoidable Mrs. Blake, with her jagged tongue, and condemnin' eyes.

CHAPTER 34

Silas – November 10, 1872

I TRACED MY finger over the letters that I carved into the heart-shaped box: *A.E.H. + S.J.P. Nov 10 1872.* I wrapped it in Daddy's old red flannel shirt and shoved it back on the shelf with bits and pieces of tools that I meant to fix.

The freezin' rain pelted against the barn roof, remindin' me that there was plenty of wood to be stacked. Course the fire always needed stokin', so I gathered an armload of the poplar, maple, and oak that I'd split in the heat of summer.

I brushed pieces of bark and sawdust from my coat before enterin' the house. The folks was in the back room bickerin'. "Come now, the trousers are fixed jest so to cover your wooden leg. Please try."

"I don't know why we gotta' go to church and be who we ain't." He shrugged his shoulders and chewed on his whiskers.

"We talked 'bout this, Hiram. We must show the Gilmans that we're decent folks. There ain't no harm in goin' to church. Maybe it'll do us good." She dropped the trousers and hurried into the kitchen.

"Mamma, if you think it best for Daddy to stay here, I–"

"Never mind." She twisted her hair into a tight knot. "I've been wantin' to go to church for a long time."

I locked eyes with myself in the lookin' glass, dipped my fingers into the lard that Daddy used for his moustache, and slicked it through my hair. The curls flattened and turned dark brown. I weren't sure if it was me lookin' back.

"Mamma?"

"Yes?"

"I'll get him." I turned away from the stranger's gaze. "I'm ready to go."

CHAPTER 35

Nellie – November 20, 1872

"I CAN'T!" SHE screamed into the darkness.

The floor was cold and bright in the new moon. I hurried to where the fire burned in the big stove, and I poured hot water over the raspberry leaf, ground hemlock needles, and yarrow.

Drops from the jug danced and hissed on the stove when I filled the pot for the next one. The lady with hair the color of a fox waited; her anger glowed in the lamplight. "Who's in here? Show your face."

I was with shaking breath. The wind blew hard. The oak branches tapped.

"I should have known it was you, Old Squaw." She set the lamp on the table. "I s'pose you're tendin' to Patience." She held a bed sheet to her breast. "Ya got some potion for her?"

Steam rose from my cup. Patience was afraid. This would help. I moved away from her questions with the answers that burned in my hand.

"I ain't never gonna' git the likes of you." She followed with lamp in hand. "I'll send for Doc Gilman."

I stood in the door. The screams came. I closed my eyes. The screams stopped. I knelt by her side and stirred the tea. The lady with hair the color of a fox went to the other side. "You shoulda' thought 'bout this when you was off strayin' with a man." She dropped the sheet and departed.

Patience spit. "Damn you! Damn you to Hell!"

The birth pains grew. I reached for her hand.

"Stay away from me, witch!"

I stepped back to wait for her spirit to change.

"Mamma," she whispered. "Mamma, forgive me."

I touched her arm. The wind stopped. The cries stopped. In the light of the moon, the spider moved swiftly across the silver web. She sat up. "I can't go on."

Mary was an elder who came to the farm a year before. She was kind. She did not remember many things and sat with the others like her. She entered the room and went to Patience. "I must ask. Who is the father of the child?"

"I cannot say." She covered her face with her hands.

"It is not a fault of yours." Mary rubbed her back.

"It's awful. I cannot bear to speak his name."

"He will not marry you?" Kind Mary asked.

"I vowed not to name him."

"Is he kin?"

"You must not speak of this." She lay back.

The lady with hair the color of a fox entered with a tall man. He carried a medicine bag.

"I cannot do this." She pleaded with the man. "Please help me."

The doctor was a stranger. He spoke soft. His eyes were kind. "Hello, Patience. I'm Doctor Gilman."

"Help me, please." She held her hands in prayer.

"I have laudanum. It will help." He held his bag under the light.

She would have dark dreams from this medicine.

He gave her twenty drops of laudanum. She closed her eyes and spoke words with no meaning.

He turned to the woman with hair the color of a fox. "May I have some tea while we wait?"

"Sure, you can have some tea, but you don't have to wait. I ain't worried with the Indian woman takin' care of her. She helps everyone around here." They departed.

The pain crouched on hind legs before the final attack. She cried. "Uncle Ephraim... father's brother!" She gripped the blanket. "My father does not believe it to be true! He goes to my sister now. I will kill him!"

Her son arrived at daybreak when the sky changed from red to pink. I held him before her to stare deeply into his eyes, to see the flickering of the purple flame, the dimming fire of the Otherworld from where his spirit emerged. This is when an infant spirit is most powerful and will try to return to the fire. If she was good, wise, and loving, he would remain.

Mary was joyful. The lady with hair the color of a fox came to us with heated water. She soaked strips of cloth. "A boy, eh?" She washed the blood away. "Another bastard." She departed in her darkness.

I washed the baby with a warm, wet cloth. His cries triumphed over the cold morning. I returned him to the breast of his mother.

She looked away from him and into my eyes. "His name is Joshua."

Chapter 36

Abigail – November 20, 1872

Broken corn stalks rattled in the wind, and ice covered branches clicked in unison. Somethin' was amiss. At breakfast, Moses, who ordinarily went on about the weather and such, joined Mrs. Blake and me in our usual grim silence. My boots slipped over frozen puddles as I made my way to the barn. I lifted the latch on the door. The clinkin' of metal against metal seemed louder than usual.

The reassurin' scent of hay and manure filled my senses. I scooped grain into the bucket for the chickens. Two white leghorns pecked by my feet. "How did you get out?" I chased them to the coop. The door was open a bit. "Pearl, you aren't doin' such a good job watchin' the ladies." There was a ruckus in the corner by the nestin' boxes.

My heart leapt at the sight of my rooster lyin' still on the floor. "Pearl!" I dropped the bucket. A handful of hens scurried around the spilt grain on the floor. Pearl seemed to be lookin' straight at me, stiff and unblinkin'. One side of his bright red comb was frozen onto the floor, and a tail feather was bent. That explained why there was no crowin' that mornin'. I didn't want to touch him. I looked for blood, but found none. He must've taken sick.

My tears were hot against my cheeks. Pearl was no ordinary rooster. I wiped my nose on my sleeve. He was clever and more affectionate than any other chicken that I came to know in all my years. My thoughts turned to Pearl as a fuzzy yellow chick that I carried around in my apron pocket. Mother warned me. *"Don't you be gettin' attached to them farm animals, or you'll be grievin' for them when they're brought to the table."* I assured her that Pearl was the only one, and besides, at the time I believed her to be a layin' hen. Mother promised me that Pearl would be spared from the pot.

Soon after his pin feathers came in, Pearl started crowin'. That changed everything. We did eat the other roosters and the hens too when they stopped layin', but Mother kept her word about Pearl. He didn't end up amongst boiled potatoes and turnips.

I took a deep breath. It was one of them things like steppin' on a spider. You want to kill it but not touch it at the same time. So I learned early on to leave the spiders alone. They don't bother me and I don't bother them. Furthermore, what right do I have to kill them?

I felt his lifeless body through my mitt and yanked my hand away. He was stiff. He musta' died early in the night. I had to get him out of the barn and return him to nature before Mrs. Blake found out. Tremblin' fiercely, I reached down and grabbed an icy leg. *Now what am I gonna' do?*

Lizzy and the other cows started lowin' when they heard the commotion. "Hush. I will be there." I pulled my cape over the dead bird, cracked open the door, and peeked out. I didn't want to invite Mrs. Blake to questionin'.

I rushed to the back of the barn and headed towards the woods. I walked fast, lookin' behind me now and again before breakin' into a run. The wind picked up, and faded, brittle leaves swept across the hayfield as it started to spit snow. I finally reached the woods.

I weaved my way through the birch trees, duckin' under branches and steppin' over fallen limbs. I stopped at an openin'. I thought it best to feed Pearl to the critters. Perhaps the vultures would get him first.

Although it was frigid, I broke into a sweat. I stood in the tranquil hush of the woods until I caught my breath. I bowed my head. "Heavenly Father, I give to You one of my dearest friends and rooster, Pearl. I return him to the earth from whence he came. He was a well-mannered rooster and did a fine job wakin' us up every mornin', and he took good care of the hens. Bless him. In the Lord's name I pray, A-men."

His body thumped against the frosted earth when I dropped him in the center of the circle. He was magnificently white in contrast to the golden leaves. I stood still for a few moments, not really wantin' to leave. A silky, white tail feather swayed in the wind. I snatched it and slid it into my apron pocket with the tip up, careful not to spoil the fine edges.

The snow accumulated quickly. I hurried back to the barn. The wind calmed, and the sun shined softly like a gauzy ball peerin' through layers of dreary gray clouds. The snowflakes became wet and heavy.

⋯⟩⟨⋯

The smoke streamed from the farmhouse chimney and the lamps were lit. Mrs. Blake sat beside the fire, sewin' garments for Moses. After finishin' the barn chores, I aimed to join her and work on the quilt that I was makin'. I wondered how peculiar mornin's would be without Pearl crowin'. There were no more roosters for makin' baby chicks. I thought maybe they'd get one in the spring from Bert Leavitt. Papa said that he had the best chickens in town.

The vultures were circlin' in the distant sky. They soared on the high winds, gettin' closer and closer. They spiraled down behind the curtain of leafless trees, where his bones would be picked clean.

No one uttered a word at supper. I had thoughts 'bout Pearl layin' in the field with all those vultures tearin' away at him. After tidyin' the kitchen, I sat on the other side of the hearth from Mrs. Blake while sewin' a soft blue patch onto my quilt.

"You're doin' good with your barn chores. Your mother taught you pretty good." Moses coughed a spell before placin' his pipe on the table.

"I told you to stop smokin' that pipe 'til your cold gets better." Mrs. Blake scowled.

"Be still, woman. I can take care of myself." He picked up the pipe and chewed on the end. I smiled knowin' that he did it to spite her.

They bickered back and forth. I kept right on sewin'. Then it happened. I felt a stirrin'. It was like someone pokin' me with a tiny finger, only on the inside. I sat very still waitin' for it to happen again.

"Ain't that right, Abigail?" Moses asked.

"What?" I knew not what he said.

"What's wrong with you, child? You look like you seen a ghost." Mrs. Blake looked at me over the rim of her new spectacles.

"No, I-I'm tired is all." I touched my stomach.

"Well, it ain't very late. Are you catchin' a cold too?" She started in rockin' again.

"Perhaps, I'll go to bed now." I gathered my quilt. "Good night."

"Good night," Moses said, not lookin' away from the fire.

"Get plenty of rest. We'll be busy tomorrow." She said those same words every night. She simply wanted me to know that she was the boss.

After I put my sewin' notions in the back room, I got the lamp and headed for the outhouse. I shivered when I opened the door. *Did I feel the baby? Or was it somethin' else?* I started countin' on my fingers. *1-2-3-4-5. I don't know for sure, but it must be the baby movin' about.* The flame flickered as the wind groaned and blew through the cracks in the wall. *I must tell them.*

I went into my room and dimmed the lamp. The almost full moon lit up the clear sky while a few fast movin' clouds rushed by. I stood by the window and looked out to where the woods met the white birches at the edge of the field. I untied my apron and set it on the chair by the table. The white feather stuck out of my pocket. I fetched the treasure chest from under the bed and placed it inside, right beside Hope. From now on, things would be different. I would have to wake up in the mornin' without a rooster crowin'. The days of relyin' on Pearl were gone.

CHAPTER 37

Silas – November 21, 1872

MAMMA TUGGED ON my foot. "Silas, wake up." The sun shone around her head givin' a false impression of an angel.

"What?"

"You overslept. I thought that you was already gone. Moses is here waitin'." She whipped the blanket off me. "Now get up."

I rolled outta' bed. I wasn't late for nothin', 'specially work. I hopped into the kitchen with one leg halfway into my trousers.

Moses's laughter rumbled within a cloud of smoke. "What a sorry sight, boy."

"I don't know what happened." I fumbled with my shirt buttons.

He tapped the contents of his pipe into his tobacco-stained hand. "You musta' been dreamin'."

"He's soft as a sour grape," Daddy said, hopin' to provoke me.

"I don't know what got into me," I said, wishin' they'd all hush.

"There ain't a lot happenin', 'cept we need to fix one of the stalls in the barn before winter sets in." Moses's eyebrows joined together in a single line, a fuzzy caterpillar. "Drink your coffee, son."

Mamma poured my coffee. "We gotta' get the rest of the firewood stacked here too." She gave me one of them looks.

After jawin' about the terrors of winter and the goin's on about town, we set out for the farm.

⋯⊱⊰ ⊱⊰⋯

I kicked the muck from my boots before headin' towards a circle of women near the fireplace. Mary stood in the center, swayin' from side to side, cradlin' a small bundle.

"Patience had her baby?" I stared down at the baby and wondered about all the fuss over what looked like a little, red-faced, old man.

"Yes, she had a boy. He's a healthy one," she said. She weren't like them other women at the farm. She didn't let things get to her. She found a way to rise above the tension.

"Tell Patience she ain't gonna' sleep in tomorrow, so she better rest up!" Miss Noyes hollered from the kitchen. "Jest another mouth to feed."

The sound of laughter tumbled down the hall. There weren't much to do in the winter. Sometimes the old men played checkers, but they mostly took to sittin' and tellin' stories about when they was young and strong, and had pride to boot. I couldn't admit to nobody that I secretly listened. I admired the old coots for bein' hard workers and providin' for their families when they was able to. They weren't afraid of a good day's work. It was a shame to see 'em sittin' at the County Farm day after day with no more purpose.

CHAPTER 38

Abigail – November 23, 1872

I DROPPED MY apron on the floor and stood sideways before the lookin' glass. I pressed my dress tightly over my stomach. All color drained from my face. I adjusted the stomacher this way and that, and I still could not hide my changin' shape. I pulled my apron over my head and stared at my reflection. *I have to wear this apron at all times.* I tied it loosely.

The door crashed. "It's too cold to be out there for long and winter ain't even here!" Mrs. Blake stomped into the kitchen.

I tiptoed out of her room.

"Where is that girl?" One would think that she had a broken bone the way she moaned as she pulled a ceramic crock from the shelf.

I loosened the apron ties a bit.

"Abigail?" She called me the way Grampa Wills used to call the pigs, startin' real low and then shriekin' up like a woman in church tryin' to hit a high note.

"Yes?" I paused in the doorway.

"Did you collect the eggs?"

"Yes. I did all my chores." I slipped my hands inside my pockets. "I put them there like always." I looked at the basket on the cabinet shelf and then quickly pulled my hands out of my pockets when I noticed the bulge. *I got to keep the apron hangin' loosely.*

"I ain't heard your rooster these days. Somethin' musta got him?" She grabbed the old, splintered broom, not waitin' for a response. "Now sweep the kitchen and hearth in the sittin' room. Don't jest stand there."

I took the broom and started in sweepin' long strokes. "About Pearl—"

"What kind of name is Pearl?"

"I named him before I knew he was a rooster, but I was accustomed to callin' him Pearl—"

"Never mind all that nonsense, jest sweep." She went into the back room.

"Well, you asked me about Pearl." I wailed the broom into the floor in short, random strokes.

"I ain't heard him for a few days now. Did somethin' git into the coop?" She put her hands on her plentiful hips, suddenly demandin' to know everything.

"I haven't seen him. I think he escaped." I refused to give her the satisfaction of knowin' Pearl's fate.

"That means someone didn't shut the coop properly." She wagged her meaty finger, grazin' my nose. "I s'pose Moses should take a look at it."

"That's a wise thing to do." I went into the sittin' room to sweep the hearth, makin' the most terrible face at her. *She is a cruel woman who already hates me. She will hate me even more after I tell her.* Black soot flew about my boots as I swept without aim.

When Moses returned from work, he went into the barn to see that all was well 'cept for Pearl bein' missin'. He didn't know what to think. If there was a raccoon or weasel, it woulda' got some of the hens and left a terrible mess of feathers and the most gruesome remains. Pearl's disappearance remained a mystery.

At suppertime I pushed my food around on my plate, wonderin' if I could actually tell them of my unfortunate news.

We collected our sewin' baskets and sat in our regular spots. I didn't care to sew, but I made the mistake of sewin' that yellow skirt and had to sew each night since. I started stitchin' a red square for my quilt.

"You know Patience Cook, Miriam?" The smoke from Moses's pipe swirled into an "S" above his head.

"Of course I know her."

"Well, she had her baby." His pipe gurgled as he toked on it.

"I pity her folks. Such shame to bring upon a family." She shook her head. "Any idea who fathered it?"

The heat rose in my cheeks, and my damp curls clung to the back of my neck.

"Nope, she ain't sayin'. That man oughta' be shot. Patience is from a good family." He leaned back in the chair and puffed perfect smoke rings.

"She has to pay for her sins too." She set her sewin' on her lap.

"Well." My voice was odd, small, far away. "Maybe she wasn't at fault."

Mrs. Blake laughed too loud. "There are some folks who pray to have children, and it jest isn't the Lord's plan. And then there's folks like Patience who don't have no husband and they fornicate, payin' no mind to what their folks would think." She rolled her eyes. "Not to mention bringin' a bastard child into the world."

I pulled the needle through the cloth and held it up close to my eyes to inspect it. *I can't tell them. I can't do it.*

"Did you go to school with Patience?" Moses leaned forward in the chair and looked my way.

"She's older than me, but we were in school together for a spell." I swallowed and the words simply escaped. "I have no choice but to tell you… that…"

"What? Is it about joinin' your sister in Fall River?" Mrs. Blake couldn't listen; she had to s'pose.

"No, it isn't that." I wiped my sweaty palms on my apron.

"Well, that would be a wise thing for you to do now that it's been a while since your mother died." She clucked and bobbed her head.

"Stop." I could not bear to hear anyone speak of Mother or Sarah. "I mean… I would like to join Sarah. I would like to work in the mills and earn a livin'."

She peered over her gold spectacles. "Go on."

"Well." I fiddled with my fingers. "I have gotten myself into a pickle."

"Go on." She leaned closer. Her eyes nearly vanished into the depths of her saggy face. "Do tell. Git to the point, girl."

"I am with child." My temples pounded. All strength was gone.

The fire crackled. Moses spoke in a deep, quiet voice, "I never thought I'd hear them words from you, Abigail."

"Sinner! You're a sinner!" Her sewin' clattered onto the floor when she bolted out of her chair. "I knew that you was hidin' somethin'. If your mother knew she would cry in shame."

"Do not mention my mother's name!" Then came a surge of pain, anger, and guilt that was so twisted up, I couldn't tell one from the other.

I fell to my knees before Moses's feet. "I want nothin' more than to be restored to a state of favor and acceptance. I grieve for my mother. I have blackened my name." I poured forth my soul in tears, but the Blakes had deemed me a sinner.

"You will pack what few belongin's you have, and Moses will take you to the County Farm." She folded her arms over her chest and looked up at the ceilin', tryin' to rustle up some tears. "Oh, the shame."

"It was simply a matter of time." I looked into Moses's eyes for a shred of compassion. "I dreaded tellin' you."

"Who is the father? He should come forward and marry you." Although he scowled, Moses remained kind.

"The father?" I bit my lip and tried to erase the vision of Silas from my mind's eye. "I do not know."

"What do you mean you don't know?" He stood up.

"She ain't tellin' the truth," Mrs. Blake said.

"I was goin' for a long ride one afternoon, and I stopped at the brook by the new railroad tracks. I was waterin' my horse when a strong man of middle age came out of the woods and chased me." I covered my face with my apron and sobbed as if there were no end to it.

"He had his way with you against your will?" Mrs. Blake was high pitched.

I dropped the soaked apron. "Yes." I wiped my nose on the sleeve of my blouse. "He fled into the woods, and I never saw him again."

"Did you tell anyone?" Moses puffed up his chest.

"No, I was scared."

"Did you get a good look at him?" He clenched his fists.

"No. I did not." The little girl in me spoke.

"Well, we ain't got a choice but to send her to the farm, Moses," Mrs. Blake said.

"Hold on," he said. "Let's think on it."

"There ain't no question 'bout it. I won't have no unwed mother livin' under this roof." She waved a fist in the air.

"I will go. I don't want to bring shame on anyone. This is my burden and mine alone." My thoughts turned to Silas.

"Moses will take you after church tomorrow." She went into the kitchen. "... give you one more chance to pray for your soul..."

"You understand we ain't got no choice in the matter," Moses said.

"Yes, sir." My body took to shakin' at that awful moment.

"Now go on to bed. You can pack your belongin's in that treasure chest of yours."

I dashed into the dark hallway and stumbled up the stairs. The moonlight streamed through the window, lightin' up the room in a dreamlike manner. I dragged out the treasure chest, grabbed Hope, and clutched her to my chest. I wept until there were no more tears to shed, until the silence of the mornin' without Pearl was upon me.

CHAPTER 39

Silas – November 23, 1872 – Gilman Residence

THE TEACUP CLINKED when I set it in the saucer. I thought it might break. "This is good tea, Mrs. Gilman." I reached for a biscuit.

"I'm glad you're enjoying it." Mrs. Gilman dabbed the corners of her mouth with the white linen cloth.

"The cup is pretty too," I said, runnin' the tip of my finger around the gold rim. "Pardon me, but is this real gold?"

"It's called bone china," she said. "And yes, it is real gold." She purred when she laughed. She weren't pokin' fun at me like some others would.

"Mother likes the finer things in life," Jessie said.

"Yes, I've been fortunate to have the finer things in life, but it wasn't always so. My father worked diligently to get through law school, and your father did the same in medical school as well." She took such a small nibble from the biscuit that I weren't sure if she even got a taste. "And that is why we are so eager and willing to help you and Silas get a good start."

I took another biscuit from the plate and put the whole thing in my mouth before realizin' that I probably shouldn't have.

Mamma gave me the eye. "Silas is excited. We all are." She dabbed her mouth with her linen jest like Mrs. Gilman. "Speakin' of Hiram, I apologize for him not bein' able to make it, he has a cold and—"

"Never mind, Mamma. Forgive me, but everybody knows his troubles." I tried sippin' my tea with my little finger stickin' up like the Gilmans did. Such an odd way to take a drink.

"It's a pity. Some of the men came back from that dreadful war in such a poor state." Mrs. Gilman shook her head and then looked out the window. "Oh good, Israel is home in time to join us." She got up and went to the door.

Jessie rolled her eyes. "I don't know much about the war."

Doc Gilman removed his hat. "It's brisk out there today. The fire is nice and cozy, dear."

"It is. Do come and join us." She poured tea into a cup and set it at the other end of the table. "We were just talking about how blessed we are to have the finer things in life and look forward to bringing Silas into the family." She patted my shoulder.

"I see." He sipped his tea with his little finger stickin' up too. "Did you discuss a wedding date?"

My faced heated up. "I didn't give it much thought, sir." I stuffed another whole biscuit in my mouth. "I think that it would be nice in the spring when it weren't so cold."

Mamma hollered at me with her eyes, about talkin' with my mouth full and such.

"That would be pleasing to me as well," Jessie said, smilin'. "And we can have the house built then too."

"We have plenty of room here if you want to live with us until your house is built. Anytime suits us, do you agree, Betsey?" He tapped his chin.

"Yes."

"We'll let Jessie and Silas talk about what suits them. In the meantime, I need you to help me rig up my sled before we get too much snow." He eyed his biscuit before barely nibblin' on it.

"Sure thing." I was eager to get out to the barn and into the cool air.

"You don't have to be formal with me, son. Call me Israel and her Betsey. We're all family here," he said.

"Uh, of course… Israel," I said. "I'm goin' to the barn to take a look at your sled."

"I'm going too." Jessie already had her cape draped over her shoulders.

"Let me know if you need any tools that I don't have." He patted his pockets as if he was lookin' for somethin'.

"Ayuh." I went out the door.

Jessie followed close behind. "This is so exciting."

We got inside the barn, and I turned to face her. Her green eyes lit up, and her cheeks was all a flush. I took her in my arms and pressed her warm body against mine. Then I held her back from me and looked her over before kissin' her soft, full lips. She responded to my touch, and I felt the fire risin' inside me.

She pulled away. "Let's not wait until the spring. Let's get married in December. We can get married right after Christmas and before the New Year, so it will always be festive when we celebrate our anniversary." She held her breath and then let it out slowly. "And, if you don't mind living with my folks for a spell."

"Uh…" I pictured cleanin' up after Daddy and listenin' to his cussin' and watchin' him soil his pants.

"That's fine. I mean, it's perfect." I picked her up and swung her around.

"I'm so happy. I want to tell the world." She buried her face in my neck. "I love you."

I inhaled her flowery scent. "I love you too." It felt odd tellin' her that I loved her. We hadn't talked about things, I mean real things like me and Abigail always did. But that was long ago, before Weston Jones, and before Doc Gilman promised me my own house and his beautiful daughter.

CHAPTER 40

Abigail – November 24, 1872

I TUCKED HOPE into my treasure chest. Mrs. Blake and Moses did not call me to breakfast, barn chores, or even to go to church. I waited 'til I heard them leave the house. Stayin' behind left a peculiar feelin' in my chest. We never missed a single sermon unless we were extremely ill. Folks would wonder of my whereabouts.

Still in my nightdress, I tiptoed across the icy floorboards and listened for the janglin' of harnesses. Then I hurried down the stairs and watched them drive away before goin' to the kitchen to cut myself a respectable piece of cheese. *It wasn't gonna' be easy livin' at the County Farm with all those filthy vagrants.* I bit into the cheese. Mother told me that some folks were mentally ill and others fell from grace. I grabbed the cider and drank straight from the jug. *Damn them!*

After I ate more cheese than necessary, I went upstairs to dress. My toe poked out of my stockin' jest enough to mock me, signalin' what would lie ahead.

I can't face Silas there. My lip quivered. I swallowed the fear.

There's no sense in cryin'. I yanked on the hooks of my skirt. *Damn… it's too tight.* I rummaged through the desk for a pin.

Maybe he won't be near where I'm stayin'. I fastened the pin on the thick material around my expandin' waist. My thoughts scattered as I buttoned my blouse and slipped my apron over my head. *I will not look him in the eye nor speak to him.*

I stuffed a bunch of curls into my snood and froze. I tossed the snood and rushed straight out to Moses's shop.

I pawed through the tools. The metal was cold. One by one, I threw them on the floor until I found the shears. I dropped them into my pocket and placed the other tools back where I found them. I started to head back to my room when I realized that I had forgotten the pencil. *I must write to Sarah.* I raced back.

I stood before the lookin' glass, rubbed my reddened hands together, and blew on them. At first, I avoided my eyes. Then I dared to look. "It will be fine, Abigail. You can do this." My body shook from within.

I tried to swallow, but I was parched. I reached into my apron pocket and removed the shears. I held a fistful of hair up over my head and snipped. My locks fell by my feet. I grabbed another handful and cut, this time closer to my scalp. I struggled to breathe. No tears.

The pile at my feet grew with each horrible cut. I cut faster, sometimes pullin' instead of cuttin'. "God, help me." I sat on the floor. My lone monocle curl trembled, danglin' in front of my eye. I rested the cold shears against my forehead and hacked it off.

The woman before me stared back. I did not know her. I was uncertain if she was even a woman at all. She looked like a child. She looked afraid. She looked sad. "The fault is your own. I must never take notice of you again." I turned my back on her, dropped the shears, and ran my fingers through the coarse tufts of hair that sat imperfectly upon my head. I collapsed in the wobbly chair and rocked for a good hour.

After returnin' the shears to their place, I had to clean the mess. Avoidin' the pathetic girl in the lookin' glass, I bent down and gathered the mound of curls. Small wisps fell to the floor. I could not leave a trace.

I fetched the broom and swept the curls into a neat pile with my monocle curl on top. I plucked it along with one lengthy, silky ringlet as perfect as if it came from Jessie Gilman's head. I tied them together with a frayed ribbon and pressed them inside the yellowed pages of Grandmother's book of prayers. I put on Mother's straw bonnet, crammed my feet into my boots, and rolled the pile of hair inside of my apron.

I hurried out to the back of the barn. The sharp wind cut through my blouse, and the bonnet rubbed and agitated my head in a most curious way. I went to the old oak tree and sat on the big rock. The last of the decayed, brown leaves drifted by my feet, mournin' for the unflowerin' woods and fields. I stood up and let the apron unfold. Curls tumbled to the ground, scatterin' in the wind, dancin' over frostbitten corn, some catchin' on tree saplin's while others proudly adorned tall dead grasses. They rolled towards the edge of the forgotten pasture, lingerin' on the white birches, makin' their way to Pearl's final restin' place.

I shook the apron clean and went into the barn. Lizzy was silent. Moses had already milked her. I opened the door. Reluctantly, she looked and then resumed chewin'.

"I'm gonna' miss you, girl." She licked my hand with her long pink tongue. I kissed her on the nose before returnin' to the house.

I started to remove the bonnet but quickly pulled it back on when cool air streamed over my head. I winced when it scratched my scalp. My dress was both moist and cold, and my thoughts leapt in many directions. *I have lost my way; my inner compass has failed. I must be calm.*

I tore a blank page from Grandmother's prayer book and rooted around in my pocket for Moses's pencil. When I sat at the table, the giant hand pressed down on my chest; nothin' seemed to afford a ray of light.

Dearest Sister,

Thank you for youre favor. I write to you conserving the sad feelings that are restin upon me. After wateing a long time, it aperes that Silas will marry Jesy Gilmen. This is a fate far worse then you can imagen. I tryd fathfuley to take the oportunite to talke to him, even sending him two letters and he chose not to replie.

I had no choyse but to tell the Blakes of my condishon. It has been desided that I will have to live at the county farm. I will leave tomorow. I have endured much conflict and humiliashon. I asked God not to turn his back on me. But I have sinned, and it is my sin that got me to where I am.

Do not worry of me dear sister. I am strong and will accept the conseqences.

Patience Cook had a baby boy. I will have a frend there & she will know the ways of the farm. All letters from you must be adressd to the county farm.

Your Loving Sister,

Abigail Hodgdon

When I heard the sound of horses, I tied the ribbon of my bonnet under my chin. It was time to pack.

I attempted to stand and thought that I might heave, forcin' me to stop and collect myself. I tried to ignore that the Blakes were speakin' in hushed tones, although I secretly strained to listen. In my silent waitin', I watched the cat chase a red squirrel, finally cornerin' it under the steps.

"Abigail?" Mrs. Blake's shrill voice caused me to flinch.

"Yes?" I thought that I hollered.

"Abigail?" she yelled louder.

I moved slowly towards the stairs. The scent of meat stew wafted up from the kitchen. "What?" I ignored the rumblin' in my stomach, not sure if it was hunger or somethin' new, somethin' I had never known before that moment.

"Come down." She walked away apparently not expectin' a response.

My feet, unwillin' and numb, lingered on each step. I took a deep breath and pushed myself closer to the lion's den.

Moses looked away. His pipe made a cracklin' sound when he toked. He stirred it with a match stick and stared quizzically as though he had never encountered the act of lightin' a pipe. He had an odd look about him, tryin' to sort out whether he should or shouldn't smile.

I fidgeted with the yellow ribbon under my chin. Bein' accustomed to his goodness, I had to sort that out too. All the feelin's inside of me raced around, threatenin' to burst. Fear took the lead. I had never been to the County Farm, and everybody said that you don't want to end up there. I was no longer safe.

"Abigail?" His voice was soft and unusual.

"Yes?"

"I'll take you in the mornin'," he said, avoidin' eye contact.

"Yes. I know."

Mrs. Blake carried on as if I were not present. "Did you tell her?"

"Ayuh," he said, lookin' quite small and defeated, like a boy who had lost his prized marbles in one wretched game with no hope of winnin' them back.

"The stew will be ready soon. She can eat when we're finished," Mrs. Blake said with her back to us.

"Miriam, she can sit with us... jest once more." The man turned boy pleaded.

She whirled around. "I ain't sittin' at the same table with no harlot. And that's the end of it."

He finally looked at me. "I'm sorry. It's the way things is." He toked on his long dead pipe.

"That's fine. I don't wish to eat at your table. I have no appetite." I turned towards the stairs. The word harlot echoed in my head. I eyed the brass candlestick holder and imagined throwin' it at her and screamin', not a scream that one would expect from a young woman but a scream from an enraged beast in the final throes of death.

"Abigail... wait."

I looked back thinkin' that he might have reconsidered. But I would refuse any offer. I would never again sit at his table.

"The money from your mother's estate went towards your expenses. The cows, pigs, and chickens will be taken to the County Farm." As a man once again, he held a match over his pipe and sucked in.

"I see." I hadn't considered the business of Mother's death. I recalled some papers, but I was overwhelmed with grief and didn't take the proper time to read them.

"We'll leave first thing in the mornin'. You can't have many things at the farm, so there ain't no use packin' your clothes, jest what you're wearin'." He looked out the window.

"Why don't I need my clothes?"

"They give you clothes to wear there."

"They do?" My cheeks got hot.

"Ayuh, but you can bring that chest of yours. I'll find a place for it." He set his pipe on the table and worked his fingers through his snarly beard. "You should eat."

"I'm not hungry." I returned to the room and lay on the bed until night-fall, listenin' to Moses rattle around in the barn and Mrs. Blake grumble and bang the dishes in the kitchen.

I ripped the bonnet off my head and felt the patchy stubble. Things would look much different without my monocle.

CHAPTER 41

Silas – November 24, 1872

DADDY WEREN'T GOIN' to church to please no one. He threw his walkin' stick clear across the room, knockin' some dishes off the shelf. Mamma stayed home to pick up the pieces and fuss. I went ahead without 'em.

I stood on the doorstep and listened to the organ while bangin' the frozen mud off my boots. The people huddled near the stove in the back. Jessie caught my eye and motioned for me to join her. I situated myself in the crowded pew in between Mrs. Gilman and Jessie.

"Good morning." Jessie wiggled closer to me than I thought possible.

"Mornin'." I stuffed my gloves in my coat pocket.

Doc Gilman nodded and then turned his attention to the organist. Mrs. Gilman smiled, looked over the top of her spectacles, and continued thumbin' through her Bible.

The Blakes walked down the center aisle and sat in the pew in front of us. I waited for Abigail to follow behind. I looked over my shoulder at the closed door.

Pastor Leighton called us to worship. I tried to listen to what he was sayin', but my mind kept wanderin'. Maybe she was sick.

At the end of the service, we stood in line to leave. Moses looked fouled up, and Mrs. Blake's mouth was in a straight line. I tapped Moses on the shoulder, seemin' to awaken him from a dream.

Mrs. Cook called out, "Hello, Miriam. Where's Abigail?"

Mrs. Blake paused. "She's feelin' feverish, so she ain't goin' nowhere for a spell." She snapped back 'round and tugged at her shawl.

"I s'pose she's got the sore throat. Mr. Tibbetts has that same sore throat." She pulled her hood over her head. "Give her our best."

"Will do." Mrs. Blake hurried out into the center aisle hangin' onto Moses's arm. They skipped right by Pastor Leighton without a word.

"Silas, do come and join us for boiled dinner." Mrs. Gilman was cheerful, unaware of my discomfort.

"Uh–" I started buttonin' my coat. "Thank you, I'd like that."

"I made bread pudding." Jessie smiled and nudged her mother with her elbow.

"That sounds real good." My stomach rumbled. I hadn't eaten bread puddin' since Mrs. Copp brung it over when Daddy came home from the war.

CHAPTER 42

Nellie – November 25, 1872

THE WINTERMAKER MOON arrived with the north wind. It was quiet inside where the fires burned. The women sewed aprons, bedticks, dresses, and nightcaps while the elders, some tied with rope, sat in chairs in the great room. The young men worked in the yard, barn, and with the animals. I sat on the floor to watch and wait.

The lady with hair the color of a fox grumbled. The white man who talked with departed ones laughed, and a young mother sang to the child at her breast.

I closed my eyes. The wind shook the windows of the great room and then blew against the windows of our house on the banks of Cold River.

⋅➤≡◉ ◉≡◄⋅

Abundant herbs hung from beams. Roots and plants filled baskets and pots. Strings of apple slices were draped by the hearth beside the sack that held scraps for doll making.

I swept the hearth. The hemlock broom was heavy. Eight days had passed since Searching Owl departed to Whiteface Mountain to hunt. I expected him to return in four days. The snow fell for six days and six nights. He wore snowshoes made by him. He carried food for five days. I called upon the mountain spirit for his safe return. Though he knew the ways of my people, I feared for him.

His song came from afar, amongst the trees and falling snow. I looked out but could not see. I waited. I saw him on the footpath pulling a great buck on his sled. I ran to him. With little strength, we hung the deer between the trees. The wind blew hard. He leaned on me and walked with much pain.

I made white pine tea for drinking and yarrow tea for bathing. I took away his outer garments. I washed him and applied the yarrow tea cloth to his wounded ankle. After he was dry and warm, we sat by the fire. He told his story.

He spotted a large doe. He did not raise his arrow; he had not yet made a tobacco offering. The doe fled.

He scattered tobacco on the ground. He honored Deer Mother and Mountain Spirit and asked for consent to take a deer to sustain his family in the harshness of winter. He continued to climb. A buck of medium size passed before him. He lifted his ashwood bow and killed it swiftly. This pleased him. With his hand on the warm heart of the buck, he offered thanks and respect to the mountain for the nurturing of the deer and all creatures that dwelled therein. He then gave thanks to the spirit of the deer before he tied it on the sled.

When departing from the top ridge and down the mountain stair, he lost his footing and fell a great distance. He returned to the sled with an injured leg. He applied sphagnum moss and balsam fir sap to the wound and wore a splint of birch bark. He made a shelter of pine boughs, built fires at night, and ate dried salt pork, hard tack, and cheese from his sack. He melted snow for drink and had a small flask of spirituous liquor. At night he covered with moose hide and warmed his feet by the fire. Four days and three nights passed before he returned home.

The deer provided us with meat to survive the winter and spring. We made clothing and bedding from the buckskin and returned the carcass to the fire so that its spirit would not depart from the hunting grounds forever.

The snowflakes brushed my cheeks. The warm fire and embrace of Searching Owl vanished to where dreams lie in waiting.

⋅→╾◉ ◉╼←⋅

A stream of water dripped from the chair where the elder Isaac sat beside me. He cried for his mother.

A boss went to Isaac. His Christian name was George; to me he was Yellow Snake – one with eyes of a snake and much yellow hair. He worked at the farm in the winter. He struck Isaac. "You pissed all over the floor, idiot." I felt the blow upon my spirit.

I rose to my feet and faced Yellow Snake. Water filled my eyes.

"Get up you fool." Yellow Snake pulled him by his shirt. He turned to me. "What do you want, Old Squaw?" His eyes were with hate.

I reached for Isaac. Again, he fell to the floor. Silas, the young man with a kind spirit, came to us. He lifted Isaac from the floor and carried him up the stairs to where the men slept. I looked upon Yellow Snake with coldness and went to the sewing room.

A sleigh arrived. The big boss helped a small woman descend. They walked together. A gust of wind came through the door when they entered. She held a box to her breast and stared with wide brown eyes. I knew her as the girl with hair the color of maple. She wore a bonnet of straw.

"Bring her over here, Moses." Polly spoke loudly. "I s'pose she's pregnant?"

There was sadness in his eyes. "Ayuh, git her one of them yellow dresses."

"Come here, child." Polly spoke louder. "Give me the hat." She raised her hand.

"No, I choose to wear the bonnet." The girl was a warrior.

Polly laughed. "It don't work like that here, young lady."

The woman with hair the color of a fox came into the room. "What's that I hear?"

The big boss spoke. "Go easy on her."

"She ain't no diffrint from the rest of 'em. And she won't get no special treatment," the woman with hair the color of a fox snorted. "Take it off."

The girl raised her fist. "Take this hat off me, and I'll kick you right in the shins."

"You'll do what?" The lady with hair the color of a fox grabbed the hat.

"Leave me alone!" the girl screamed.

Polly smiled. "What's her name? She looks familiar."

"Abigail Hodgdon. I got her papers. She's expectin' a baby, and there ain't no declared father." He looked at her. "What happened to your hair?"

There was a crash. Silas stood with broken glass by his feet. He had the look of fear.

"What happens to me is no longer of your concern."

She pulled away from the lady with hair the color of a fox and stood silently before Silas. The shouting stopped. The sewing stopped. And the wind was no more.

"Here." Polly held out the yellow dress. "Now follow me."

The big farm boss took the box away from the girl. "I'll put it in a safe place, Abigail."

She wilted before surrendering.

"Careful of the glass." Polly gripped the girl's arm. "Mary, sweep it up."

CHAPTER 43

Abigail – November 25, 1872

MY THOUGHTS CHURNED about as I watched the snow collect on the window panes. I waited for daybreak, starin' out at the mountains until they were consumed by the billowin', dark clouds. Moses and Mrs. Blake shuffled about the kitchen in muted disgrace. I finally mustered the strength to remove the heavy quilt and step onto the icy floor.

I tucked Hope into the chest. The howlin' wind reminded me of the woolen shawl that Mrs. Blake gave to me. *Will she take it back?* Although out of season, I placed the straw bonnet upon my tufted head. With barely enough strength, I managed to tie the frayed ribbon under my chin.

I made my way to the top of the stairs and hesitated. The shutters wailed against the house, thumpin' within the walls of my chest. Heat prickled my cheeks in spite of the bitter cold. I stopped halfway down the stairs and watched as Moses drummed his fingers on the table. Mrs. Blake's face was scarlet. Her unruly hair sprouted out from her snood as she wildly stirred some sort of batter. The door shook in the wind and a trace of snow blew in through a wide crack beneath it.

"After you eat somethin', we'll go in front of the board and then to the farm." Moses bent down and examined the door. "I gotta' fix this before too long."

"I don't feel much like eatin'." I watched Mrs. Blake scrape the sides of the bowl without lookin' my way. *Board?* My insides fluttered.

"You oughta' eat now. It'll be a long time before the next meal." He walked out the door.

I sat down at the table. Miss Emily raced inside and wove herself in and around my ankles.

Mrs. Blake shoved a plate of eggs, bread, and molasses in front of me. "What are you doin' in here?" She scooped up the cat and tossed her out into the snow.

It was too quiet. The sound of my chewin' was unbearable, and the bread wanted to stick in my throat. I washed it down with milk. To take my mind off of my entire tremblin' self, I looked out the window and watched Moses hitch up the horses. The snow was at least as high as his knees. The fire crackled, and bright yellow flames glowed through the seams of the stove. I wanted my mother. I closed my eyes and took a deep breath. "Thank you, Mrs. Blake."

She continued workin' as if I hadn't spoken. She spilt flour on her calico apron and grumbled. Then she took to hummin' quite loud in her usual sour voice. I left the room and went into the bedroom. I straightened the bed and took a last look around to see if there was anything more that I could stuff into the treasure chest. Moses told me not to bring any other belongin's, so I left the shawl and drab clothes that Mrs. Blake gave me. I picked up my letter to Sarah and tucked the chest under my arm.

I paused by the door. "Goodbye, Mrs. Blake." I cleared my throat. "Thank you for your hospitality." I set the letter on the table in hopes that it would be sent.

She marched into the back room and took a crock from the shelf. I waited to see if she would answer or speak a word. She did not.

Like an uninvited guest, the blizzard lingered outside the door, greetin' me with a sharp blast. I came quite close to fallin' on the ice that had formed on the ground beneath the fresh snow. Moses dashed over and took a hold of my arm. "Careful."

He boosted me onto the sleigh. I glanced over at the barn. I had not said goodbye to Old Gray Mare. With no good rooster to keep them in line, the chickens chattered nervously inside the coop. The wind howled. I pulled the hood of the cape over my straw bonnet and attempted to withdraw into the safety of my deepest self.

Moses hoisted himself up onto the sleigh. "We'll go before the board first and then get ya settled." A fine white crust of ice clung to the tips of his moustache and beard.

The sleigh glided over the snow, and the brawny beasts huffed into the crisp air, keepin' a steady rhythm with their hooves. Their harnesses jingled, creatin' the false illusion of a festive event. "What board?" I shouted, competin' with the wind.

"Speak up. I can't hear a word you're sayin'."

"What board are you talkin' about?" I hollered.

His shoulders dropped. "The Board of County Commissioners… it's jest procedure. It ain't nothin'."

It ain't nothin'? We passed by the remnants of our farm. A soft white mound of snow atop the blackened chimney wisped in the wind, imitatin' smoke from days past. A blue jay fluttered by and perched upon the wooden fence post. Moses continued to look straight ahead. "Ya sure that ya can't name the father?"

"Yes, sir." My eyes watered from the cold.

"It ain't no good keepin' it a secret."

"I'm certain. He was a stranger."

"So be it." He focused on the unendin' whiteness ahead.

The heavy snowfall continued as we wound through the trees where the road must have been. I had to squint to see the grayish shadow of the courthouse over the knoll. Moses drove the team around to the front. He hopped off first and then came over to my side. I ignored his outstretched hand and tumbled into the fluffy white powder. I looked up into the spiralin' flakes as they fell from the sky. Somehow the eerie, rushed silence brought about a much desired inner peace. I tried to feel my toes inside of my stiff, wet boots as I trudged behind him, carefully placin' my feet in his huge footprints.

He stopped in front of one of the doors in the long hallway. "Wait here."

"Yes, sir." Although quiet, my voice managed to echo.

He disappeared for a short spell. I focused on a series of cracks in the wall that looked like an evenin' primrose. His deep voice brought me back to the present with a start. "Follow me."

Three men sat at a long, dark, shiny table. I recognized Alan Peavey and Daniel Stiles from church. I had seen the other man, Mr. Nichols, around town and even met him once at Mr. Tibbetts' store. Mother told me to be careful if I shook his hand, and if I did, to count my fingers in case he stole one or two.

Mr. Peavey's buttons looked like they might burst from the coat that he had stretched over his belly. His face and bald head flushed, and he spoke quite anxiously. He looked over his spectacles at me and then down at the papers on the table. "M-Miss Abigail H-Hodgdon?"

"Yes." My inner child was at the helm.

"You are to be admitted to the C-Carroll County Farm?" He tapped his double chin. "I-Is that c-correct?"

"Yes."

"You are the daughter of S-Samuel and Annie H-Hodgdon?" He leaned back in his chair and continued peerin' over his spectacles. "Both deceased?"

"Yes." It was as if I was hearin' the word deceased for the first time.

"You are being a-admitted to the Carroll C-County Farm because you are with ch-child and no man c-claims responsibility, and you bring no charges?"

"Yes." I began swayin' from side to side.

"A portion of the estate of your parents' p-property has been awarded t-to M-Moses Blake for providin' r-room and board, a-and the remainder goes to the Carroll C-County Farm. One cow, four pigs, and t-twelve chickens will be brung to the farm on your behalf."

I smiled at the thought of my beloved Lizzy. "Yes, sir." I bit my lip. "What about Old Gray Mare?"

"There is nothing e-else on this list." He glanced at Moses, who shook his head regretfully and turned away.

Daniel Stiles listened intently. He had a head of full black hair with a few gray strands at his temples, sideburns, and no other facial hair. I had never seen anyone as tall as him before. He crossed his arms. "Abigail, do you understand that by not namin' the father, there is no one but yourself to take responsibility for your condition and your child?"

"Yes."

"Are you protectin' someone?"

"No, sir." I set the treasure chest down by my feet.

"Why is it that you name no one?"

"Because... I do not know his name, sir. A stranger approached me in the woods by the railroad tracks and forcefully had his way with me and fled. I had never seen him before and never saw him again." The room appeared blurred through my tears.

"You spoke of this to no one?" He sat with his huge hands folded primly upon the table.

"That is true." My knees wobbled. The room took on a grayish hue.

"Would you like to sit down?" Mr. Nichols spoke as he walked to the corner of the room and dragged a chair across the floor.

"Thank you." I sat down jest before I might have fainted.

"Moses?" Mr. Nichols pointed at the cluster of chairs.

"Nope." He leaned against the wall.

"When do you approximate the birth?" Mr. Stiles asked.

"In April." I found it difficult to swallow, as I knew it to be March.

"The only kin that you have is your sister, Sarah, who resides in Fall River, Massachusetts. Is this true?" He dipped his quill into the inkwell and scratched loud, dramatic loops on the paper.

My breathin' quickened at the mention of her name. "Yes, that is true."

"She shall be notified." He continued with his agitated scribbles and nodded at Mr. Nichols. "John?"

"I don't have anything to add." He wove his bony fingers through his wiry, white hair. "Such a shame, your folks were good people."

They talked amongst themselves while I watched the golden pendulum swing and listened to the deafenin' tick, tick, tickin' of the enormous grandfather clock. The snow didn't let up. My thoughts returned to the days when Sarah and I would celebrate the first real snowstorm by runnin' outside and makin' snow angels.

"Miss Hodgdon?" Mr. Nichols interrupted the clock.

"Yes?"

"Please sign this, and then you can go." He slid a paper to the edge of the table.

The chair creaked when I stood, and I felt that quickenin' like before — the slight twinge, pokin' from the inside out. Mr. Nichols pointed to the line where I was to sign. I looked at the words but could see nothin' but a black blur against the white page. I took the quill pen from him, dipped it in the inkwell, and signed my name in thick, shaky letters.

Mr. Nichols snatched the quill pen and nodded. "Good day, Miss Hodgdon."

"Good day." I think I said aloud.

Moses was in the doorway with his back to me. One wouldn't have known of my presence by the way the men chatted after my dismissal. I was forgotten before the ink dried; there would be no wastin' of tears. I pulled on my cold, soggy gloves, fetched my treasure chest, and followed Moses out into the blizzard, where our previous footprints had all but disappeared.

→⟫═◎ ◎═⟪←

We arrived at the County Farm. Moses drove the team up to a large ghostlike house which, until that day, I had only seen from afar. The pungent scent of wood smoke struck me.

Moses brought the horses to a halt. "Abigail, you ain't s'posed to have things with you at the farm. So, I'm gonna' take that chest of yours and put it in a safe place."

He tried to take it from me, but I held tight. "You said I could have it!"

He got off the sleigh, hurried over, and lifted me from seat. I flopped in his arms and dragged my feet, leavin' a trail behind me in the snow. The house smelled like burnt bread and some kind of medicine that Doctor Wentworth gave us when we were young.

Women sat in straight rows, sewin' and pretendin' not to notice us. I knew some of them from town and some I hadn't seen before. I scanned the room for Patience Cook but didn't spot her.

I looked down a long hallway where some old folks were tied up and slumped in chairs starin' straight ahead. Mother told us that some of them weren't right in the head. The old Indian woman, known to be a witch, sat on the floor with her eyes closed. She looked dead, yet peaceful.

A tall woman, with gray teeth, sallow skin, and dark hair pulled into a painfully tight knot at the nape of her neck, approached me. "Bring her over here. I'll fit her for a dress." She scowled. "Another pregnant one?"

Moses nodded. "Git her a yellow dress, Polly."

"Don't jest stand there. Come here," she said, smilin'. The stench from her sweat gagged me. She grabbed at my straw bonnet.

"No." I stepped away from her. "I choose to wear the bonnet."

Foam settled in the corners of her mouth. "It don't work like that."

A very large woman with startlin' red hair burst into the room. She echoed the other woman in sound and stench. "She ain't gonna' take off the bonnet?"

Moses had a stern look that was most unfamiliar. "Go easy."

"She ain't no different from the others." The fat one shook her chicken wattles. "And she won't get no special treatment. Now take it off."

I gripped the corners of my hat. I would have died before givin' up Mother's bonnet.

"Take this hat, and I'll kick you in the shins." My wet boots slipped on the floor.

"You'll do what?" With manly strength, she ripped the hat from my clenched fists.

The commotion stopped. Everybody stared at my scruffy head. I screamed and kicked at everything and anything. "Leave me alone!"

Polly smiled. "What's her name, Moses? She looks familiar."

"Abigail Hodgdon. I got her papers and—" his eyes widened when he looked at me. "Your hair!"

Glass shattered behind me.

"It's none of your concern. Now let go." I tried to wiggle away from the fat woman. I broke free and fled towards the door. Silas, as pale as a corpse, watched. My chest heaved. No one moved or uttered a word. An old man in the corner whimpered, unaware of the world around him.

Polly interrupted the quiet and held out a dingy yellow dress. "Now follow me."

Moses took the box from my limp arms. "Remember, I'll put this in a safe place."

Silas and I were face to face and eye to eye. I was an onlooker, no longer truly present. My boots ground the broken glass into the floor as I passed him by. I held my head up high, although my spirit had come undone. I felt that stirrin', that little poke inside of me, and I stood up even straighter with the yellow dress bunched under my arm and the cool air rushin' over my head.

CHAPTER 44

Silas – November 25, 1872

THE SKIES WERE heavy with snow. We had plenty of wood stacked in the shed, but not enough for the big house, so I got the men to haulin'. I stopped when I heard hootin' and hollerin' in the great room. It sounded like George Durgin, a local codger, was actin' up. He finally returned to work after bein' away for the summer.

The old Indian woman, Nellie, sat on the floor in the corner by a handful of elderly folks. She liked to be nearby so that if things got bad, she could lend a hand with her potions and such. It seemed George was irritated with Isaac Weeks, who was slouched over in the chair, sittin' there in his soiled pants, cryin' for his mamma and watchin' his piss stream across the floor. I went over to get him outta' the chair. George wasn't no small man, at least a foot taller 'an me.

George cuffed the old man upside the head. "Get up, fool." He yanked him by the scruff of the neck, causin' him to scramble with his feet dancin' this way and that.

Nellie tried to catch him, but Isaac fell to the floor, hittin' his head on the edge of the chair.

At first George raised his hand, and then thought better. "What do you want, Old Squaw?"

I stepped in. "George, don't be hittin' ole Isaac here. He ain't doin' no harm."

I picked the old man up from the floor. "Now, now, Isaac. It's gonna' be fine." Bein' accustomed to carryin' Daddy and all, I hoisted Isaac over my shoulder like a sack of grain and lugged him up the stairs. He weren't nearly as heavy as Daddy.

George jest didn't git it, and he had to have the last word. "Goddamned fools." He shook his head and went off to find more trouble.

I took Isaac to his sleepin' quarters and laid him down on his bed sack. He pulled his crusty, old blanket over his head and whimpered.

I jammed my hands into my pockets. "Stay here. I'll get you some dry trousers."

He flipped the blanket down and looked up at the ceilin' with that blank stare like most of the other old folks, 'cept for the Indian; she was always thinkin'.

I went to the launderin' room and found a pair of trousers, and then I headed for the medicine cabinet for a bottle of elixir. I stopped cold when I heard a woman puttin' up a howl in the great room.

Miss Noyes was right in the middle of it. "You'll do what?"

A shrill scream caused me to flinch.

"What's her name?" Of course, Polly was part of the rumpus.

My stomach started in on me, and beads of sweat dotted my forehead.

Then I heard Moses. It weren't typical for him to be in the house that time of day. "It's Abigail, Abigail Hodgdon."

My heart raced.

"I got her papers right here... "

I thought I didn't hear him right.

"What happened to your hair?" he shouted.

I approached the doorway. She stood there as plain as day with short clumps of hair coverin' her head where them beautiful curls used to be. She seethed like a rabid fox.

Tears stung my eyes and my chest tightened. I dropped the bottle of elixir. It shattered on the floor.

"It is none of your concern... Let me go!" She tore away from Miss Noyes and slowly turned and glared at me with cold, dark eyes, not warm and brown like I knew 'em to be. I froze and kept thinkin' that Mamma would wake me.

"Here's ya dress," Polly said.

It was yellow. Yellow. *Dear Lord, I'll kill Weston Jones. It can't be mine, she woulda' told me.*

Without takin' her eyes off me, she snatched the dress from Polly.

"Follow me." Polly rolled her sleeves clear up to her elbows.

Moses took a box that Abigail held under her arm. "Remember, I'll put this in a safe place." He glanced at me.

She stepped on the broken glass as if it weren't even there, and then she stopped and looked me straight in the eye. It seemed like a long time passed before she turned and followed Polly up the stairs.

I didn't move while Mary swept the glass by my feet. I draped Isaac's pants over the back of a half busted chair and ran out the back door to the wood-shed where the men was stackin' wood. I pushed by Cyrus Trask, bumpin' his shoulder. He puffed up his chest, ready to fight. I flung open the door and leaned over the railin'.

Cyrus shouted, "Looks like ol' Silas drank too much rum last night, and he ain't got the stomach for it." The men was laughin' and howlin' along with the wind against my back.

After a short spell, I went out to the horse stalls. My thoughts crowded in so fast I couldn't sort one from the other. I pictured Abigail standin' there with jest about no hair while holdin' onto a yellow dress. *She's havin' a baby. Goddamn. My sweet Abigail is here at the farm like a good for nothin' whore.*

I hadn't cried for some time, but them tears let loose, and I couldn't do nothin' to stop 'em. *So that explains why she'd been avoidin' me. Folks tried to tell me 'bout Weston and her carryin' on, while I was busy carryin' on myself, about to marry Jessie.*

I punched my fist into the rough-cut barn board, rippin' the skin from my knuckles. I wanted to kill Weston. If I saw him then, I woulda' tore him to pieces. I slammed my fist into the wall again, leavin' a splatterin' of blood.

"What are you doin'?" Moses came in from the back of the barn.

I stood in silence.

"I'm talkin' to ya, son."

"I wanna be left alone." The warm blood ran down my fingers.

"Well, somethin' ain't right. It's 'bout Abigail." He walked in front of me and held a match over his pipe.

"Never mind. I got nothin' to say." I wiped the blood on my trousers.

"I know you was sweet on her. I was fond of her myself." The tobacco glowed in his pipe with each long draw. "Course, not in a fanciful way."

"She was my girl, only we was secretive because of her mamma." I paced.

"Secretive?"

"Her mamma didn't want her courtin' no one, so we met secretly like I said. Then after the fire, she started carryin' on with Weston. She avoided me." I dragged my sleeve across my runny nose. "And Jessie jest came outta' nowhere."

"You been intimate with Abigail?" He raised an eyebrow.

"Only once."

"More than four months ago?"

"Yes." I thought back to the barn dance, countin' the months.

"She claims to have been taken by a stranger who forced himself on her by the railroad tracks, and she swears she don't know him. I think she's protectin' Weston."

"Then bring the son-of-a-bitch here and make him take responsibility." I wailed my fist into the wall. "I'll kill him." I pulled back to strike again.

He grabbed my wrist. "He left town. He went to work up to Bangor in the lumber mill with his brother-in-law John Garland."

"He left on the account of Abigail bein' pregnant?" I was ready to make the trip up to Bangor and drag him back to do right by Abigail. But I woulda' had to kill 'em first.

"Let it be. You got a nice girl and a plan for your new house. You don't want to get tangled up in this."

"What makes you think it's Weston? What if it were some stranger comin' through town?"

"Me and Miriam have been watchin', and we seen her bein' familiar with him on more than one occasion. They sneaked off into the barn and in the field right in the light of day." He shook his head. "Miriam warned her, but she didn't take no mind."

I closed my eyes and leaned back against the uneven, splintery wall.

"Besides, why would he go leavin' town so fast if he weren't in some sort of trouble?" Moses held a match to his pipe. "If Abigail would name him as the father, we'd go fetch him. But she signed a paper sayin' that the father was unknown, and there ain't a thing we can do 'bout it, 'cept pray that Weston don't come back."

The starless night was darkenin' over the fresh white snow. Moses patted me on the back. "Come on now, son. Let's forget all this. Come and join Miriam and me for supper. You can tell us all about the weddin'."

I stood still, starin' up at the house as the lanterns were lit one by one. It was quiet, 'cept for the random thump of snow fallin' from weary trees and ice covered branches brushin' against each other in the wind. I winced when the jagged, raw flesh on my hand rubbed against the inside of my pocket. Heck, it was 'nuff to bring any man to tears.

CHAPTER 45

Abigail – November 25, 1872

"TAKE OFF THAT dress and git into this." Polly gritted her teeth and ripped the yellow dress away from me. "Since you ain't got much hair, we don't have to chop it off."

I unbuttoned my blouse and noticed the tattered and filthy bed sacks settin' on the floor along the walls. In one corner was a bed that showed no promise of holdin' together for a night. A woman in the far corner held a baby in her arms. Matted bunches of yellow fuzz covered her head. I tried to see her face as she walked through the vague shadows.

"Patience." I grinned.

Smudges of dirt dotted her small heart-shaped face. "Abigail Hodgdon?" The baby squirmed in her arms. "What are you doin' here?"

I looked down at my feet.

"Oh Lord, of course."

"Never mind all ya jawin'," Polly said. "Git back over here and git dressed."

I hesitated before undoin' the last button and dropped my blouse on the floor. "What is the purpose of hurryin'?" I unhooked my draggled skirt and stared at the severe lines on her face, warped and misshapen, infected by years of hatred.

"You better not sass me back, or you'll be in a heap of trouble."

The old Indian woman came into the room, scrapin' her feet as she walked across the uneven floorboards. She stood quietly in the corner, watchin' us with steady brown eyes. I remembered her from the room in the back of the store. She was a curious sort.

"Off." Polly yanked on the corner of my camisole. "Your fancy days are over."

"It's cold." I rubbed my bare arms.

"Don't worry. You'll work up a good sweat when you do chores." She leaned into me.

My stomach rebelled when I tasted her foul stench in the back of my throat. I cupped my hand over my nose and mouth. "So be it," I said.

I stripped down to my pantaloons, leggin's, and boots, and stood before her, shiverin' more from her penetratin' eyes than the icy wind blowin' through the cracks. I covered my breasts with my hands.

She cackled and tossed the yellow dress at my feet. "Put this on. Ain't no use hidin'. You ain't got nothin' I don't see every day." She continued to stare.

I pulled the crudely sewn garment over my head. It scratched my skin and hung loosely on my body in the least flatterin' manner. I removed my soakin' wet boots and peeled my leggin's off of my cool, damp skin. I clutched my skirt tight to my chest.

"Give me them clothes. You don't need them." She inched closer to me.

"Uh, I need one thing." I reached down and untied the ribbon that held Hope to the underpinnin's of my skirt.

"What's this?" Her warm breath washed over my face.

"Somethin' that I will be keepin' in here with me." My voice faded like a window closin' down on the last hint of fresh air. I tightened my grip on Hope.

Suddenly the Indian woman shuffled in our direction.

"Hold on there, Missy." Polly dug her bony fingers into my arm.

"No! You can't have her! She's mine!" I held on, prepared to fight.

"Hand it over! Rules is rules, and you ain't allowed to keep nothin' right now!" Her dirt-encrusted fingernails scratched three perfect lines of blood down my arm.

"I must have her. Papa gave her to me." Tears spilled from a place unknown before that moment. The fight inside of me trickled down to a plea. "Do you have to strip a girl of everything?"

The Indian woman stepped between us and faced Polly with her arms crossed high on her chest. She didn't utter a word, yet oddly Polly responded.

"Oh well, you can keep it, but jest for tonight, and then I have to take it from you. Them's the rules." She scowled and crumpled my clothes into a ball.

I looked away from Polly and into the warm, chocolate eyes of the old woman.

"Don't be thankin' me. Thank Nellie here." She nodded her head towards the old Indian woman, who I then knew as Nellie. "And this is your bed." She kicked at the yellow stained, straw-filled bed sack on the floor. "You can set it on one of them bed frames over there; that's up to you."

Patience sat on a board positioned between two blocks, nursin' her baby. "Nellie has some dried moss that you kin stuff in with the straw, and it ain't so bad." Her son bobbed his tiny head in search of her breast.

"When you hear the bell, come to the dinin' room with the others." Polly marched off, leavin' behind a trace of her most unpleasant odor.

I turned my attention to the reassurin' sound of the sucklin' baby as he nestled in his mother's arms, blissfully unaware of the awful place in which we were. Nellie tapped my arm. Her eyes sparkled when she laughed an odd, soundless laugh. She pointed at my doll.

"Hope?" I handed her the doll.

She smiled. I thought it peculiar that she took a likin' to my doll. No sooner had she smiled than her shoulders drooped and she released a heavy sigh. She traced her crooked finger over the frayed doll and stared blankly.

I wanted my doll. *Does she think that Hope is hers now?* I waited. All I could hear was my own breathin' and a woman in the hallway softly singin' as she lit the lamps. Nellie walked away and sat on the floor with her back to me. She rummaged through some things, makin' a slight clatter. I tiptoed closer. She sat up with a start.

"Nellie's got a secret place over there; pay her no mind." Patience placed the baby over her shoulder and patted his back. "She don't talk neither."

A bell sounded and folks shuffled down the hall in small herds. Nellie, illuminated in soft amber light, grunted and struggled to her feet holdin' somethin' in each hand. I took two or three steps towards her and stopped. She had another doll that resembled Hope 'cept for the color of the dress and fewer beads.

"You have a doll too?" I grinned. "Sisters?"

Nellie shook her head no. She pointed at Patience and then to the baby. "Is it Patience's doll?"

She shook her head again and then motioned as if she were sewin'.

"You are Hope's mother?" My face flushed. "You made Hope?"

She smiled and pressed Hope to her lips before handin' her to me. I never expected to meet the maker of my faceless companion, especially seein' it was the Indian woman.

"Is Hope that doll you was hangin' onto?" Patience asked as she wrapped the baby in a sling.

"It was a gift from Papa. I have always cherished her." I choked up. "Nellie made Hope. Nellie is a doll maker." Warm, salty tears slid down my cheeks.

"Well, I'll be darned." Patience paused in the doorway. "Ain't that somethin'."

When Nellie reached for Hope, I handed her over, knowin' that I had a friend. She returned to her corner and shuffled things about, puttin' both dolls in her safe place in the floor.

⋅⇥ ⇤⋅

I stood in line tryin' to make out the faces of folks that I knew. We all filed into the kitchen together, but in the dinin' room, the women sat on one side and the men on the other. My hands trembled as I constantly looked for Silas. *What will I do if I see him? I will run. No, I cannot run. I have nowhere to go.* I moved forward in the line stayin' close behind Nellie. *I will stare at him until he leaves the room.* I imagined his face and his eyes lookin' back at me. *I will look away and pretend he is not present.*

"Hey you." A woman's sharp nasal voice snapped me back into the moment. It was that enormous, red haired woman they called Miss Noyes. "Take this." She thrust a bowl towards me.

I snatched it and glared at her with false courage.

"You watch yourself or you'll wish you ain't never been born." She wiped her grubby, dimpled hands on her apron and flashed her teeth like one of the huge boars from the piggery.

Nellie tugged on my elbow and brought me to a long table, where six ragged women sat in anxious silence. Everyone focused on a pot in the middle of the table that contained some sort of colorless stew. A loaf of crusty bread was ripped into small pieces and scattered about.

After a spell, folks whispered behind their hands, starin' at me with hollow eyes. I saw Mrs. Piper, the widow of Solomon Piper, who ran the gristmill. We were in the garden when we learned of his death. I heard Mother's ominous voice in my head. *Poor woman has no kin and will end up at the County Farm. Such a shame.*

A thin, scared woman ladled the stew into each bowl, splatterin' and makin' a fine mess. Then everyone knew to grab one piece of the brick like bread. Of course they used lard instead of butter. I closed my eyes and thought of Lizzie. Nellie nudged me. I took a spoonful of the light brown, watery broth. Without thinkin', I blew on it. As vile and lukewarm as it was, the gnawin' inside forced me to taste it. I glanced around the room. Everyone shoveled it down like it was a feast, 'cept for Nellie. She had her head bowed in prayer. Then she took a piece of bread and left the table.

She went to a table of old men. They simply sat there as if they had no sense. Then she approached a skeleton of a man with gray eyes, untamed white hair, and a badly bruised face. He looked familiar, almost like Isaac Weeks, the blacksmith who shoed our horses before Papa went away.

He flinched when Nellie touched his shoulder. She fed him his stew. Like a child, he stared at her while she scraped the spoon on his chin to catch the drippins'. She dunked his bread in the broth and fed it to him along with her own bread. No one seemed to notice or care.

She stopped at a table of older womenfolk. She reached into her belt and took out somethin' small and dark and handed it to a woman who sat with her head layin' on the table. I could have sworn it was Mahitable Colby, but she looked quite aged. She lifted her head and took the mysterious object into her mouth with her eyes fixed on the ceilin'.

Nellie returned to our table. I tried another taste. I couldn't decide if it was pork or not. A few salty carrots and about a third of a potato sloshed in my bowl. In an attempt to soften the bread, I dipped it in the stew, soppin' up the broth. My thoughts turned to Jessie Gilman sittin' next to Silas eatin' a roast duck dinner with all the trimmin's. I dropped my spoon.

A slight woman sat across from me watchin' my every move. Her long silver braids were coiled neatly around her head, and her blue woolen shawl hung loosely off of one bony shoulder. "If ya ain't gonna' finish yer stew, I'll have it." She slid her shaky, frail hand across the table.

I pushed the bowl in her direction. "Here, you can have it. It's not fit to eat."

The mysterious meat, potato, and carrots splattered when she dumped them into her bowl. "Mighty thankful." She grinned before plungin' in, slurpin' and drippin' all over her chin as though it were her last meal.

Miss Noyes pushed her way to the table. She swiftly cuffed the old woman aside the head. "No talkin'."

The woman's head snapped forward and she started chokin'. She looked at me with her eyes burstin' and broth runnin' from her nostrils.

I opened my mouth. I had to say somethin'.

Miss Noyes crossed her ample arms and glared at me. "You ain't s'posed to fraternize. She knows better." Another bell sounded. People arose and shuffled into lines. I jumped, knockin' my chair onto the floor when a man of at least forty years ran his calloused hands down my arms. I knew he wasn't right in the head. I looked away from his cloudy, gray eyes and devilish grin. I stepped behind Nellie, keepin' a safe distance away from the rest of them.

We returned to our sleepin' quarters, where Polly waited. "You'll be needin' this." She held a stiff, wrinkled nightdress in her hand.

I took it. I did not have the strength nor will to defy her.

The other women kept to themselves while they stripped down and got into their nightdresses without one bit of modesty. Polly was in the middle of the room watchin'. I hadn't undressed in front of anyone 'cept Mother and Sarah, and even then it was not intentional. I went as close to the wall as I could and turned my back, took off the yellow dress, and slipped into my nightdress.

After Polly left, Nellie approached. She got on her knees and filled my bed sack with straw. Then she reached inside of her belt and pulled out Hope and handed her to me.

I had a strong urge to embrace her. I hesitated. She patted my head. We stood together for a moment before she went to the other side of the room and blew out the lamp.

I pulled the blanket up to my chin and stared at the ceilin'. All the groanin' and screechin' scared me and prevented me from movin'.

"Abigail?" Patience whispered.

"What?"

"Don't be scared."

"I'm not." I squeezed my eyes shut tight.

"They can't take away your soul."

I watched her shadow on the wall. "I know." I rolled onto my side.

"Heavenly Father, I have sinned... There is no turnin' back. I am fully aware that I must surrender to that which is my fate. I pray that You take me into Your hands and in Thine own time, restore to my bosom the enjoyment of peace. Though I am poor and needy, I pray that You think of me. And while reviewin' my life, my sins, and forgetfulness, that You will guide me through my distress in my needful time. I pray for strength and forgiveness. In the Lord's name I pray, A-men."

CHAPTER 46

Silas – November 26, 1872

"You don't look so good." Mamma poured steamin' coffee into my cup.

I inhaled the scent of the fresh brew, always bitter and too hot.

"You ain't sick are ya?" The pot rattled when she set it on the stove.

I wished her away, knowin' she'd still be right there pickin' and talkin' as she had a mind to.

"Some folks got the sore throat." She twisted the corner of her apron 'round and 'round in her raw, red hands. "I can tell when you're sick. You get that glazed look."

"I s'pose I caught a cold." The coffee seared my tongue and the roof of my mouth. "I ain't worried."

"Well, make sure that ya boots are by the fire so they dry." She carried 'em over by the stove.

"Ayuh." My head throbbed. Nothin' would ever be the same. I couldn't look at Abigail. I couldn't stand knowin' that she was at the farm, carryin' Weston's child. My stomach rumbled as I poked at the hash in my bowl.

"Don't starve yourself. You'll git sicker if ya don't eat."

"I ain't got no appetite." I went over and fetched my almost warm, damp boots.

"You're bein' wasteful. You know how I hate wastefulness."

"I'll bring it to the pigs." I struggled to get the wet boots over my dry stockin's.

"Them boots didn't have half a chance to dry. And you wonder why–" She stopped at the sight of Daddy.

"Where's my coffee, woman?" He sat on his chair, lookin' around the room through puffy, red eyes. "What's this 'bout feedin' your breakfast to the pigs?" He bobbed his tousled head and squinted like he was lookin' into the bright sunlight instead of a dreary, dark kitchen.

"Never mind, Daddy." I reached for my coat. "I'll feed the animals and collect the eggs, and then I'm leavin'. You got 'nuff wood stacked."

I closed the door on their naggin' and bickerin'. The sun warmed my face, and the snow slid off the roof in broken, flat sheets.

After I finished in the barn, I headed out. Major plodded through the slush. I got to thinkin'. I preferred to never set eyes on Abigail again than to see her at the farm wearin' a yellow dress. The thought of her with no hair and that wild look in her eyes made my stomach roll.

After thinkin' about how to see and not see Abigail and reachin' no conclusions, I arrived at the farm. I stopped when I heard men hollerin' from inside the barn. I went in. Cyrus Trask had George by the collar. Cyrus had his fist drawn back, about to punch him. George picked a fight with the wrong fella.

"Let go!" I jumped right in the middle. "Are you crazy hittin' a farm boss?" I grabbed Cyrus by the arm.

"He asked for it." Cyrus tried to wiggle away. "He was insultin' me and eggin' me on."

I tightened my grip. "It don't matter. When you're here, you got bosses and rules, and you can't go around fightin' all the time, or you'll be thrown in lock-up."

"He was mouthy." George wiped a trickle of blood from the corner of his mouth.

"You oughtn't to be gettin' in fights, George. Seems you're always in a scrape." I released Cyrus. "Now George, go clean up. Cyrus, follow me."

"You ain't in charge," George muttered.

"You're right. So go see Moses and tell him what ya done." I walked towards the house with Cyrus stumblin' along behind me.

One of the wings of the house had rooms sorta' like stalls. They had locks on the outside door, no windows, and with the exception of a straw bed or bench, had no furniture or fixin's. Large hooks and chains hung on the walls for restrainin' the folks who got outta' hand. We used lock-up for the crazed folks or men who got to be too much of a handful.

I didn't like usin' them quarters unless I had to. I decided to put Cyrus inside of lock-up for the day in hopes to break him of fightin'. Trouble is, both he and George are fightin' men with a fine line between 'em.

I didn't mind havin' to walk through the launderin' room to get to the back stairs. The new women usually started out in the kitchen, leavin' no chance of seein' Abigail. I pushed Cyrus through the doorway.

"Ooh. A pretty new face." He threw his head back and laughed.

I looked over Cyrus's shoulder and stopped dead. Abigail stood over a steamin' tub workin' a wash pole. She glanced at me, makin' me red-faced and useless. She turned away and continued stirrin'.

"Hey." I dug my fingers deep into his shoulder bone and pushed him ahead, keepin' him at arm's length.

"You're hurtin' me for Chrissakes." He shrugged, tryin' to free himself.

As we neared the stalls, I hesitated at the sound of a woman's cry from behind one of the doors. I loosened my grip on his shoulder and cleared my throat. I couldn't be gettin' soft.

The heavy oaken door squeaked when I pulled it open. Cyrus stopped. His shoulders sagged when he saw the chains and a board propped on two crates. "You ain't gonna' chain me are ya?" He peered at me from under his thick, filthy hair. The cries on the other side of the wall continued.

"Nope, jest stay in here for the day and think 'bout it next time ya wanna fight." I left the dark room, pullin' the door tight and then hitchin' the outside latch.

To avoid seein' Abigail, I walked all the way to the staircase down the hall past the men's sleepin' quarters. When I hit the bottom step, I bolted, headin' straight out the front door.

I spent the rest of the day workin' in the barn, even tendin' to chores that the inmates should have done. In the late afternoon, I sent Asa to let Cyrus out of lock-up. Heck, I didn't even go into the house for lunch.

At the end of the day, Moses came into the pigsty, where I was watchin' the men replace one of the stall boards. He took his pipe from his pocket and packed it with fresh tobacco. "You ain't gonna' be able to avoid her forever ya know."

I didn't move.

He held a match over the bowl and toked a few times before puffin' a trail of smoke rings. "It'll get easier in time."

"I know I can't avoid seein' her forever."

His pipe gurgled as he jest stared at me.

"You're wrong. It ain't ever gonna' be easy." I grabbed my coat. With Moses followin' behind, I left the pigsty and went to fetch Major. Without a word, I mounted my horse and galloped into the curtain of darkness that snuffed out all possible light that remained.

CHAPTER 47

Abigail – November 26, 1872

I AWOKE TO my own terrifyin' screams, standin' before a fogged window with a ragin' crack down the middle. My nightdress was damp and clingin' to my skin, and I had my hands coverin' my ears. *Where am I?* Two women sat on the floor starin' at me, and at least four others lay in motionless bundles along the wall. Only one woman bothered sleepin' on a bed with a frame.

My heart pounded. I touched my head, and my fingers happened upon a tuft of stiff hair. A baby cried from across the room. It was no dream. I was in the most wretched place on earth.

Sarah used to calm me. "Breathe in through the nose and out through the mouth." I stood motionless as the cool air whistled through the cracked window, dryin' the sweat on my skin. I jumped when someone touched my arm. As quickly as she appeared, Nellie vanished into uncertain shadows.

"Folks probably heard you all the way down at the train station," Patience said. "Don't worry. I had nightmares at first too. I still do from time to time." She situated herself on the bench with the baby.

"It wasn't a nightmare." I sat on my bed and pulled my knees to my chest. "It was somethin' else, somethin' more terrifyin' than a nightmare."

"Shhh." Mahitable pulled her blanket over her head.

"Sorry." My breathin' returned to normal.

"She ain't one to talk," Patience said. "She screams more than anyone."

The murky, gray skies surrendered to gauzy pink and amber clouds. A rooster from the barn crowed, soundin' almost like Pearl but higher pitched. I smiled when I thought about him lyin' alone in that field with his bones picked clean. "Live free or die." I finally understood what Grampa Wills meant when he ranted about that old general.

The men's voices from outside competed with rattlin' pots in the kitchen. One by one, the others began to rise. Their murmurs joined in the chorus of clangin' chains and cows that lowed in the barn. I looked, but Nellie wasn't over by her medicine place or within the herd of cheerless women. Her empty bed sack sagged in the middle. Without her, I did not know what the day would bring forth.

Jest as the door opened, the rooster crowed again. Nellie walked across the room and sat down beside me. She carried an old, crumpled tin of brew that she stirred with a notched twig. She stared into the cup with great interest before handin' the cup to me. I brought it to my lips and blew on the steam. It smelled familiar. I was pleasantly surprised when the brown and greenish speckles lingered on my tongue. It tasted like sweet dirt and smelled like a pine grove. I drank it all.

Unconcerned with their surroundin's, the women dressed in silence. After Patience nursed the baby, she got into her yellow dress and pulled a holey snood over her snarled hair. "Nellie's got secret potions." She buttoned her dress. "She's better'n most doctors."

Miss Noyes started in hollerin' and ringin' the bell. "Breakfast!"

"I don't want to get in trouble for bein' late." I tumbled out of bed, droppin' Hope and kickin' the tin cup across the room.

The women filed out of the room mumblin', detached from themselves and each other. When Nellie touched my arm with her warm, yet calloused hand, I felt safe and loved in an unexpected manner.

"Stay with Nellie!" Patience called after me.

Nellie brushed past me and picked up Hope and went to her secret place. I looked away so that she wouldn't think that I was snoopin'. She waited by the door while I ripped off my nightdress, stuffed it under my pillow, and wiggled into my yellow dress. The rumblin' in my stomach seemed to get louder as I neared the kitchen.

I tried to merge with Nellie. When she moved a certain way, I moved that same certain way. Polly handed over my bowl and spoon without speakin'. We went to the same table, only this time the pot contained brown, runny gruel instead of stew. The bread and lard were in the center of the table. Folks ate desperately with a hunger that I had never witnessed.

The brown gruel dribbled off my spoon and back into the bowl. I watched Nellie walk about, helpin' folks eat as she broke her bread into pieces and parceled them out.

She addressed a woman with a boy not more than three years old. She pulled out what looked like berries and gave them to his mother, who in turn gave them to the boy. He made a fuss and looked away with his arms folded over his chest. His mother tussled with him before he threw them onto the floor. Jest as the mother was about to strike him, Nellie caught her hand and retrieved the berries. She gave the boy a stern look, pried open his fingers, and dropped them in his hand. He smiled sheepishly and popped them all in his mouth. Nellie patted him on the head and returned to our table to eat her gruel.

At first I thought of givin' away my gruel, but my stomach protested. I found that swallowin' hard made eatin' gruel easier. I tore off a piece of bread and hid it inside of my pocket for later.

"You're goin' into the launderin' room today." Polly drove her sharp fingertip into my shoulder. I followed her down the hallway to a room filled with washboards, poles, tubs, shelves of soap, and lines for hangin'.

Polly approached a girl in the corner of the room. She was movin' slow, leanin' on a pole, and hummin'. She looked up. Betty Wallace. I gulped. She was s'posed to have gone to work in the mills. She was a bit younger than me. A crop of brown curls fell in front of her eyes, and the disgraceful yellow dress, the dress of a sinner, fit snugly around her slightly swollen belly.

Polly nudged her shoulder. "You ain't gettin' much done. If you don't keep the clothes movin', they'll have yellow spots."

Betty straightened up, lookin' pale as death, and started in stirrin' the clothes. She glanced at me and then back at the tub.

"Mary, show her what to do," Polly said.

The woman named Mary smiled at me. She wore a blue dress like the other inmates, but she acted like a boss, a nice boss. "Hello, dear. Abigail?"

"Yes." I was startled at the meekness of my voice and how much strength had dwindled away. No longer bright or free, I had faded. I concluded that God had misplaced my true self in this place of misery.

"It works like this. On Sunday night, we put the clothes in the vats with warm water and let 'em soak all night. On Monday, we scrub 'em on the wash-board with lye soap. On Tuesdays, today, we put the clothes in boilin' water and stir 'em with these long poles. Then we take 'em out with a wash stick and put 'em in warm water one more time, wring 'em out, and hang 'em on the lines to dry." Quite pleased, she put her hands on her hips.

"Yes." I thought of how I tended to put off launderin' more than all other chores.

"The men bring in the water durin' the winter. So all you gotta' do is stir, rinse, and wring 'em, and then hang 'em on the line."

"Yes." I turned to discover that Nellie was gone.

Mary led me to a vat of steamin' water that had a pole in it. "Here."

I started stirrin'.

No one spoke. No wonder Betty was hummin'. However, I decided to use this time for earnest prayer, to ask the Lord to find a thought for me and to forgive my broken, unclean spirit so that I may return to what is good and righteous.

We simply stood over vats of boilin' water and swirled clothes around, and then rinsed them around, and then wrung them out before hangin' them on the lines. If I looked into the water too long, the room would spin about.

Mary peeked over my shoulder. Concerned that I was goin' too slowly, I stabbed at the clothes with the pole. I felt the stirrin' inside – the pokin' finger. I stopped.

"Here, do you want to wear this?" She waved a yellow cloth.

"Wear it?" I started stirrin' again.

"Yes, on ya head." She draped it over her head in a silly fashion and smiled.

I laughed. "I would like to wear it, thank you." I tied the cloth around my head and knotted it in the back.

The sweat on the palms of my hands started to sting with blisters. I wiped my hands on my dress. A sharp pain shot through my neck and shoulder muscles, bringin' me to my knees.

"It ain't time for a rest now." Polly was right there at every move and in every thought. "Toughen up, girl. Soon you'll have calluses."

I scrambled to my feet and spun around, holdin' back the urge to strike her. I had never struck a person before. I looked into her eyes. I did not know that I was capable of such feelin's. I returned to my pole and swirled the clothes, watchin' the trail of whitish lye on the water. I thought of Mother and how she put a drop of lavender oil in the water. "That little extra sweetness makes a difference," she told Sarah and me.

"Ooh. A lovely, new face." A man's voice interrupted my thoughts. His laugh was loud and deep.

Without liftin' my head, I glanced up at him. My knees about gave way when I saw Cyrus Trask. Sarah spoke of him often. He always took to boastin' and fightin' in town when he got all liquored up. Silas pushed and poked him from behind.

I can't run. I can't hide. Our eyes met. I returned my sights to the clothes in the warm, gray water. My temples throbbed. I thought that I might faint.

"You never mind."

His familiar voice reached a different place, a place where I kept all of the love that I once had. It was a sort of flower garden. However, I could not see the flowers, touch them, or even smell them. I could only conjure up an image. When that garden gate opened, it was simply to remind me that the flowers were there, and if I dared to pick even one, they would all die.

CHAPTER 48

Nellie – November 26, 1872

THE STARS FLEW from the fire to Father Sky to join the others. The maple burned brightly. I danced with song in heart and wings upon my spirit. In the Planting Moon, we celebrate fertility, birth, and all that nourishes body and soul. We gather courage, nurture dreams, and call upon the sweetness of truth stored deep in the heart of Our Mother. We depart from the quietness of our cave and enter into the wildness of living things.

My husband carved a flute for me to make music. He carried it with him when we were together. *Play for me, Nanatasis.* This made him proud.

I danced with the cool and quiet wind from Cold River as her voice blended with the music of crickets and giant pines.

Searching Owl spread our blanket before the fire. *Come and sit, Nanatasis.*

I sat with my head on his shoulder. The night chorus swelled and begged me to join. I put the smooth wood to my lips for the birth of a new song. I closed my eyes. The fire warmed me, and music filled Father Sky. Harmony in creation is where all energy flows.

After the songs, I gave thanks to the Great Spirit. Searching Owl took the flute. The moon cast a glow on our nakedness as we united in body and spirit.

The barred owl flew with silent feathers, watching and waiting nearby. The embers glowed and the night fell quiet, awaiting the colors of morning.

⤜⊙ ⊙⤛

A scream pierced the darkness. The owl departed from the withering tree. The steady currents of Cold River ceased, and the strong arms of Searching Owl fell away. I opened my eyes. Shadows of the oak tree swayed on the ceiling. The Planting Moon was no more. A cold moon took its place.

Abigail stood before the window. She was gripped by the hand of fear. Some of the women awakened as the baby cried. I would help her to find peace. Fear destroys. I went to her. She jumped at my touch. I looked into her brown eyes with my own before going to fetch tea.

The sun was rising. Men filled the stoves with wood. I poured the heated water into the cup. The lady with hair the color of a fox did not speak.

I went to my medicine place and took two pinches of dried yarrow flower, a piece of inner white pine bark, and burdock root. I put them into the medicine pouch, bruised them with my fingers, and placed the pouch into the cup of water. I approached Abigail. She watched me stir with the pine twig.

I offered her the brew. At first it did not please her. I warmed her cold hands in mine as she watched others prepare for the day. Fear returned. She took the tea and hurried. She drank it all away.

The bell rang and the women departed. I placed the cup and doll in my medicine place.

She walked close to me. We joined the others for food. I took my bread for the wounded ones and for those who needed more. The old man called Captain was weak in body and spirit. His eyes held no spark and did not see. He struggled to lift his head. I went to him. I tore my bread making three.

"No, no." His cry was soft and childlike. "No, no, no…"

To bring him back and to clear his pathway of fear, I held his face in my hands. He became silent. I fed him gruel until he would take no more.

The woman called Jane sat across from Captain with her silver head bowed in quiet. Her husband Henry was at her side. He wore spectacles with one broken glass. His hands shook and his gruel fell from the spoon. Jane reached for the spoon. He pushed her away.

I went to them and wiped clean his spectacles and returned them to his face. I gave to each a piece of bread. He dropped the spoon to take the bread.

The woman called Emily shouted at her son. He had the sore throat. I brought dried juniper berries for him. Later, I would give him medicine of the elder and white pine twig tea.

After her anger departed, she took the berries. "Daniel ain't feelin' well, and he ain't behavin' well either." He rebelled when she gave him the berries.

When she raised her hand, I stopped the blow. A mother should not strike her child. I gathered the berries and gave them to the boy. He took them. I stroked his head before returning to the table to eat my own gruel.

Some elders were tied to the chairs. Some were not. I stayed nearby as they waited for the passage from their earth walk to the Otherworld.

When the farm bosses left, I went to the tied ones and rubbed dried yarrow and plantain leaf on the skin, where redness and pain left marks. I wrapped them in blankets.

"No! No! You can't have him! He's my baby!"

The call of a mother fell upon my ears and heart. I was still.

"Take him, Asa." It was the voice of the big farm boss, Moses.

Daniel cried. I went into the hall. Polly and the lady with hair the color of a fox held Emily. The strong man called Asa carried the boy as he reached for his mother.

"Them's the rules, Emily." Polly did not know the ways of Our Mother.

"He's my son! Don't take him!" Emily fell to her knees. "Daniel!"

"You knew this day might come. You could get righted around and try to get him back." The lady with hair the color of a fox spoke without care.

"You said that he could stay."

"It don't always work that way. Now Daniel can go to a nice family." The farm boss walked away smoking his pipe.

"Mamma! Mamma!" His voice faded with the sound of hooves drumming against the earth.

Emily broke free and ran to the door. Polly chased her. The lady with hair the color of a fox followed.

"You ain't gonna' change nothin'. You'll jest make matters worse," Polly said.

The lady with hair the color of a fox stood over Emily. "Are you all done scrappin'?"

Emily kicked and clawed at the two women. "You can rot in Hell!"

Polly took one arm, and the lady with hair the color of a fox took the other, and they dragged her to where people are locked in stalls.

I waited for them to leave. I tasted the salt of sadness upon my lips.

Time passed. I went to the stalls where Emily wept behind the heavy door. The latch was not locked but kept her confined. I removed it and entered. I held her in my arms. Her tears soaked through my dress and into my spirit.

CHAPTER 49

Abigail – December 13, 1872

MY SLEEP WAS broken by the harsh duet between Miss Noyes's hollerin' and the kitchen bell. When I attempted to rise, a burnin' pain threatened to devour my entire body.

Nellie stood at the foot of my bed.

"Yes, I know. I must get up." I rubbed my shoulder.

I was the last one to leave the room. I lost sight of Nellie and rushed out the door, quite pleased to catch sight of her at the top of the stairs.

"You waited for me," I whispered.

She smiled. We walked down the stairs in unison, Nellie in the lead and me tryin' to go unnoticed.

Emily, the mother of the boy taken away for adoption, moved ahead of us in line. She had the same vacant look as the men who came back from the war. Patience said that she stayed in lock-up because of her tantrums.

Then I spotted a girl with short, golden curls and a unique beauty that enveloped her. She had perfect posture, and her slender, white neck begged for an ornament, maybe a velvet choker or pearls. She said to Nellie, "We're havin' biscuits." Her eyes sparkled, and she had a dimple in her left cheek.

Nellie patted her arm. I wondered how a girl could be so happy in such a wicked place. Surely, it was a sign from Heaven.

I gasped when I saw a shadowy figure pass by the window. The familiar pressin' down on my chest returned as I watched Silas standin' outside with his hands in his pockets, talkin' to Moses and another man. I stumbled along behind Nellie and the flawless girl, beggin' myself to look away.

A tall, handsome man with black hair and light blue eyes looked my way and smiled. I fumbled with my spoon, wishin' that I were in another place, sittin' amongst familiar folks, wearin' a fine red dress with perfect seams, a stylish bustle, layers of flounces, and a silk bonnet.

"Bella," he said jest loud enough to hear over the clatter.

The edge of my dress caught on the chair and ripped when I tugged at it. Red-faced and breathless, I dropped my bowl on the table.

The girl sat down across from me. With graceful hands, she arranged her spoon and bowl in front of her. *How did she primp herself in the likes of such an intolerable place?* I fiddled with the frayed, yellow cloth upon my head and then hid my red, cracked hands beneath my skirt.

She peeked over her shoulder at the man and blushed openly before returnin' to the business of breakfast. "That's my husband, William. We were married two years ago." She plopped the brown gruel into her bowl and reached for a biscuit as if it were a fancy teacake.

"He seems nice," I said. "It must be difficult to see him from a distance."

She carefully ladled the runny slop into my bowl and glanced around the room. "We have our meetin' places," she whispered. "And I will not tell where."

I broke my biscuit in half. "Secret places and goin' off to be with that forbidden person is quite excitin'."

"I think we'll be leavin' in the spring. William's uncle wrote in a letter that he would send for us. He moved to Ohio." She took a small bite. "We must see ourselves clear of this place, and then we'll pay our debts." The dimple in her cheek vanished along with the sparkle in her eye. "We are quite fortunate to be able to come here durin' difficult times."

Nellie did not take notice of us. She made her way to the old folks, spoon feedin' some and sharin' her biscuit with others. She stirred a pinch of somethin' into Mahitable's cup.

I felt the scrapin' of spoons against bowls inside of my chest, and the occasional coughin' seemed to get louder. I tried to sing a song in my head, but I couldn't concentrate.

If I leaned forward a certain way, I could see Silas. A spirit of unknown origin seemed to push me towards him. I bit my nails and tried again to remember a particular song that we learnt in school. I found comfort in this, as hymns reminded me of Mother. I fought the persistent spirit and looked away from the window.

My eyes rested on Emily, who sat with her head bowed until Nellie approached her with bread and a cup of steamin' brew.

After we ate, we gathered in the great room waitin' to be assigned our daily chores. I never knew what to do from one day to the next.

Polly shouted, "Abigail, Bella, Sarah, Louisa, Nettie... you'll be in the sewin' room." She pointed down the hall.

I followed the women to a large room lined with sewin' machines and tables. I went straight to the fireplace. My fingers weren't good at sewin' on a warm day, never mind durin' a cold snap. I rubbed my hands together over the fire and smiled. It was better than launderin'. I turned to see a perfect view of the barn and yard outside the window. I watched Silas lead a draft horse towards the field.

Crack! Polly's stick whipped past my face and onto the sewin' table. "You won't git work done lookin' out the window!"

I took a deep breath and sat up straight. Tears threatened to spill while Polly set a yard of cloth down before me. I could see Bella out of the corner of my eye. She was singin' and stitchin' and bein' quite merry. "What are we supposed to do with this?" I asked meekly.

"You ain't been listenin'." Polly waved her stick in the air.

"I'm not feelin' well," I said.

"Well, you ain't no diff'rent from the rest." She glared at me with her black, birdlike eyes. "Bella, show her what to do."

Bella showed me how to sew the light blue night caps. Her dainty hands moved about on the material with confidence. I forced myself to look away from the window, but I could still see him.

Polly drifted in and out of the sewin' room, and every so often Asa came in to stoke the fire. Other than that, it was the same women sewin' together harmoniously. I tried to still my heart but found it impossible with Silas passin' by the window for a better part of the day.

The afternoon brought with it a gray mist and longin'. When Silas finally left, I wandered over to the window, pressin' my nose against the cold glass, leavin' a foggy smudge. Bella sang softly in the background.

I sat down beside her, riskin' Polly and the stick. "You are quite happy for someone locked up in this dismal place."

"I know that my days here are numbered." She smiled and examined her stitchin'. "I'll be with William again as it should be. We're burdened with debt. We find comfort knowin' the relief to be temporary, yet necessary. I make the best of it. You should do the same."

>⊨⊙ ⊙⊨<

We retired each night at eight o'clock. I was rightfully exhausted, yet I wanted to see Lizzy. If I went to the barn in the day, I would risk meetin' up with Silas or another farm boss. The women generally stayed inside, 'cept for goin' to the outhouse and in the summer when they worked in the gardens. Even though we were referred to as inmates, they told us that we weren't prisoners. However, it was understood that the doors were locked every night. The matrons' quarters were at the far end of the hall. Because of the loud moans and cries each night, I thought that I would be able to sneak out the sewin' room window unnoticed.

Mahitable finally stopped whimperin', and baby Joshua was asleep in Patience's arms. Nellie snored in a light, steady rhythm. I pulled the blankets away and waited. No one stirred. It was time. I held my breath and walked as quietly as possible on the creaky floorboards. My heart pounded when I reached for the door and felt a hand on my shoulder. I spun around to face Nellie.

"You frightened me."

She crossed her arms.

"Well, I was goin' to fetch the chamber pot." I looked down.

She did not move.

"Ah, you sense that I'm not tellin' the truth." I bit my thumbnail. "Alright, I'll tell you." I feared that I might wilt. "I'm goin' to the barn to see my cow, Lizzy. I haven't seen her since I came here. She's my only kin now."

The lines on Nellie's face softened when she smiled.

"I mean there's Old Gray Mare, but she's still at the Blake's farm," I said. "And my sister Sarah is away at the mills in Massachusetts. But Lizzy is here."

Nellie walked away. I thought that she returned to her bed, but she came back with a shawl draped over her shoulders. I started to head for the stairs, when she tugged at my arm. "What?" I asked, realizin' that my agitation was actually relief.

She lifted her shawl and gave me a stern look.

"I'll get my blanket and boots." She was right. I needed to wear more than a night dress.

I yanked the blanket from my bed and paused when Mahitable stirred. I waited until she resumed her snorin'.

Nellie and I walked together to the sewin' room. She didn't pay any mind that we might get caught and punished in an unthinkable manner. I expected someone to come out and shine a lamp in our faces. No one did. They were accustomed to Nellie wanderin' about.

She stopped by the window in the far corner of the room and watched as I tried to open a window by the fireplace. I struggled, and it didn't budge. "Does that window open?" I whispered.

She nodded. I went over and opened it with ease. I was met by a blast of frigid air. I sat on the sill for a moment before turnin' to help the old woman. She was not in sight.

I closed the window and hurried, narrowly escapin' a spill on the ice. I finally made it to the rear of the barn. My eyes adjusted to the darkness as I fumbled with the latch. I pushed the door ajar and stood quietly in the wide-open area. After bathin' in the aroma of hay, wood, and farm animals, I moved on.

I looked out the window to see the light of a lamp accompanied by the sound of footsteps crunchin' upon the frozen earth. A nearby horse snorted and stomped. I crouched into a corner and pulled my blanket over my head.

The door creaked open. I peered out from behind the blanket to see Nellie's silhouette in the glowin' lamp light. "It's you," I said. "How did you get a lamp and climb out of the window?"

She walked ahead, lightin' the way. My heart beat faster with each step as I followed behind her. A critter scampered out in front of me causin' a fright. I stepped back, and the creature wound its furry body around my ankles. "Miss Emily?" I gathered her in my arms and held her purrin' softness against my chest. "This is my friend from the Blake's farm. Moses must have rescued her from his vicious wife."

I handed the cat to Nellie, and she carried it as we made our way to the cows. There were at least twenty, most of them brown and white. Some were layin' down while others were standin'. Nellie hung the lamp on a hook. The mellow, golden light spilled forth, providin' much needed reassurance. Puzzled by the late night visitors, the cows stirred.

"Now, now, be still. It's only Nellie and me lookin' for Lizzy." I ran my hand over the back of a curious yearlin'. I squeezed through a tight knit group of cows before I saw her. "Lizzy! There you are!" I draped my arms around her warm neck and imprinted her scent upon the deepest part of myself.

Nellie weaved in and out of the herd, enjoyin' the gentle beasts. They responded differently to her, gatherin' around as though were a preacher about to give a sermon. I continued to watch her when Lizzy nudged me with her nose. Suddenly I became very tired. "Come on, Nellie. We must get back," I said and kissed Lizzy's head.

I led the way, stoppin' now and then to examine assorted tools that hung on beams and in chosen nooks. Papa said that every barn has its own unique character; you simply have to open your eyes and see.

Hopin' that Nellie wouldn't mind, I slipped through an open door, which would bring me to the blacksmith shop – the heart of the barn – as Grampa Wills would say. I spotted the well-used anvil and passed by shelves of hammers, rows of shovels, pitchforks, and hoes waitin' for handles. I rummaged through some odd bits and saw yet another room.

"What's in here?" I continued explorin' as Miss Emily found me again.

The door moaned at the light touch of my fingertips. I felt a cold air current when I pressed my face against the crack and looked into the blackness. The distinct fragrance of pine overwhelmed me.

At first the door resisted, but then I pushed it hard. It opened. I lifted the lamp over my head. A sawhorse and tools were scattered about in disarray. Someone left in a hurry. A tall stack of millboards reached the ceilin'. I slowly turned around. The light fell upon a long pine box set on the floor. I backed away.

Nellie waited in the doorway. I stumbled into a board propped against the wall. My thoughts turned to Silas and the other men when they buried the child. I supposed it was Mahitable's son.

I jumped when I heard a racket. Miss Emily leapt from a beam to a pine box. "Let's leave now, Nellie."

We wove our way through the maze of doorways and uneven sections of the barn. I darted across the yard, headin' straight for the window. Nellie tugged my arm. I followed her to the kitchen door in the back, not realizin' that it was unlocked the whole time. I hurried up the stairs.

"Thank you," I whispered. I pulled off my boots and slipped under the blankets. I squeezed Hope tight to my chest, closed my eyes, and attempted to erase the relentless images of pine boxes.

CHAPTER 50

Nellie – December 13, 1872

DARKNESS CAME EARLY in the Wintermaker Moon. The women did not leave the house when the thick white blanket of snow covered Our Mother. We waited patiently for the great rebirth.

Emily lost her spirit when they took her son. I brought her into the circle of mothers that share sorrow and seek healing.

The lamps in the hall shined in on Patience as she held her child to her breast. The other women were scattered around the room going in and out of sleep. They mistrusted the night and were too tired to weep. Mahitable wept softly, welcoming the cover of darkness, fearing the dream world and seeking visions of her son. Before her loss, she walked the good road.

Abigail sought after what she remembered to be beautiful and good. Her heart was dark after the loss of many. She hungered for truth and fought to stand in it. With her inner eye, she saw beyond what she could hold in her hand. Our spirits communed many winters before, when she became the caretaker of the doll. She knew the spirit born from the labor of my hands and elements of the earth from which it derived. She was a daughter, not of my own blood.

The song of the wind swept into the valley like a deep mourning chant. I waited for the vision that would carry me to dawn. Small branches tapped against the window of the big house, bringing me home to Cold River.

⟨⟩

The snow was deep. I walked on snowshoes into the woods, where wisdom lies within leaf and rock. I followed the path of a doe by the river's edge. Two white birches grew as one and creaked in the wind. Our eldest brother, the sun, broke through milk white clouds, and the dust of snow sparkled in the light.

Nanatasis! Searching Owl called into the fading day.

I blew my wooden whistle hard. The creaking birches grew loud.

I opened my eyes to see rising stars and the face of my husband.

⇢▶◉ ◉◀⇠

The creaking – no longer trees by the river – came from floorboards. A dark figure moved towards the door. It was Abigail. Her spirit was restless; she was not in harmony with the present moment. I approached, only to frighten her. She spoke false words. Her inner truth would emerge.

After her quiet rebellion passed, she told me of her cow and that she would go to the barn to see it. We covered in our blankets to keep warm and to fearlessly face the shadows of the unknown.

In her haste, she did not wait for me. She climbed out of the window. I carried a burning lamp and walked through the door. Only a brave and unwise girl would go into unfamiliar darkness.

I found her. She hid beneath her blanket. "It's you." Her round eyes reflected the light. "How did you get a lamp and climb out the window?" She stood before me shivering.

I walked before her, lighting the way. I knew not of her plan. A creature ran before us. I moved the lamp to see a cat familiar to her.

The reunion of Abigail and the cat brought gladness. I stroked the soft fur before we continued on. I followed and watched.

She passed through the cows and stopped and embraced the black and white cow that she called Lizzy. She had found another that was lost to her.

"Come on, Nellie. We must get back." She gave the cow a parting kiss.

Having met with her animal friends, she continued to explore the barn, led by the brave spirit of the night. She took the lamp. We went to where the men made shoes for horses. She moved the light in many directions.

She walked to the room where the white men prepared for the dead. She pushed open the heavy door. "What's in here?"

She saw the pine boxes. Thoughts of death and dying darkened her face. The cat leaped, and the light and shadows shook on the wall. She ran swiftly through the barn and to the house, where she stood waiting before the window. I continued to walk. She followed me into the kitchen. The coals burned hot in the stove.

CHAPTER 51

Silas – December 14, 1872

"SILAS, TAKE A few men with you to make more coffins. Now that it's winter, the fever will be creepin' in." Moses leaned against the barn door and cupped his hands around his pipe with a match stuck between his fingers. "Them old folks don't stand a chance." He frowned through a haze of smoke.

"We started one Friday," I said. "We jest need to make a top is all."

"We gotta' make at least a few a week from now 'til spring. It don't hurt to pile 'em up. I'd rather have too many than not enough. Eventually we'll use 'em."

"I 'spect you're right. I'll get Billy and Timothy." I blew on my cold, red hands. "They're good at workin' with wood."

He stirred his pipe with a match stick. "Jest git it done, son."

"Ayuh." I looked at the house.

"You're gonna' have to go in there to fetch Billy and Timothy. Like I said, ya ain't gonna' be able to avoid seein' Abigail forever. Besides, you're gettin' married in two weeks for Chrissakes."

My cheeks burned. "I ain't tryin' to avoid no one."

Moses laughed himself into a coughin' fit. "You can't fool me."

I went up to the house grittin' my teeth. I refused to take any guff from no one, includin' him. The heel of my boot slid across the icy step. I grabbed the rail, avoidin' a spill.

"You can't fool me, boy!" Moses yelled out from the barn.

I opened the door to be greeted by a surge of heat and the scent of wood smoke, lye, and bread. I leaned against the wall and waited a spell.

Polly burst into the kitchen. "Whatcha' want?" she asked, wipin' her hands on her apron.

"I'm lookin' for Billy Peavey and Timothy."

"They're haulin' wood into the woodshed off the kitchen." She shook her head. "Ain't no good reason why I know that and you don't." She left the room mutterin'.

My feet didn't cooperate one bit. I knew I needed to move, but I jest stood there like a scared schoolboy in disbelief that I was actually fightin' off tears.

I puffed up my chest, removed my hat, and headed for the muffled chatter of women and the hectic crashin' of kitchen utensils. Puttin' one foot in front of the other is what I was aimin' for.

I stopped dead in the doorway at the sight of Abigail leanin' over the table, rollin' out dough. My face heated. Everyone gawked at me as if I was standin' there naked.

She glowed with her rosy cheeks, a smidgeon of flour on her chin, and a crown of chestnut curls settin' atop her head. She managed to look like an angel in that vile yellow dress. Heck, she'd look pretty in a potato sack. She looked up quick like and continued on with the rollin' pin, takin' no notice of me.

I stumbled through the kitchen like a puppet with someone else pullin' the strings. I cleared my throat and bowed my head, bustin' past the fear to speak. "Mornin', ladies."

The whole place went quiet 'cept for Abigail's hummin'. The others jest froze. Polly slammed a crock on the table and gave me the evil eye.

"Jest bein' pleasant on a cold mornin'." I tried to smile.

Abigail paid me no mind and continued on hummin'. She glanced at me outta' the corner of her eye. I know. I saw her as plain as day.

I clenched my fists inside my pockets, diggin' my fingernails into the flesh of my palms. I followed the sound of tumblin' wood and hollerin' men. They lugged in enough wood to stack clear up to the ceilin'.

"Billy! Timothy!" I shouted.

Billy scratched his shiny, bald head and whined like a boy about to be whooped. "Yessah?"

I threw my shoulders back. That's how everyone shoulda' addressed me, by Jesus. "You and Timothy come with me." I looked around. "Where's Timothy?"

A clear stream of mucus ran from his nose into his mouth. "He's comin'." He stood hunched over with his head hung down, lookin' up at me so that you could see the whites of his eyes. He wiped the stringy slime on his hand.

The door crashed open, smackin' the wall. Timothy had near a dozen pieces of wood stacked in his arms. He dumped 'em onto the pile 'cept for a few that toppled over the side.

"You lookin' for me?" Bits of bark and chips stuck in his gray beard. He crossed his beefy arms across his chest and stared. I'd hate to come up against him in a fight. I seen him take on three men all at once at Jones's Tavern, knockin' 'em out cold. He could drink Daddy under the table on a good night.

"Ayuh." I too crossed my arms over my chest and quickly dropped 'em by my side. He mighta' thought that I was testin' his manhood. "First, pick up them logs, and then you and Billy Boy follow me."

I stopped when I heard Abigail hummin'. "We'll go the other way, so not to make a mess in the kitchen."

Outside, I pushed my way through men and wood piles in knee deep-snow. I was pleased to see Moses with Asa in the blacksmith shop. He wouldn't invite me to talkin'.

I opened the door to the coffin shop. "Start a fire. It's cold."

I saw somethin' white settin' on the floor by the toe of my boot. I bent down to get it. It was a handkerchief or somethin'. I unfolded it. My mouth went dry when I saw the initials, *AEH*, embroidered in the corner below a tattered butterfly. I held it to my face and inhaled her faint scent.

Timothy rooted around inside the potbelly stove in the corner of the room. "We'll go get some kindlin'."

I stuffed the dainty handkerchief into my coat pocket. "You do that."

The men left, and I pulled out the handkerchief, tryin' to sort it out. I traced my fingers over her initials.

I thought I heard footsteps. I looked up, and there was Moses standin' in the doorway starin' at me, so I shoved it back into my pocket.

"I'm bringin' Abigail's horse here next week. I ain't got no use for it."

"She won't have no use for it neither." I rubbed the soft cloth between my fingers.

"Well, come spring after she has the baby, she can come out and see it from time to time." He started in coughin'. "The poor girl ain't got nothin'."

"Are you gonna' tell her 'bout it?" I rubbed it some more.

"Nope." He turned around and left.

Billy came in with a bunch of kindlin', and Timothy balanced an armload of wood.

"You boys know what to do. Get to work. We need boxes in three sizes. We might need 'em faster than we can make 'em. I hope not." I sat down on a rickety stool. I almost fell over when a cat howled and leaped right out in front of me.

The men laughed. Timothy picked up the cat and rubbed behind its ears. "What's the matter, boss, afraid of a harmless cat?"

"You never mind and get to work." I kicked at a piece of wood on the floor and wound the handkerchief tightly around my fingers.

CHAPTER 52

Abigail – December 19, 1872

I FOUND IT difficult to imagine Christmas at the Carroll County Farm. I didn't think it possible to miss Sarah blastin' that horn of hers, but how I longed to hear even one pitiful note. We used to spend a full week bakin' merries and decoratin' the house with pine boughs and red ribbons. When Papa was alive, we journeyed through the woods to cut down a tree.

After Papa's death, Sarah and I took it upon ourselves to go into the woods and cut down our own tree. Mother waited with warm milk and sweets. It was an all-day affair to wander about in the deep snow, pick the best tree, and then cut it down with Papa's saw. We took turns draggin' it home, leavin' a path adorned with snow angels and speckled green pine needles.

Before fetchin' the tree, we spent many a night sittin' by the fire stringin' apples and special cranberries from Mr. Tibbetts' cousin in Cape Cod. My favorite decoration was the abandoned bird's nest that I found in the barn. Sarah played festive music on her cornet and even played for the special church service. Together we sang hymns and Christmas carols and planned for the annual gatherin' of neighbors to share wassail and sweet cakes. Sarah always wanted to start a song, but Mother would not have it because she was the unmistakable leader when it came to the business of singin'.

My circumstances seemed far worse than when I first arrived and became more unbearable with each passin' day. My first concern was that I had not heard a word from Sarah. I sent her four letters since my arrival and had yet to get a response. If it were someone else, I would understand, but it was not of her character to forget about me and not fuss about my existin' conditions.

The mood of the folks seemed generally depressin' without much change in the daily chores. I agreed with Patience, stretchin' in the mornin' did not prevent me from bein' sore. My hands, always wet and cold, had become raw from lye. I despised doin' the laundry most of all, but if I uttered a word in protest, I would feel Polly's stick upon my shoulders. I swear she could sense when I was about to have an outburst. She seemed to be waitin' behind me, so I held my tongue as Mother would have advised.

Mary worked hard to lift our spirits. She seemed to be stuck somewhere between the matrons and us inmates. She talked sweet but didn't put up with any nonsense. She stood up to the bosses, yet she didn't raise her voice, and she always had a plan.

After a long debate between Polly and Miss Noyes, they concluded that we would start stringin' apples followin' the supper chores. Patience and Bella buzzed with the notion that we would be makin' somethin' for ourselves. Emily simply sat with her hands pressed together lookin' scared and continually checkin' the door in hopes that it would fly open and her boy would return.

The child inside of me continued to move and grow and poke me as if I needed remindin'. I saw no point in tryin' to hide it. God would never allow me to forget. I prayed every night. My misshapen stomach and the fact that I wore the yellow dress, the symbol of a whore, was a sharp reminder. Although, Patience said that she couldn't even tell that I had a baby inside of me, 'cause she looked like she had a watermelon inside of her from the start. Nellie acted peculiar from time to time when she would place her hand on my stomach, close her eyes, and then jest walk away. Of course, I didn't understand her, but I had no fear.

A woman shrieked from the great room. Other folks carried on with their business, but I felt every inch of that scream. I walked closer.

I stood behind the doorway and peeked through the crack. A heavy woman, wearin' a badly worn shawl and boots with holes in both of them, snorted like a bull backed into a corner. She had a gray smudge on her cheek, and she wore a crumpled, black hat with brown patches peelin' off one side.

"You let go of me." She spat in Miss Noyes's face.

Miss Noyes hauled off and whacked her with her open hand right across the face. "You'll never do that again." She wiped the white foam from her cheek with her apron.

With one hand coverin' her face, the woman teetered a bit before spittin' again, this time hittin' Miss Noyes on the front of her dress. "Burn in Hell!" She cowered in anticipation.

"Polly... where are you?" Miss Noyes grabbed the woman's elbow and twisted it behind her back. "This one's trouble."

The woman started kickin' Miss Noyes right in the shins, and the two of them fell to the floor like roly-poly pigs. I secretly hoped that she would get Miss Noyes a good one.

Miss Noyes always carried on, lettin' the new people know who was in charge. I looked out the window, as I had acquired the habit of doin'. I hadn't seen Silas for a while.

I pulled my sleeve down over my hand and scraped the beautiful ice patterns on the bottom of each pane of glass, makin' the outside world a dreamlike vision. A string of black spindly trees backed by several rows of pointed, green firs lined the graceful hills.

Polly seemed to be more agreeable on the account of Christmas. I thought that I might get permission to cut down a small tree, but I realized that draggin' a tree into this lifeless place would not change a thing. I blew on the glass and rubbed it again with my fist. The life inside of me nudged. *Was it possible to make Christmas merry in this hellish place?*

It seemed like an entire lifetime had passed since the day I fought and kicked at Polly and Miss Noyes. They didn't know what it felt like to lose everything near to your heart, to be standin' in the stench of the place, with people pullin' at you, takin' away your last bit of dignity. I had an urge to hug the vulgar woman, the crude old soul that I would have avoided a few months earlier. I wanted to fight Polly and Miss Noyes myself, but it wasn't my fight. I already had my battles and didn't have enough strength for hers too.

When she caught me lookin', she stopped fightin' for an instant. It was one of those moments when all things around you sort of slow down and hang in the air, like the restless fog that lingers before rollin' in over the hay field in the mornin'. She turned her attention to Polly and Miss Noyes, threw her head back, and let out another scream, makin' my insides rattle.

Nellie shuffled up behind me and we watched together. It took two of them to bring her down. She clawed and twisted her body until Miss Noyes raised her fist and slugged her under the left side of her jaw, causin' her to faint dead away. I started to run to her, but Nellie grabbed my arm.

"Why not?" I tried to wiggle away.

She held tighter.

"We must go to her aid." I shook free of Nellie. "Two against one isn't fair."

The look in her eyes outgripped her hand on my arm.

"Fine." I rolled my eyes.

Polly and Miss Noyes gave each other the nod of victory and pulled the half-conscious woman to her feet. Her eyes fluttered, and a trickle of blood dripped from the corner of her mouth and onto her filthy shawl. They each took an arm and dragged her towards the stairs. It was time for her to put on the blue dress. She was too old to be with child.

The scruffy woman stared at us as she went by. Nellie and I stood with our shoulders touchin'. We watched her, silently knowin' that soon we would hear all about her, where she came from and where she was or wasn't goin'.

The sky darkened, and a flurry of fine snow blew outside the window. I pulled my shawl around my shoulders and decided that I would try to make merry with at least one small pine bough. Leavin' Nellie behind, I barely touched the latch when the door burst open with a fiery gust of wind. I gasped when I found myself face to face with Silas. I stepped to the left. He stepped to the right. I stepped to the right. He stepped to the left. Only inches apart, we looked away from each other, both wishin' to escape the awkward dance.

"Abigail! Where are you goin'?" He finally managed to speak.

"Excuse me. I'm not goin' far... only to the edge of the field for a pine bough, sir." I kept my eyes down and pinched my cape around the base of my neck. "Now if you don't mind steppin' aside." I ducked under his arm and dashed down the icy walkway.

The air was sharp and thin. I stopped and leaned against the barn, keepin'
my back to him while he continued to stare. I was surprised that I managed to
utter a word. I jumped when the life inside poked, like a compass pointin' me
in the right direction, any direction, urgin' me to get on with it.

Except for the women shoutin' upstairs, I heard not a sound. I was tempted to listen in on all of the commotion, but I changed my mind and continued
to venture into the night. I paused where the lamplights cast long, sparklin'
rectangles on the snow. I looked up at the tiny snowflakes that swirled from
endless black tunnels, racin' towards me.

With outstretched arms, I spun around, makin' my way down the trodden
path through the fresh, virgin snow. I closed my eyes and held my hand out
to where Sarah would have been and fell straight back into the snow. I imagined her laughter. "Abby, you must fall back neatly or your snow angel will be
spoiled."

I extended my arms and legs, moved them back and forth across the snow,
makin' an impression of an angel beneath me. I stood up carefully, turned,
and looked at the angel. It was perfect, certainly the most perfect snow angel
I had ever seen. Hot tears streamed down my face. The shakin' started in my
knees and travelled quickly throughout my body. One solitary angel brought
forth more pain than I thought possible. I wrapped my arms around myself
and squeezed tightly while the snow started to blow sideways.

I turned away from the angel. *This angel cannot exist without her sister.* I fell
back into the snow beside my angel and made another. I stopped with my arms
above my head and feet out to the side. "Sarah. Oh Dear God, what good is
it to have one angel when there were always two?" I lay still with tears flowin'
from a deep place that was without end.

I pressed my hands against my hot eyelids and tried to stop convulsin'. I
couldn't. The life inside poked, but it didn't matter. When his strong arms slid
beneath me, I cried harder. I clung tightly to his neck and buried my face in his
shoulder, into his musky shirt. All was quiet 'cept for the flurry of wind that
whistled recklessly through the tops of the trees.

He pulled a handkerchief from his pocket and dabbed my tears. "Please,
don't cry."

"I'm fine." I released my arms from his neck and squirmed away. "Where did you find this?" I snatched my handkerchief from his hand.

"It was in the barn, in the woodworkin' shop."

"Oh." I looked down at my wildly shakin' knees, fearin' that I might collapse.

"You should be careful and not go out to the barn. It's off limits to…"

"Inmates?" I forced a laugh. "Go on and say it."

"No." He stuffed his hands into his pockets. "I don't want nothin' to happen is all."

"I will be fine." I spun around and stomped up the pathway. I looked back at him. "You spoiled my snow angels." I kicked the snow off my boots, opened the door, and stopped. My body tingled. Senseless laughter drifted down the stairs. The ragin' heat of the wood fire and the smell of apples and urine washed over me. The wind caught a hold of the door, closin' out the wintery night that left me dead with sorrow. The garden gate would never open again.

CHAPTER 53

Silas – December 19, 1872

A WOMAN'S SCREAM echoed over the frozen hills. *Another wild one.* I watched the shadows of a rumpus through the window and heard more cuss words than I cared to remember.

Polly and Miss Noyes grappled with the woman, one of the Smith clan from Effin'ham. I knew her husband, Frank, before he up and left. Some say that he hopped on a westbound train to work on the railroad. No one heard from him again. She let out another scream, carryin' on like most all of 'em did when they were taken to the farm against their will.

I usually weren't at the farm after dark, but I agreed to tend to the fires and watch over folks while George recovered from the sore throat. I scooped a bucket of grain for the cows and looked out over the snow-covered fields that matched the grayish clouds overhead.

I liked it when the cold air stung my cheeks, keepin' me from driftin' away with my thoughts. All the fussin' and bickerin' about the weddin' got to poundin' in my head. I was thinkin' that it didn't matter much if I wore a fine suit or my work trousers. Jessie wanted me to go to a tailor and such, but I didn't see the purpose of that jest to stand in her parlor with friends and family.

I went into the cows' pen and dumped grain into the trough. My favorite time in the barn was jest before nightfall when the animals was all tuckered out and gettin' settled.

Abigail's cow stood out, bein' the only black and white one in the herd. She nudged me and stomped her foot, demandin' to know what was a doin'.

"I know. She'll be fine. You wait and see." I scratched her head and then returned to the grain bin. I thought about Moses bringin' Abigail's horse to the farm, not that it would do a lick of good. Old Gray Mare was a fine horse in her better days.

I looked up at the house. It was all quiet again. I s'posed they wore her down and was ready to bring her to the women's quarters, where she'd take it all in. The fact that she had arrived at the County Farm was a turnin' point. For some it was a nightmare and for others a great relief to have a bed, shelter, and a meal. This woman was probably happy for that, but jest ornery by nature.

I moseyed through the barn with lantern in hand. I knew every nook in that barn and could find my way without any light at all. I tossed the last of the grain in to the cows and headed for the chickens.

Now they was a different story. They marched from the yard right on into the coop jest a hair before sunset. They have their peckin' order and don't need the likes of folks tryin' to manage 'em. Nope. I learned that early on. After spendin' a good part of an evenin' chasin' a buff rooster and red hen around the yard, Daddy hollered, "Whatcha' you doin', boy? You don't have to herd them chickens; they do fine roostin' all by themselves!" From then on, I made sure that the door to the coop was open. They went in one by one and perched on the roosts.

When I approached the chickens, I was met by a slight rustle, feather against feather, cooin' and scratchin'. A red cochin watched me with one drowsy eye.

"Whatcha' lookin' at?" I poked a stick into the top layer of ice that formed on the water. I leaned against the wall. "Damn, I'm gonna' have to go inside before too long."

I latched the door of the coop. I knew that Asa made sure that the men buttoned up the pigs and horses, but I thought I'd see to it jest the same. I took my time walkin' down to the other end of the barn. It was quiet, and everything was in order.

I whistled and stumbled along the uneven floor on my way to the pigsty. The stench burned the back of my nose and into my throat. In addition to grain, we fed 'em all the leftovers from the kitchen, makin' 'em the healthiest pigs in all of Ossipee. When I opened the gate, two of 'em bumped my leg with their snouts, while another one nibbled on my boot. They was as content as pigs could be and had fresh water. I had nothin' left to do but go to the house.

My stomach rumbled. I hadn't eaten nothin' since midday, when I hid in the back of the kitchen and put away some of Polly's salt pork and beans. I couldn't bring myself to goin' into the dinin' room and seein' Abigail in her yellow dress with her chestnut curls growin' like fiddleheads around her pretty face. I knew I had no business thinkin' in such a way, but it was true. I simply couldn't figure out why she took up with Weston and never told me or anyone else about the man who had his way with her by the railroad tracks. I'd have surely beaten him senseless if she'd jest told me.

I stopped outside the barn and watched the snow flurries for a spell. I brushed the bits of grain and hay from my trousers. It was my duty to go inside. The wind whipped my face as I stood starin' at the house. I paused. *She's probably not even downstairs.* I yanked on the door handle, nearly fallin' on the icy step. There she was all bundled up and ready to go outside. *There are rules. She can't jest go out.*

I didn't know what was a doin'. She darted back and forth tryin' to escape. "Abigail Hodgdon, where are you goin'?" I cleared my throat. I hadn't ever addressed her like that.

"Excuse me, but I am not goin' far. Jest down to the edge of the field for a pine bough, sir." She fluttered her dark eyelashes.

I searched for words and found none. Unable to trust my legs or my feelin's, I leaned against the door for support.

"Now if you don't mind steppin' aside." She ducked under my arm and fled. I wouldn't have let any other inmate walk out like that right in front of me, but it was as if I was pinned down by an ox.

I closed the door; the heat of the wood stove scorched my face. Folks scurried this way and that. I looked at the clock. It was too late for all the fuss.

"Damn fool." Polly stomped past me with a bowl filled with bruised apples.

I kept my eye on her 'til she disappeared into the kitchen. *I should go get her. It's cold. She ain't s'posed to leave the house, 'specially at night.* The ox pressed harder.

"Come now. Let's begin." Mary led a procession of women into the kitchen.

Mary was a pleasin' woman, quite clear and happy. Folks on all sides took a likin' to her. She helped with the inmates, even though she was one, and she kept Polly and Miss Noyes from killin' someone.

I dragged the stubborn ox with me into the kitchen. A handful of women sat around the table with the apples and pieces of string. Polly rolled her eyes.

"What's a doin', Polly?"

"Mary talked me into stringin' apples," she said.

"Ayuh." I nodded. "It's Christmas."

"You never mind." She pointed at me. "They can do this until eight o'clock, not a moment longer." Her eyes were small and dark and lost under the deep lines that creased her forehead.

"I'll check the fires." I ducked into the woodshed off the back of the kitchen, not waitin' for a response.

I loaded up my arms 'til I couldn't hold another stick of wood and re-turned to the kitchen. I dropped the wood into the box. When I stoked the fire, the heat from the deep bed of coals singed the hair on my knuckles. I stayed for not more than a minute to watch the yellow flames lick between the spaces of the perfectly round logs.

Miss Noyes and that Smith woman continued hollerin'. Somethin' moved outside the window. It looked like a figure in front of the barn. I looked through the ice-covered glass.

Seein' it was Abigail, I sprinted across the room and out the front door. I came close to fallin' at least twice on my way to the barn.

She cried and screamed, layin' in the snow with her hands coverin' her face. Everythin' raced through my mind. *Maybe the baby is comin'. Maybe she got hurt.*

I gathered her in my arms. Her body shook, and her cry sounded like a wounded animal. She jest clung to me. Without givin' too much thought, I reached into my pocket and pulled out the handkerchief that I found in the barn. I wiped the tears from her face. I started to lose my balance and stumbled towards the barn. "Please… don't cry." I felt my own tears risin' from inside my chest.

She wiggled away. "I'm fine." She tossed her head the way she always used to. "Where did you find this?" She snatched the handkerchief away from me.

"It was in the barn, in the wood shop." I felt boyish and meek.

"Oh." The wind blew hard and she looked away.

I wished that she would look at me. I had to say somethin'. "You should be careful and not go out to the barn. It's off limits to… "

"Inmates?" She stuck out her chin, as I had seen her mother do so many times.

"No." I swallowed. "I jest don't want nothin' to happen." The words inside me refused to budge. They was trapped. I no longer tried to speak.

She stormed towards the house and stopped in the doorway. The light framed her rounded belly beneath the yellow dress and cast an angelic glow around her curls. A shriek of laughter from the insane folks on the second floor caused me to stiffen. First one, then two, and then at least five or six of 'em laughed and shouted along with the howlin' wind as it wailed the door shut with a forceful crash.

CHAPTER 54

Nellie – December 19, 1872

THE BIRDS CIRCLED high above. Father Sky was clear and blue during the Wintermaker Moon. The trees shook in the wind. It was cold, but we were warm in our clothing made from hides.

The blood on the white snow was like a bold red flower. We gave thanks to the mountain spirit and to the spirit of the rabbit. We moved from the woods to the clearing.

I followed my husband's tracks in the snow. The small black and white birds called, and the tapping birds drummed in tall trees. The song of Our Mother brought about thoughts of my earth mother who I would see again in the Otherworld. The rabbit hung from my husband's pack. Its silken fur parted in the wind.

We walked along the snowy banks of Cold River, towards our home. A wisp of gray smoke rose from the chimney. The fire still burned. *We're almost there Nanatasis.* My husband took long, quick strides.

He reached the place where we made fires to prepare meat and hides. He shed his pack, removed his snowshoes, and rushed into our home. My heart soared in his presence.

We honored the change of season with a feast and the exchange of one gift. He no longer belonged to the black robes, the ones who celebrate the birth of their dead king.

My friend the crow landed on the long branch of a maple, looking first with one flickering eye and then the other. In the light, his black feathers shined green, purple, and blue. His wing brushed against me as it passed from the world of my dreams to the present dimming light of day. His cry became the scream of a woman.

⋄═◉ ◉═⋄

There was much anger and fear when the new ones arrived. The lady with the hair the color of a fox brought pain with her hands and her words. The woman in the great room had the strength of a warrior and the ways of a fool. She spoke words with little meaning, born of fear.

The one with the hair the color of a fox called for Polly. I stood with Abigail to protect her. She wanted to save others because she believed that she could not save herself. She watched the battle. I watched her.

I moved closer to Abigail as the fighting woman took the final blow and fell to the floor. She wanted to run to the beaten woman, to wake her from the shadows. I held her back.

She was unknowing. "Why not, Nellie?" She spoke my Christian name, a name required by White Man's law to become the wife of Searching Owl.

I held firm, and I looked at her, brown eyes to brown eyes. It was then that she knew. She surrendered.

We remained silent as the beaten one passed. I would give her medicine. She wore blue, the color of a woman without a child in the womb.

I waited. The kitchen fire burned bright. The women made symbols with apples to honor the birth of their dead king. The sounds of struggle faded as the woman lost her will.

Abigail left the house and went into the darkness. I did not follow, for I knew she would return. I would wait for the beaten woman to find her place.

I looked upon the woman as she lay crying. I went to my place of many medicines, removed the board, and reached inside the floor. In darkness I searched. My fingers traced the damp outer edges of bark. I broke a piece. I felt for my cup and pouch that held dried yarrow flower and leaf. I snapped a small twig from a hemlock branch.

With cup and pouch in hand, and medicines in my belt, I passed the crying woman. I went to the kitchen, where women gathered around the apples. I poured hot water from the kettle into my cup. I rolled and crushed the flowers and leaf into the steaming water. I stripped the hemlock needles from the twig, added them, and stirred with the bare twig.

"I s'pose you're gonna' tend to Ole Martha Smith, ain't ya?" Polly's voice was harsh.

"If it weren't for Nellie, more people would be dead 'round here than there already is," Patience said. She was in her place away from the table with her baby cradled in her arms.

"You jest tend to your own matters," Polly said.

I left the women and the apples and the warmth of the fire. The smell of sweet earth medicine grew as I neared the crying woman. I stood in the light for her to know of my presence.

She sat on her bed sack facing away. She listened. I took another step closer. With great effort, she climbed to her feet and looked into my eyes. "What do you want?"

I held out the steaming cup and moved closer. The laughter of men, who spoke words with no meaning, drifted down the hall like the calling of loons on Bitawbagok.

"Whatcha' got there?" she asked.

I waved my hand over the warm hemlock oil and yarrow.

The light from the hall showed the wounds on her face. The laughter came longer and louder. She spoke with fear that tried to replace anger.

"I ain't seen you for a long time. You used to wander 'round the village. People said you was a witch. I thought you was dead." She did not move.

I waited in silence.

"I don't drink nothin' unless I know what it is." She turned away. "If you're a witch like some folks say you is, then why should I trust ya?"

I brought the cup to my lips. The tea was good and hot. I would gain her trust.

She took the drink I offered. Her hands shook. "I s'pose if it don't hurt you, then it won't hurt me or nothin'." She drank swiftly. "I ain't tasted nothin' like this before. It ain't too awful bad."

I found the inner bark of white pine in my belt and rubbed it my hands.

"Now what are ya fixin' to do?" She stepped back.

I touched my face in the same place where she had wounds on hers. I pressed the bark to my skin and then pointed at her.

She did the same. "It hurts." Tears returned.

I pressed the bark to her cheek and placed her hand over it.

She sat on the bed with the bark on her bruised flesh. Her gaze turned to the ghost shadows on the wall. Small grains of hemlock lined the empty cup that warmed my hands. Soon she would find her way to where life begins, where visions live in the dream world.

CHAPTER 55

Abigail – December 25, 1872

A STREAM OF frigid air whistled through a wide crack in the outhouse wall. I looked out at the pinkened sky, and a shiver ran down my back. I tried to push away memories of hot chocolate, corn bread with pumpkin butter, and the sound of Mother's laughter. When I stood up to fix my leggin's, I heard a ruckus comin' from behind the barn. I pressed my face up to the nubby wood and peered through the crack.

"Heeyah!" The quiet mornin' was interrupted by the clatter of horses in the barn and the echo of Moses's voice. I wondered why he was there on Christmas.

The door groaned when I pushed it. I inhaled the crisp air. "Your curiosity always gets the best of you Abigail Elizabeth," Mother used to say.

I held on to the door and let it close slowly to avoid that telltale creakin'. I waited, and then I took a few baby steps on the pathway and stopped, hopin' to hear somethin'. However, Moses barely spoke above a whisper. My heart thumped when a door slammed. I dashed to the back of the barn and watched him lumber up to the big house.

It was warm durin' the better part of the previous day and then chillin' to the bone again at night, causin' a blanket of ice to cover everything. To avoid takin' a spill, I slid my boots across the crusty snow without liftin' them. After a quick look around, I opened the door jest enough to slip into the barn. I leaned against the wall.

Moses's boots crunched on the ice as he departed. I pulled my shawl tightly around my shoulders and held my breath. I thought about hidin', but my feet remained firmly planted. The tinklin' of harness bells and wooshin' of his sleigh broke the silence. I gathered my wits about me and stood starin' at the sparklin' flecks of hay that filtered through the cracks in the beams.

I wandered through the mazes in the barn, which had become familiar to me. The hens squabbled, and the rooster that sounded like Pearl stopped midway through a crow when I passed by the coop. A deep pitched drone came from the cows, followed by the clankin' of thick iron bars. I ignored my instinct to offer Christmas cheer to Lizzy and went to the horse stalls.

The beasts stomped and snorted when I rounded the dark corner. The silhouette of horses' heads, framed by the risin' sun, bobbed up and down in silent harmony. I walked past a line of stalls, givin' an occasional stroke on a soft nose, while curious about my own sense of urgency. I forced myself to stop in front of a white and black speckled mare. She nudged me when she raised her head. I offered some stray pieces of hay that I picked up from the floor. Her warm breath moistened my palm. "Merry Christmas," I whispered.

I had taken too long. It was daybreak when I went to the outhouse. I had to get back to the big house without anyone realizin' that I was at the barn. Three heavy thumps shook the floor from behind. I turned towards the rows of stalls on the other side. I thought that surely my eyes were deceivin' me. It looked like Old Gray Mare tossin' her silky mane and murmurrin' like she always did.

It was no mistake. I ran to her and threw my arms around her neck. Joyful tears rushed like a river, and I didn't attempt to stop them. Moses did tell me that he would get Old Gray Mare to the farm, but I didn't expect that he would keep his word.

Laughter and voices twittered from outside along with the steady squeakin' of the outhouse door. I kissed Old Gray Mare on the nose and headed back into the heart of the barn, promisin' that I would return at the earliest opportunity. The sun blinded me when I stepped outside. Forgettin' about the ice and simply hurryin' to get to the outhouse, my feet went out from under me.

I sat on the ground waitin' for the usual commotion, but no one paid me any mind. My left wrist throbbed. I moved it around and knew that it wasn't broken, only cut a bit from the ice.

I got to my feet and slid across the ice to the side of the outhouse. I waited until Lidie closed the door and for the path to be clear. I coughed loudly. "Lidie? Are you about finished with your business?"

"I jest got in here. Don't be rushin' me."

"Merry Christmas." Thinkin' 'bout Old Gray Mare brought forth a smile.

"I ain't celebratin'," she replied flatly.

I turned and walked towards the house, unwillin' to permit a soul to spoil my cheer.

"I said I ain't celebratin'. Whatcha say to that?" she grumbled from the outhouse.

"Good mornin'." I nodded at Betty as she slid down the path on her bottom.

"Good mornin'." Her soiled, yellow dress flapped in a wind gust, exposin' her holey leggin's. The women wore yellow even after the child inside was gone, which was the fortunate case for Betty after the seemingly uneventful loss of her child jest a week before. I imagined that folks wanted to remember the sinners and keep them separate from the others.

Polly took charge, as Miss Noyes was visitin' family. There were helpers from the Methodist church fixin' breakfast and such. I walked inside, tryin' to conceal my unusual gladness. I passed Nellie on the stairs. "Merry Christmas."

She stopped and smiled. And then she reached over and wiggled her fingers through my hair before returnin' to her methodical steps.

Patience sat on the board nursin' baby Joshua. "Where on earth 'ya been?"

"I went out for a short walk." I straightened my bed sack and tucked Hope under the foul blanket that I had learned to appreciate.

"It ain't a warm summer day or nothin'." She shifted the child onto her shoulder. "And besides, we ain't s'posed to wander outside."

"Maybe I like the winter." I turned away and primped my undersized curls. "And I think that we can take some liberties if we're mindful."

She shook her head as if I was one of those senile folks. I didn't take kindly to her judgment. I smoothed my hand down over my dress, leavin' a trail of spotted blood from my wrist. I felt a pang in my chest as I thought that

I wanted to look my best. I blushed and attempted to erase Silas's face from my thoughts. Besides, it made no sense for him to be at the County Farm on Christmas. I walked towards the stairs. *He doesn't matter.*

Somewhat lively chatter replaced the usual faint murmur that blended with the clangin' of plates and forks. We were served a special chicken dinner with potatoes, beans, biscuits, strawberry jam, and fruit. The Methodists were friendly, but careful not to look us in the eye. After we cleaned our plates, Polly herded most of us into the great room. The wooden chairs were placed in rows in a semi-circle around the fireplace. I sat with Nellie on one side and Betty on the other.

Mrs. McCormack, one of the Methodists, clasped her hands together and spoke to us in the same manner in which one speaks to children. "Now we're gonna' sing some carols." Strands of gray locks fell onto her wide forehead. She wore a dark woolen skirt and a green apron with very long strings. "I will lead." Her pinched face turned a deep shade of red when she smiled.

After a time of singin' traditional Christmas songs, some of the other women of the church gave us each a neatly bound Bible and a bright red Durgin apple.

Polly, on her best behavior, stood in the middle of us tryin' to conceal her discomfort, as kindness was a stranger to her. "Now you have time to do as you please." Her voice was unnatural without the shrillness.

We all sat there for a spell, not quite comfortable openin' what we knew to be a book, as some of our books were taken from us when we first arrived. I did learn, however, that havin' a book was possible, providin' that one did not make such a fuss of it.

Finally, folks started millin' about. Some of the old men played checkers and others, even though most could not read, leafed through their new Bibles. Mother used to say that no matter whether we are old or young, if we hold fast the profession of our faith without waverin', we will be prepared when it is time to die.

Isaac Weeks stared longingly at his apple before he put it up to his toothless mouth. He dropped it, and it rolled along the floor and rested next to the toe of my boot. I bent over and picked it up. He sat still lookin' at the floor, pinin' away silently for the apple. I went over to him and set it on his lap. He made a moanin' sound, and a puddle formed on the floor by his feet. I took a few steps back and bumped into my chair, and then I dragged it up close to the fire. I took to shinin' my apple on the skirt of my dress.

The apple crunched when I bit into it, and the juice dripped onto my new Bible. I wrinkled my nose and stuffed the apple into my pocket to give to Old Gray Mare later that night.

I gazed into the fire on that bittersweet Christmas day. Nellie stood behind me with her weathered brown hand on my shoulder. The joy of seein' my horse vanished into the loss of all of those who I once loved, those wilted flowers, rattlin' in the frozen earth of my forbidden garden. The ache soon became what sustained me.

CHAPTER 56

Silas – December 28, 1872

WE WAS ON the road early. The massive snowdrifts blown along by the wind made it nearly impossible to pass. Harness bells echoed over white powdered fields as the team of rust colored draft horses hauled the sleigh. Their black, ice peppered manes shook with each step. I held tight to my hat and buried my face into the collar of my frock coat. Moses scowled openly. We sat shoulder to shoulder in the front seat, and Mrs. Blake and my folks huddled under woolen blankets in the back.

I fancied the notion of spendin' the rest of my days with Jessie, to no longer be a witness to Daddy's drunkenness and Mamma's feeble excuses. Although he was referred to as a survivor, to me he died some years before. I didn't know the broken man who returned home to us, the one who had lost his own compass and ability to stand in every possible manner.

"If we get through this damn blizzard, it'll be a miracle." Moses ducked under a snow-laden branch, keepin' his eyes on the road ahead. "You shoulda' waited 'til spring."

"It weren't my idea to get married now. Jessie and her folks wanted a Christmas weddin'!" I shouted into the wind and gripped the seat as the sleigh lunged forward.

"Soon as the ground thaws, they'll start buildin'. With all the men that Doc Gilman intends to hire, it won't take long," he said. "Course it'll be a bit different livin' with the Gilmans."

"Ayuh." I wiped my nose on the back of my glove and looked away from the rubble of the Hodgdon farm. The dim golden sunlight tried to break through a cluster of clouds while a handful of crows cackled and cawed, bringin' me back to the moment. One of 'em stopped to preen on a mound of snow that covered the chimney. "It sure is perlexin' how things can change."

"Yes, it is," Moses mumbled. "We both know you got a soft spot for Abigail. You still ain't good at hidin' it." He tugged the reins. "But you gotta' do what's best for you."

Preferrin' silence to all that talkin', I didn't say nothin'. My eyes watered in the gusty wind.

"This is a perfect chance to have the good life: a pretty wife and a well-to-do family that takes a likin' to you." He sniffed. "Poor Abigail didn't have a chance. First her sister up and left, then the fire, and her mother dyin'. All that after bein' raped."

"She shoulda' come forward." I thought of her warm body pressed against mine when I picked her up. She weren't heavy at all. I figured if she was carryin' my child, she'd be a bit heavier and showin' her condition. It was nearly six months before when we was intimate.

"I s'pect she was scared," he said.

"When will the child be born?" I asked as the crow swooped in front of us and then off into the woods.

"She said in April or May." He snapped the reins. "You got plenty to think about. Unless you got somethin' ya ain't told me."

I tapped my fingers on my leg... *six, seven, eight, nine*. "Like I said, we was familiar once." I cleared my throat. "At a barn dance. That's it."

He squinted and his voice deepened. "Are you sure about that?"

"Course I'm sure. It was in June, so if she's havin' that baby in April or May, it ain't mine."

The sleigh jerked to a halt. We was the first ones on the road since the storm started, so the horses muscled their way through a snowdrift. They pounded their hooves into the frozen earth, finally regainin' their rhythm.

"By the sounds of it, she got around, though she seems like a good Christian girl."

"She is." I started in sweatin' in spite of the cold. "When we was familiar, it was the first time for her. She ain't no whore, Moses."

"Well, she might not be a whore as you see it, but she fornicated with you, then she claims the man at the railroad tracks had his way with her, and then there's Weston Jones." He paused. "All in such a short time, ain't that somewhat immoral?"

I stiffened. "How do you know she was with Weston?"

He stared straight ahead. "I jest do."

"Well, it don't matter. I ain't the father of no child and today's my weddin' day," I said. "So what's the purpose of all this talk 'bout Abigail?" I looked back at Mamma, Daddy, and Mrs. Blake all heaped together and shiverin'.

"That's right, son." He slapped my knee. "We're gonna' celebrate. You got yourself a fine woman."

I worked up a smile, even though I despised the thought of that baby bein' someone else's and not mine.

We arrived at Water Village. The snow let up some, but the wind continued to shake its angry fist. We passed the church and turned onto the Gilman's road. Even though it neared eight o'clock in the mornin', the murky clouds and the glow of lamps through frost covered windows made it seem like night.

We stopped. I slung my sack over my shoulder and climbed down from the sleigh. I helped Mamma, Daddy, and Mrs. Blake, while Moses unhitched the horses and led 'em into the barn.

Mamma, who seemed more like my child than my mother, gripped my arm real tight. We made our way to the house. Daddy trailed along behind, still vacant from the hard cider that he polished off the night before. He'd jest as soon fall on his backside than let anyone help him.

I stepped out of the cold and into the hot, stuffy room. Mrs. Leighton sat on the piano bench with her face up close to the music, lickin' her lips and plunkin' on the keys. Pastor Leighton nodded his head as he spoke with Doc Gilman.

The room was festive with the likes of pine boughs and white ribbons strung with cranberries, apples, and cinnamon sticks. A feast of pies, cakes, and merries covered the table. The scent of bacon, chocolate, coffee, and wood smoke hung thick in the air.

A strikin' young woman stood next to the fireplace. She was wearin' a fancy, blue dress. She had them green eyes like Jessie and black, shiny hair piled up high on her head. She fiddled with her pearl necklace and stared into the cracklin' fire.

Mrs. Gilman rushed over to me. "Good morning. The special day is upon us."

"It is a fine day, indeed." I stuffed my hands in my pockets.

"I'd like you to meet Margaret. She's my niece from Arlington, Massachusetts." She cleared her throat. "She's the maid of honor."

"A pleasure to meet you, ma'am." I bowed.

Then Sally Smith wandered over. She worked for the Gilmans. I weren't used to seein' her away from the County Farm. She took my hat and grinned, displayin' that her front tooth was missin'. I found myself smilin' at the sight of her freckled face all lit up and her kinky pumpkin colored hair goin' this way and that. I was accustomed to the small, spunky girl who could change from sweet to hellfire in a snap, cussin' like the best of 'em. She weren't more than fourteen years old when she had her baby girl. Some well-to-do folks from Tamworth adopted the baby, givin' her a good home.

Margaret curtsied and offered me her dainty hand. "The pleasure is mine."

I shook her hand real hard, probably too hard, before realizin' that I was s'posed to kiss it or somethin'.

"Jessie mentioned you in her letters." She smiled jest like Jessie.

I nodded. "Excuse me." I went over to help Daddy with his coat.

Pastor Leighton stepped in front of me. "Silas, what a wonderful and important day." His white eyebrows clung to his gold spectacles.

"Yes, sir." I kept my eyes on Daddy as he struggled with one arm all tangled in his coat.

"You have the ring?" He spoke slowly, as if I had trouble hearin', and he ended each sentence with a big smile. I found myself starin' at his peculiar expressions and not listenin' to his words.

Daddy whipped his coat sleeve madly. "Goddamn thing."

"Yes, I do." I patted my breast pocket and felt the tiny gold ring that I got from a jeweler in Wolfeboro. It cost me nearly all the money I had saved in my tin. Since I didn't have no house to buy or barn to build, I had money to spare. I took it from my pocket and handed it over to him.

Mamma pushed through a small crowd and yanked Daddy's coat off him with one good tug. Her hair, still wet from the snow, stuck to her red face in wayward chunks.

"That's fine then…" He went on talkin' and smilin', but I didn't hear a single word 'cause I was busy eyein' Daddy, hopin' that he wouldn't yell or nothin'.

Upstairs, Jessie primped and fussed and waited to make her entrance jest as I 'spected. She did look like the finest lady in these parts. Her weddin' dress was probably worth more than a good horse.

I met all of Jessie's aunts, uncles, and cousins. And I met old grandmother Gilman. She was sittin' in a wheelchair all bundled up in a red blanket, wigglin' her nose like a rabbit, and starin' at nothin' with her colorless eyes. Other than some folks in Wakefield, who I never really knew, I didn't have no relatives to speak of. The Blakes was there on my behalf. Moses was my best man.

Mrs. Gilman's warm breath tickled my ear. "Do you have a special song you want to hear? Mrs. Leighton plays quite well and can play just about anything, I'm sure."

"Uhhh." I looked up at the ceilin'. I'd be damned, as I realized that I only knew them drinkin' songs that Daddy sung and a few others that I couldn't name. I rubbed my chin. "I'll think on it."

"You do that, dear." She looked at the clock. "Do you want to change into your wedding clothes?" she asked. "It's almost time."

"Ayuh. I would, indeed."

She led me to a room off the kitchen. I pulled my clothes from the sack. The shirt and the gloves were no problem, but I couldn't get that tie straight. I poked my head out the door. Margaret posed near the stove hopin' that all eyes were on her for the time bein'.

"Excuse me." My face heated up.

"Yes?" She tilted her head with an air of false virtue, like some of them women down at the tavern, only this one had money and class.

"Please ask Moses to come here."

"He's the man who accompanied you?" She acted concerned, but she was only concerned with herself. I knew her kind.

"Ayuh."

She came back with Moses followin' behind her.

"What is it, son?"

"Come in."

"Is the tie givin' you a tussle?" He yanked proudly on his tie.

"Ayuh." Ignorin' his braggin', I handed my tie over to him.

He weren't so good at it either. He fumbled with it for a spell and put it on the chair.

"Damn thing." He turned to leave.

"Where are you goin'?"

"I'm goin' to get Miriam. Hold tight."

I picked up my work shirt from the floor and twisted it in my hands.

Mrs. Blake burst through the door with Moses followin' behind. "You should have told me that he needed help before now." Her face wrinkled up like she was suckin' on a sour lemon drop. She grabbed the tie.

"I appreciate it, Mrs. Blake."

She whipped it around my neck like she'd been doin' it every day.

Mrs. Gilman rapped on the door. "Are you ready?"

Moses looked directly into my eyes and said, "This is it." It didn't come to mind at the time that those words ought to have come from Daddy.

"Yes, ma'am." My voice cracked. "I'm ready."

"Come on out now." She trailed off into the parlor.

Margaret, Moses, and I waited in the kitchen. The folks sat in chairs, which were arranged in the shape of a horseshoe, around Pastor Leighton. Mrs. Leighton wailed on the piano keys in her usual manner.

Pastor Leighton waved to me. I walked around the folks and took my place beside him. He nodded, clutched his well-worn Bible, and rocked from side to side. Mamma started in cryin' and dabbin' at the corners of her eyes with her handkerchief.

Margaret walked in holdin' on to Moses's elbow. She held her head high, wearin' the same bright smile as her cousin.

The music changed. All heads turned towards the back of the room. Some of the women gasped. Jessie was a sight from heaven. She stood in the doorway with her father. Small ringlets fell about her face. She wore a wreath of white lace, silk blush roses, and tiny wax orange blossoms with a veil.

She had a fancy silk shawl draped over her shoulders, and her ivory dress, embossed with white and silver satin flowers, flowed when she walked. She carried a bouquet made from firs and winterberry, tied with red and white ribbons.

Sweat dripped down my back and under my arms. Afraid to take my eyes off her, I joined in with the pastor, rockin' from side to side. She smiled, not the bright smile that I saw at the barn dance or at the store, but a smile that held some sort of secret.

They stopped before us and the pastor started in. "Dearly beloved, we are gathered here in the sight of God, and in the presence of this company, to unite Silas and Jessie in holy matrimony. Marriage was ordained by God in Eden and confirmed in Cana of Galilee—"

The old grandmother began talkin' nonsense. No one paid her any mind, 'cept for Daddy who seemed willin' to respond but thought better of it when Mamma gave him the elbow.

Pastor Leighton took a deep breath and continued. "Who gives this woman in marriage?"

Doc Gilman didn't speak. He stood erect in his fine black cutaway suit and white silk shirt. He peeked at Jessie, nodded, and hurried to the chair by his wife.

Jessie seemed to float over to my side. All that tingled inside of me surely showed in my face. I couldn't hold back from grinnin'. At the direction of Pastor Leighton, we kneeled down on the small bench for a silent prayer. I tried to think straight, to take the time to do what we was supposed to do. Every time I thought of somethin' private to say to God, somebody coughed or wiggled in a creaky chair. I cleared my throat and collected my thoughts as best I could.

God? I know You don't hear much from me and all, but it ain't 'cause I don't think highly of You. I jest get tied up in everyday affairs. With all the work at the farm and takin' care of my folks, I don't take time out to talk to You. I'm thankful for all this… Jessie and the house and good folks like the Gilmans. I pray that Jessie and me can be happy. I pray that I can take my mind off Abigail and be a good husband and…

"Silas?" Pastor Leighton whispered. "You can stand up now."

Jessie smiled down at me. It weren't like me at all, but my knees almost gave out. Every time I looked at Jessie, I sweat like it was August. We exchanged vows, repeatin' the pastor word for word and answerin' all them questions that they ask at weddin's.

"Do you, Silas, take Jessie to be your wife? Do you promise to love, honor, cherish, and protect her, forsaking all others and holding only unto her…?"

The words sounded far away, like I was watchin' from across the room. I paused. Jessie blushed. Her eyes darted back and forth between me and the pastor, finally restin' on me.

"I-I do," I said quietly.

My mouth was parched, and I struggled to catch my breath. I tried to get Abigail's face from bein' fixed in my mind. The dampness spread across my shirt as if I had put in a few hours at the wood pile. And to top it off, I jest couldn't hear right.

"I do." Jessie's bright voice snapped me back.

The pastor handed me the ring and started in talkin'.

My hands shook when I tried to slip the ring on Jessie's finger. It wouldn't go over her knuckle. When I tried to pull it off, it fell to the floor, makin' a clinkin' sound and rollin' right under Daddy's chair.

"Uh… I'll get it." My heart pounded clear down to my feet as I got on my hands and knees in front of him.

At first he chuckled, and then he got to coughin' and gaggin' and howlin'. "Jesus Christ, son. You ain't off to a good start." Tears rolled onto them prickly whiskers that started on his cheeks and ended in his long untamed beard.

"Hiram." Mamma nudged him hard with her elbow. "That's enough," she whispered and gave me a regretful look.

I reached way under his chair and snatched the ring. I took my time standin' up, not takin' my eyes off Daddy. He kept on laughin' in spurts under his breath. He quieted down, and I returned to Jessie. Her bottom lip quivered and the red in her cheeks up and left.

I smiled. "Let's do this agin'." I lifted her hand and forced the ring on her finger. She let out a long breath, and we turned to the pastor. I held on to her hand, and I felt them fires burnin' jest thinkin' about the consummation of our marriage. Then the pastor pronounced us man and wife. We walked proud as could be through the crowded room. Some laughed and others cried, while Daddy peed in the chair makin' a real mess of things.

We enjoyed a weddin' breakfast of hot chocolate, pear pie, warm pumpkin bread, and buttered toast with strawberry jam, eggs, bacon, and a rich, dark fruit cake with white frostin'.

After a spell of dancin' them awkward dances like minuets and waltzes, folks waited in line to wish us well. Moses kept slappin' me on the back, while Mamma whimpered, and Daddy stood there with a big wet spot on his trousers, cussin' 'cause there weren't no liquor.

All the guests had to stay 'til the next mornin', after the storm passed. I thanked the good Lord that the Gilman's house was as big as any barn.

CHAPTER 57

Abigail – December 28, 1872

ANXIOUS VOICES MERGED with my dream. I opened my eyes to see Miss Noyes and Polly in the pale yellow light as they crouched over Mahitable's bed. Nellie sat motionless on the floor with her eyes closed and head bowed. The snow whipped against the cracked windowpane, leavin' a fine line of powder along the sill.

"She's cold." Miss Noyes pulled her hand away from Mahitable's forehead.

"She's been dead a while then," Polly said.

Nellie remained still.

"What?" I rubbed my eyes and focused on the circle of women.

"Never mind," Miss Noyes snapped. "We'll get Billy and Charles."

Mahitable was dangerously ill. Her cries, which I had become accustomed to, fell silent in the night. The brittle straw in my bed sack crinkled when I pulled my blanket up under my chin. *She wasn't that old.* I reached for Hope. *She died of a broken heart.* I felt a quickenin', a nudge, the perpetual reminder of my sin.

Polly and Miss Noyes left the room grumblin' about bein' awakened and havin' to start the day early. Accompanied by shrill laughter, a light flickered from down the hall, matchin' God's cruel joke. I watched Nellie go to her secret place in the floor as the baby whimpered and stirred.

I had never seen a dead person, only pine boxes containin' them. I hesitated before lookin' at Mahitable, expectin' her to move. She lay with the bleak mornin' light gleamin' in her eyes, and her mouth was still open.

My shoulders ached from constant shiverin', and I could see my breath. I supposed that they would take her to that room in the barn and put her in one of the pine boxes. I envisioned the numbers etched in granite and wondered what number Mahitable would be. I was saddened to think that she would be buried without her name. Her greatest crime was bein' immeasurably poor, grievin' the loss of her son, and then becomin' weak of mind, body, and spirit. I swallowed my fear in one gulp. *In through the nose.* I struggled. *Out through the mouth.* I gasped when the usual nudge inside my belly became a good hard kick.

Nellie rooted around beneath the floorboards. Patience finally arose and went to her usual spot with a blanket draped around her and the baby.

"Patience?" I whispered.

"What?"

"It's Mahitable." Tears threatened.

"What about her?"

"She's…"

"She's what, Abigail?" She looked towards Mahitable.

"Dead." I surrendered to the tears.

"She's dead?"

"Yes," I said, still waitin' to wake from a terrible dream. "She died in the night."

"Oh." She sat quietly. The top of Joshua's fuzzy head poked out from the blanket.

"What do we do?" I stared at the lifeless woman with the silent scream of her dead son imprinted on her lips.

"What can we do?"

"I don't know. She can't simply lie there like that."

"The men will come and take her." She stroked Joshua's head.

Nellie returned to Mahitable. She had a plan. She knew what to do. My breathin' returned to normal. I watched. She massaged Mahitable's face and arm with some kind of oil. Then she placed her fingers over Mahitable's eyes and gently closed them. She reached into her belt and pulled out a dried leafy plant. She brushed it lightly over the woman's body before placin' it upon her unmovin' chest. She paused and then kneeled before Mahitable.

My head throbbed. The other women in the room continued to sleep. I sat frozen in my bed, watchin' and waitin'. Patience turned her baby to her breast with her eyes set on Nellie and Mahitable. The wind moaned pitifully. There was not a thing I could do.

Nellie pulled the blanket off of Mahitable and then grabbed her by the ankles. I covered my eyes only to peek through my fingers. She dragged her, stopped, and then looked over her shoulder before movin' her a few more inches. She finally covered her body with a blanket.

I forced myself away from the safety of my own blanket and collected my ragged, yellow dress from a pile of clothin' on the floor. I faced the wall and removed my nightdress. A current of cold air washed over my nakedness, so I quickly pulled my dress over my head. I hesitated before puttin' on my panta-loons, which were dingy and gray from goin' too long without bein' laundered. Mother would have been fitful.

The mornin' bell vibrated in my head, and the usual shuffle of boots and muffled voices drifted from the hallway as folks made their way to breakfast. We walked single file past Mahitable. Some gawked in horror; others offered a silent prayer, while some did not look at all.

Nellie was last in line and followed close behind me. I stood before Mahitable, who lay with a sprig of Nellie's plant restin' upon her. Although Nellie had closed her mouth, I could not escape the desperate cries that would haunt me for all of my days.

I closed my eyes. *Heavenly Father, I pray that You take Dearest Mahitable to be with You and her boy in Heaven, and rejoice with the angels for all eternity and that she may rest in peace. Bless her Father. In the Lord's name I pray, A-men.*

"Hurry up and git down here!" Miss Noyes barked as if it were another ordinary day, as if one of our beloved women did not lay dead on a soiled bed sack on the cold, splintered floor.

Nellie wrapped her warm gnarled hand around mine. The angry voices of the matrons and farm bosses escalated as we neared the kitchen. The three men who were to take Mahitable to the barn rushed into the room.

"Moses ain't gonna' be here, so I decided that we'd jest go ahead and bring her out to the barn like we always do." George puffed up like a mean ol' rooster.

"There ain't nothin' to decide, George." Billy sounded more like a whinin' child than a man.

"When's Moses comin' back?" George asked.

"It's jest a weddin'. And they're gettin' married down the road apiece for Chrissakes." Charles's voice rose above the others.

"Yep. They're gettin' married right there at Doc Gilman's," Billy said as he reached the top of the stairs. Then he uttered somethin' that I couldn't understand.

"Ayuh. Silas is like a son to him," George mumbled.

I tried to free my hand. She tightened her grip. The kitchen stench, wood smoke, and lingerin' smell of death made me heave. I leaned against the wall. Nellie embraced me.

"Hurry up! Now!" Polly shouted.

I jumped when an armload of wood toppled beside me. Cyrus smiled. "Sorry if I startled ya, Missy."

Nellie led me to a table and sat me down in a wobbly chair. Folks anxiously devoured the brown, watery gruel and crusty bread. The hunger had returned.

One biscuit sat in the middle of a plate beside an empty crock, which moments before brimmed to the top with strawberry jam. The chicken and potatoes from Christmas were gone. The pine boughs were gone, and every last wrinkled apple had been eaten. Even Mahitable Colby was gone. I picked at the scab on my wrist. And at that moment, I knew that jest as sure as the warm blood trickled down my arm, that Silas Putnam was gone too.

CHAPTER 58

Nellie – December 28, 1872

DEATH CAME WITH the harsh winds of the Wintermaker Moon. A mother's heart broke into many pieces, scattering love that reached the furthermost corners of Our Mother. Those who dwelled in the dark shadows of hate and greed were revealed. A motherless child remained in the Other World to wait for the grieving earth mother. Freedom was death.

Her cries quieted. She dimmed like the waning moon. The veil that separates this world from the Other World grew thin. She took no food for many days and nights. The last flame of light departed from her eyes.

The storm came from the northeast. The fires did not make us warm. I wrapped her first with her blanket and then covered her with my own. I embraced her frail body. Once a maiden bearing fruits of motherhood, nurturer, and sustainer of life, she would never become a wise woman elder. Her head fell forward like the animal that remains warm after the kill. She stared without seeing when I lay her down for the last time.

Polly and the lady with the hair the color of a fox spoke with anger, looking and pointing at Mahitable. The others were quiet and unaware.

I closed my eyes.

"I s'pose we oughta' at least take another look at her." Polly's voice came with her footsteps from beyond the room. The door opened. The lamp shone bright. She walked over to the other side of Mahitable's bed and held the light near her face. "It won't be long," she said. "I'll be damned if they don't always go in the night."

Mj Pettengill

"She ain't been right since Josiah up and died," the lady with the hair the color of a fox said.

"We'll come back in the mornin'. Nellie will tend to her like she always does." Polly spoke as the women departed.

The night cries of those who were without dreams blended with the wind and grinding wheels from my distant past.

→=⊙ ⊙=←

The cart shook hard. *Witch! Witch! You killed my boy!* The young mother ran beside us on the dusty village road.

I leaned into the strong shoulder of my husband to shield from fear and hate.

Three days before, the woman went into the store. Her child was ill and lay bundled in her cart. She spoke to the storekeeper with worry. *Please rush. My child is sick.*

Searching Owl filled our cart with goods he traded. I followed weak cries that led to the young boy wrapped in a blanket. He shook. His face had many angry sores, and his fever burned my hand.

I hurried to our cart and searched in my baskets for medicine. I broke a piece of white pine bark for the fever. The boy coughed and tried to sit. I touched his arm.

The mother cried. *Take your filthy hands off of my boy!* She dropped her sack of goods.

I stepped away and looked into her eyes, as one mother to another.

Did you cast a spell on him? She looked at her child and then at me.

I offered the bark to her.

What is this? She struck my hand. The bark fell to the ground. She gathered her goods and returned to the child. *Stay away from us with your wicked ways, the ways of the devil!*

She departed. Searching Owl came out of the store. *What is all the commotion about?*

I watched until I could see her cart no more. I picked up the bark and returned it to my basket.

Folks don't understand you. He patted me on the knee. *Tho' some folks do know how smart you are.* He took my hand in his. The face of the boy would not leave me. The wheel of our cart struck a hole. I started to fall. My husband held tight. He would not let me go.

◦◦◦

I returned to her deathbed. She gripped my hand. Before the first light, her spirit departed with the cry of her son's name in a final breath.

The wind blew hard, and the snow grew deep when her spirit departed. The ones before her waited in the Other World. Her spirit would smile. Her spirit would sing. I thought of when I would reunite with Mamijôla, Searching Owl, and the others. It was not a time of sadness.

I released her hand and placed it on her heart. Pain rested in my neck and shoulders from sitting long with no blanket.

Polly arrived with the lady with the hair the color of a fox, and she touched Mahitable's head. "She's cold." She looked at me with surprise. "She's been dead a while."

The lady with the hair the color of a fox spoke. "George and Billy will get her."

The women left. I went to my place in the floor to gather oil of juniper and fresh hemlock twigs to prepare her for burial in the white man's garden. I returned to Mahitable and massaged her with the oil and cleansed her with boughs of a hemlock before I closed her eyes and positioned her to face west, the Looking Place.

CHAPTER 59

Silas – January 26, 1873

"I DON'T UNDERSTAND why you dislike going to church. I find it refreshing to see folks after being shut inside all week." Jessie primped a perfect curl.

"I jest think it's dull sittin' there listenin' to Pastor Leighton go on and on 'bout sinners and repentance." I sat on the bed.

"You must be aware of what he says and learn the ways of the Lord." She fussed with the next curl. "Besides, that is how we will make our way to heaven. We must always strive for that."

"I think that God hears me no matter if I'm sittin' in a church pew or out muckin' stalls," I said.

"That isn't good." She pulled at her corset. "Will you get this for me?"

I walked over to her and tugged on the laces. "I really do believe that."

"Tighter," she whispered, tryin' to hold her breath.

"I mean, it jest don't make sense that you have to go to a buildin' to talk to God."

"Well you need to have faith," she said. "You can't go around questioning everything."

"Some folks do bad things and think that jest 'cause they go to church on Sunday and ask for forgiveness, that it's all good," I said.

She rifled through her dresses and held up a bright red one as if it were somethin' of great importance. "What do you think?"

"It don't matter."

Her smile faded. "Why? Don't you care if your wife looks her very best when she goes out in public?" She tossed the dress aside.

"You always look good." I imagined Abigail on her knees in front of the laundry, wearin' her yellow dress and scarf wrapped around her head. "And you can choose what to wear." I turned away from her. "Some folks is lucky to have anything to wear jest to keep warm."

"That's nonsense." She rolled her eyes. "I know that there are poor folks, but we always take them into account and donate to charity."

"I know. It ain't that. It's jest that your appearance means an awful lot to you, and I ain't comfortable with that."

She sunk into the bed with her arms crossed, poutin' like a little girl. "You lost interest in me already? You don't care if I'm the prettiest woman in town or not."

"Look, Jessie, you are the prettiest girl in town, but it ain't what counts." I sat beside her and put my arm around her slight shoulder.

"I want you to be proud of me." Her eyes filled with tears, and her lower lip quivered.

"I am proud of you. It ain't the most important thing is all." I kissed her on the forehead. "So wear whatever dress you like, and let's have breakfast."

"I'll join you in a moment."

⊶⊷

"Sit down and eat some pancakes." Mrs. Gilman set a pitcher of syrup in front of me. "This syrup is from last year. We take great pride in it."

The butter slid off the stack and onto my plate. "I love maple sugar. I must confess that I have a love of sweets." I dribbled the golden syrup over the fresh melted butter and thick pancakes.

"I do too," Doc Gilman said with a chuckle. "You can help the men tap the trees and boil the sap." He looked out at the sugarhouse. "I'm hoping for another good season. We had nice warm days and cold nights last March, perfect for the running of sap."

"Here she comes." Mrs. Gilman's eyes lit up when Jessie entered the dinin' room.

"Good morning, Mother. Father?" She sat down slowly, careful not to spoil her dress. "I only want one pancake. I must watch my figure." She spread her linen carefully over her dress.

"You must eat, child. Your body needs extra nourishment in the winter months." The doctor pushed his spectacles up on his nose and stared at his daughter.

"That doesn't mean to become a sow." She cut a tiny piece off the corner of her pancake and stabbed it with the fork.

"So how are things at the farm?" Doc asked.

"Same as always. Nothin' much changes." My face reddened as I realized that I talked with my mouth full.

"Well, I know that some of the inmates have had the sore throat and fever. Moses told me that it was starting to spread. I'll go there tomorrow to assess the situation."

"There's always somethin' a doin' with sickness and all."

"Moses asked me to check the Hodgdon girl as well," he said, lookin' over the rim of his spectacles.

"Oh?" *Somethin's wrong.* "Does she have the sore throat?"

"No, but her child will be born soon. He wants to make sure that she's well."

"That's unusual for Moses." I started in on the mental math thinkin' of April or May. I sensed Jessie's eyes on me.

"That's true, son. Well, he was her caretaker after her mother perished, and I expect that he still feels some responsibility."

"I s'pose." I swallowed the last mouthful of coffee.

"Well, she's probably perfectly fine," Jessie said. "If she didn't partake in sinful behavior, then none of this would have happened."

"Now, now Jessie. You are right of course, but it isn't up to you to be the judge," Mrs. Gilman said while reachin' for the doctor's plate.

"Betsey, get Sally to do that. I kept her on here so that you could play the piano, do your needlework, and paint." He cleared his throat. "In any event, we must leave for church. Silas, please ready the sleigh."

Sally rushed into the dinin' room all a flush. "Are you folks finished?" Her snood fell off to the side of her head with sprigs of orange hair stickin' out. She was eager to please and thankful to be away from the County Farm. She was a good sort to have around, if she didn't get too fired up.

"Yes, Sally. Thank you," Mrs. Gilman said with a quick nod.

Jessie sat beside me wearin' her red cloak with the hood pulled over her head and her hands wrapped inside of a white fur muff. We rode in silence while the sun warmed our faces, and the sleigh pushed through the steamin', slushy snow. I enjoyed what folks referred to as the January thaw. Dark gray clouds gathered over the ridge, threatenin' the clear blue sky. If we left right after church, we would miss any snow squall comin' in our direction.

CHAPTER 60

Nellie – January 26, 1873

I CARRIED THE empty cup and walked slow in the night shadows. Sickness came with the harshness of the Wintermaker Moon. Soon, Jane Norton and Mrs. Kennison would depart to the Other World. The husband of Jane would follow, not from fever but from the desire of his spirit to join hers. I cared for both of the women throughout the night. I met with Abigail in the darkness. After I stirred the tea, I gave it to her. I watched her gain the wisdom of healing.

"What do you mean? I ain't been hidin' nothin'. I jest forgot!" Polly shouted.

"When a letter comes for anyone, you see that it's delivered. You hear?" Moses tossed the papers on the table.

"Yes, don't be frettin'. I'll give 'em to her."

I followed Polly to the great room. Abigail sat before the fire looking but not seeing. Her hair fell from the cloth that she wore on her head. She spoke less with each passing day. I made her take food and drink. The child would come after the passing of two moons.

"Abigail?" Polly stopped before her.

"Yes?" Abigail did not look away from the fire.

"These are for you." Polly dropped the papers on her lap.

Abigail gathered them with joy. "Thank you, Polly." Her eyes were wet with tears. She held the three papers marked with the symbols of the black robes. She carefully tore one open to find another inside.

I returned to the kitchen for water. The sun came through the windows, warming the floor.

⇥⊚ ⊚⇤

The heart of Our Mother beat with my own. I ran my hands over the dark green moss, listening to the giant pines whisper in the quiet winds of the Planting Moon. The long shadows were safe. Icy remnants of the dying winter roared from the waters of Cold River, carrying with it visions of Mamijôla. Soon the orange and black butterfly would bring comfort.

My friend the crow perched high above on an outstretched limb. He cried out to all. *Caw! Caw! It is the time for coming again.*

Nanatasis! Searching Owl called from our home. The flapping of the crow's wings broke the light of the sun. I reached for my whistle. I blew three times to guide my husband. The sounds of snapping twigs and earth beneath his boots came swiftly.

He held a white paper in his hand. *Nanatasis, we've received a letter. It's your mother.*

He pulled a paper from inside of the other, both marked with the familiar symbols of the black robes. I waited. I looked up at Father Sky through the green, rushy boughs. The time for Nigawes to join Mamijôla and the others had arrived.

Come, Nanatasis. We will return home and I will read the letter.

I pressed my face into his red shirt that smelled of sweat from swinging the axe. Sorrow mixed with joy. Silence fell upon the giant pines. I pulled away. I would hear the words within the safety of the trees. I pointed to the earth.

You want to sit? My husband held the paper from the wind that wished to steal it.

We sat face to face. Fury rose in the song of the many-voiced river and the wind blew bitter. My black hair fell from my hat and into my eyes.

Searching Owl unfolded the paper. He spoke in a quiet voice.

Dear Mrs. Baldwin,

This letter is to informe you of the death of your mother, Kchi alakws. She died of a fever two weeks before the writing of this letter. She was withe her people at the time of her death and was as comfortable as could be expected. Many other Indians have been afflicted with the fever. We pray earnestly that it will pass as spring arrives. Your father's brother requested that notificatione be sent to you.

As God's Willing Servant,

Eliza Jane Cress

Mission of St. Marie Church, St. Albans, Vermont

The wind triumphed. Searching Owl chased the paper until the wispy fingers of a sapling caught it. I waited, listened, and watched all that surrounded me until the sun neared the ridge. I felt her arms around me.

Many of my people died that year. The Black Robes took them in to become part of their village, to take Christian names, and to give up the secret ways of the fox, abandoning the shores of Bitawbagok. It pleased me that she remained Kchi alakws.

I called for the rain – for the falling of tears from Father Sky – to celebrate the life, earth walk, and mourn the loss of Nigawes, Kchi alakws.

CHAPTER 61

Abigail – January 26, 1873

I GAVE UP thinkin' about that which was easy and pleasant, only to be discontented because I couldn't have my own will. I gave up all wishin' and longin'. I only thought of bearin' what lay upon me and acceptin' God's will.

Bein' crowded into that miserable house – confined for room, neither wind nor watertight – became my own hell. Gone were the days when we relished the January thaw, the short-lived warmth in the midst of winter.

When the cryin' and moanin' ceased, the snow melted in thunderous drips on the roof, on the sill, and into the pot in the middle of the room. I pulled my blanket over my ears, but the relentless cries kept me awake through the night. Nellie shuffled up and down the stairs to fill her cup with hot water for medicine tea.

Old Mrs. Kennison, from across the hall, coughed and gagged. "I need water. Somebody please get me water."

"Jest quiet down and go to sleep," the new lady said, hopin' to get a reaction. "Ain't nobody gonna' fetch you water at this time of night."

I sat up and whipped the blanket off me when Mrs. Kennison started gaspin' for air. I listened for Nellie's footsteps.

"You ain't goin' in there are ya?" Patience's voice came out of the dark corner.

"Nellie can't do it alone. And I can't sleep with all this turmoil." I wrapped my shawl around my shoulders and headed for the dimly lit hallway.

"You're gonna' catch the fever," Patience called after me.

I met Nellie on the top step. She held a steamin' cup in each hand. She stopped and smiled.

"Is one of these for Mrs. Kennison?"

She handed one of the cups to me. Both of them had what looked like reddish brown oil and green dirt floatin' on top of the water.

Careful not to scald my hand, I kept it steady. "I'll bring this to Mrs. Kennison."

Nellie nodded and followed me into the room. She reached into her pocket and pulled out a notched stick and stirred slowly as I held the hot cup in my hands. She concentrated hard and closed her eyes every so often. Mrs. Kennison started coughin' again. Nellie took the stick out of the brew, twisted it so that you could see the white inner bark, and then put it back into the cup. She pointed at the oil as it swirled out from the stick and into the brew, and she nodded towards the old woman.

I took small, uncertain steps over to the side of the bed sack. Nellie watched from a distance. "Here, Mrs. Kennison, drink this and you'll feel better. The coughin' will subside." I couldn't stop my hands from shakin'.

She sat up. Her silver hair was flattened in the back, and her eyes were blood red. She reached for the cup. "It hurts to cough. I can't stop."

"Hold your head up and sip this." I held the cup close to her lips. My thoughts turned to Mother. When Sarah and I had coughin' spells in the night, she came to us with honey and whiskey.

Mrs. Kennison gripped my arm and took to drinkin' the tea. I placed my cool hand on her burnin' forehead. "Now lie down and go to sleep."

She whimpered and spoke in a childish voice. "I can't."

"Stop carryin' on for Chrissakes." Martha Smith pulled her blanket over her head.

"Mind your manners. She's ill," I snapped.

"That's what they all say at this damn place." She turned away.

"Do not listen to her or anyone else who doesn't have a good word, Mrs. Kennison. Have bright thoughts. You'll feel better if you rest and take Nellie's medicine."

"I soiled my bed," she said. "I'm wet and cold." She let out a long, woeful cry.

I spun around. Nellie was no longer in the room. Mrs. Kennison curled up in a ball. I ran my fingers through my snarly curls and stared helplessly at the old woman, whose trials and afflictions seemed to bind us closely together. "What do I do?" I whispered under my breath.

I paced around the room once and stopped. "I will return with dry clothes and beddin'. You'll be fine." I wrapped my shawl over her bony shoulders. *Dear God, let her be fine.*

I clutched the sides of my nightdress and hurried to the launderin' room. The pungent scent of lye and wood smoke assaulted my airways. The maze of washtubs and long sticks took on an eerie glow as I stumbled my way through to the dryin' lines. I set my eyes on one blanket hangin' amongst a variety of garments. I felt a twinge in my chest when I squeezed the blanket to find it still to be quite damp. "Heavenly Father, please help. Show me what to do next." My words echoed in the large, empty room.

Swallowin' my frustration, I grabbed at the other items, tossin' them on the floor. Two pairs of trousers, an apron, leggin's, leggin's, and more leggin's. Jest as I thought that all strength had left me, I saw a blue flannel nightdress. I held it out in front of me. It was large enough to fit the likes of Miss Noyes. I conjured an image of the frail, old woman on the floor clingin' to life, wet, and shakin' with cold and fever, and tucked it under my arm.

I took hold of the lamp and went to the back room, where we stacked dry clothes. I rummaged through the piles until I found a coverin' for her bed. It wasn't a blanket, but she could have mine. On my way out of the room, I snatched a pair of mismatched leggin's and a nightcap.

The moanin' swelled as I climbed each step. Nellie met me in the hallway. We stopped and looked at each other. At that moment, I simply knew what to do. It was clear to me that I would watch and learn and most importantly, trust myself. It was God's will for me to care for the sick and dyin'. He brought me to Nellie so that she could teach me the ways of nature, nurture, and healin'.

I went to Mrs. Kennison, who snored lightly, her damp hair pressed onto her troubled, ashen face. I bent over and shook her lightly. "Wake up." I took a deep breath. "We need to get you into dry clothes."

She started thrashin' her arms about. "Go away. Don't touch me."

"It's Abigail. I won't hurt you." I wanted to flee, but I remained calm.

She sat with her head hangin' and shoulders slumped forward. "Jest let the good Lord take me."

I struggled to untangle the nightdress from her limp body, surprisingly heavy for such a small frame. Her wrinkled skin hung loosely from her bones. Shiverin' and pantin', she reached for her wet blanket.

I helped her to her feet and then slipped the giant nightdress over her head. It fell off her shoulder and dragged on the floor. "It isn't the best fit, but it's clean and dry."

Ignorin' the stench, I yanked her foul blanket from the bed sack and fixed it up with a dry cover. When I returned to our room, Nellie was sittin' on her bed unbraidin' her hair. I ripped the blanket off of my bed and rushed back to Mrs. Kennison, who was layin' on her back takin' short raspy breaths. I covered her with my blanket and tucked in the corners by her feet. I touched her head. It was warm but not scorchin' like before. "Sleep well." I collected my shawl and returned to my room.

"I think Mrs. Kennison feels a bit better." I looked over at Nellie. She was asleep with a peaceful expression on her gentle, old face. I wrapped my shawl around me and fell asleep to the sound of meltin' snow drippin' from the eaves, makin' long pointed icicles.

When the mornin' bell rang, I opened my eyes with a start. My feet were no longer covered and had become numb. Patience nursed the baby while the others got dressed. My head pounded, and I reeked of Mrs. Kennison's urine. I looked out the window. Rows of crimson clouds gathered over the ridge and the snowfield had a gray look about it.

With Nellie watchin' closely, I ate my gruel and browned ash potatoes in silence. My eyelids felt thick and my back hurt. Nellie looked no different. She was accustomed to gettin' up and tendin' to folks.

After I forced down the last bite, I went into the great room and sat in the rockin' chair before the fire. Ladies would be comin' from the Methodist church to sing and read from the Bible. The inmates were permitted to have leisure time on Sundays. Usually I preferred to sneak into the barn and visit Lizzy and Old Gray Mare, but on this day I required rest.

Polly came into the room with Nellie behind her. I did not look at them. I watched the cracklin' flames and relished the warmth on my face. The child in me stirred.

"Abigail?" Polly stood before me.

"Yes?"

"These are for you." Three letters tumbled from her hands onto my lap.

I stared at Sarah's familiar handwritin'. "Thank you, Polly." My eyes filled with tears as I ripped open the one marked November 29.

My Dearest Sister,

I write to you with a heavy heart. It is tragic that you are at the county farm. I lie awake at nighte thinking of how to save you from such missfortune. It is not justifyed that I am working hard and living a life of independense while you are in the likes of such a place. If you were not withe child, you could join me and we wuld work together.

My days are long. I work from before the sun rises until after sunset, wich is the way of all of the women here in Fall River. Many are sick and without hope, but many are strong too. I find kindred spirits when all seems unfavorable and grim. It remains a challenge to find the time and place to practise my cornet, but I shall not give up.

What about Silas? What has becom of him? Did you not tell him of the child? Oh sister, I pray that you will have love and support from him as you shuld. I must retire. I will think of a way for you to join me and to leave your sorrow behind.

Pray, sister. We shall be together again one day.

Affectionately,

Your Sister, Sarah Hodgdon

I poured forth my soul in tears. The taste of salt lingered on my lips as I pressed the letter to my chest. Folks started to come into the great room and set the chairs in a circle.

My conflicted heart — both heavy and filled with joy — broke when I read and re-read the remainin' letters from my dear sister. I vowed that after the birth of the child we would leave together, and I would find a way to work in the mills.

"Let us bow our heads in prayer." Mrs. Brown's voice wavered when she spoke. The other women from the church scampered around helpin' folks get situated. I closed my eyes and drifted into a light sleep.

The ache that has settled in my bones, is proof that I am still alive. To stop yearnin' for what I know to be good and wondrous, is to surrender to hopelessness.

CHAPTER 62

Silas – February 26, 1873

"Finally." Jessie stared into the lookin' glass with swollen, red eyes. "You could have come home." She pulled the brush through her hair.

"I had to wait 'til the storm passed. It ain't good for the horse to lose footin' on the ice. As it is, I shoulda' stayed another night." I yanked off my wet boot and dropped it onto the floor. "And it's my job to help out at the farm when things get rough. The woodpile was covered with ice, and with folks bein' sick with the fever, I had to stay."

"The woodpile here is covered with ice too. Besides, we are a priority over those people." She changed from a wounded duck to a cluckin' hen.

"But the back shed off the kitchen is chock full of wood. You weren't in any danger of freezin'." I dropped my other boot. "And with your folks here and Eb comin' to check up on you, you was fine."

"I get scared when you aren't here." She pulled her hair back from her face, cocked her head to the side, and sort of smiled. "Does it suit me to have my hair like this?" She looked at me in the mirror.

"Why are you scared?" I sunk into the bed.

"Because when the wind blows it keeps me awake, and I'm scared. I don't know," she said.

"You're safe here. Don't worry 'bout such things." I closed my eyes.

"You didn't answer me. You don't like it."

"Like what?"

"You aren't listening to me. All you think about is that awful place, and you don't even notice me." She stared at her reflection.

"I'm listenin' to you. I'm tired is all." I watched her sittin' there with her fancy red nightdress fanned out on the floor like a queen. All of her things for primpin' were made of porcelain with hand painted pink flowers.

"I asked if you liked my hair." She turned and glared at me.

"Aw... come on, Jessie."

"And you did not respond. So, I take that as a no. You don't like my hair pulled back, or you simply don't care." She crossed her arms.

"Any way you fix your hair is fine. I can't decide when it comes to the likes of them things. Jest keep doin' what you feel is best; you're beautiful."

I started noddin' off when a vision of Abigail appeared outta' nowhere. I sat up and tried to shake it off.

"You mean it?" She giggled.

"Of course I mean it."

"I'm eager for spring to arrive so that I can get a new hat." She spun around in the chair. "A woman has to feel special, and nothing does that more than a stylish new hat."

"I see." I unbuttoned my shirt.

Unable to resist herself, she returned her gaze to the mirror. "One like they wear in Boston. Not some pathetic straw thing from Tibbetts' store."

"All I know is that I'm tuckered out and should get some sleep," I said.

"I was thinking of getting a bright yellow dress with a bustle. Did you know that it's the latest fashion? Yellow is such a bright color. I feel so drab after a long winter."

I burrowed under the soft quilt. My shoulders ached from choppin' ice and carryin' bodies. Even the small folks felt heavy when they was dead. I couldn't help but think of poor Mrs. Kennison, such a kind soul.

"Do you think yellow will look good against my fair skin?" She turned down the lamp.

Abigail's face returned. I tried to blot out her curls spillin' out from the yellow cloth that she wore on her head and her blushin' cheeks and sweet laughter when she fussed over Patience's baby. I tried to blot out the sadness in her eyes. And I tried, but couldn't blot out the fact that she looked beautiful in the dirty yellow dress that clung to her round belly. "Yes," I replied. "Yellow."

"Not every woman can wear yellow. But I think that it will be eye catching on me." She climbed into bed.

"Yes, that's true."

She kissed my cheek. "Good night. I'm pleased that you're home."

"Good night." I drifted to sleep thinkin' of the events of the day. The last thing I had 'spected was to come face to face with Abigail.

Jessie inched closer to me. "Pleasant dreams."

CHAPTER 63

Abigail – February 26, 1873

THE STORM LASTED for two days. I looked out over the glazed earth. The ice pounded against the roof and felt like tiny needles against my face. I took a cautious step, but the sole of my boot skidded across the ice. I scrambled back to the safety of the step. With no luck, I tried to dig my heels into the frozen snow.

I had no choice but to slide on my bottom to the outhouse. I slid over the glasslike surface and came to an abrupt halt when my feet slammed against the rock at the bottom of the hill.

A gust of wind caught the outhouse door, bangin' it against the wall. Martha Smith stood before me yankin' on her undergarments. "What the hell are you doin' settin' on the ground like that?" She fumbled with her laces and scowled. "You're lookin' foolish like ya always do."

"It's too slippery. I'd take a spill if I walked on the ice." I got to my feet.

"Damn fool." She shook her head.

I entered the outhouse and latched the door. I sat on the cold wood, lookin' down and tracin' my fingers along the outline of my misshapen belly. "You'll be here soon. Then we will leave for Fall River," I whispered.

"Set her down on the board and we'll slide her down the hill!" a farm boss yelled in the distance.

"Damn ice! Sure can't wait 'til spring!" Silas's voice carried over and above the downpour of freezin' rain.

"Then we'll be workin' overtime." Benjamin Wallace broke out laughin'. "We'll be eaten alive by black flies and sore for weeks from diggin'."

I waited until they got into the barn before I left the outhouse. When I reached the steepest part of the slope, I got down on my hands and knees and crawled to the steps.

The women had jest finished with the dishes and were settin' out to do the launderin'. Mary talked Polly into lettin' me do the sewin' until the birth of the baby. I slipped quietly down the hallway, where I caught sight of poor old Mr. Norton sittin' in the Great Room. He had a fearful look and his face was quite pasty. He was rollin' a cloth around in his hands and trembled in spite of himself.

"Mr. Norton?"

He stared straight ahead.

I tapped his shoulder. He gasped and looked at me with wild eyes. "Mr. Norton, I'm sorry about your wife," I whispered. My heart wilted at the thought of her cries in the night. When Nellie and I went to her to administer comfort durin' her final moments, it was too late.

He mumbled somethin' impossible to understand and returned his gaze to the fire.

I was headin' for the sewin' room to gather cloth for night caps when I was overcome with the desire to see Old Gray Mare. I hadn't been to the barn for some time, and the last time I saw her, she looked awful thin.

I thought of my dear horse as I carried on sewin', already workin' on my third cap. Without warnin', a wicked pain shot down into my lower back. I got up to stretch and walk about. Mr. Norton still sat in his chair rubbin' that cloth in his fingers. He didn't make a move or seem to notice when I passed by him.

I scurried into the kitchen. Polly hollered at the women in the launderin' room while Miss Noyes cleaned up after the dead. Other than in the dark of night, I hadn't seen much of Nellie since the fever took hold.

I went into the back room off the kitchen. I took a quick look around before tuckin' two rather large carrots inside the sleeve of my dress.

I heard the sound of heavy boots headin' straight towards me. There was a pause. I could hardly realize my fear of gettin' caught.

The door flung open. I gasped at the sight of Silas and dropped one of the carrots on the floor. We stood motionless.

He put his hands in his trouser pockets. "Good mornin', Abigail."

"Good mornin'." I studied a meanderin' crack in the floor.

"It's a pleasure seein' you on this otherwise dreary day." He smiled. His face was covered with short, dark whiskers.

"I see." I continued starin' at the crack, which had become blurred.

"No, I don't think that you do." His voice was quiet and deep.

"You're right. I don't understand why seein' me in this place on a miserable mornin' would invite any sort of pleasure." I started to wither, but rallied almost immediately.

"Well, let me try to explain. First of all, you dropped this." He reached down and picked up the carrot.

I stared at it in his outstretched hand.

"Aren't you gonna' take it?" He had a look of boyish virtue about him.

"I don't know." My heart pounded. "Are you gonna' tell Polly?"

"Nope."

"What if I told you that I don't know whose carrot it is?" I looked him right in the eye.

"I would tell you that you ain't a good liar," he said with a smirk.

"I don't see the humor in that." I turned away.

"I know exactly what you are up to, Miss Hodgdon."

"Oh? Do tell."

"You're goin' down to the barn to give Old Gray Mare a treat. That's what you're up to." He chuckled as if we were sharin' a cup of tea on a bright afternoon.

I snatched the carrot away from him. "And that is a crime?"

"No, it ain't."

His very blue eyes still made my knees wobble a bit.

"But it sure is icy. So, be careful. And, uh… Abigail?"

I rested against the wall in order to remain vertical. "What?"

"I 'spect that it is a crime for you to be goin' down to the barn. I mean, it's against the rules and all. But in my mind, givin' your horse a carrot ain't a crime." His smile caused my heart to weaken within my wretched soul.

"I see."

"You might not want to go down there. Of course, I can look the other way." He glanced over his shoulder. "But the others might not."

"Well don't worry yourself about the others. I am capable of takin' care of myself."

"I know. You're one whippah snappah."

"What does that have to do with the pleasure bein' all yours?" I thought about Jessie. "I find that interestin' comin' from a married man." I looked at him through a small, new monocle curl.

"We've been luggin' the dead out of the house. That ain't no picnic." He coughed in a forced sort of way. "So seein' the likes of you on such a gray day after a night like last night is, well... a pleasure." His smile vanished.

"It is not my intention to bring you pleasure, Mr. Putnam. So I apologize on my own behalf. Now, if you'll excuse me, I have aprons to sew." I started towards the door.

He raised his arms, blockin' the door. "Don't leave."

I stood before him. "Move or I will scream." The child inside nudged.

"In here, no one so much as blinks when someone screams. You know that."

"Fine, if you don't move, I'll scream for my own benefit." I bit my lip.

"Abigail..."

"So, if you don't mind?" Desperate to appear unshaken, I looked squarely into his fright.

He stepped aside. "Take care on the ice, and you best wear a shawl."

"I will skip and dance on the ice and leave my shawl behind." I curtsied. "I do not need advice from you or anyone else for that matter."

I grabbed the corners of my dress as if it were a three-boned, flounced hoop and marched off. The rain pounded against the roof, and the wind groaned as it swept over the abandoned fields. I stumbled into the Great Room, where two men dragged an unknown dead woman across the floor on a torn bed cover. Her vacant gray eyes stared into nothingness. I rushed to the back door. I stood alone with death behind me and before me. The earth wept in the bitter cold, amidst the sorrowful cries of trees that cracked and fell to their deaths from the intolerable burden of ice.

CHAPTER 64

Abigail – March 21, 1873

WHEN I HELD Betty in my arms, she wailed inconsolably, drenchin' me with her tears. She endured much conflict after she gave birth to a baby girl, who died only moments after her entrance into this pitiless world.

The commissioners sent a letter to Betty's folks informin' them of the news, in hopes that she could return home. It took a good three months before her family replied.

"How could they do this to me?" She dabbed her eyes with the corner of her yellow dress. "Nobody has to know about my baby," she said. "And she's dead." The pages of the letter scattered about her feet.

"I know." I hugged her.

"I can't stay at this place. I would rather die than live here another day," she cried. "What will I do?"

"I'll write to my sister, Sarah. She lives in Fall River and works at a textile mill." I forced a smile. "You can go there to live and work." I brushed a tight, brown curl away from her eye. "You'll even earn wages."

"You'd do that?" She retrieved the crumpled pages from the floor.

"Yes. In fact, I'll do the same after the birth of my own child." I patted my stomach. "It'll be adopted by a fine family, and I will leave this dreadful place once and for all."

"Get that stick turnin', Betty." Polly edged between us. "You go to the sewin' room. Pretty soon you'll be back to launderin'." She jabbed a bony finger into my chest.

I glared at her horrible face, prematurely wrinkled from years of bottled up hate, knowin' full well that we would go toe to toe someday.

"Go on, Betty. We'll talk later," I whispered. "We'll read from the poetry book that I found in the barn."

"I can't read," she said.

"Stop the idle chat! Get to work!" Polly reached for her stick, the stick that would earn her an unquestionable passage through the gates of Hell.

I hesitated, disregardin' the unspoken threat. "I will teach you."

"Wait, before you go…" She handed me the letter. "Will you toss this in the fire?"

"You should keep it."

"I don't need it." She lowered her eyes. "I will never forget."

I tucked it into my pocket and rushed past the Great Room, where Nellie sat on the floor listenin' to Henry Norton. Since the death of his dear wife, he tells long-forgotten, muddled stories of life on his chicken farm.

I stopped in the doorway of the sewin' room. Bella, who was always hummin' in a most pleasin' manner, smiled at the sight of me. Lidie, on the other hand, continued on sewin' with her face inches away from the material, on the account of her needin' spectacles.

Bella stopped hummin'. "Hello, Abigail."

"Good mornin', ladies." I avoided lookin' at Silas in his usual spot near the horses, where the men were workin' on bar posts. I experienced a peculiar and unwelcome happiness at the sight of him. In an attempt to shake it off, I rummaged through a pile of blue cloth, relieved at the well-timed surge of anger that was takin' hold.

"Are you makin' aprons?" Lidie looked up. "Or shirts?"

"I don't know." I fiddled with the letter inside my pocket.

"Aprons is the easiest." Lidie squinted to see the seams on the shirt that she was workin' on. "But you can't use blue fabric for 'em."

"That's a fine shirt." I examined the perfect seams that even Mother could not have matched. "You should leave this place and work as a seamstress. The way that you sew, you certainly don't need to stay here." I settled into a tired rockin' chair by the fireplace.

Her shoulders drooped. "Who would hire me?"

"You should try somethin'. You have God given talent—"

"You mustn't let Miss Noyes see you bein' idle," Bella cut in. "She's apt to throw a fit."

"Let her throw a fit. It doesn't bother me at all."

"So be it." She returned to hummin'. "Remember that I warned you."

I unfolded the crumpled letter. *Lord, please forgive me.* Mother used to scold me for bein' a busy body. This was different, and besides, Betty gave it to me herself.

Dear County Commishionners,

We are respondin to the leter that you sent to us in January conserning our daughter Betty. She has shamed us & blackened our name. We did not speake of her sinful ways to folks in town, but we carry the burden evry day. Many folks know the fate of Betty as most other girls who leave home do so because of shame. It is the unspoken truth.

Even thoughe the child did not live, it is after much thoght that we have desided that we cannot have Betty return home as ther is no longer a place for her. It is a great strugle to feed our young ones as is. The weight of this desishion brings us much heartache but we see no other way at present.

Please do not contact us agan with any more informashon regarding Betty. We have donated a small sum of money to the County Farm in return for her not comeing home.

Sincerely,

Mr. & Mrs. Jonathan F. Wallace

Freedom, New Hampshire

The handwritin' melted into squiggly black lines on the white paper. *She has shamed us and blackened our name?* I choked back the tears.

Bella's hummin' suddenly became agitatin', and the poundin' hammer rattled my insides. *The unspoken truth?* I bit my lip and wondered if my own mother would have turned away from me. The paper shook in my clammy hands. If Mr. and Mrs. Wallace were present, I feared that I would be arrested because of my powerful urge to attack them. I had forgotten how to respond to my own emotions.

I laughed aloud. "How could I be arrested? I am already a prisoner." I tore the paper into pieces and threw them into the hungry yellow flames.

"Who are you talkin' to?" Bella stood up. "Have you gone mad?"

"No, I am not mad. Everyone else has gone mad."

Lidie set the shirt on the table. "What did you throw into the fire?"

The bright flames sparked to life. "Betty's folks wrote a letter to the Commissioners." I sat down. "They claim that she has shamed them, blackened their name. There is no place for her in their family." The room blurred through my tears.

"Poor baby." Bella came to my side. "She is but a child herself."

"And her cousin is responsible," Lidie said, blurtin' out the secret she swore she would never reveal.

I jerked at the odd sensation, a tightenin' in my stomach. I turned towards Lidie. "Please... Please tell me this is not true." My voice cracked.

"Betty told me herself. And her folks jest looked the other way," Lidie said. "She told her father once, and he beat her. And her mother didn't believe it to be true."

The sun peeked through the broodin' clouds and streamed in through the window. I studied my shadow on the wall as I rocked hard in the chair. "It isn't right."

"What in blue blazes are you doin?" Miss Noyes marched in through the doorway with her ample cheeks matchin' her red dress.

"We're about to return to work." Bella dashed to the sewin' table.

"Abigail?" She put her face close to mine. Her warm breath reeked of onions.

"I am feelin' poorly today, Miss Noyes." I held my breath.

"Do ya think it's a holiday?" She clamped her thumb and finger on my elbow and squeezed 'til it tingled and became numb. "I'll show you what it's like to feel poorly."

I squirmed, unable to free myself from her grip. "No, I simply feel a bit uneasy." When I attempted to stand, she squeezed harder, almost bringin' me to my knees.

"As long as you're drawin' a breath, you have to work." She dragged me towards the sewin' tables.

"Damn you!" I yanked my arm free. "Leave me alone, old biddy."

As soon as the words escaped my lips, everything slowed. Her cheeks turned even redder than before. She slapped me across the face, about knockin' me to the floor. I covered the hot skin on my cheek with my hand.

"Don't sass me back!" She struggled to jam her wiry, red hair into her snood. "I don't take no cussin' from nobody, 'specially a whore."

I was like an outside observer watchin' myself grab the front of her apron. "Who are you callin' a whore?" I hollered so loud I thought that my own head might burst.

"You let go, girl, or you'll wish you ain't never seen the light of day." White foam gathered in the corners of her mouth.

"I don't care if you beat me to death." I pulled her apron harder, yankin' her apple face close to mine. Her foul breath washed over me again, and it didn't matter. "I am no whore. And no one, not even you, will talk to me that way." I staggered but maintained my grip.

"Well the fact is, you are a whore, and there ain't nothin' you can do to change that. Even after you have your bastard child, folks will always know the truth." Her eyes disappeared into thin green slits when she smiled. "It's a small town and folks don't ferget. 'Cept for when you die, then no one gives a damn."

Heated and quite disturbed in mind, I raised my fist, and then someone grabbed my hand from behind. "Don't do it, Abigail."

I froze. All strength was gone. My chest heaved and sweat trickled down my back. I managed to take hold of the strong hand.

"You can go now, Miss Noyes. I'll take care of this," Silas spoke in a quiet, unfamiliar voice.

"What are you gonna' do with her?" She smoothed the front of her apron. "She ain't deservin' of a second chance. She ought to go into lock-up after that episode."

I tried feverishly to catch my breath. I waited for Silas to respond. My knees weakened when the peculiar tightenin' across my stomach returned. It wasn't a pain really; it was a slow, deliberate squeeze.

"I will report to Moses and then, uh… maybe to lock-up. I don't know." He coughed slightly. "Abigail don't usually give no one any trouble; she must not be well."

"Are you favorin' her?" She gritted her teeth.

"No, I'm jest diffusin' the anger." His warm hand tightened around mine. "You go on to the kitchen."

"You ain't heard the last of this." She started to walk away and then stopped to give me the evil eye. "And you and me?" When she shook her head, her jowls quivered like the wattles of a nervous hen. "Well, don't cross my path, or you'll regret it." She stomped away grumblin' and cussin' under her breath.

Snow clouds blanketed the sky, and the room darkened. He held my hand firmly and lingered before lettin' go. I feared that if I exhaled, my very life would escape in a final breath. Bella and Lidie pretended to be workin' as if nothin' happened at all.

He guided me to the chair and knelt in front of me. "What's got into you?" He touched my cheek.

His eyes were bluer than I remembered. "I – I can't take it anymore." My monocle curl fell over my eye.

"You can't be fightin'. It'll get you in trouble." He stroked my cheek, invitin' me into a false sense of safety. "We both know that you're a lady."

The bitterness returned, givin' me much needed strength. I pushed his hand away. "I do, do I?" I felt the tightenin' again, only this time it was harder but still without pain. "Nobody calls me a whore." I looked out at the snow spittin' in the yard.

"You're right. But things is different in here." He leaned closer to me.

With a heart full to overflowin', I pressed my back into the chair, fearin' that I might give in to him if I looked into his eyes a moment longer.

There is no hope of healin' wounds made in the past. No hope. I rocked hard in the chair, all done talkin'. I stopped when I heard the sweet sound of Nellie's moccasins scuffin' across the floorboards in the hallway. Silas scrambled to his feet.

"There she is." Miss Noyes rushed past Nellie with Moses followin' close behind. "If she gits away with it, I'm all done. Somethin's gotta' happen to her, or they'll be takin' over the place."

Moses toked on his pipe. "You can go now, Miss Noyes."

"You make sure to punish that wench!" She craned her neck around for one last look.

I stared right back with the same stern look that Mother had when she was cross. Knowin' that Nellie was nearby gave me comfort. She would protect me.

"So, Miss Noyes tells me that you had trouble." He held his pipe in one hand and tugged on his beard with the other. "We can't be havin' that sort of thing here."

"She hurt my arm, struck me, and called me a whore." Suddenly I was a fidgety eight-year-old explainin' why I retaliated against Ben Sawyer for spoilin' my bonnet when he hid it in the tree trunk.

"As you know, you jest can't go around raisin' your fist either." Moses looked down at his boots. "So in fairness we got to follow the rules, and you need to go to… the…" His pipe gurgled when he sucked in. "… the quiet room."

"You mean lock-up?" I glared at him, knowin' that he lacked the courage to answer truthfully.

He shifted from one foot to the other. "Well, some folks call it that." He cleared his throat. "It ain't that bad."

How did he know? Did he spend so much as a minute in there? A sharp nudge came from inside, bringin' me back into the dreadful moment.

Silas pushed up his sleeves. "Jest for a few hours?"

"Overnight." He looked at Silas out of the corner of his eye. "If she don't act up, she'll never have to go there again. Rules is rules, son."

"Ayuh, but she's…" The color drained from Silas's face.

"Rules… " Moses ran his fingers through his beard and avoided eye contact with him.

Nellie gazed out the window, and Lidie and Bella continued sewin'. Moses started to leave but then he stopped. "I'm sure you learned your lesson, Abigail. Tomorrow's a new day." He put a match to his pipe and drew in slowly. He let out three short puffs, followin' them with his eyes. "Silas come see me after… well, you know."

"Ayuh." Silas reached for my arm. "Come on now."

"I can walk on my own." I jerked away from him and rubbed my tender elbow.

We walked together in silence. The heavy wooden door whined when Silas pulled it open. We stopped in the doorway. The dim light in the hall revealed a rickety chair in the middle of the room and a chamber pot in the corner beside a stained, crinkled blanket.

"I can't do this," he whispered.

I entered the room and stood by the chair with my back to him. "Leave." He paused. "No."

I sat down in the chair. "Suit yourself." Laughter and screams from the folks who weren't right in the head echoed behind us.

I could hear him breathe. "I'll be back." He closed the door.

I waited but did not hear the latch. I focused on the thin line of light from under the door until it faded away with his footsteps. I kicked at the stiff blanket on the floor. The child inside of me shifted when I patted my stomach. "And no one will call you a bastard."

Perhaps it was an hour, maybe two or three. I could not determine how much time had passed before I heard the sound of his boots rise above the hideous laughter that ebbed and flowed in short bursts.

Suddenly, the door flew open. He walked in with blankets under his arm. I twisted a curl around my finger and watched him. Without sayin' a word, he bent down and prepared a bed on the floor. "I will see to it that someone brings you food. You'll be able to leave here in the mornin'."

I stared at the chamber pot in the corner.

"Goodbye." His voice wavered.

I shuddered when his leg brush against mine.

"I'm sorry." He fled from the room, away from the inconvenient wretchedness of my situation, careful not to allow even the tiniest amount to spill into his perfect world.

I flinched when he closed the door. The sound of metal grindin' against metal gnawed inside of me. Accompanied by a chorus of janglin' keys and vile cacklin' from down the hall, his footsteps vanished with the only thin ray of light. My heart leapt when he started whistlin' the same sad song that he whistled when he buried Mahitable's son on that hot summer day.

I held my hand in front of my face and could not see it. My breathin' got louder and louder. I swallowed and tried to quiet it down. I pressed my hands over my ears, but it got worse.

I closed my eyes. *In through the nose... out through the mouth.* Visions flashed in my head as I drifted in and out of consciousness.

Papa's shiny pocket watch dangled before me. *May I hold it?* I begged.

Why do you want to watch time pass? He smiled with half of his mouth, not wantin' to commit himself to the pleasure he found in my endless curiosity. *There's too much to do, little one.* He towered over me.

His woody scent overwhelmed my senses as I stood stubbornly before him with Hope tucked under my arm.

You can hold it, but not for long. We have to pick butternut squash.

I beamed as the gleamin' circle caught the light. At first, it was cold in my hand. I looked at the numbers and then held it close to my ear. *Tick, tick...*

I bolted from the chair, knockin' it over as I raced towards the door. I ran my hands over the wood in search of a handle. I found nothin'. I wailed, "I cannot escape... I'm imprisoned! How could he lock me in here? He walked away." I rubbed my stomach. "He left us alone. Dear God, he left me and his own child behind."

I lay down on the crude bed, pullin' the top blanket up to my chin. I had never seen a place so dark. It was not possible to hold body and soul together.

However, I finally managed to fall asleep amidst mindless chatter and the smell of lye hangin' thick in the air.

I shot up when I heard a rattle. The door opened. I winced and shielded my eyes from the bright lamp light. The pressure on my chest lifted when I recognized Nellie. I wrapped the blanket around my shoulders and climbed onto the chair. She carried a bowl of meat stew and a crust of bread.

I ate the warm carrots and meat and sopped up the watery broth with the bread while she stood behind me lightly caressin' my shoulders. "Why do they send you?" The spoon clanked in the bowl when I set it down.

She looked at me with warm, chocolate eyes before reachin' inside her belt. She handed Hope to me.

"Thank you." I stared at the worn faceless doll. "You're so kind. I'll hold her close." I bit my fingernail. "I'm scared. I don't think I can do this."

She pressed her hand gently on my stomach and closed her eyes. I was stunned when she kissed the top of my head and left the room. I cringed, anticipatin' the scrapin' of the metal lock, but it didn't happen.

With Hope at my side, I sat on my bed, took the yellow cloth from my head, and ran my fingers through my stiff, knotted hair. The crazed laughter from down the hall turned to shoutin'. A man moaned and called for his mamma. I entertained the thought of joinin' in and callin' for my own dear mother, but preferred to sing instead.

"Rock of Ages, cleft for me,

Let me hide myself in Thee;

Let the water and the blood,

From Thy wounded side which flowed—"

I heard a thump outside the door. "Nellie?"

Silence. I wasn't certain if I shivered from the cold air that streamed in through the cracks in the wall or the expectation of findin' out who was out there. The laughter subsided leavin' the howlin' wind and my heartbeat as the only sounds in the darkness. After several moments of quiet, I continued to sing.

"Be of sin the double cure;

Save from wrath and make me pure…"

I couldn't find the words. Mother always insisted that we sing every last word of any song. She would remind us that if we were gonna' bother singin' it, then sing the whole song or never mind. I fell asleep with a vision of her standin' with her eyes closed and arms uplifted – like an angel – singin' directly to God.

A surge of thick, warm fluid gushed from between my legs. I lay still. "Lord, what is happenin' to me?" Was it blood? I pulled the saturated blankets away and stared into the dark with my yellow dress clingin' to my sticky, wet legs. I started to stand when a sharp pain gripped my stomach, bringin' me to my knees. I leaned against the wall. "Dear God, it's time."

Consumed in blackness, I glanced around the room quickly. At last, I could move. With drenched garments still stuck to my skin, I sat in the chair. *Now what?* I shuddered and remembered the blanket on the other side of the room from the person before me.

I thought of those who may have been in this room and wondered who used it. I peeled the pantaloons away from my skin. *Perhaps it wasn't soiled.*

When I got to my feet, a pain far worse than before seized my body. I knew that it must have been the Devil squeezin' so tight that there was no breath left in me. I toppled into a heap on the floor and bit so hard on my knuckle that I could have drawn blood. I shrieked when the pain swelled.

I released my finger as the pain subsided. "No one told me about such pain. This can't be from God. Surely, my sins have summoned the Devil himself."

I pounded my fist on the wall and screamed, "Damn you, Eve! It's your fault for eatin' that apple!" Immeasurable tears flowed, as I thought it best to die rather than lay alone in a dark, filthy room accompanied by the Devil while givin' birth to my child.

They will come to fetch me in the mornin', and I will be lyin' dead on the floor with a lifeless baby in my arms. I staggered across the room and grabbed the old blanket, which was stuck together in a stiff clump – it was dry. "No." I tossed it.

I felt for the hook on my dress and ripped; it dropped to my ankles. I tripped over the chamber pot before makin' it to the chair. The folks who weren't right in the head had quieted down, and the wind slammed branches against the outside wall of the house. I sat with my legs stretched out in front of me and rubbed my arms to keep warm. I managed to take a thin, shaky breath before another pain struck. "Mother!"

I knew then that I would die. I clutched Hope. "God, forgive me. Please don't let me die. Not now... I'm not ready."

The pain passed, leavin' me weak. I was hot and cold at the same time. I ran with my arms flailin' about, crashin' into the wall, kickin' the chamber pot, about to scream again, when I saw a soft yellow light barely glowin' through the crack.

The door opened. "Nellie, how did you know?" I threw my arms around her neck. She set the lamp on the floor, took me in her arms, and held me close to her warm body.

When my breathin' returned to normal, she retrieved the lamp, and we walked hand in hand down the hall. "Nellie," I whispered. "The baby is comin 'now, tonight. I've had awful pains and a great deal of water came."

She squeezed my hand.

"I'm scared."

We entered into our room. The women were asleep, and beside my bed were all sorts of Nellie's healin' things. She brought me a dry flannel night-dress. I bent down to undress and the pain struck. I clutched my stomach and gasped for air. "Oh no, Nellie... here it comes."

She rubbed my arm. "Shhh." She put her finger to her lips. Then she took a slow breath in through her nose and out through her mouth. She stopped and looked at me and waited.

The excruciatin' pain was risin'. I had no time for such foolishness. "Oh Dear God... help me!" I fell onto the floor.

Nellie reached down and cupped my face in her hands. She gave me a stern look and pointed to her nose as she took in a deep, slow breath. Then she pointed to her mouth and exhaled.

"I know all about that." I closed my eyes and shook my head. "I can't."

She continued to hold my face. She repeated her breathin' while my pain slowly vanished. I did not take my eyes away from hers.

I leaned against the wall. "I'll try that." I lifted my chin and took to the required breathin'. "My sister used to rescue me the same way. In through the nose and out through the mouth."

She patted me on the head and left the room with her cup in hand. I thought of all the times that she brought medicine made from roots, bark, and leaves harvested throughout the year. Some folks lived and some folks died. Nellie tended to them all. It was my turn.

"Abigail, it's time?" Patience called sleepily from across the room.

"Yes." I closed my eyes and braced for what was to follow. "I've never felt such pain. Why didn't you tell me?"

"Even if I did tell you, it wouldn't do no good. Ain't a thing you can do to stop it."

I thought for a moment and asked, "Why do women suffer?"

"Because of Eve. It's all her fault." Patience draped her blanket over her shoulders and sat beside me. "Didn't you pay attention in church?"

"Of course I paid attention in church. I'm well aware of Eve committin' the original sin. I would like to meet her and tell her a thing or two."

"It won't change a thing," Patience said with a grin.

No sooner had a smile formed on my lips when I doubled over in pain. "Oh no, Patience. Help me." I started to cry.

"Breathe like Nellie showed you." She rubbed my back.

"No! Don't touch me!" I held my breath and cried, "I want my mother."

"You must breathe, or it'll be worse." She looked over at baby Joshua who was startin' to stir in his crate.

Sweat ran down my face as I fought for each breath. The pain happened to vanish when Nellie arrived with a steamin' cup.

Her face glowed. She set the cup on the floor and stirred it with a fresh white pine stick. I watched her all hunched over with her lined face and long silver braids hangin' down. *She is no witch.* She left the room. I stiffened when

I heard the likes of Miss Noyes. The thought of seein' her was unimaginable. My stomach tightened, but fortunately she did not come in.

I drank the earthy, hot tea — dried raspberry leaf, hemlock needles and yarrow flower — and sat with Nellie on one side and Patience on the other, breathin' slowly until the break of day. The pains came one after another, and with each one, I squeezed a thick birch stick that Nellie got from her place in the floor.

Then Nellie tried to lift me off the bed. She motioned to Patience.

"I can't move." I licked my cracked lips and prepared myself for the next swell of pain.

Ignorin' my pleas, the two women guided me over to the wall in the corner. Then Nellie had me squat, sort of like sittin' down without a chair. The two women sat on each side of me as I dug my fingers into their arms. Soon the flesh on my back became raw from grindin' against the wall, but I didn't care.

"I see the head! Oh Lord in Heaven, I see the head," Patience said and she laughed. "It's almost over. Keep breathin', Abigail."

"Don't laugh," I whined.

"I ain't laughin' at you." She dabbed my head with a damp cloth.

The room whirled about when a great urge to push overcame me.

Nellie knelt before me and caught the baby in her hands. The blood continued to rush from me like a river in the spring. At first, no one said a word. Patience wept as if there were no end to it.

I slid down onto the floor. "Somethin's wrong."

"It's a boy," Patience said. "You have a son."

Bella came runnin' from across the hallway. "Can I come in?"

The uncertain wind pelted snow against the window while buttermilk clouds spilled across the bleak mornin' sky. In the midst of the muffled voices swirlin' about, all I could see was Silas's face. Even when I closed my eyes, he would not go away.

It was too quiet. Nellie held the baby in front of her and studied him before cleanin' him with warm water and cloth strips, careful of the cord that still pulsed between us.

He cried. I flinched. I did not expect such a loud cry. I couldn't bear to look, and I couldn't bear not to.

A rush of warm blood streamed down the insides of my thighs when I stood up. I thought that I might collapse. Leanin' on Patience, I walked to the chair leavin' a trail of bloody footsteps on the cold floorboards. My shakin' body felt tremendously empty.

My thoughts turned to the day I fell from the white pony and landed on the stone wall by the pasture at the Forbes farm. Papa rushed over to me. *Abigail, are you hurt?*

I can't breathe. I tried to sit up.

You got the wind knocked out of you. He inspected me all over for broken bones.

Can you pick me up? I looked up at Papa from under my straw bonnet.

His laugh was deep and hearty as he scooped me up in his arms. *You will get breathin' again and climb right back on that pony, Buttercup.*

I smiled and buried my face in his shirt, inhalin' the perfect earth scent that I was never to experience again. *Thank you, Papa.*

Papa's face departed into a mix of blood and warm water as it filled the chamber pot. Patience carefully cleaned my feet. Her son fussed, but she ignored him 'til she finished dryin' each one of my toes. She helped me to my bed sack. *I will awaken soon. It's a dream. I got the wind knocked out of me is all.*

I lay down on the cool beddin' and closed my eyes. Nellie placed my warm, naked baby against the gritty film of dried sweat that cloaked my breast. I felt stiff and unnatural when I embraced him. She leaned over us with her heavy tears spillin' on my face.

I sensed somethin' new and peculiar at the touch of his soft hair against my neck. Nellie wrapped a linen cloth around my waist and under me to soak up the blood that flowed from within. She carefully cut the cord that connected us with a crude knife from her secret place.

"Ain't ya gonna' open your eyes and look at your son?" Patience asked while carryin' her own son in her arms.

I opened my eyes enough to see the golden fuzz on his small round head. I winced when I tried to sit up. I held my breath and took a long look at him. "It's a miracle. He's a miracle."

"As I see it, he's all you got in this place." Patience kissed her son.

I stared at his petite nose and pink mouth. I felt a pang when I noticed that he had a dimple in his chin. *Dear God, I cannot deny that he is his father's son, but I must. I must part with the memory of my love for Silas.* I attempted to swallow my pain, but the tears would not wait.

I tingled all over when he found his way to my breast. I was convinced that my spirit might depart once and for all. "I will never leave you." He grasped my finger with his tiny hand.

"So, what's his name?" Bella sat beside me on the bed.

"Samuel."

He fell asleep at my breast. Nellie took him to the wooden crate lined with blankets. She returned with another cup of tea. I sipped from the cup and watched my son as he slept, bewildered that I longed to hold him rather than see him in that decrepit crate.

"You oughta' git some rest. He'll be awake before you know it," Patience said with a wide grin.

I handed the cup to Nellie and she handed it right back. There was still some tea left in the bottom. I swallowed the last of it. With great effort, I rolled onto my side and watched my son until I fell asleep.

I dreamt of Mother and Papa. I tried to show them the baby, but they couldn't hear or see me. I shouted to them, but they faded away, and then Sarah emerged wearin' the most elegant blue taffeta dress. I handed the baby to her while Silas stood beside me with his arm around my waist. We beamed with pride. Then Sarah became Jessie, and she looked at Silas and said, "What a beautiful son we have."

I sat up and clutched the blankets. "Thank God, Nellie's tea helps the bleedin' but makes my dreams strange." I glanced over at the crate; it was empty. I scrambled to my knees, lost my balance, and fell back onto the bed. Each part of me throbbed, but I had to find my son. Tears filled my eyes when I saw Nellie's shadowy figure approachin'.

"There you are my sweet." I reached for the bundle in her arms, ignorin' the surge of blood that flowed, soakin' the beddin'. "You are a gift from Heaven."

Patience, Nellie, and Bella surrounded us. I felt a twinge of guilt when I remembered the loss of Bella's baby. She whispered, "He's beautiful." She smoothed her dress. "And healthy."

"I think that Samuel suits him." I kissed his head. "God Hears."

CHAPTER 65

Nellie – March 20, 1873

SEARCHING OWL BRUSHED my hair. He traded syrup of the sugar maple for a brush. He said that this was to please me, but I knew it pleased him more.

We sat on the flat rock. It was warm from the sun and smooth where the river carved her name. The water rushed beneath us. The golden grasses on her banks parted, giving way to kasko, the great blue heron that came to fish.

You have already bathed. Are you returning to the water?

I pointed at kasko. I would swim where he fished.

But I call to you as well.

He took me into his arms. We joined in body, making one in spirit. When I became his wife, I had many fears in the ways of a man and a woman. He showed me the splendor of our sacred union.

The surging river united with our passion, lifting us to Father Sky. I lay my head upon my husband's chest and watched the painted turtle bask in the sun. Then, I walked to the river's edge, ready to bathe in her smiling spirit.

Beneath the water, I opened my eyes as my finned brothers did, so to see the yellow sand and gray rocks. I swam out of her slow current and watched the tall bird. I honored his skills as he stood still and quiet.

Nanatasis, I wait with the blanket.

The blue heron smiled and flew above my head, beyond the giant pines. The leaves on the tall oaks shook and bowed to the wind.

⤙⊙ ⊙⤚

The thin branches of the oak tree tapped against the window. Mr. Norton spoke quiet, hurrying his words and whistling where his teeth once were. "When our son Ira swung that ax, he cut enough wood in an aftahnoon to burn nearly the whole wintah. He was strong as an ox, that boy was. Jane used to feed him five times a day. He had arms as big as a tree trunk." He smiled. "Sometimes Jane cooked corn puddin'."

I no longer heard his words when Abigail's spirit called upon mine. The child would be born in twilight, neither night nor day – the sacred place between here and the Other World.

I struggled to stand. I would not surrender to pain that dwelled within. I lay my hand upon Mr. Norton's shoulder. He stared with clouded eyes and talked more. I walked away, leaving his words to fade away behind me.

The lady with the hair the color of a fox hurried. She shouted and her face was red. Moses followed behind. They went to the sewing room. Abigail rocked in the chair with much anger. I stood nearby, prepared for what would follow.

Moses sent away the lady with the hair the color of a fox. He spoke quiet to Abigail. Silas waited. He took the path that fled from his spirit, the path that strayed from his truth. Love would not hide.

Moses smoked his short pipe and talked about locking Abigail in one of the dark rooms, where people were separated from others.

Silas took Abigail away. They shared the fear in their eyes.

The sun was down when I brought her food. The heavy lock moved with difficulty. I entered the room to find her on the floor.

The pains of birth had arrived. First, she ate the small food offering that I brought. Then, I gave her the doll that she called Hope. I placed a parting kiss upon her head before I left. I did not lock her in.

I passed through the long hall where people laughed and cried and spoke words with no meaning. I went to my place of many medicines and filled a pouch with dried wild raspberry leaves, hemlock needles, and yarrow flower – mothers' tea. I gathered strips of cloth. I would rest until the arrival of the final pains of birth, until the daughter not of my blood, needed me.

I heard her cries together with the wind. Wrapped in my blanket, I left my bed and fetched the lamp. In my mind, I would run like a deer. The inner, wise counselor took slow steps.

Upon the birth, I would look into his eyes to see the violet flame, the veil that separates this world from the Other World. I would then hold him in front of her. She would love him with a fierceness known only by a mother. The truth would be revealed after the passing of many winters.

She lay on the floor. I helped her to stand. The pain of birth raged. She screamed and fought, making the path difficult and the journey long. I embraced her.

Into the darkness, she screamed again. We stared, brown eyes to brown eyes. She quieted. Together we walked down the long hall, through moaning and laughter and the shouting wind.

She would not watch or listen. She panted like a hunted animal. After much time, she watched and did as I did. I recalled forgotten fear from winters past, when I gave birth to Mamijôla. I soothed her, as my own mother had soothed me.

It was time. I left her side. I took the pouch, cloth, and my cup for hot water.

The lady with the hair the color of a fox was in the kitchen. "What's all that commotion? Is the whore havin' her baby?" She looked into her tea. Her face showed lost beauty, before anger took root in her spirit.

The water from the steaming kettle splashed onto the table when I poured.

"I s'pose I should go up and see what's a doin'. I ain't gonna' get no sleep with her screamin'. If things get too bad, we'll send for Doc Gilman."

I stood quiet.

"What's the matter with you?" she asked.

Her words were bitter and her deeds fueled by hate. I departed. I would keep her away.

Abigail cried for her mother, her sister, and her father. And she cried for her God in Heaven. I held her hand, caressed her head, and looked into her eyes as we breathed in unison. She did not want to drink the tea.

I guided her from the bed to stand and crouch. Her son entered our world in twilight, as I knew he would. I searched his eyes while the veil from the Other World was thin. His cries rose above all else. She looked away, as I did at the birth of Mamijôla. I placed his warm body upon hers, melting fear and anger.

It was two winters past when I saw Abigail and Silas. I walked in the woods near the Blakes' farm when I heard laughter beyond the trees. Their love was strong, like the love I shared with my husband. Carried by the four winds through time – love does not die. A love harmed and denied, wilts on the vine.

I bathed Abigail with a tea wash made from dried leaves of plantain and ash before she took her son to her breast for nourishment and bonding.

When I cut free the birth cord that joined them in life, my mother's words came to me. *Nanatasis, the twine of love and life that connects a mother and child will not be severed. It grows longer and longer, and it roots as one.*

I set out to fetch the father of the child. He was near the door with his coat in hand. I stood before him. He placed his hands on my shoulders, and his eyes held many questions. He took another as his wife. His spirit knew the truth, but his mind would not allow it.

I pulled away from him. He was good and kind, but other than my husband, I did not like the touch of a white man.

"How is she? Is she well?" He searched my face.

I cradled my arms to show him what he already knew.

"I heard a baby cry. Everything is fine?"

I smiled.

"Does she have a son or a daughter?"

I took his arm to lead him to his son. His fear of being watched vanished. "I will follow," he said.

I would not bring him into the room. Abigail could not know. He stood outside the door while Abigail slept in peace. I took the child to his father, who waited with fear and hope. I held his son before him.

"He's, he's… so small… and perfect."

He reached for him. "May I hold him?"

I placed the child in his arms. He found the other love, the joy never known to him before. Voices came from below. I took the child away and hurried back to the room.

Abigail sat up. "There you are my sweet."

A group of women – the inner circle – formed around mother and child, making bonds where there once were none and making strong the ones before. She would love and protect him as mothers will.

The women pulled the circle closer. "I think that Samuel suits him," she whispered. "God hears."

The father fled on swift feet, leaving behind his son and the woman of his heart and spirit.

CHAPTER 66

Silas – March 22, 1873

FAINT AMBER LIGHT streamed in, framin' her yellow dress. I reached for her. She smiled with her soft brown eyes lookin' right at me. Then all of a sudden she faded into the mist. I tried to holler, but nothin' came out. Darkness engulfed me.

She emerged again and appeared close. I could see through her, and she rippled as if she floated on water. I tried to move, but my hands and feet felt like they was in iron chains. She laughed before she slipped into the shadows. The invisible chains fell away. I ran until I bumped into the thick wooden door as it closed. The heavy metal echoed when she locked it.

"No, no! Wait! Open the door!" I gulped for air and sat up. My nightshirt was soaked.

"What is it?" Jessie stroked my arm. "You had a bad dream."

My heart hammered away in my chest as the sweat on my face evaporated in the cool air. When I closed my eyes, I could still hear her laughter from behind the door.

"Tell me about it," she said. "What's troubling you?"

"I don't know." I imagined Abigail alone in that dark, dingy room.

"It must be something. You were shouting and thrashing about."

"Sometimes I have to do things at the farm that I don't like." I tried to shake her image – her brown eyes.

"It must have been awful for you to get so worked up." She paused. "What was it?"

"Well… I had to put a woman in lock-up today."

"She must have done something awful to deserve it."

"She was protectin' herself from Miss Noyes." I swallowed and continued even though I knew I was invitin' questions. "Old lady Noyes is mean spirited."

"What did this girl do?"

"She was sassin' and ready to haul off and hit Miss Noyes." I warmed inside thinkin' about the feel of her hand in mine.

"Then she should have been disciplined and rightly so."

"You don't understand."

"I understand quite well." She tucked a strand of hair into her nightcap. "She was unruly, and you can't have that with those people."

"Miss Noyes called her a whore. And her baby a bastard."

"Well is she a whore?" Her voice became high pitched. "Is she an adulteress?"

"No, she ain't. Well… I mean… Yes, she is."

She laughed like she always did when I was ruffled. "Make up your mind."

"She ain't no whore." I bit my thumbnail. "And I s'pose she is an adulteress."

"Who is it?"

"You don't know her."

"Then there is no harm in mentioning her name."

"Molly Smith." The name jest came out. I didn't know anyone by that name.

"Hmmm. You're right. I don't know her. She has a child?"

"Not yet. She'll be givin' birth at the end of April, beginnin' of May."

"I'm impressed."

"Why?"

"That you know precisely when her child is expected to be born."

"Moses told me. I don't know much else about her." I straightened my tangled, damp nightshirt, thinkin' 'bout Moses scoldin' me: "You have to stop showin' favoritism towards Abigail. No more leapin' to her defense. Ya hear?"

"So you were just doing your job." She patted my leg.

"I know. Lockin' up a woman inside a dark, bare stall doesn't set right with me."

"You're too sensitive. If you carry on like this, you won't ever be the big boss."

The wind picked up like it tends to in March. I always thought of it as spring blowin' winter away. My thoughts turned to how cold it got in that big place and hopin' that she was warm.

"Get some rest. It's almost morning." She kissed me on the cheek. "And stop fretting."

I lay awake through the night and into the mornin', listenin' to the wind and thinkin' of that dream. When I heard Sally rummagin' around in the kitchen, I was more than ready to get out of bed.

Jessie slept soundly in spite of all the bangin'. I tied my boots and shuddered at the thought of the bitter wind blowin' snow in through the cracks of the walls and windows at the farm.

"I'm going to sleep late this morning. You kept me awake with all of your silly nonsense." Jessie buried her face in the pillow.

I fastened my suspenders and walked to the top of the stairs.

"Silas?" Her muffled voice came out from under the pillow.

I stopped. "What?"

"Aren't you going to say goodbye?"

"I thought you was goin' back to sleep. I didn't want to bother you." The bacon hissed and popped and smelled wicked good. I looked down at the top of Sally's head as she dashed over to the stove.

"You should always kiss me goodbye... under all circumstances," she said.

I walked over to the bed, bent down, and kissed her forehead. "Bye, Jessie." I followed the scent of a hearty breakfast, where nothin' was 'spected other than polite conversation.

"You don't really mean it," she said. "And now I'm wide awake because you didn't kiss me on your own. You had to be reminded."

"I didn't wanna' disturb you."

"Just go." She fluffed her pillow and settled into the bed.

I stood watchin' her for a spell. She didn't move. Her dark eyelashes fluttered as she tried to keep her eyes closed. She was like a painted lady in one of them art books from school. They looked good on paper.

I ducked my head and rushed down the stairs. Sally had to stop herself from gigglin'. With them orange freckles and her wide toothless grin, she looked more like a little girl than a grown woman. "Good mornin', Mr. Putnam."

"Good mornin'." I sat down at the table. "There ain't no reason to call me Mr. Putnam. Silas will do fine."

"I'm jest bein' proper is all." She watched me outta' the corner of her eye, not mindin' the spatterin' bacon grease.

"My daddy is Mr. Putnam."

"If you say so." She set a cup of coffee in front of me.

I shoveled my breakfast down quick in hopes to avoid seein' the Gilmans. They was good folks, but I weren't in the mood for idle talk. Sally prattled on about little to nothin'. I enjoyed her company 'cause she was simple and didn't put on no airs. She could be pleasant, and she knew what life was like on the other side.

When I reached the farm, I led Major into the barn and brushed him. He still had some good years left, but the cold, wet weather got to him. I looked up at the wing of the house where Abigail spent the night. My breakfast churned away in my stomach.

I went into the kitchen, right into a heap of commotion. Usually the folks weren't up and about for another hour. The sound of women's chatter replaced the usual silence. I waited and listened until I caught sight of Nellie. It was common to see her. That woman never got much sleep to speak of, takin' care of folks the way she did.

I hung up my coat and approached Miss Noyes. I 'spected that she would take to cussin' and complainin', but I greeted her nonetheless. "Good mornin'."

"What's so good 'bout it'?" She wailed the spoon on the edge of the pot. A grayish, brown clump plopped and then disappeared into the bubblin' gruel. "It's jest like any other mornin' at this God forsakin' place."

"Seems to me that somethin's abuzz."

"Only thing new here is that whore had her baby this mornin', 'bout an hour ago." She wiped her hands on her apron.

My mouth went dry. "Abigail?"

"Of course, Abigail." She gritted her teeth. "Ain't nobody else 'spectin' right 'bout now." She took two loaves of crusty bread from the pantry and dropped 'em on the table.

"I thought she was havin' her baby in April or May?" I stuffed my hands in my trouser pockets and started tappin' away on my fingertips.

"What the hell possesses you to know these things? It ain't a man's business to know."

"How is she?" *June, July, August, September, October, November...* I tapped.

"Well, I went in to see her and was chased away, so I don't know." She dumped a chunk of lard into a bowl. "Don't make no difference."

"Chased away?" *December, January, February, March...*My cheeks burned, and I perspired right through my shirt.

"After yesterday? I don't give a damn 'bout her, and she certainly don't want nothin' to do with me, 'specially in the throes of childbirth." She scratched her head. "But there sure was lots of screamin'."

I caught a glimpse of Polly passin' by carryin' an armload of blood soaked garments and beddin'.

"Was she in lock-up? I-I mean when the child was born?"

"No, I'll be damned if Nellie didn't get to her in the middle of the night. That old Injun knew somethin' was a doin'."

"Should we go...?" I froze right there in my boots when I heard a baby squealin'.

"Should we what?"

"Never mind. I'm goin' out to the barn." My hands shook. Either the baby came early, or...

"Men." Miss Noyes rammed a piece of oak into the stove.

I headed for the door but stopped when I saw Nellie. She approached and looked me square in the eye. Of course she never spoke, but I sensed somethin' big. "Nellie." I grabbed her shoulder.

She pulled away.

"Is Abigail well?" I glanced around the room to see if anyone was listenin'. Her face softened. She smiled.

"I heard the baby." I lowered my voice to a whisper. "Is it okay?"

The old woman raised an eyebrow.

"Did she have a son or a daughter?"

She poked her finger into my chest. Her smile faded. Her eyes darkened.

She knew. I ripped the edge of my thumbnail off with my teeth and spit it out. Knew what? I looked away. I was gettin' all riled up. I needed to think.

Nellie glared at me.

"What?" I looked towards the stairs.

She took a hold of my arm and rushed towards the stairs, haulin' me like a child about to get walloped.

I took a quick look around. The only person nearby was Miss Noyes, who couldn't hear a word above her own cussin'.

We hurried down the hallway, and then she motioned for me to stop. I waited while she disappeared into the room. I bit at my thumbnail, that had started bleedin', and leaned against the wall wonderin' what in the Lord's name I was doin'.

After a short spell, Nellie came into the hall with a bundle in her arms. I closed my eyes knowin' that once I looked at this child, nothin' would ever be the same. There was no turnin' back this time.

She came towards me. When I finally looked, I had never felt nothin' like it. A fine layer of honey colored hair covered the head, and its cheeks was pink. When she pulled the blanket away, it squirmed and looked right at me. There weren't no question that it was a boy.

I guess you could call it instinct that caused me to take him from Nellie. Daddy often spoke of instinct, 'bout the animals doin' what nature intended. I always thought it best to follow your instincts.

I pressed my cheek against his soft face. He weren't a small baby, and he looked sturdier than most. He started to wiggle, and his bottom lip quivered, but he didn't cry. I hadn't ever held a baby. It felt right, downright good. He held his tiny clenched fists against his cheeks and rolled his head from side to side. I knew then and there that he was a miracle. I pulled him close to my chest, wantin' to protect him but havin' no business to.

Jest like that, Nellie reached 'round and plucked him away, leavin' a peculiar hole where he imprinted on my shirt. I could still smell him.

Abigail's voice drifted out from the poorly lit room, from within a gatherin' of women folk that surrounded her. "You are a gift from Heaven."

I pressed my sweaty palms against the walls and leaned my head as close to the door as I could without bein' seen. The women spoke in hushed tones in clear admiration and support.

"I think that Samuel suits him," Abigail said. "God Hears."

The sound of her voice touched a place deep in me that I never felt before that particular moment. I wasn't even sure how I would move from that spot. Everything had changed.

All of a sudden, I jest knew that I had to run. I ran straight to the barn, climbed the ladder to the loft, and fell back on the stiff bundles of hay. Tears felt good and tears felt bad. I didn't fight 'em. I knew that I had to let 'em out or be all busted up inside. "God, what do I do now? I got a son. Why didn't she tell me?"

All them questions and answers raged out of me. Every time I tried to stand, it started in all over again – the heavin', the ache inside my gut that seemed new but was there all along.

I got to my feet. "Why didn't she tell me she was carryin' my child?" I slammed my fist into the wall, numb to the pain that shot down my arm. "Why?" The boards creaked as I paced.

Was she intimate with Weston near the same time? I wiped my runny nose on my crumpled, damp sleeve. She weren't no whore.

Harness bells jingled below as Asa fixed to bring the team out to the front yard. I knew they searched for me, but I weren't about to move. That baby was my son.

"You ain't seen Silas have ya?" Moses shouted from below. His tobacco smoke meandered through the cracks and into the loft.

"I ain't seen his scrawny hide since early on this mornin'."

"That's odd. He ain't in the house and he ain't out here." Moses took to coughin'. "If you catch sight of him, tell him to come see me."

"Ayuh." The horses stirred. The bells shook. "Will do, boss."

I waited 'til the barn was quiet 'cept for a few chicken squabbles and a moan from a milkin' cow.

I peered out a crack and watched the men go about their business. I had to take it like a man with no carryin' on. I gripped the ladder so tight that my knuckles turned white, and I almost fell when I jumped off. I brushed away the strands of golden hay that stuck to my trousers. I wondered how I'd face Jessie knowin' that I had a son.

"There you are. By Jesus, I been lookin' all over the damn place for ya." Moses walked in tappin' the ashes from his pipe into the palm of his hand.

"Ayuh." I moseyed over to the snow shovel. "Here it is." I grabbed it and stood facin' the wall.

"We ain't got enough snow to worry 'bout, son"

I stared at the thick smoke as it curled out of the big house chimney.

"Where've you been?" He pinched a wad of moist brown tobacco into the bowl of his pipe and packed it with his thumb.

"I, uh…" My nose ran down into my mouth. I sniffed and wiped it on my sleeve. "I was in the loft seein' to it that we had enough hay to make it through."

"Through to what?"

"You know… 'til the end of winter."

"Come here." He rested his paw-like hand on my shoulder. "Let's talk straight now." We left the barn and headed for the house.

We walked through the kitchen. The women washed pots and kettles, and Lidie scoured the floor. We passed by Polly, who cussed a streak while strugglin' to put an oversized log on the fire. Then we went into the great room where old men and women, most tied in their chairs, sat with their eyes fixed on nothin', jest waitin' to die.

I paused at the bottom of the stairs and looked up to where my son lay with his mother. The heavin' threatened to start, but I covered my mouth and had a coughin' fit instead. I hurried ahead to Moses's room. *This ain't no place for a child. This ain't no place for my child.* I walked faster and faster, finally sprintin' and gettin' to the room before Moses.

"For Chrissakes, this ain't no race," he said between raspy puffs.

I bolted through the door and sat on a stool at the long oak table that served as Moses's desk. He dragged a spindly chair over the uneven floor and sat. He said nothin'. He jest stared at me with his steely eyes. I swore he could see clear inside of me to find all them answers that he was after.

I shifted on the stool. "So, what do you want?"

"It's always her."

"Who?"

He forced a deep laugh. "Don't be playin' dumb with me." He stirred inside his pipe bowl with a matchstick. "Abigail."

"What about her?"

"She had her baby."

"What's that got to do with the likes of me?" I swallowed hard.

"I don't know. That's why I'm in here invitin' you to talkin'."

I looked out the window. "I ain't got nothin' to say."

"You're full of horse shit." The tobacco in his pipe glowed and crackled under the match flame.

"What the hell do you want from me?" I jumped to my feet. "I have a wife. Abigail is nothin' but an old friend." I shoved my face up close enough to feel his rotten tobacco breath.

He smiled and blew a cloud of smoke in my face. "It ain't so."

I walked away from him. "Her child was supposed to be born in April or May."

"Well he weren't born in April or May now, was he?" He chewed on the stem of his pipe, squintin' to see me through a smoky cloud.

"And he sure as hell weren't born early. He's a strappin', healthy boy."

"You saw him? What the devil did you go and do that for?"

"Like I told ya before, I was intimate with Abigail, jest about nine months ago at your barn dance. I had my way with her in the loft." My voice cracked.

Moses kept tokin' on his pipe, not talkin' or nothin'.

"He's my son. I know it." I started bawlin'. "My son is layin' up above us right now, and there ain't a thing I can do about it."

"Get a hold of yourself, boy! You can't be sure. What about Weston Jones?" He chewed on the stem of his pipe. "And why didn't she fess up?"

"I don't know!" I banged my fist on the table. "I jest don't know. I woulda' done the right thing. I loved that woman."

"There ain't no turnin' back now," he said. "She made up her mind to leave you out of it for one reason or another. The fact is, you might never know her reasonin', and you might not even be the daddy."

I closed my eyes.

The chair toppled when he jumped to his feet. "Pull yourself together. From now on, you won't think of that child as yours. The little bastard will ruin what you got goin' for ya."

After he left, I sat on the edge of the table lookin' out at the patches of rotted, brown leaves beneath the dirty snow. I didn't move. The wretchedness was gone. I felt an odd sense of peace as I watched and waited for the sun to set over Brown's Ridge. I listened for the folks to shuffle to their quarters for the night and for the last stroke of the splittin' maul to ring out from behind the woodshed before I mustered up the strength to leave.

It was well below freezin' on the ride home, perfect weather for tappin' maple trees, warm in the day and cold at night. The arctic wind stung my eyes and snapped against my face. It was time to go home to my wife.

CHAPTER 67

Abigail – May 23, 1873

MOTHER USED TO tell us that the scent of lilacs was intoxicatin'. She preferred it to the likes of the hard cider that Papa kept in the root cellar. Every spring she filled the house with the heady blossoms that lined the road.

She said that we were blessed to have all shades of purple and many white ones as well. She would exclaim with an armful of blossoms, "Now don't jest stand there, fetch me some water!"

She lamented when they passed, leavin' them drooped in jars in the fragrant splendor of death until they wilted and turned into weightless, brittle leftovers of what once was. She even used the dried flowers to sweeten tea or add to a sachet. I never really knew what all that meant until the first spring of my own motherhood, when my senses had fully awakened.

I reached for a lilac stem and snapped it free. Samuel wiggled a bit inside of the blue sling that Bella made for him. It was the same material used for the men's shirts, but I liked it all the same.

I thought of how fortunate I was to have Samuel with me throughout the day. The farm bosses didn't complain, as long as I got to my chores and didn't dilly-dally. At night, I tucked him in close to me rather than in that rickety crate beside the bed. He was a good-natured baby and didn't take to fussin'. In fact, he smiled at me quite regularly. Patience said that it was on the account of gas, but I knew better.

With Mother in mind, I held a white lilac close to my face and inhaled. She always prayed for a cool, dry spell, so they would last a long time. I slipped the stalk into my apron pocket and approached the next tree, one of pale purple blossoms. I reached as high as I could and broke off a woody stem.

I heard a rustlin'. I whipped around to face Nellie with her cheeks all ab-lush. "Nellie, you shouldn't sneak up on me like that."

She laughed and pointed at the lilacs burstin' out from my apron pocket. The slight breeze blew strands of her silvery white hair in front of her eyes and across her lined forehead.

"Aren't they lovely?" I snapped another stem.

She opened her arms in front of all of the lilac bushes and then looked up at the sky.

"What on earth are you doin'?" I plucked the green leaves from the lower part of the stem and placed it in my pocket with the others.

She looked stern and then acted as if she was pickin' all the beautiful lilacs in a frenzy. She sighed and walked away.

"You're a silly woman." I felt the blossoms in my apron pocket. "I should leave some and not be so greedy."

Her eyes widened and she moved closer.

"Who am I to pick all of the lilacs, jest to have them die in a bucket of water?" I sat down on the cool, damp grass. "I should leave some behind for the butterflies, bees, and hummin'birds."

She smiled and sat in front of me pokin' her finger into her chest.

"Nellie, you're actin' peculiar. What are tryin' to tell me?"

She glided her hand through the air, jabbed her finger into a cluster of blossoms, pulled it back out, and repeated the process.

I watched in amusement as she slowly danced around the tree, flappin' her arms and dancin'. "Are you a hummin' bird?"

She bobbed her head in agreement.

"You're a hummin' bird?"

She bobbed again.

I had never seen her so pleased. I could only suppose that her Indian name was Hummin'bird. I felt quite warm and tingly when I watched her wander over to the pond, still flappin' her imaginary wings. It was odd that I learned more from her – a woman who never uttered a word – than any other.

"Abigail!" Polly shouted, slicin' through the tenderness of the moment. "What in Heaven's name are you doin'?" She marched towards me like a foot soldier.

"I was pickin' some—"

"You never mind." She shook her head and said, "This ain't no holiday. Now you get down there and start hangin' the laundry on them lines out back."

"Yes, ma'am." I swallowed. Samuel started to fuss and fidget.

"And I mean now." She stormed down the hill.

"Shhh. It'll be fine." I kissed Samuel on top of his head, sat down on the grassy knoll, and held him to my breast. "She'll have to wait. A hungry child comes first."

I pulled my shawl around Samuel when the wind picked up. I heard the snap of a branch. "Nellie, is that you my little hummin' bird?"

No one answered. I looked and saw no one. I scrambled to my feet when I heard the swishin' of old dead leaves. "Who's there?" I pulled Samuel in close to me.

My heart raced at the sight of Silas duckin' out from under some branches. I stepped backwards, about to flee.

"Wait." He stayed within the safety of the bushes. "Please, don't leave."

Since my arrival, I did my best to avoid Silas. I did well with the exception of a few scrapes. After the birth of our son, I managed to escape him altogether. "What do you want?" The ragin' fire of passion, anger, and fear crackled inside of me.

"We need to talk." He retreated into the bushes.

"There is nothin' to be said." I turned away. "I must go to work now, or they will not allow me to keep my baby with me."

"I can't wait no more, and I won't let them take him."

"Polly said that if I don't do my share of chores, the baby would be sent away to a family that will give him a good home." I wilted.

"We jest hafta' talk." He peered out from behind a branch.

"She said that chances are, since he's so healthy and all, they might take him whether I work hard or not."

"Abigail—"

"They'll have to take him over my dead body. I will run away first, and they'll have to—"

"Listen to me." He grabbed my arms, pullin' me through the thick branches and into the edge of the apple orchard.

I shielded Samuel's head with one hand and pushed the leafy branches away with the other. "I'm goin' to let out a scream, Silas, if you don't—"

He put his hand over my mouth. I thought of bitin' him but stood tremblin' and wantin' to flee.

"Now sit." He took his hand away from my mouth and pointed to the ground.

"No. I'm standin' right here."

"I gotta' know." His eyes filled up with tears.

"Know?" I started makin' my way back through the lilac bushes. "There is nothin' that you don't already know."

"Wait." He squeezed my elbow.

"Let me go."

We were interrupted by the sound of horses headin' in our direction. I broke free and hurried out the other side of the bushes as Asa galloped by with William followin' close behind. Silas ducked back into hidin'. I held tight to Samuel and dashed down the hill towards the barn.

I stopped abruptly at the pump to gather my wits about me. I tucked my loose curls under my snood and glanced around the yard. It seemed that no one was lookin'. I dipped the ladle into the barrel, and brought the water to my lips. Samuel squawked when the icy water dribbled down my chin and onto his head. I wiped the droplets away with the corner of my apron. He looked up at me with his big blue eyes, Silas's eyes.

I wondered why he would come forward then. He had a wife, and for all I knew he had his own child on the way. I dabbed the sweat from my brow.

"We don't have all day, Missy." Polly jabbed me in the small of my back with her newer, longer, sharper stick that she must have found after the snow melted.

CHAPTER 68

Silas – May 23, 1873

DADDY ALWAYS SAID that when somethin' is born, somethin' dies, and when somethin' dies, somethin' is born – livestock, deadstock.

Two days after Samuel's birth, Daddy became deadstock when he up and died, leanin' against the woodpile with a half a jug of whiskey froze in his hand.

I guess I shouldn't have 'spected nothin' more from Daddy. He weren't ever the same after the war. He lived by the jug and died by the jug. I thought it were a blessin' for Mamma not to have to put up with his cussin' and carryin' on, but grief hit her hard. Jessie weren't pleased when I invited her to move in with us come September, but Mamma didn't want no part of leavin' the house she was born in.

When I was a young boy, Grandpa Putnam gave Daddy a two-drawer pine cigar box. Even though he never had more than a handful of cigars at one time, Daddy beamed with pride because the box held up to a hundred cigars. When Mamma gave the old wooden box to me after he died, I didn't have no desire to look inside.

Other than accidental bits and pieces of useless things that Daddy had a knack for collectin', the only thing I 'spected to find was the stench that he carried with him as far back as I could recall. I hauled the box into the house and left it on the floor by the foot of the bed. Jessie bothered me every day to open it, beggin' me to look inside. I couldn't get her to understand that Daddy didn't have nothin' worth savin'.

I was about to get some breakfast, when I found myself reachin' for the box. I held it in my hands for a spell before finally openin' the top drawer. Jest as I 'spected, the familiar rotten smell hit me. I slammed the cover shut.

I sat in silence with the box restin' on my lap waitin' for a feelin'… any feelin' at all. Like when he died, I waited for tears, but none came. After his service, when the folks was all gone, I still felt nothin'. Why didn't I grieve for the bastard? He managed to kill any hope of grievin'.

Then I felt somethin' odd, too odd to accept or speak of. So, I pushed it way down inside. I kicked myself for havin' such feelin's. I preferred to feel nothin' than to feel so much joy and relief that I wanted to dance.

I rubbed my hands together and re-opened the drawer. I unfolded the crumpled receipt for the cow that he bought from Clarence Hutchins, dated June 10, 1868. She was a fine black and white cow that followed me around the same way a dog followed its master.

Next, I happened across a neatly folded paper with, "Volunteer Enlistment," printed boldly across the top. It broke the barrier. I felt a twinge of sadness or maybe somethin' else when I recalled all them nights we sat by the fire. He told stories about his heroic deeds: bein' shot in the leg, mouthin' off to a Reb, and the other gruesome tragedies of war. I knew most of the words by heart. As the years passed, he often relied on my memory to help him so he could conjure up some well-earned tears.

I pulled out the soiled handkerchief pressed into the corner of the drawer amongst brittle tobacco crumbs. It had been many years since I had seen Mamma plyin' the needle. I shook it and tried to smooth out the wrinkles before droppin' it back in the drawer.

The yellowed newspaper clippin', from when his regiment returned from the Great War of the Rebellion, had tears in the creases from frequent handlin'. I leaned over to show Jessie. She didn't move, sleepin' soundly with her new flowered nightcap snug on her head. I envied her. Ever since the birth of Samuel and the passin' of Daddy, I lay awake wonderin' how everything got all knotted up. I tried to figure out why Abigail didn't tell me about the child, or why she chose to go to the County Farm. I thought about it over and over again, 'til I finally fell asleep, only to wake up thinkin' 'bout it again.

I returned the papers to the smelly box. I wanted to check the progress of the buildin' of our house before goin' to the farm.

Jessie stirred. "Are you leaving now?"

"Yep." I tied my bootlaces. "Shortly."

She climbed out of bed and wandered over to me. "Why are you leaving so early?"

"I want to see how our house is comin' along and then go straight to the farm." I kissed her forehead.

She pouted as she often did, and I didn't have the mind to question it.

"Have yourself a good day, and get some fresh air. Winter's gone." I headed downstairs.

The bright sun streamed in through the kitchen windows. "Are you stoppin' long enough for breakfast, Mr. Putnam?" Sally stood proud in front of a freshly baked loaf of corn bread.

"It's Silas." I stopped with the door slightly open.

She dimmed.

"And, yes, I have to have at least one piece of your bread." I closed the door and sat down at the table.

Her shiny, scrubbed cheeks blushed beneath all 'em freckles. "Thank you."

"No." It felt good to smile. "Thank you."

"You missed Doc and Mrs. Gilman. They was out early." She flipped a generous hunk of bread onto my plate.

"Oh." I stuffed half of it into my mouth. "Mmm. You're a heck of a good cook."

"You embarrass me, Mr. Putnam."

"Silas." I shoveled in the rest of the bread and paused in the doorway. "Mr. Putnam was my daddy."

"Silas." she said, rollin' her eyes.

I stopped on the front step. *Was my daddy? Was? Where is he now? Surely not in Heaven — wherever that is.* I buttoned my coat and started for the barn, the place where everything made sense, where I could have thoughts without judgment or invitin' anyone to talkin'.

The door flew open. Still in her nightdress, Jessie chased after me. "Wait."

"What is it?" I took her into my arms, noticin' that her flowery scent – all but gone since the weddin'– had returned.

"Oh, Silas." She wrapped her arms around my middle and rested her head on my chest. "I'm so anxious to move into our own house."

"If all goes well, it'll be done before September."

She pouted.

"You ain't fussin' are ya?" I stepped back, searchin' her face for a clue. From day to day, I never knew what her concern would be jest as I was about to leave.

A big tear slid down her cheek. She looked up at me. "It's been nearly five whole months, and I'm still not with child." She buried her face in my shirt.

"Now, now." I patted her head. "There ain't no hurry." My thoughts turned to how I found myself watchin' Abigail while I oversaw the men plowin' the field. She sat amongst the lilac trees singin' to the baby.

"I know there's no hurry for you. But I'm ready now." She dabbed the corner of her eye with her fancy handkerchief, tryin' to capture that one tear, and maybe find another.

"Maybe it's jest as well until we move into the house." I swatted at the cloud of black flies swarmin' 'round my head.

Her body stiffened, and she pulled away. "These black flies will be the death of me. I'm going inside." She stormed up the front steps. "Come on."

"Like I said, I'm goin' to check on the men at the house. They got the cellar hole dug and are puttin' in the floor beams." I squinted and looked beyond a grove of hardwood trees towards our property.

"Suit yourself." She slammed the door.

At first, I thought about ridin' Major but decided to walk. I kicked through leftover patches of snow scattered in the deep, shady part of the woods and whistled what I supposed was an old drinkin' tune. The hammer stopped ringin' as I approached. I wanted to join in, but Doc Gilman hired about seven men to build the house so that I could concentrate on the County Farm.

"Good mornin'!" I called over to the circle of workers huddled in the corner of the newly dug cellar hole. "Jest stoppin' by to see what's a doin'."

They glanced at me and then returned to their manly circle as if I weren't there. That's what happens when someone else pays 'em. They don't answer to ya.

After seein' that nothin' much changed, I left, stumblin' over uneven ground, kickin' at dried, curled up ferns mixed with new green shoots pokin' through. Moses and I coulda' built that house without the likes of them big-headed men from outta' town, and we'd probably done a better job.

I fought the urge to return to the cellar hole and knock their heads together, but I knew it weren't my place to complain. By payin' no mind, I'd shorten the uphill of life.

I snuck to the back of the barn and slipped out with Major, hopin' not to attract attention from the kitchen, where Jessie roared aimlessly at Sally.

⋅►═◉ ◉═◄⋅

We had to bury the rest of them folks who passed away, so I spent a good part of the mornin' overseein' the men load up the cart with the last of the pine coffins that Billy Peavy and Timothy Hutchins made.

We made several trips to the cemetery that day, which was generally pleasin' in spite of the black flies. Benjamin Wallace, Charles, and I had the miserable task of buryin' 'em. The inmates were strugglin' with their own health and generally took no part in buryin' the dead. On occasion, they paid their last respects, and folks from town might come along with the pastor to offer a few good words.

"This is the last of 'em." Charles hopped onto the cart.

"Ayuh." I caught movement outta' the corner of my eye and heard a tinklin' of laughter comin' from the lilac bushes. My face reddened at the sight of Abigail and the baby.

The leather harness squeaked, and the carriage rumbled. "Go on ahead. I'll catch up to ya." I slapped the rump of the horse.

"I s'pose you'll be in that outhouse for the rest of the afternoon." Ben burst into a hearty laugh. I couldn't determine if he thought himself to be amusin' or if he was plain nervous, but he laughed louder and more often than most folks.

"That's one way to get out of a good day's work." Charles spat on the ground. "Don't take too long, Silas. It's your turn to dig."

The cart creaked and lunged forward, carryin' the stinkin', cussin' men, who told them same old stories that happened to change a bit with each tellin'.

After they disappeared, I went around to the backside of the lilac bushes near the apple trees. I watched her. She looked so beautiful in that same old dress, speckled with faded bloodstains and no longer clingin' to her round belly. I felt a tightenin' in my chest when she spoke to the baby in soft musical tones. Then Polly let out a good holler causin' me to jump. She got right up in Abigail's face and cussed a good one. I ducked behind the leafy branches, watchin' and waitin'.

After listenin' to the ornery old hag long enough, I had a mind to step in but thought against it. It would have appeared odd for me to come barrelin' out of the bushes. I didn't want no tongues waggin'.

The baby fussed and squirmed. Abigail must have learned her lesson because other than havin' a face redder than an apple, she kept her anger under a bushel. I was proud of her for that.

I peeked through the branches and waited for Polly to leave while Abigail sat down on the grass. She slipped the yellow dress off her shoulder and placed the baby at her breast.

When I watched the golden sun glow on her thick curls and his small perfect round head against the fair skin of her breast, I became all too human. The pressure built in my chest and tears stung my eyes. I took a step closer.

"Nellie, is that you my little hummin' bird?" she called.

Twigs snapped under my feet. I stopped.

"Who's there?" Her voice cracked.

I parted the branches. She gasped.

"Wait. Please don't leave."

"What do you want?" She pressed the baby close to her chest.

"We need to talk." I remained hidden.

"There is nothin' to be said." She turned her back on me. "I must go to work now, or they'll take my baby away."

I swore I wouldn't beg. "I can't wait no more, and I won't let 'em take him, don't worry."

"Polly said that if I don't do my share of chores, the baby would be sent away."

"We have to talk."

"She says that they might take him whether I work good or not."

"Abigail –" I touched the soft skin on her arm.

"I will run away first and..."

I no longer cared if anyone saw us. "Listen!" I dragged her into the bushes, stoppin' abruptly when I saw fear in her eyes.

She fumbled with her dress, coverin' her exposed breast. I thought she might scream. I cupped my hand over her mouth. All I wanted was for her to jest listen to me.

"Now sit." I released her arm.

"I'm standin' right here."

"I gotta' know." I had all I could do to keep from bawlin'.

"Know?" She gathered up the folds of her shabby dress as if it were an elegant gown. "There is nothin' that you don't already know." She whirled around.

I grasped her elbow. "Wait."

She jerked away, and we both stopped at the sound of horses.

I crouched down. Sweat soaked my shirt, and my hands shook as Asa and William passed so close I coulda' touched 'em.

When Abigail fled, I stared numbly at her yellow dress flappin' in the wind. That ole heavin' started comin', but I wouldn't let it.

I took off down the hill with black flies swarmin' around my head. I kept my eyes down and paid 'em no mind. When I got to Brown's Ridge Road, my breathin' had returned to normal, and I was whistlin' by the time I reached the cemetery.

"Well that didn't take too long." Ben jabbed Charles with his elbow.

"He jest wanted a chance to peek at the Hodgdon girl," Charles said.

"She's quite a beauty considerin' she's one of 'em." Ben wiped his brow.

"I know I'd have my way with her if the opportunity came up." Charles snickered and handed me the shovel. "Your turn to dig."

In my head I was fixin' to kill him with that shovel. Instead, I whistled even louder and drove the shovel into the earth. I kept diggin' without a word, without stoppin', 'til the sun was about to set on Brown's Ridge, 'til that hole was dug deep.

CHAPTER 69

Nellie – May 23, 1873

THE WATERS OF Cold River joined with sister streams, rushing from the mountain. Many voices sang in her currents. Offerings of hope were wrapped in tight buds within fingertips of crooked white birches. Trees once cloaked in frigid whiteness, baring souls in the dim light of winter, stood before Father Sky. It was time to rejoice. The Planting Moon was upon us.

I was to crush bone meal with the elders. Before joining them, I went to the edge of the pond to await the return of the butterfly. I sat on the soft grass and closed my eyes. I leaned into the uplifting rush of wind that carried his voice. *I am with you.*

⋅⊱⊰⋅

Emily approached. She lived on the other side of the river. *Sorry to hear 'bout Mister Baldwin, Ma'am.*

I looked to the banks of Cold River, where Searching Owl lay in the earth beside our son.

Ah… he was quite nice.

The smell of purple flowers summoned the day that men shouted, and the sound of horses drummed in the distance, the day that my husband's spirit departed.

⋅⊱⊰⋅

I fell to the ground when the men came. The song of the woods was not the same. The wind, river, and birds flushing from the trees made a silent scream. Sickness grew in my stomach. I lay on the earth and waited for them. The others came first. My husband was the last, draped over his horse and covered with a blanket that was red with his blood.

Mister Cook spoke. *Mrs. Baldwin?*

My eyes rested on the blanket.

He led me into our home. I pushed him away and ran to my husband and fell to the ground. The gray clouds swallowed the great flame that burned in Father Sky. The men took my husband off of his horse.

Get her away from here. A man stepped between my husband and me.

Darkness fell upon my spirit. I took flight from my body and sat beside my friend the crow in the great white pine and watched from above.

I knew he weren't gonna' make it. One man said.

He was reaching for this when he fell. He gave something to the other man.

What is it? He held it up. *Some sort of bird he whittled.*

Give it back. He snatched it away from the other man.

I descended from my perch, reuniting with self. I stepped lightly as I approached the men. I pushed through their circle and extended my hand. The man dropped the carving into my palm. I wrapped my fingers around the smooth pine and looked away from the red blanket. The shadow of my friend the crow passed overhead, clicking and knowing.

I opened my hand. My heart soared. The slender, wooden beak came to a point. I traced my finger along the lines carved by his knife. I turned it over to see his symbol, the heart, cut into the grain. I held it tight.

There was an accident at the mill. Apparently your husband dropped that carvin', and when he reached for it, he got pulled right in. He fought for courage to speak. *We tried to save him. He lost his arm... The blood...* tears came.

The wind did not speak. When I kneeled before my husband, the trees, river, and birds were soundless. I pulled the blanket away. Blood covered his face and his body where the great jaws of the white man's beast tore his arm. In death, he wore the mask of pain. I touched his face. The coldness passed through my fingers, reaching my heart. I pulled my hand away and looked at Father Sky. Searching Owl's spirit had departed. He was with our son and Mamijôla and the others. The tears did not come.

We should take him now. The tallest of the white men spoke.

Mister Cook touched my shoulder. *We must take him Ma'am so that he can have a proper Christian burial.*

I looked him in the eye.

You can come with us. We'll fix him up with a coffin and…

I shook my head. We did not go to the white man's church to worship their dead king. I pointed to our burial ground by Cold River.

They ain't church goin' people. She'll probably have an Injun burial. A short man with much hair covering his face spoke.

Yes, Elijah was born as one of us, but he shoulda' been an Indian. He lived the Indian way, had an Indian wife. He would want it the way that Mrs. Baldwin wants it. A young man with kind eyes and a gentle voice spoke for the first time.

Well, we oughta' go into town and report his death. Mister Cook spoke. *Will you be needin' some help, Ma'am?*

I kneeled beside my husband, covered him with the blanket, and bowed my head.

There ain't nothin' for us to do here. I'll come back and check on her in the mornin'. Mister Cook tipped his hat and mounted his horse. The sounds of men's voices and running horses became one with the river.

I went into our home to prepare for the burial. When I returned to him, the sight of the red blanket brought forth many tears. At our circle, I made a fire with small branches of pine and maple, dried leaves, and bark of the white birch. Much smoke kept the small black flies away.

I placed the kettle of hot water and many pieces of cloth by his side. I closed my eyes and called upon my ancestors to stand with me.

Shedding many tears, I took the blanket away and fell upon him. I dreamed of his embrace. My heart beat against where his lay silent. The warmth of my breast ached upon his coldness.

I moved away. *I call upon the Great Spirit to give me the strength of the bear and the wisdom of the owl.* I covered my face with my hands and swayed to the river's lament.

The white-tailed hawk cried from the inner sky. I gathered the blanket – thick with his blood – and went to the fire. I released it into the flames and stepped away. The fire grew hot. The blanket burned brightly, throwing sparks into the leafy trees and Father Sky.

I returned to my husband. The jaws had torn his body and his garments. With much force, I ripped the shirt free from his body. My hands quaked as I set his arm in place. I poured hot water from the kettle into the oaken bucket and cleansed his body, making my hands red with his blood. I filled the bucket with fresh water and washed his hair with juniper oil.

After I made pure his body, I rubbed mullein flower oil on his skin. He was ready. With great strength, I wrapped him from his neck to his feet in a thick, brown woven blanket.

With his shovel, I dug. I struck many rocks and roots. I prepared his burial place beside our son on the bluff near Cold River. The call of the red-winged blackbird rose above the river song. Sunset was near. It was time to return him to Our Mother. Many tears came.

I rested before moving him. I dragged. I cried. I dragged. The sunset made red, pink, and golden clouds, and the fire burned low. I placed more branches on the fire and returned to my husband. The blood from his wounds spread on the blanket. I held his feet and pulled again. I screamed. I pulled. I cried at the sight of him. I cried from his weight. I pulled him once more, not stopping until I reached his place of rest. I laid him on his left side, facing the west – the Looking Place.

I ran swiftly into our house. I took a feather of the barred owl from the spruce box and two of his arrows and returned to my husband. I placed the feather upon his chest, the arrows beside him, and I spread pine boughs around him. I silently said the death prayer and gave a tobacco offering before covering him with earth. After much time passed, I left his side.

I returned to the fire and stripped away my clothes. The flames leapt high into the darkness. I poured red clover water over my body to wash away tears, blood, and the rich earth of Our Mother.

I wore the dress made by my mother from many winters past, and with my flute, I returned to my husband. There was no moon. The only light came from the fire. I stood beside him and raised my flute to my lips. Quivering and seeking the flow of air, I waited. Softly and gently I played. The waters of Cold River hushed. The brightest star looked down upon hearing my song of sorrow. I played until the night chorus emerged. I prayed to the Great Spirit.

Death comes to all living things that dwell upon Our Mother. Our powers are great and small. We are with both strength and weariness until death comes upon us. The great flame in the sky rises and shines until it is overcome by darkness. The moon swells to fullness and then fades. Flowers bud, bloom, and then wilt. Trees boast green leaves and then die in glory. The wind blows and then calms. All things die. All things are reborn and live again. I call upon the Great Spirit, guides, and ancestors to give him guidance as he departs from his earth walk. I will honor his spirit within mine.

→══● ●══←

I returned to Emily, whose eyes were the deepest blue. *I sure like them lilacs. Ain't they special?*

I smiled and embraced her.

The sound of one horse came from beyond the trees. We stood together and watched as the tall, strong man stopped before us on his brown stallion. He was a town leader. Searching Owl did not care for him. *Nellie Baldwin?* He lifted his hat.

I nodded.

I'm here to collect the payment that you owe on the property here. He held the reins tight with two hands and kept his eyes upon me.

She don't speak. The girl looked up at him.

I don't care one way or the other. I have to tell her in the name of the law 'bout her debts. I'm here to notify her. The horse trotted in a small circle.

Mister Baldwin jest died; ain't you got no respect? The girl was brave.

I'm sorry 'bout your loss, Ma'am. He lifted his hat again. *I knew Elijah. He was a good man. It's a tragic thing to die like that. But this is simply business.*

Again, I put the flower up to my nose. I did not look away from where my husband lay in the bosom of Our Mother. The wind rose in the tallest part of the giant pines, releasing fine yellow dust.

Well, I'm obliged to give you this, ma'am. And I'll be back to collect in about a week. He held a paper in his hand and reached towards me.

I did not move. The girl took the paper from him. *Mister, you should leave. God forgive you for thinkin' of money at a time like this.*

I stepped in front of his horse. He pulled back hard on the reins. *Whoa! What in the devil's name are you doin'?* The horse reared.

I stared into the man's gray eyes. He did not smile. I turned and walked into our home. He talked to the girl. I reached for the small spruce box, one of many made by my husband. He was a man of his word. Inside were coins and bills.

I returned to the man and offered him the box. *What's this?* He seized it.

I looked to the place where my husband lay beside our son on the bluff by the river. I reached in my pocket and felt the smooth wood of my whistle. *I do not need this, for Searching Owl is with me always.*

He opened the box and counted. *This is too much.* He reached down with one gold coin in his hand. I did not accept it.

The wind in the tall pines swelled to a longing cry. My hair blew before my eyes as fierce, gray clouds swallowed the light.

Ain't you gonna' take it? The girl touched my arm.

Despair fell upon me. I could not move.

Here. You take this. He gave the coin to the girl.

What about the box? She called to him.

I sort of like it. I don't think the squaw minds if I take it with me. He put it inside his pocket. *Good day, ladies.*

Here's your coin. He says that you gave him too much. Her face glowed with hope.

I remained still. I looked to Father Sky and waited for the time when I could return to our home alone.

I gotta' go home, or I'll be in a heap of trouble. She held on to her hat and ran downstream to the footbridge.

I stood before my husband, son, and Cold River until the clouds became a soft blanket of deep yellow. I went to my house, and I sat before the fire, wrapped in the shirt that I made for Searching Owl two winters past. I could not take food. I drank tea of the yellow lady slipper. I stared into the fire until sleep found me and took me to where dreams live.

When I awoke, I did not move. I searched the room to see if my husband would come from the Otherworld. It was quiet inside. The small black and white birds called to their mates and fluttered amongst leafy limbs. Wrapped in the red and green woven blanket, I went outside. The sun warmed my face. I looked to where Searching Owl lay and closed my eyes. The water tumbled over rocks, playing and singing. I opened my eyes. There was brightness shining by my feet. I reached down and picked up the gold coin that the girl had left in the night.

CHAPTER 70

Silas – September 13, 1873

THE FULLY LOADED carriage rocked from side to side. The sun peeked through the trees, flickerin' on Jessie's face as she rested her head on my shoulder. The sky was always bluest in September, and the leaves was on the verge of turnin'. The bugs was gone, the nights cool, and the days warm.

The new house had been finished for nearly a month. When it was time to move in, she weren't in no hurry. As much as she complained, she was bothered about leavin' her folks.

"I'm eager to spend our first night in our new home," she said.

"Ayuh, it sure is special." We turned onto the rocky path that led to our house. "A cause for celebration."

We came to a stop beside the oxen cart that Moses brung from the County Farm. He waited on the porch with his arms folded across his bulky chest, studyin' me through a thin trail of smoke that curled around his face. "Is that the last of it?"

"That's the last of it," I said.

I was carryin' the rockin' chair up the stairs when I heard a clatter. Stern-faced and thin-lipped, Mrs. Blake and a worried Mrs. Leighton bobbled on the seat of Moses's carriage, makin' their way towards us.

"Hello." Mrs. Blake pushed her way past me carryin' a bean pot. Mrs. Leighton smiled apologetically, as she always did when she weren't wrapped up in the safety of her organ keys.

"Hello." I followed them into the kitchen. "Jessie, come see who is payin' us a visit."

"I can't hear you. How many times must I remind you—" Jessie marched into the kitchen, stoppin' short when she saw the women.

Moses wandered in from out back. "Hello, Miriam."

She dismissed her husband with a nod and glanced at Jessie. "We have beans and molasses, salt pork, and fresh zucchini bread."

"That is so thoughtful and kind." Jessie clasped her hands and giggled the way that she did when she wanted folks to notice her. "I don't know how to repay you."

"There's no need to repay us," Mrs. Blake snapped. "It's what decent folks do. Now Moses, don't leave here without makin' a fire and helpin' with the wood."

I bit the inside of my cheek to keep from grinnin'. Moses didn't much care for bein' pecked. I learned quick to jest let it go, but Moses weren't that way. He didn't take sass from nobody, includin' his wife.

"You ain't gotta' tell me what to do, woman." He stuffed his pipe into his shirt pocket.

George Durgin came with Moses to give a hand. He burst through the door carryin' an armload of wood. "Where do you want it stacked?" He looked at Moses instead of me.

"Jest on the hearthside for the time bein'." I spoke a little louder than usual, probably even hollered, invitin' everyone to stare. I had a belly full of bein' ignored by the men who built the house.

"Would you all care to join us for beans and zucchini bread?" Jessie flitted across the room, seizin' the opportunity to make a food offerin', seein' she weren't much of a cook. "I also have some fresh piccalilli from Tibbetts' Store."

Mrs. Leighton was ready to oblige when Mrs. Blake blurted out, "No, no, no. Of course not. We brought this for you."

Even though I was tuckered out, I needed to unwind and settle down. Jessie went on to bed before me. I leaned over and positioned one last piece of poplar on the fire. The flames scurried along the edges of the bark, brightenin' the room. Daddy's old cigar box caught my eye. I picked it up from the floor, where Moses set it. I sat down in the rockin' chair, enjoyin' bein' housed up in my own place. *What should I do with this old thing?*

I opened the top drawer, and that old rotten smell hit me again. I rifled through the papers supposin' that perhaps I should keep my own papers in there.

I reached underneath, and the second drawer slid out in my hands. My faced reddened, as I always thought that the second drawer was for show.

I came across some papers crammed inside like they was crumpled up in a hurry. I unfolded the top wad of paper. Someone had scribbled the word *taxes* in unfamiliar writin' across the top. I flattened the creases with my fingers. As I started to read it, I had an urge to heave.

"God, no." I held the letter by the light of the fire to see if what I was readin' was real, that my eyes wasn't playin' tricks on me.

Dear Silas,

I do find that it is nessesarie for me to speake with you, so I am penning you this letter. This is an importint mater. I have not had the oportuntie to see you privatlie since the death of my beloved mother. It is with a heavy heart that I write to you. I am in such a way that time is of the esensse. Please meet me at our spot in the field behind the barn. I will arrive at 3:00 on Saterday and I will wait there after meeting on Sunday if Saterday is not goode. If you cannot meete me, please send a reply note and leeve it under the bench in the stall beside Lizzy. I left a small box for your use. I will waite for you and know that if you do not arrive, that it is true, you have given your heart to Jesy. I pray that this is not so, as it is you who I profess my love to.

Faithfully Youres,
Abigail

I read it again. Why was the letter in there? I paced in a circle, shakin' from the inside. She did try to tell me. Dear God, she thinks I ignored her.

"Silas, are you coming?" Jessie called from upstairs.

I choked.

"Silas?" Her light footsteps stopped at the top of the stairs. "Do you hear me?"

"I'll be up shortly. I'm stokin' the fire." I dropped the letter and grabbed a fistful of my hair and pulled.

"Oh, God." I reached for the other crinkled paper. There was more? I unfolded it. My chest tightened.

Dear Silas,

I write to you in despiration. I waited for you Saturday & Sunday last & you did not show. Peple talk about you and Jesy Gilman getting maried. Surely that canot be true. For if it is true, I shall lament for the rest of my days.

What it is that I must talk to you aboute is an urgent matter. Remember when we were intimat in the hayloft? There is a conseqense for our behavore. I am not free to write it in a letter and would prefer to tell you in person.

I remain in anguish here conserning the sad feelins that are resting upon my mind. My life has becom lonely & filled with drugery and tiresom work. I miss our talks and genrally being close. What I have to tell you is without questhion the most important thing in our lifes.

Come to our spot when it pleases you. Place a letter in the stall beside Lizzy under the bench to tell me when we shuld meet. I will check it evry day. I do not beleve it to be true that you love any other than myselfe.

I waite faithfully.
Abigail

I rocked in the chair with the letter in my fist. How could that goddamned drunk bastard have kept these from me? The tears came, and I let them. I had no choice in the matter.

Jessie stood behind me and massaged my shoulders. "Now, now. It's about time you mourned the loss of your father."

I crumpled the letter in my hand. "I s'pose it caught up to me is all."

"We've been under a great deal of pressure. Now you have the opportunity to grieve. I understand." She walked towards the stairs. "You need to do what is necessary."

I stared into the fire, distorted through tears, and tried to clear my head.

"I'm worn out. Come to bed when you're ready." She disappeared up the stairs wearin' her fancy blue-checked nightgown and matchin' cap.

CHAPTER 71

Abigail – September 14, 1873

I WAS ABOUT to pluck the biggest apple that caught my eye. I stopped, realizin' that I already had two in my apron pocket. I had learned from Nellie to take from the earth what is needed and nothin' more. I returned to Samuel, where he lay on my cape, squirmin' and lookin' up at me.

I plopped down and gathered him into my arms. The sun was agreeably warm as high noon approached. I took an apple from my pocket, rubbed it against my yellow dress until it was shiny, and then I bit into it with a snap. My lips puckered until the meat of the apple sweetened.

Samuel reached for the apple and smiled. His tiny white tooth sprouted out from his bottom gum. I took another bite. "No, no my sweet, you have but one tooth. It's much too soon." I laughed and wiped the juice from my chin with the corner of my apron.

Often, Sunday afternoons afforded a time of leisure. We did some harvestin' in the mornin' because the gardens were abundant, and there was still some corn and butternut squash to pick. I enjoyed workin' in the fields. I was accustomed to it. I generally preferred the outdoors to the stiflin' launderin' room or the kitchen, where scourin' the floor and cleanin' pots was the order of the day.

I had taken issue with the fact that it was a man's job to milk the cows. I requested to do barn chores, but Miss Noyes laughed loud and hard when I mentioned it. She wagged her fat finger in my face and said that the men were the only inmates who could work in the barn. I had to do launderin, sewin, cleanin', or gardenin'. Unless, of course, I wanted to grind bone meal.

I meandered through the fields and orchards whenever possible. I must confess that I longed for the days when I had the freedom to be my wild self and bathe in the solitude of the woods, which were completely off limits.

I carried Samuel in the sling. When it got too hot, I doused us both in cool water from the spring-fed pond. I could take the black flies in May, followed by the wood ticks and the mosquitoes, as long as I used Nellie's oil to keep them from bitin'.

I had a hankerin' to see Lizzy and Old Gray Mare. I went to the barn now and then durin' the summer, but it wasn't as easy sneakin' around with Samuel. I never knew when he might make a noise.

I bundled Samuel in my cape, snatched an apple for Old Gray Mare, and dashed down the grassy hillside, avoidin' the bees on the half-rotted apples that lay on the ground.

There wasn't much activity in the barn on Sundays, so I thought it a good time to go inside. When we reached the pasture out back, Old Gray Mare trotted up to the fence. I broke the skin of the apple with my teeth, pried off a section, and fed it to my horse. She ate it quickly and nudged me for more. I fed her the rest of the apple bit by bit and gave her a handful of red clover. Samuel squealed with delight when I took his small hand in mine and rubbed it on the horse's nose.

"This is Old Gray Mare, dear heart," I whispered in his ear. "Someday I will teach you to ride."

Someone gripped my shoulder.

"Abigail?" Silas's voice rushed past my ears and into my chest. He turned me around to face him. He did not look well. His eyes were red, swollen, and with dark circles beneath them.

"What is it?" I leaned against the wooden fence while he maintained his hold on me. Old Gray Mare nibbled on the back of my neck.

"You mustn't run or hide from me." His eyes were especially blue.

"We have nothin' to discuss." I shrugged my shoulder in an attempt to free myself.

"Stop." He squeezed tighter. "You're comin' with me, where we can talk without anyone buttin' in." He loosened his grip. "Oblige me."

I followed behind him, barely able to keep up. We went to the back of the barn and ducked inside the half-open door.

Enterin' into the blackness from the bright sun caused me to stumble over the uneven boards. I stopped and tried to focus.

"Abigail?" He came towards me.

"I'm here."

"We have to go where no one will see or hear us." He took my hand.

"Why?"

"Shhh." He looked around quickly before steppin' into the blacksmith shop.

I looked at all of the tools and such hangin' on the walls as we neared the coffin room. I shivered. The warmth of the day never reached that part of the barn.

"Come here." He pushed on the thick, heavy door. "Don't be afraid."

When he opened the door, the aroma of fresh pine swept over me. Gone were the days when this scent transported me to a place of comfort and safety. I was certain that I would drop. First my thoughts turned to Papa, and then to the coffins that we saw on that dark winter night. I stopped. "I don't like it here."

"It'll be fine. There's nothin' to be afraid of."

The room looked different than it did when I was with Nellie. There were boot tracks and sawdust piles coverin' the floor and only one pine box instead of a stack of them.

"I'm cold." My voice was flat and louder than I expected.

"Here, wear this." He draped his coat over my shoulders. He lit a dusty lantern.

"Why did you bring me here?" I asked.

"Sit." He dragged a barrel across the room and set it in front of me.

Samuel squirmed in my arms and started to fuss. I stroked his head and kept my eyes on Silas as he sat upon a rickety sawhorse.

He reached inside of his trouser pocket and pulled out two wads of paper. One at a time and with tremblin' hands, he carefully spread them out on his knee. He attempted to speak.

I leaned closer to get a better look. My stomach rebelled when I recognized the writin' as my own. I covered my mouth with my hand and closed my eyes. Samuel wove his tiny fingers into my curls and pulled.

"Abigail?" he whispered. "I found these letters last night. I found 'em last night." Tears streamed down his cheeks.

I feared that my heart would stop beatin'. The entire ache that I tucked away inside started to gush out like a waterfall. The room whirled about.

He grabbed the letters and held them in his fist. "I never got these letters!" He hollered as loud as any man could. "I thought that you avoided me to be with Weston!"

Miss Emily walked into the room, purrin' and weavin' around my ankles. Samuel laughed and reached for the cat. I tried to awaken from what I imagined was a horrific dream.

"And I jest knew that if a man had his way with you at the railroad tracks that you woulda' told me." He shook his head. "Moses tried to convince me that if it were my child, you would have come to me."

I stared, unblinkin' while his mouth moved and all sound diminished.

"And you told the commissioners that the baby would arrive in April or May. So, I didn't think it was possible for me to be the father," he cried.

I was numb. I tried to see beyond the shadows and beyond the flickerin' light. I swallowed, unable to speak.

"I found these in my daddy's cigar box." He jumped to his feet. "I hate him! I hate him! If he weren't already dead, I'd kill him." He wept like a child, leanin' against the wall with his head buried in his arms.

The cat jumped onto my lap and found a way to nestle into Samuel. I tried to wiggle my toes inside of my boots, but I could not feel them. I realized then that I was awake. I felt my forehead for fear that I was gravely ill. I opened my mouth. No words.

"I married Jessie." He clenched his fist and hit the wall. "I don't love her!" He struck it again. "I love you. I always have and I always will." He stared at me. "I thought that you didn't want me."

I pushed the cat away and covered my face with my hands. I recalled the night that I served Silas, Jessie, and the others while at the Blakes, no longer carin' if my spirit lived or died. I had accepted my fate and learned to dwell in endless misery.

He wiped his bloody hand over his face and stood motionless with the letters by his feet. "Abigail, I would have married you. I would have made a life with you and our son. We could have had many more children." He got on his knees before me.

I turned away from him with my chest risin' and fallin' dramatically as I tried to breathe. I looked up at the ceilin'. *Oh God, please shine a light to show me the way, for I am eternally lost.*

He put his hands on my knees. "What do we do?" He lay his head down on my lap. His tears soaked through my apron and into my dress. "I would never have kept you waitin'. It's no wonder you hated me."

I hesitated and held my hand over his head. I trembled, finally summonin' the courage to reach down and touch him, which caused him to cry louder.

Where was my voice? The urge to scream rose in my chest but came out as a soulful, deep cry. The gateway had opened, allowin' my sorrow to escape. "Oh my God!" I sobbed. I leaned over and lay my head on his, and we cried together. Our son looked on, releasin' one tiny hand from my hair and weavin' it into his father's curls, holdin' us all together.

After several moments, I sat up. "I don't know what to say." I wiped my face with my apron. "I am stunned and sickened to hear of this… but relieved too."

"I don't know either."

"You have a wife. You must honor your vows," I whispered.

"We can go away together. The three of us… where we don't know a soul. We can start fresh." He looked boyish and innocent.

I felt ill. I pushed him away and walked to the other side of the room. "You cannot do that. Your name will be blackened, and it isn't right."

"I can't go on like this. I love you." He came over to us and took Samuel from my arms. "He's my son." Samuel smiled at him, revealin' his one tooth. The afternoon bell rang, signalin' folks to get ready for dinner.

The tears started in again at the sight of Silas holdin' our son. "I have always loved you too, and I always will," I said. "But God has a plan."

"I was tormented before I knew the truth about you and our son; now it'll be hell." He held Samuel close to his chest and kissed his head. "My son can't be raised here."

"It's God's will." Samuel fussed when I took him away from Silas. "Perhaps it's because we sinned? I don't know. I have learned to accept my fate." Samuel reached for his father.

"I can't accept this." He picked up the letters from the floor. "My drunken daddy stuffed our fate into his cigar box."

"Do you think it's easy for me to say this? Do you know how I have wept and cursed you and your prim and proper wife? How my name is tarnished about town? I wear this yellow dress to alert others and to be reminded of my sordid behavior. You locked me in a room with a soiled blanket, chair, and chamber pot the night I gave birth to our son. The world knows of me as a whore." I wiped my tears on the sleeve of my dress. "And you will not accept it?"

"Abigail." He reached for me.

"Wait." I jerked away from his hand. "I am called a harlot to my face and our son a bastard. I have been spit upon, beat, poked and prodded with a stick. I've been hungry, cold, and wet, and had letters from my dear sister withheld from me. I waited for you to come to me or to write me a letter, instead you come to dinner with Jessie and talk about your home and future plans. I was nothin' more than a servant."

I paced, makin' a trail through the sawdust with my shoes. "You cannot accept this? We have no choice. His will be done."

"But, Abigail..." He put his hand on my shoulder. "I didn't know..."

I turned to face him. "God knows how I love you. I love you more than life itself, and there will not be another. But it can never be."

He pulled me and Samuel into his arms. "It has to be. This ain't of our doin'." He kissed my forehead. His lips lingered.

My heart pounded wildly, nearly out of my chest. My brow was moist, and I was losin' my footin'. I looked into his eyes. "We were wrong to be intimate before sayin' our vows. Now we're facin' the consequences of our sinful ways. God has spoken and I have listened." When I kissed him on the cheek, my entire body quivered. I didn't ever want to let go.

"No, it ain't right. What kind of God does this?"

"Silas?"

"What?"

"Do you know what Samuel means?"

"Well, it's his name... your father's name?"

"Do you know the biblical meanin' of Samuel?"

"No."

"God hears."

I backed away from him and paused at the door. "In my silent waitin', I have learned to accept that I must part with everything and everyone I loved and cared for. The most painful is that I must part with you. We must never take any notice of each other again." It was as if someone else spoke. It was impossible to imagine that those words came from my lips.

Miss Emily followed me through the blacksmith shop and into the main part of the barn. I rushed out the door, passin' by Old Gray Mare and on to the main house. Folks straggled in line for supper. I stopped to collect myself and to find Nellie, but I couldn't see her anywhere.

CHAPTER 72

Nellie – September 26, 1873

THE DAY BECAME night as a cloak of darkness fell upon me. Those with no thoughts were silent and sat in the circle tapping bones for meal. Their rhythm joined with the drumbeat of my people, becoming my pulse. The cry of the red-tailed hawk accompanied those who danced before me in shadows, and my friend the crow looked upon us with a cold eye. The heat of the great flame that burned in Father Sky did not give warmth. The icy winds that warned of the coming of the Wintermaker Moon lay a hand upon me. My arms lacked strength to lift my blanket.

The voices of men joined with the shaking leaves of the giant oak. I sat by her roots, where wisdom lay in waiting for those who listened. The drumming grew loud within me until I rose up to meet the spirits of my ancestors.

We danced with the oak in the center of our circle. We prayed for all creatures and thanked the stars and the seasons that always change. *Great Spirit watch over me. I am old and weak. Give me guidance as I leave my earth walk.* Heaviness lifted from heart, spirit, and mind.

Waiting to return to Mamijôla, Searching Owl, our son, and those who went before, I looked upon the wise medicine woman who leaned against the heart of the tree. The great light shined brightly. I left the circle and stood before her. She looked at me within the light. I kissed her forehead. Her silken, white hair touched me as she spoke. *No, Nanatasis. It is not time.*

CHAPTER 73

Abigail – September 26, 1873

IT HAD BEEN nearly two weeks since Silas told me about the letters. I was accustomed to avoidin' him. I didn't want to encourage him, yet I could no longer ignore him. As Mother often said, I had gotten myself into a fine pickle.

I was hangin' the last of the laundered garments on the line when suddenly the usual grindin' of bone and murmur of voices ceased. I dropped a clothespin into the bucket and waited. Still nothin'.

The wind whipped up the hill, flappin' the clothes on the line. I hesitated when I heard a woman's cry and men shoutin' in the distance. The quiet returned.

I looked at my son. His bottom lip quivered, and he wrinkled his nose before he cried. I whisked him into my arms. "Shhh."

I parted two damp nightshirts on the line and looked down at the yard. The old folks and the weak minded were causin' a stir. I went to the edge of the house to get a closer look.

My heart quickened at the sight of Asa and Silas crouched by the oak tree with folks standin' around them. Keepin' my eyes fixed on the troublin' scene, I slipped Samuel into the sling.

"Nellie, can you hear me?" Silas shouted out over the others.

Nellie? I held Samuel's head firmly, grabbed onto my skirt, and ran.

"Back away, folks," Asa said in his usual gruff voice.

My knees almost gave out as I pushed through the crowd. Silas held Nellie's head as she sat propped against the tree, starin' wide eyed at the sky. "Is she dead?" I couldn't really bear to know.

He kept his head down. "No." He pressed the back of his hand against her cheek. "She's havin' some sort of spell."

"Get some water!" Asa yelled.

I hurried over to the pump and wailed on the handle. I whimpered as the water gushed into the oaken bucket. "I need a cup." I pumped again and again.

Miss Noyes waddled over to me. "What's the ruckus?"

"Nellie's havin' a spell. Somethin' isn't right." The bucket was almost full and wobbled in my hand with water sloshin' about. "I need a cup."

"Where's that ladle?" She walked away cussin', yet genuinely concerned.

I held tight to the water bucket and ran to Nellie. Silas plunged his hand into the icy water and rubbed it on her face. She still did not blink. He slapped her face gently.

"Nellie, Nellie. Wake up," he said.

"Don't look good. Oh well, it happens to them ol' geezers." Miss Noyes had returned to her wicked senses as she handed a cup to Asa.

He snatched it from her, filled it up, and crouched down beside Nellie.

"C'mon now, Ole Squaw, take a drink." The water dribbled out the sides of her mouth.

"Wait. It ain't workin'." Silas reached into his pocket and pulled out a handkerchief. He dunked it into the water and pressed it against her forehead.

"And yes, she is quite different, Miss Noyes," Bella said as she joined in the circle.

"Let me." I thrust Samuel into Bella's arms and took the cup from Asa. "Nellie, drink this right now." I brought the cup to her lips. The water trickled out of her mouth and down her chin.

She jerked forward, blinked, and started chokin'.

"Nellie." I cradled her in my arms. "Nellie."

Silas dipped the cup into the water. "She needs more water, Abigail."

He wrapped my handkerchief around the cup and handed it to me. I held it to her lips, and she drank slowly.

"Let's git her in the house," Polly said.

"She needs to stay here... by the tree," I said.

"You must know somethin' that I don't," she said, chewin' on a piece of grass.

"I jest know," I said. "She wants to take a good look at the sky, the trees, and hear the birds sing. Then she can go inside."

Nellie smiled weakly.

"Folks, git back to them bones!" Miss Noyes hollered. "You'll use any excuse to keep from workin'."

"I'll take Samuel with me," Bella said. She had become a second mother to my son, makin' it less of a challenge to navigate the murky waters of the place, ensurin' that he would be able to stay.

"Thank you." I pushed a strand of long white hair away from Nellie's eyes.

Silas squatted down beside us. "I'll leave you for a bit and will come back to bring her to the house."

"Thank you." With my sleeve, I wiped away the tears that had spilled from my own eyes and onto Nellie's face. "What would I do without you, Nellie?"

Silas and Miss Noyes wandered off, leavin' Asa to tend to the folks who had returned to crushin' bones as if nothin' had happened. I rested against the tree.

"Dear Lord, thank You for sparin' Nellie. I know she's far along in years, but I'm not ready for her to be with You or to go where Indians go. I pray earnestly: please allow her to stay with me a bit longer. I regret that I am selfish in this request and know that I have not been perfect in any way, but I do ask with a humble heart. In the Lord's name I pray, A-men."

My tears washed over me like a drenchin' spring rain. I reached into my sleeve and pulled out the handkerchief that I hadn't seen for several months. I ran my finger over the familiar butterfly that took many long hours to stitch.

Amongst a chorus of grindin' bones and hushed voices, I sat for a good hour and caressed Nellie's arms. I sang softly and watched her fearful eyes search the sky and canopy of leaves flutterin' high above our heads.

Polly stopped in front of us with Silas a few steps behind. "Time to bring her in."

I shivered as the sun slipped behind the barn, and my legs tingled from sittin' in one place for too long. "I'll help."

"Asa, come give us a hand!" Silas shouted to the burly man, who was leanin' against the fence.

Together we lifted Nellie. Her skirt was damp and soiled, and she couldn't walk. We summoned the strength to carry her limp body up the hill and to the house. We finally got her upstairs, where Patience had fixed her bed.

"It will be fine," I said, takin' a deep breath.

We set Nellie down on her bed sack and stood around her. She did not take her eyes away from me.

"She needs rest and to be bathed. But first, I'll make her tea." I dabbed my forehead with my handkerchief while starin' directly at Silas, who quickly looked away.

Women folk from down the hall drifted in and out of the room. Some poked their heads in and then left, whisperin' to one another.

Asa scowled and said, "Everybody git back to their business. Nellie's fine."

After the room cleared, I went to Nellie's place in the floor. She turned her head to watch me. As far as I knew, no one else had rooted around in there besides her. I pulled out a bundle of pine needles. "Should I use these?"

She shook her head, no.

I picked up a well-worn satchel that rattled with small nuts or seeds inside. "These?"

She shook her head, no.

"This might take a long time, Nellie. You have so many things in here," I said.

I continued to ask her about different barks, dried plants, roots, and needles. After many tries, she nodded yes.

I left the room with her tin cup and a blend of dried red clover blossoms, yarrow flower, and plantain leaf packed into the medicine pouch. The kitchen buzzed with talk of Nellie while folks filled their bowls with thin meat stew. Miss Noyes glared at me.

Polly nudged her. "Not now, she's takin' care of Nellie."

"I don't trust her," Miss Noyes said, continuin' to stare.

"Nellie does, so this time we gotta' let her go and do what need be done."

Miss Noyes spun around to face the line of folks waitin' with their bowls in hand. "Don't jest stand there, git movin' and quit talkin'."

When I returned, Nellie was sittin' up lookin' straight ahead. She didn't take notice when I entered the room. She jumped when I touched her shoulder. I sat down beside her and brought the steamin' cup to her lips. She turned away.

"What is this?" I set the cup on the floor and pulled her face towards mine. "You agreed to this brew."

She sighed. With great effort she made a stirrin' motion with her hand.

"Of course." I went to the corner, removed the floorboard, and found a small pine twig – a stirrin' stick. For several minutes, I stirred the brew while it steeped and the amber oil swirled from the twig. I poked at the herb-filled pouch to release the healin' properties.

Nellie looked odd when she smiled a sort of half smile. She drank from the cup, pausin' between each sip with tea spillin' out of the side of her mouth.

Nightfall was upon us and Nellie needed bathin'. I fished around in my pocket for one of the two matches that I took from the kitchen earlier on. I lit the hangin' lamp in the hall and carried it into the room. "I must get you cleaned up." I hung the lamp on a nail by her bed. I had only seen Nellie wearin' her brown dress with a belt on the outside and one inside that held the most interestin' things.

Patience came into the room with her son perched on her hip. She stopped at the foot of the bed. "How is she?" The light illuminated half of her face.

"She's better. I need to bathe her and get her into a clean nightdress." I paused, hopin' to find one. "Will you fetch a kettle of water from the stove, and a basin and cloth from the launderin' room?"

"Who will mind Joshua?" she asked, knowin' quite well that he had become difficult, screamin' for a better part of his wakin' hours.

The womenfolk filed in through the door, each stoppin' to look at Nellie and me. I pointed at the crowd. "Ask anyone... Lidie, Betty, Emily?"

Bella came through the door holdin' my Samuel. I took him in my arms. "Someone look after the children while we take care of Nellie, please."

Betty came forward. "I will."

Samuel shrieked when she took him. I pried his little hands from my yellow dress. "Now now, dear heart, go with Betty." I kissed his cheek. He wavered for an instant and started cryin'.

Bella cleared her throat. "Patience can stay. I'll help you, Abigail."

"Fine. Let's gather what is needed." I patted Samuel's fuzzy curls and headed for the launderin' room. I stopped and pressed my ear against the kitchen door. Bella started to talk.

"Shhh." I put my finger to my lips.

"Well I s'pose we should keep the fire goin' so that there's coals in the mornin' for cookin'." Polly's flat voice rose above the creakin' stove door.

"I ain't too pleased that winter's around the corner," Miss Noyes said.

Their voices lowered as the dinin' room door swung open. I sneaked into the kitchen, grabbed the kettle from the long-dead stove, and ran out of the room.

Bella gawked at me. "What are you doin'?"

"Quick." I tugged her arm, and we dashed down the hall and into the warm launderin' room. A bed of red-hot coals pulsed inside the stove from heatin' water throughout the day; I set the kettle on top of it.

"We have to find a night dress for Nellie while we wait for the water to boil." I quickly rummaged through piles of folded clothes, not mindin' the mess that I was leavin' behind.

Although Nellie was a strong woman, her frame was small, and she barely reached my chin. The first few nightdresses were much too long. I dropped them on the floor and continued rummagin'. I held up another one. "This is perfect." I draped it over my shoulder and tapped the kettle on the stove. "It isn't warm enough." I paced.

Bella picked up a neatly folded pair of pantaloons. "Does she wear these?"

I laughed. "We don't even wear the likes of those anymore." I looked them over. "Lidie must have made these; they're very fancy."

Bella examined the elaborate stitches. "Who are they for?"

"I don't know who they were intended for, but they're Nellie's now." I let loose with laughter that I hadn't experienced since before Mother died.

"Get a hold of yourself. You'll attract attention."

I gripped the edge of the table. "I can't help it. I haven't seen pantaloons like that for quite some time. And to see them here." I wiped the tears from the corners of my eyes. "And to think that Nellie will be wearin' them would cause some kind of stir."

"We can't jest take them," she said, backin' away from the table.

"Why not?" I shook the kettle as it started to hiss. "Who will know what Nellie's wearin' under her dress?" I asked, and started in gigglin'. "I'm not tellin'. Are you?"

"Well, no…"

"Make yourself useful and carry the kettle and that basin." I pointed to the basin on the floor. "I have cloth strips here too." I turned and left the room with Bella chasin' behind me like a delicate field mouse.

As soon as Samuel saw me, his thumb popped out of his mouth, and he started fussin'. I rushed over to the corner of the room, pulled up the floorboard, and poked around. I was stunned when my fingers stumbled upon a pinch pot of lavender oil and beeswax. I held it up to my nose.

Bella stood in the middle of the room with the kettle and basin. "What now?"

"Fill the basin with warm water and add a bit of this." I pulled the pinch pot out of my pocket. "I will return to bathe her."

Red-faced, Betty tried to hold my son as he squirmed and fussed in her arms. I took him from her. He smiled, pleased to be with me and pleased to get his way. I sat on the wooden crate beside my bed sack and put him to my breast.

⊷⊶

Although very much out of place, the heady aroma of lavender filled the room. I looked down upon my sleepin' son, who resembled his father more with each passin' day. I tucked the blanket in around him.

Bella and Betty were sittin' next to Nellie as she stared blankly at the ceilin'. Bella wrung her hands. "I think that she's havin' another spell."

I knelt beside Nellie. "She's waitin' is all." I smiled when she looked at me. "Now please come and help me undress her."

They were afraid, afraid of seein' what a hundred-year-old Indian woman would look like under all the layers of clothin' that she wore. Before I had gotten to know Nellie, I would have been scared too.

"What are you waitin' for?" I reached behind Nellie's head and lifted her to a sittin' position. She let out a deep sigh, and her head dropped forward when I untied her belt. I pulled it away from her body and gave it to Betty. "Put her clothes in a pile; we'll launder them ourselves tomorrow."

Betty nodded.

Bella went around to the other side of Nellie and together we pulled her outer dress over her head and gave it to Betty.

She had another belt over her dress with pockets in it. I reached to untie it, and she let out a wistful cry.

"Nellie, we won't wash it. We'll keep it here with all of your trinkets inside. I'll put it safely inside the floor." I stroked her cheek.

Her eyes filled with tears.

I carefully took the belt away from her. Somethin' fell on the floor. She whimpered when I reached for it and held it up to the light. It was a beautiful hand-carved hummin' bird – true to size. There was a heart carved into the belly. It was magnificent.

"Nellie, this is beautiful," I said. "I'll put it back in here, where it's safe." I tucked the wooden bird into the inner pocket of the belt.

My eyes watered. I tried to conceal that Nellie's unpleasant scent and soiled clothin' made me feel ill. At first, Betty wilted when I handed the dress to her, but after lookin' into my eyes she knew better.

I slid the basin across the floor, added more hot water, and dotted the cloth strips with oil of mullein flower. I carefully rubbed the warm cloth over her seasoned skin. I then dried her off with the clean linen intended for makin' men's work shirts.

I held up the pantaloons. "These are for you, Nellie." I contained my laughter.

She shook her head, no.

"You must wear these. It will help to keep you warm until your clothes are cleaned, and then you may dress as you wish." I struggled to pull the pantaloons over her one heavy leg that she couldn't move.

She lay down on the bed, makin' dressin' her a difficult task. I brushed her thick, white hair, surprised at its silkiness. I braided it the way I braided Sarah's hair, and then I tied it with a strip of cloth.

"Nellie, you're beautiful." I put my arms around her and kissed her cheek. Not knowin' where she kept her doll, I set my own faceless doll beside her. "Here, keep Hope with you until you recover."

Weary and silent, the others gathered around in a circle. Her kind, wise face glowed in the golden lamp light. She smiled with a slant. Her skin looked darker than usual next to the light blue nightdress. Except for Jessie, I supposed that she wore the fanciest pantaloons in all of Carroll County.

CHAPTER 74

Abigail – October 26, 1873

I COULD SMELL the seasons. October was an honest, clear month. The hardwood trees were bare. No more hidin' behind safe, leafy cloaks. I shielded my eyes and looked out over the garden, where a good armful of frost-covered pumpkins remained.

"Abigail!"

I pulled my hood over my head and continued down the slope into the long rows of papery cornstalks.

"Wait!" Silas called out.

I kept my head down. "What is it?"

"I saw you and jest wanted to see what was a doin'."

"Shouldn't you be at church with your family?"

"I chose to be here today, to do some preparations before the cold creeps in, to oversee the men splittin' wood… " He seemed uncommonly tired and disheveled.

"No one works on Sunday." I bit my lip.

He stepped in front of me. "Where's Samuel?"

"He's in the house with Patience and the others."

"You usually don't go nowhere without him."

"I know."

"I jest wanted to make sure that he was well, since there's been some fever." His eyes were bluer that day.

"He's well." Ignorin' the rush in my heart, I bent over and picked up a shiny pumpkin.

"You're beautiful." He spoke so fast, I wasn't sure if I heard him right.

"You make a girl blush." I embraced the cold, wet pumpkin.

"Well, I can't help myself. You're—"

"Please don't." I tightened my grip on the pumpkin.

"Well..."

"We don't have a life together. You're married and shouldn't have those feelin's towards me. It isn't right."

"You must have them same feelin's. You can't deny it. I see it in your eyes." He searched my face.

"I have learned to quell those feelin's that you speak about." I set the pumpkin on the ground by my feet. "God has a plan. We must abide." I looked beyond him, focusin' on the big house.

"God knows I try. My heart won't let me forget."

"You have a wife." Tears threatened. "Please don't follow me around. You'll invite folks to talkin."

"I don't give a damn what folks say."

"That's foolish. You have too much to lose. Now I must bring this to the house." I picked up the pumpkin again.

"Jest admit it." He moved close enough for me to detect his musky scent. "Admit that you love me."

"What will it prove? It makes no difference. I will always love you." The heavy hand pressed down hard.

"I needed to hear it."

"I must get back before folks notice." I brushed past him.

"Abigail?"

"What?"

"Our son is a handsome boy. Do you think he takes after me?"

I smiled. "He is handsome, indeed. But I think he looks like Papa."

"Oh."

"You best be gettin' to that wood before the men get too content playin' cards." A gust of wind whipped through the yard, makin' my eyes sting.

"You make a good point." He paused. "I'll see to the men."

"Good day."

"Good day… " His voice trailed off.

Suddenly my heart quickened. I watched him walk to the pasture, where Major grazed on dead, yellow grass. I struggled with my desire to run after him.

He mounted his horse and turned my way for a few seconds. I stared at him, unable to move. "Yes, your son looks like you, exactly like you," I whispered. I kept him in my sights 'til he vanished around the corner.

"You're lettin' the heat out," Polly said, pointin' a long, crooked finger at me. "Either go in or out, for Chrissakes."

I hurried out to fetch the pumpkin from the step. "There are more. I'll bring them in. We had a hard frost last night and Mother always said that—"

"Will you stop all that jawin', and jest go get 'em? I ain't got time for it. And you broke the stem."

"What does it matter? Do we eat the stem?" I slammed the door behind me, shuttin' out her unrelentin' chatter.

⋅⊷⊷◉ ◉⊷⊷⋅

Every mornin' and night, I spent time helpin' Nellie to get her strength back. Ever since she had her spell, walkin' had come hard for her, and she lost use of her left arm. She was relieved to get her Indian clothes back, but she decided to keep the pantaloons.

Each mornin' I lifted her legs and moved them several times so that they wouldn't become stiff. Then I helped her up out of her bed, and we walked slowly to the outhouse.

At first, I had to assist her until she was strong enough to go in by herself. Then we went into the kitchen to get her gruel. I found it hard to imagine that even when she moved as slowly as she did, she still managed to help folks.

We spent long hours at night sittin' by her special place in the floor. She showed me how to make medicine from that which grows wild. When it was time, I would carry on as the healer for the folks at the Carroll County Farm. God had a plan, indeed.

CHAPTER 75

Nellie – October 26, 1873

MY FRIEND THE crow perched on a pine bough overhead, scratching and peck-
ing and watching. I looked upon our home. The time had arrived. I could
no longer pay the white man. For many winters after my husband's spirit departed, I made snowshoes, baskets, and dolls for selling and trading. I sewed
shoes, hats, and coats from the furs that he left. I traded or sold all and kept
only one from the beaver.

I'm sorry. You fell too far behind, Mrs. Baldwin. The man with green eyes spoke.
It's awful kind of Mr. Burrows to take you in.

I walked to the resting place of Searching Owl and my son. Golden pine
needles from the past season scattered in the wind as I knelt by their graves.

It's best for us to be on our way, ma'am. The men will be comin' along.

I dug my fingers into the earth and pulled out a small purple flower that
is the first to grow after the Wintermaker Moon. I tasted the salt of my tears.
*I ask Our Mother for forgiveness, as I have plucked that which comes forth from Her womb
for matters of the soul and will not use for medicine. I honor this brave warrior as it fights to
survive in snow and cold winds.* I approached the man and his brown horse.

It's a long walk to Burrows' store. Do you want to ride? He spit.

I shook my head, no. Walking long was good.

Are you certain?

I nodded and held my sack close.

He needed not go with me. I knew the way and preferred solitude. Except
for the fallen branches that snapped beneath our feet, warning creatures of
our presence, we journeyed in silence. Songbirds followed us to the edge of the

safety of the trees, bidding farewell amongst the shaking leaves. The rushing waters of Cold River faded behind me.

I followed the white man and his horse into the village. The sun was low. He stopped and spoke. *So long, Mrs. Baldwin.* He rode away, leaving his dust around me.

I waited. A woman with a boy child stopped and stared long. *Come Joseph... don't be lookin' at her.* She pulled him into the store.

Mister Burrows came out. *Nellie, follow me.* He led the way. *You can put your belongin's in here.* He pointed. *This is where you'll sleep.*

The room in the back of the store was small and had no window. Mister Burrows made a bed of straw in the corner beside a broken crate. A lantern hung on the wall.

Make yourself at home. I'll tend to these folks and be right back. He talked and moved swiftly. He was a small man with a long beard and white hair that covered his face and ears.

I placed my sack in the crate and hung the beaver pelt over the spaces in the wall. I spread my blanket on the bed and sat and listened to the changed world. The woman's laughter echoed like the black and white loon on Bitawbagok.

⊷⊷⊙ ⊙⊶⊷

Abigail's laughter trickled into my dream. I opened my eyes. She held her son before me. "Samuel wants to lay with you."

"I will hold him while you are with Nellie." Bella took Samuel from Abigail's arms. She carries the love of her lost child with her.

After placing the herbs of the day inside my belt, we walked to the outhouse and then to the kitchen. I carried my bowl of food to the table and helped the elders and those who were not well.

When the night had fallen and her child was in slumber, Abigail sat with me. I taught her of many medicines. I prepared her. She would care for the sick and the elders. She would become a wise woman.

CHAPTER 76

Nellie – November 2, 1873
– Morning

THE BRUSHSTROKES OF the setting sun painted the afternoon red. I sat on the pickle barrel and watched as the white men carried the body of Mister Burrows to the cart. There was no one to show sorrow or joy when his spirit departed. I alone would miss his goodness.

What about the ole squaw? He kicked open the door. His voice was too loud. His clothes were with holes and his face with scars.

I dunno. The other came inside. He stood tall with yellow hair and blue eyes. I saw him with his wife. He did not hate women, children, or my people.

The door closed hard. I stared at the place where Mister Burrows fell to the ground with great pain in his heart. He would reunite with those in the Other World. I thanked the Great Spirit for his generosity and kindness.

Then the glass broke. I thought to flee. The loud man charged as does a moose during the rut. *You're comin' with me!* He reached with both hands.

I ran to my room in the back. I closed the door and locked it with the hook made by Mister Burrows to keep me safe. I pressed my back against the door and felt his angry fist strike the wood.

You ain't stayin' here. Now that the ole man is gone, you're goin' to the County Farm. He hit harder and harder. *Now come out nice-like so it don't git ugly.*

The tears came. The wood broke into pieces and his hands bled. I covered my face and crouched as he came to me in violence.

I told you to come out nice-like. Now look at what you went and made me do. He held his bleeding hands before me. *It's all your fault.* His eyes were black.

I pulled the blanket over my face and moved deeper into the corner. The pain came when he pulled my hair to make me stand.

If you fight, you'll git hurt. I'm givin' you fair warnin'. He pulled my hair again.

My foot struck the crate, and I fell to the ground. A thunderbolt struck upon me when he kicked my side. There was no air for breathing.

You think you're somethin' special livin' here when you should be locked away. He breathed spirituous liquor. I looked away. The other man who may have helped was not in sight.

Show me some respect, Injun! He raised his hand to strike. I looked into his eyes. I would not cry.

Hey! A different man came and helped me to my feet. He had a pleasing face and a dark beard. He smelled of tobacco. *This ain't how we do things.*

She weren't cooperatin' so I had to use force. His eyes were small with lies.

I don't want to hear any more of that. He wiped blood that flowed from my mouth with his sleeve. *Looks like they took Mr. Burrows. God rest his soul.* He held my arm.

Moses, why did he let her stay? Folks say she practices witchery.

Never mind all that. I talked to Mr. Tibbetts, and he ain't gonna' let her stay, so I'll bring her on down to the farm. It ain't right for me to discuss her business. The strong man called Moses walked to the water barrel and dipped his cup.

Weren't she married to Elijah Baldwin? The one with hate put a plug in his mouth.

Moses offered me the cup. *Yep. That was a long time ago, and then he had that terrible accident at the mill.* He watched me drink. *They call you Nellie?*

I nodded, yes. The sun departed. Moses took me in his cart. We went to a place called the County Farm. I had seen it when I gathered plants for many medicines. Strawberries, nettles, yarrow, and mullein grew where they buried their dead.

He drove the cart into the yard. A young man came around and took the horse inside a barn with many animals. I waited and then followed him on a path that led to a big house. We stepped inside, where cries of elders, children, men, and women fell on my ears. It was cold and filled with death.

⊷⊨⊚ ⊚⊨⊷

Samuel cried hard. Abigail hugged him. "Hush now."

The rain came in the night and was hitting the window. The pain that rested in my neck reached my shoulder. I tried to sit.

"Patience, bring him to the launderin' room, and I will join you after I help Nellie." Her smile warmed me.

"Ayuh." Patience tied her apron.

Abigail lifted me from the bed. I was weak and moved slow. After the stairs, I walked alone. More rain fell. Father Sky was angry. The tall grasses swayed in the wind that blew hard from the north. I was the last to eat the cold gruel.

In the Great Room, I sat on the floor amongst the elders and those who spoke words with no meaning.

"Are you comfortable?" Abigail placed my blanket on my shoulders.

I nodded. I would not hear the cries around me, for I could no longer give them what they needed. I would wait until she came for me at the time of the setting sun.

The heat of the wood fire warmed my face. I closed my eyes and saw a woman.

⊷⊨⊚ ⊚⊨⊷

The rushing water and song of the red bird filled the air. It was Mother standing before me in the waters of Crooked River.

Mother, why do you smile? Joy is in your eyes, heart, and spirit. It is all around. I walked closer to the banks. The wind caressed my face.

I smile because you speak. She stood tall. *Look, Nanatasis.* She parted the golden grasses, giving way to a girl who was naked with her back to me. Her long black hair draped over her bronze skin.

Who is she? My heart beat hard. *I know, yet I do not know.*

You know her. Mother smiled again. *Trust yourself. Find your courage.*

The girl turned and stared with deep blue eyes. She held something in her hands.

What does she hold in her hands? The sun warmed all of me.

It is yours and will be for all of time. Mother spoke gently. *Go to her and see what she carries.*

I took small steps towards her. She held out her hands. The song of the red bird filled Father Sky. My heart danced. *What is it that you carry?*

She revealed an orange and black butterfly. Its wings unfolded before us as it rested in her hands.

A barred owl swooped down from high atop the giant pine, brushing away the butterfly with the tip of its wing. With great talons and wings spread wide, it hovered, and looked upon me with large golden eyes.

⋗⋙⊙ ⊙⋘⋖

"Come now. We must have some meat stew and corn bread. If we go quickly, it will still be warm." Abigail wrapped her arms around me and helped me to my feet.

CHAPTER 77

Silas – November 2, 1873

I ROLLED OVER to an empty space. It weren't usual for Jessie to be up and about before me. I turned down the quilt and stepped onto the cold floor. I could barely hear Jessie and Sally talkin'.

"It's an awful thing, yearnin' for a child," Sally said, speakin' in an odd, wispy manner with her front tooth missin' and all. Even though Jessie wouldn't admit it, she had become fond of Sally, goin' so far as to say that she was amusin'. After Jessie whined and carried on about needin' help with the chores, her folks sent Sally to stay with us.

"What do you know about yearning?" Jessie asked. "You had a child."

"I know all too well," she said. "My yearnin' is diff'rent from yours."

"Do tell."

"'Tis' true, I gave birth to my sweet baby, Rose. But I ain't never gonna' hold her or watch her grow up." She paused. "She's got a real family in Tamworth."

"So you must yearn for her now?" Jessie tinkled the spoon in her hand-painted tea cup.

"I don't s'pose that I could take proper care of her, but she is my child, and I do love her."

I went down the stairs, makin' a bit of noise to warn 'em. I liked that Sally invited Jessie to talkin', although I had trouble sortin' it all out. I stood in the doorway. "Good mornin', ladies."

"Good morning." Jessie looked like a school-girl with her braids coiled neatly on each side of her head and tied with blue ribbons. She had dark circles under her eyes, and her mouth turned down in a perfect pout.

I smiled at the two of 'em. "The coffee smells pleasin'. I'd love some before headin' out." I sat across from Jessie at the long pine table. I 'spected her to ask me about workin' on Sunday, but she was quiet.

"Will you have some pumpkin bread to go with it?" Sally asked.

"I wouldn't pass up nothin' that you baked, Sally." A plump Rhode Island Red caught my eye as it perched on the porch railin'. "Darn chickens got out of the pen again. If I don't fix it, the coons will git in there."

"I heard some commotion in the yard last night. I hope it isn't too late," Jessie said, flutterin' her eyelashes and pretendin' to be concerned, when it weren't no secret that she despised most all critters.

My mouth watered when Sally set down the warm pumpkin bread covered with fresh butter. The smell of ginger and cloves was like medicine, like the days before Daddy went to war, and Mamma used to bake all them merries. I tried to take my time, but I wolfed it down. "You must be the best cook in all of Carroll County."

A wave of pink washed over her freckled face as she stirred the hot coals in the stove. "My grandma showed me everything that there is to know 'bout cookin'."

"I would like to learn to cook one day," Jessie said. She looked out the window and sighed. The few times that she did try to cook was downright wicked. I s'posed that she was best at lookin' pretty and makin' artificial conversation.

Sally put on her ragged shoulder shawl. "Jest tell me when that would be; I'd be happy to 'blige." She picked up the egg basket and shooed the hen off the railin'.

"You have a pleasant day." I kissed the top of Jessie's head, careful to avoid spoilin' her hair.

"Winter's nearly here," she said, hopin' to get a response.

"I know. We're well prepared." I buttoned my coat.

"Yes, we are," she said, keepin' an eye on Sally.

I was relieved that her folks would fetch her to go to church. I didn't invite her to talkin' because it was the same thing nearly every day. She wanted a child, but it didn't happen. I told her that it didn't matter much. She didn't believe me. Maybe it was 'cause I had a son and I saw him jest 'bout every day. I knew it weren't right thinkin' in such a way, but I couldn't help it.

"Here chick, chick, chickies!" Sally sung out the way she always did.

Filled with the excitement of rufflin' feathers, peckin', and nervous chatter, I entered the coop and looked over the door and fence. "The pen don't need fixin'. You need to close the door behind you at night."

"Yes, sir," she said. "I guess I didn't latch it."

"Well now that we have that settled, it's time to go to the farm." I left.

"But, it's Sunday!" she called after me.

"I have to make preparations before winter sets in." I whipped open the barn door. I would be damned if Sally was gonna' start in on me, 'specially if Jessie didn't fuss.

I spent most of the day overseein' the men workin' the woodpiles. With the onset of winter, folks at the farm often worked seven days a week, enablin' me to catch a glimpse of Abigail in the launderin' room. She tended to Samuel, makin' sure that he was outta' harm's way while keepin' that stick turnin'. Patience, on the other hand, didn't have it so easy. Lil' Joshua crawled about, gettin' himself into one fix after another.

It weren't usual for children to stay at the farm after they reached three years of age. I took comfort when folks' conditions improved and a family could leave the Poor Farm together. It was a sad state of affairs when an outside family adopted one of the children. It came about when the young mothers' families turned away from their daughters in shame. It didn't happen much, but happened 'nuff times. The mothers suffered unbearable torment, but rules was rules.

"Why are you pokin' about?" Polly stopped, about to jab Emily Drew with her stick. She acted spiteful and all, but I 'spected there was a soft spot inside.

"Ah—" I got stuck on the sight of Abigail's curls fallin' about her face as she scrubbed. "—have you seen Moses?"

"Moses? What makes you think he'd be in here?" Polly replied while tryin' to get Betty a good one with that damned stick of hers.

"I thought I saw him comin' this way." I stuffed my hands into my pockets. "If you see him, tell him I'll be out at the woodshed." I started to leave but hesitated when I heard Samuel's laughter.

"Pick up them bed ticks and stop mussin'!" Polly shouted, payin' me no mind.

Most of the time the men took to sawin' and splittin' the wood, but no one liked stackin' it. I was no exception. As an overseer, I could decide when I wanted to pitch in. Some of the bosses never so much as lifted a finger, but I liked workin' up a sweat. Moses nagged at me to sit back and supervise, but I jest liked good hard work.

Sweat and rain soaked my shirt, and my arm muscles burned when I picked up the axe and wailed it into the thick maple log. The wood split in two and fell onto piles on each side of the choppin' block. I swung harder each time, and the pile kept on growin'.

"Silas." Moses came up from behind.

I delayed my swing, holdin' the axe in midair. "What?" I slammed the axe head into the wood.

"It ain't necessary for you to be doin' all that." He struck a match and held it over his pipe. "That's what the folks here is s'posed to be doin'." He puffed. "It's Sunday."

I leaned the axe against the choppin' block. "You ain't tellin' me what I don't know." I 'spected a talkin' to because he was always watchin' out for Jessie and me.

"We have more than enough wood and more than enough men to split it. You should be home with the Misses." He kicked at the pile. "What's a doin', boy?"

I crossed my arms and stared at him. "Wood is good."

He laughed hard, so hard that he held his stomach and leaned against the rail. "Wood is good?" He doubled up and went from laughter to a coughin' fit.

I shook my head, picked up the axe and swung, splittin' it right down the middle with one strike. The wind blew my shirt up, exposin' my back to the rain. I reached into the pile for another piece of wood, the biggest one I could find.

After he collected himself, he started in on me again. "Son, what are you avoidin'?" He tapped the ash from his pipe onto the rail. "You come here seven days a week now, and it ain't necessary."

"You know?" I sat down on the choppin' block. "I ain't sure."

"Let's get out of the rain," he said, hurryin' into the woodshed.

I followed him, carryin' the axe with me to keep it from rustin'. The smell of molasses and rice drifted out from the kitchen. My stomach rumbled as I watched the folks standin' in line with their bowls in hand. Even though the food weren't much good, bein' so close to supper and all, I s'posed I might jest as well eat.

"I know what it is," Moses said. He picked the bark off a piece of wood in the pile and examined it. "You jest can't get those thoughts of Abigail out of your head. Can you?"

I took a deep breath. "No, that ain't it. I'm all done with that." I wished that he would pay me no mind. I did my job, took care of Jessie, and the house. Hell, I even took care of Mamma now that Daddy passed away.

"I don't like to say it, but you're lyin', son." He chewed on the end of his pipe.

"What difference does it make? I ain't doin' nothin' to hurt you or anyone else." I stood up to him with my chest puffed up like a big ole rooster.

"Simmah down. We ain't never raised a fist…" We was interrupted by the rattle of a carriage approachin' from down the road. Moses peered out the window, but we couldn't see nothin'.

God help me if Moses and I ever got into a scrape. I would fight like hell, but he'd clout me a good one. I dashed out the door towards the carriage with Moses at my heels. "Looks like the folks from Berry's Tavern over in Wolfeboro!" I hollered.

I had seen that shiny black chassis once or twice; it was a corker. I couldn't figure out why it was at the farm. We only had visitors when someone had bad news or delivered an inmate and never in such a fancy manner.

I could see the dim outline of the two Foss brothers perched on the carriage. "Whoa!" James, the taller of the two, shouted as they neared the yard.

Although his brother John didn't offer up many words, he was a darn good arm wrestler and the ladies seemed to fancy him.

"Evenin'," Moses said.

"Good evening, Mr. Blake." John shook Moses hand with vigor.

"What brings you out here, gentlemen?" Moses asked.

He didn't say a single word, and then he motioned for his brother to open the carriage door. "We have a woman here who has no money, no kin, and needs tending to."

"What else do you know 'bout her?" Moses asked, lookin' inside the carriage.

"She came to the inn about a month ago and said that she was looking for a distant relative. It wasn't clear. She might not be quite right in the head."

"I see." Moses lit his pipe while James lifted the elderly woman from the seat. She was a small thing, with silvery white hair pulled back away from her face. Her cheeks was flushed.

"Bring her inside," Moses said, pointin' to the house. "Silas, the folks is 'bout done with supper. Go fetch Polly and Miss Noyes."

I touched the woman's forehead. She was burnin' up. She looked at me with fearful blue eyes. "It's gonna' be alright," I said and smiled. I knew I'd seen her somewhere, but I'd be damned if I knew where. I hurried up the pathway to the house jest in time to see Abigail helpin' Nellie climb the stairs.

CHAPTER 78

Abigail – November 2, 1873

POLLY'S SIGH WAS well rehearsed. "Nope. She ain't got no kin." She hovered over an elderly woman who was strugglin' to breathe.

"Seems she's got the fever," Miss Noyes added.

"Well, I s'pose we should put her up with the others." The lamp light exaggerated Polly's thin red lips and frown lines.

"Who is she?" I asked and stepped closer to the women.

"Mind your P's and Q's," Miss Noyes said, givin' me the evil eye.

"I jest want to help."

"Go find Silas then, and tell him that we need to get this one upstairs," Polly snapped.

"Where do you think he might be?" I peered timidly into the darkness towards the dim golden light that burned in the barn window.

"Damned if I know." Polly rifled through the woman's reticule. "There ain't nothin' in here worth keepin'."

I stopped and looked at the woman lyin' on the bed. Her silky, white hair was braided and twisted into a loose bun. The deep set lines around her eyes showed signs of laughter.

"Do you know her?" Miss Noyes asked.

"No, I was thinkin' that perhaps I did, but I don't." I placed my hand gently on her forehead, which was hot to the touch. "I'll fetch Silas."

"Don't dawdle," Polly said.

I fiddled with a curl and pressed the front of my yellow dress, tryin' to smooth out the wrinkles, thinkin' it shameful for takin' notice of my appearance. I marched into the barn, nearly collidin' with Silas. I gasped.

"Well, good evenin'," he said. His eyes lit up when he smiled.

"Good evenin'." I thought of returnin' the smile, but the chill had settled in. How I longed for a good hot bath to lie in.

"What is it? I ain't accustomed to seein' you out at this time of night."

"The woman inside…" Imprisoned for what seemed an eternal moment, I blushed at my inability to form a complete sentence.

"The woman they sent over from Wolfeboro?"

"Yes. Polly and Miss Noyes need help bringin' her to the sleepin' quarters. She's nearly out cold with the fever."

"The folks from the tavern told us that she seemed to come from nowhere 'bout a month ago. She had money to pay for her room for a spell, but then she fell ill and no one seems claim her. So they sent her here."

"Pity no one claims her. She must have kin somewhere."

"I don't know. That's the case with most of the old folks who end up here."

"I think I've seen her before." I brushed over a tuft of hay with the toe of my boot. "But I don't know where."

"Abigail?" His tone was gentle.

"Yes?" I looked up at him through the curl.

"How's Samuel?"

"He's well. He was not well a few weeks back, but it was only a cold."

"I watch you with him."

"I know. I mean, I see you sometimes." I avoided his eyes.

"You're a good mother."

"I had a good teacher. Mother was testy at times, but she loved us."

"Are you comin' in here to help?" Polly hollered.

"We're comin'," I said.

When we got inside, the woman was leanin' on her elbow strugglin' to get up. "I must go home now."

"You never mind. You ain't goin' nowhere. You're sick," Polly said.

"What's your name, woman?" Miss Noyes pecked.

"Isabelle," she whispered. "Isabelle Smith."

"Do you have any kin?" Polly pressed.

"No, my husband and son died many years ago." Although quite wobbly, she had an air of great strength and fortitude.

"Silas, help git her other arm, and let's bring her upstairs." Polly said as she bent down to lift the frail woman. "Miss Noyes, we can take care of this."

Miss Noyes sighed and looked my way. "Abigail, go see to it that there's a bed ready. Should be one where Sadie Hunt slept."

I balked. "She's dead..."

"I know. I know. Go see that it's ready."

"I'll fetch clean beddin'." Tears stung my eyes.

"The beddin' up there will do," she called after me and started in cussin'.

I ignored her and continued on. I would not allow this Isabelle Smith woman to lay down where another had died. I threw open the door and grabbed a bed coverin' from the stacks of folded linen and rushed upstairs to get the white pine for tea.

When I entered the room, Silas gave me an apologetic look as he and Polly lowered Isabelle onto the intolerable worn sack of straw that was fallin' through the knotty cord and splintered frame.

"Wait!" I shouted.

Polly frowned. "We don't have fresh husks or straw on hand to make a new bed."

"She can use my bed. I put in fresh straw and husks about a month back." I dropped the linen and peeked over at Nellie, who had stirred from her sleep. I dragged my bed sack to where the sick woman lay.

"You're goin' to too much trouble. Now what will you use for a bed, fool?"

"I'll go to the barn and gather a few flakes of straw and make a fresh bed for myself." I rushed past her and Silas. "Now help me."

The woman groaned as we lifted her, and Polly slid my trusted sack beneath her sweat-soaked backside.

I covered her with my blanket. "Now I'll get my pillow and then make tea." I left the room, not givin' a damn about Polly's disgraceful opinion.

I slipped into the room as quietly as possible, so as not to disturb Nellie, and returned with a pillow for Isabelle. "I'll bring you tea for your fever." Although I felt Silas's eyes on me, I remained focused on the present situation. I patted her limp hand and left once again.

The light from the hallway lantern was barely bright enough for me to determine which pouch in the floor contained the pine needles and twigs. I quickly made a blend of crushed pine matter, pleased that I remembered the stirrin' stick as well.

Polly and Silas followed me into the kitchen. I poured steamin' water into the cup. "This will help to bring her fever down." I set the cup on the table and reached for a crock of lard.

"Did Nellie show you all this?" Polly asked. She leaned over my shoulder as I scooped out a small amount of lard and rubbed it on my hands.

"Yes, she's been showin' me how to use different plants, roots, and bark to help folks." I withered away from her warm breath.

"What are you doin' that for?" she demanded.

"Oh, this is to remove the pine pitch from my fingers. It's wicked sticky and makes such a mess of things." I wiped my hands on a nearby kitchen cloth.

"That's why Nellie is always comin' after the lard," she said with an unexpected smile.

"Yes." I stirred and stared into the swirlin' hot tea. "Medicine."

"How did she teach you if she don't speak?" Silas asked.

"We sit together at night and she shows me."

Polly wrinkled her nose. "Shows you?"

"Yes, she shows me."

As I picked up the cup, a disturbin' peculiar cry shattered the stillness. I had never heard a sound like it before. I got a chill. A bit of tea splashed onto the floor, and I nearly dropped the cup. I followed what had become a loud moanin' sound.

Silas and Polly darted up the stairs, trippin' over one another. I took a deep breath and deliberately put one foot in front of the other, holdin' the cup firmly. When the wind picked up, causin' the shutters to crash and the branches to bang against the windows, I wanted to flee.

The tea scalded my hands as I rounded the corner and headed for the sick woman. The voices of Silas and Polly mixed in with that odd cryin'. I couldn't hear what they were sayin' with all the commotion. I stopped in the doorway.

Nellie was kneelin' over the woman. The cryin' ceased. The room fell silent. With her hands pressed together, she looked upwards; her chest heaved with each breath. The lantern danced behind her on the wall, illuminatin' her face enough to see tears glistenin' on her cheeks.

I slid down onto the floor, spillin' more of the hot tea on my hands and legs. I watched without believin' what was before my eyes.

Polly and Silas were still. Curious folks streamed down the hallway and stood in the doorway lookin' on.

CHAPTER 79

Nellie – November 2, 1873 – Evening

WHEN THE CORN Making Moon passed, the barred owl came to me by the silver light and shadows of the moon. My woven circle hung in the window. I made it with grapevine and bittersweet, adorned with feathers of the crow, jay, and red-tailed hawk. Those in the Other World came closer and beckoned. The elder with flowing white hair appeared for three nights. It was time.

Abigail and I walked together. The cold wind rushed in from the open door when I reached the top step. I stopped.

"Come now, Nellie. We must retire." Abigail urged me to continue.

While her child slept, she brushed my hair and made a firm braid. "Your hair is silky. I prefer that to my wild, curly mane." She caressed my arm when she spoke.

I wrapped a curl around my finger and smiled. White women are never pleased and seek beauty in falsehoods. I released her curl.

"Nellie, I know that you wish me to be thankful for what God has given me. Mother said this as well." She helped me to lie down.

I nodded and pulled my blanket over my shoulders. I looked at her, brown eyes to brown eyes. She is a wise young woman who has learned many lessons. She will learn more as she grows. My work is done.

"Sleep well, Nellie." She kissed my cheek.

The golden lamplight illuminated her. I watched her read her book until my eyes would not remain open. The flowing spirit of the river beckoned.

->=● ◉=<-

I returned to Mother and the girl at Crooked River. The sun warmed us. All of the pain that I carried departed. My hair was black and my skin was without lines. An elder stood in the distance on the great rock by the water. His long white hair swirled like that of a river current.

Nanatasis, come. The river spirit calls to you. Mother's face was filled with love and laughter. Her dark eyes held the light.

Is it cold? I held my dress close.

Why do you ask many questions? It is pure and you will rejoice. She opened her arms to Father Sky.

Why does the girl not speak? I sat on the silken grasses of the riverbank.

Why do you not ask her? She disappeared under the water, leaving perfect, silent rings.

The girl came closer. Her eyes were deep blue like the clear sky during the Corn Making Moon. Her black hair shimmered in the sun. She was graceful in her nakedness.

Why do you come to me? I leaned forward to see her better.

She came closer. Her lips were full and red. Her arms and legs were strong like one who lived close to the breast of Our Mother.

Why do you not speak? I stepped into the waters of Crooked River, closer to her.

She smiled before vanishing beneath the surface of the still water.

Where is she? I returned to the bank and stood amongst the tall reeds.

She is here. You must find your courage to believe, Nanatasis. Mother cupped the water in her hands, and it trickled over her youthful body.

An orange and black butterfly flitted before me, followed by another and another. Soon delicate wings of orange and black butterflies filled Father Sky. The girl reappeared and stood strong in their presence. They landed on her hair, her arms, her face.

She reached out for me. *I am here.*

I left the shadows of the reeds and went to her. All of the orange and black butterflies departed except for one; it landed on her neck and became one with her. I took her small hand in mine. *I know of one girl who was born with the sign of the butterfly.*

Find your courage, Nanatasis. Always is forever. Mother spoke quietly. *Believe.* She swam away, past the rock where the elder stood in his truth, silently overlooking the river.

Mamijôla.

⋅→⊨◉ ◉⊨←⋅

Hoo-hoo, hoo-hoo! I sat up when the messenger came. The strength that I needed was with me. I rose from my bed and walked to the room across the hall. She was lying on the bed. Her eyes were closed. Her white hair was braided. She had a beautiful face. I unbuttoned the collar of her dress. She opened her eyes – the blue eyes of the girl by the river – and looked into mine. The sign of the butterfly was upon her neck.

I looked up to Father Sky. I saw the face of my mother. *Find your courage, Nanatasis.*

Many tears flowed.

"Believe." My spirit shook at the first word uttered from my lips for many seasons.

Mamijôla looked upon me. "Is it you, Mamma?"

"Yes, Mamijôla. I am here."

CHAPTER 80

Abigail – November 3, 1873

ALTHOUGH THE SPARSE and twisted bed sack offered no promise of seein' me through the night, I somehow managed to sleep. I looked over at the sun streamin' in on Nellie's empty bed and realized that I had lost the ability to comprehend my own feelin's.

My son fussed, so I wrapped my shawl around my shoulders and quickly gathered him into my arms.

"Did I hear Nellie talkin' last night?" Patience asked. She struggled with her squirmin' child, who had become increasingly difficult to hold down.

"Your ears did not deceive you. Nellie spoke," I said. "We witnessed a miracle."

"Who's the woman?" Patience asked. "Is she ill?"

"I don't know, really." I bundled Samuel and held him to my breast. "I'm confused. The woman is said to be one Isabelle Smith, yet Nellie uttered another name."

The breakfast bell rang. What used to be a time of comfort and bondin' with my son had become somewhat frantic. "I know that I can't and shouldn't hurry you, but there's so much that needs tendin' to."

"Would it help if I took Samuel to the sewin' room?" Bella asked. She was always willin' to help when it came to the children.

"Yes, thank you." A dozen thoughts rushed in. "I must see to it that Nellie and Isabelle are cared for."

"No one offers to mind Joshua," Patience said.

"I don't mean to offend you, but I'm not spendin' leisure time. I'm tendin' to Nellie. She needs me." I pulled my yellow dress over my head. "And it isn't becomin' to complain. You should know that." I twisted my curls into my snood.

"You think you're somethin' special. Well, in here, you ain't no different from the rest of us." She stumbled away with her boy fightin' her every step.

Jarred at how she mirrored Miss Noyes, I could only bite my tongue and pray harder for her.

As soon as Bella took Samuel, I dashed to the room across the hallway. I came to a halt when I saw the two women lyin' together in the bed. Nellie was whisperin' to Isabelle, who rested peacefully in her arms. Nellie looked up at me.

"Uh... I don't want to interrupt. I wanted to look in on you." My heart pounded in anticipation of a response, of the unusualness of hearin' her speak.

Nellie motioned for me to approach. I hesitated. She then patted the floor. I sat down beside her.

"Abigail." Her voice was frail and shaky, and her eyes filled with tears. "I have stories of the one who was silent for the passing of many seasons." She placed her worn hand upon mine.

I became the silent one. I searched for words but could not find a one. Hunger growled in my stomach.

"First eat. Then return and we will talk." She stroked Isabelle's forehead as she spoke.

"What about her?" I looked at Isabelle. "What are her needs?"

"Plantain, burdock root, pine bark... and mullein leaf," Nellie whispered.

"And you?" I asked timidly. "You must take nourishment as well."

"No." She turned away.

I stared at the two women. My sound mind had finally unraveled, and my other self was to take the helm.

"Go now," Nellie said without lookin'.

I went downstairs towards the clatter of breakfast. I was able to eat a bit of sticky, cold gruel before Polly started hollerin'.

Bella patted Samuel's head as he fussed. "Is Nellie well?" she asked.

"Yes, it's quite peculiar."

She followed me into the kitchen. "What?" Samuel's cries became more persistent.

"Nellie is talkin'." Samuel left her arms and fell into mine.

"What?" Bella asked. "What does she say?"

"Very little." My gaze followed Silas when he walked by the window.

"Who is this woman?"

"I don't know."

"Bella, git down to the sewin' room!" Polly shouted and waved her stick wildly.

"Here, take him." I pushed my fussin' child into her arms.

"Abigail?" Polly's tone indicated rare fatigue.

"Yes?" I fiddled with my snood and blushed shamefully when Silas and William entered the room.

"I s'pose you're all in a snit about Nellie and that other woman."

"Well..." I cleared my throat. "Yes."

"You should be down in the launderin' room with the others." She nodded at Silas and William when they passed by.

"I couldn't do that when Nellie's—"

"Never mind, I'll decide what's a doin' 'round here."

Silas paused in the doorway. "Polly, I suggest that Abigail tends to Nellie and the other woman."

"You do, do you? What does it matter to you?"

"Nellie has always helped folks 'round this place." He went on. "And Nellie told Abigail about her remedies and all."

"I see." Polly picked at her gray teeth with a splinter of wood.

"I'm only askin' that..." My thin voice faltered.

"It's settled. Today you are permitted to tend to Nellie and the other woman." She walked away hummin' out of tune and swingin' her stick.

"Thank you," I whispered.

Silas turned to me. "Abigail?"

"Yes?"

"I don't know what's a doin' with Nellie, but she deserves our help."

I was certain that I saw a tear. "I know."

He wavered. "Do good… do good." He turned and left.

I poured the steamin' water too close to the top of the cup, thinkin' that I might scorch my hands, but I hurried up the stairs in spite of it.

Durin' all of the commotion the night before, I left a medicine sack beside the hole in the floor, somethin' Nellie never did. I blended the leaves, crushed root, and needles inside the pouch and placed it in the cup. I took a deep breath and entered the room. The two women held tight to each other.

Isabelle remained asleep. Nellie looked up and raised her hand. "Come."

Keepin' my eyes on the brew, I knelt down. "I brewed it as you said."

"Mamijôla." She shook Isabelle gently. "Awaken. You must drink good medicine."

Isabelle's eyes fluttered. She looked around the room. Her cheeks were quite red, and her lips were cracked and dry from fever.

I handed the cup to Nellie. She snapped the stirrin' stick to release the pine oil. "Drink, my daughter."

My daughter? I bit my lip and watched Isabelle sip the tea. She did look at Nellie with the eyes of a child.

Nellie set the empty cup beside her on the floor. "Sit, Abigail. We shall talk."

I sat with my shoulder shawl wrapped tightly around me. The familiar echoes of workin' draft animals, the splittin' axe, and men's voices were louder than usual. My heart thumped as if it might come undone.

She spoke slowly and gazed out the window. "Many winters ago, I lived on the shores of Bitawbagok, in a place that white men call Lake Champlain. I am Nanatasis. In Abenaki, it means hummingbird or muted one. My mother said that I did not cry at birth."

I smiled as my thoughts turned to that warm spring day when Nellie showed me that she was a hummin'bird.

"My people moved with the passing seasons to many hunting and fishing grounds. We honored the Great Spirit for plentiful bounty. We did not choose to live amongst the white man. We lived quiet like the fox in the woods." She stopped and looked into my brown eyes with her own.

"When I was a child, I helped to make snowshoes, canoes, baskets, and garments. My father, mother, and the elders showed us the ways of Our Mother. We made medicine from herbs, roots, seeds, plants, and all that grew. The men were hunters." She closed her eyes.

I ran my finger over a string of holes that dotted across the bottom of my dress. "Do you need food? Tea?" My pulse quickened as I wondered if she had died at that moment.

She remained still. I stared at her chest to see if it still moved. Isabelle shifted and Nellie's eyes opened with a start. "No food or water, my spirit is nourished."

A woodpecker drilled consistent, short bursts into the outside wall. A few folks who weren't right in the head shrieked and broke into disturbed laughter. I focused on a single yellow leaf as it shivered and clung fiercely to a branch outside the window.

After determinin' that she hadn't died, I settled down and studied her face. The tappin' on the house got louder and closer.

She took a deep breath and carried on with her story. Isabelle was soaked with sweat. She whimpered and tried to focus on her mother's face. I held back my tears when Nellie told us that she had been raped, resultin' in her pregnancy. Although she was faced with becomin' a mother at such a tender young age, she loved her daughter deeply. She told us of her vow to remain silent followin' the devastatin' accident at White River in which Isabelle was presumed dead.

Nellie turned and looked at Isabelle and then closed her eyes. I kept watch over the yellow leaf. *Would it hang on for another day?*

"More tea." She tipped the empty cup over on the floor. "She burns with fever." The black and white wings of the woodpecker fluttered outside the window.

"I will return." My legs tingled from sittin' for so long. I went across the hallway to our room, to the hole in the floor. Nothin' was the same. My hands trembled when I grabbed the pouch.

Although Nellie and Isabelle were waitin', I had an urge to see my son. I set the steamin' cup on the table and dashed to the sewin' room. Breathless, I stopped abruptly at the door. The women talked casually while Samuel slept in the crate. In some ways, it was a relief that he took to cow's milk and the nursin' can. In other ways, I would miss our bond.

"Abigail." Bella looked up from her sewin' and smiled.

I put my finger to my lips. "Shhh." I tiptoed over to the crate. My heart brimmed with love. His dark eyelashes fanned out over his pink cheeks, and his curls resembled my own.

I slipped out of the room and into the kitchen, thankful for not seein' a soul. I stumbled up the steps, splashin' a trail of water behind me. I paused and stood in the doorway. The two women appeared to be sleepin'. I studied their faces. They were identical, 'cept Isabelle had blue eyes.

Nellie awoke when I knelt down beside her. She took the cup. "Mamijôla, you must drink."

The outdoor farm chorus that was previously distractin' had become oddly reassurin'. At some point, I had gathered my wits about me. I understood that I was witnessin' an extraordinary event. Bein' clear and present was a priority.

"I learned of a mother's love." Nellie smiled and looked to shed a tear. "It does not die."

The yellow leaf shook in a flurry of bitter wind. She went on to tell us about her life with a man who the townspeople knew as Elijah Baldwin, but in her rich silent world she referred to him as Searchin' Owl. It was his tragic death and most unfortunate circumstances that brought her to the County Farm.

She smoothed the tangles of her daughter's white hair as she filled in the story of their long separation. I struggled to breathe at the mere sound of her voice, once silenced by tragedy, pourin' forth the words she longed to release.

A sliver of orange sun slipped behind the greyish clouds, and the sly shadow of the tree disappeared from the wall beside me.

She slowly turned to look at me. "She is here because of the doll she calls Hope, which was made by my hands. Our bond was meant to be. I passed on the ways of healing to the daughter not of my blood." She smiled. "She is a red maple with roots planted firmly in the breast of Our Mother. She is Abigail."

The wind blew hard. The branches scratched against the window, and the yellow leaf fluttered. I wiped a tear from my cheek. "You must have food and water."

"Not now," Nellie whispered and looked at Isabelle. "How is it that you came to me? I have lived one hundred winters. I have been without you for eighty."

Isabelle spoke so softly that I had to strain to hear. She did not open her eyes. "I held you in my dreams." She drew a deep breath. "The story was told to me by my folks, Ezra and Mariah Smith." She paused. "My father and uncle were fishing when they found me on the riverbank. They searched for my kinfolk. After several months, they gave up and took me into their home. We lived well on a small farm in North Troy, where my father was a blacksmith."

"At times I saw your face. I called you the River Woman, and I waited for you to appear in my dreams. And I knew the river's deepest secrets. They too came to me when I dreamed and were chased away by the morning birdsong. The sunlight laughed at me and filled me full of doubt. I could not curse the day, but I welcomed the darkness when you would come. Even when I dozed, you came through the narrowing doors, finally becoming a pale ghost washed away by the swift river currents. Until I met White Flower, you were my own divine secret. I almost forgot, but I always remembered."

We sat in the dark while the folks below us shuffled in line to have supper. The predictable stench of beef bone soup and rusty beans drifted into the room. I ignored the hunger in my belly, gladly tradin' it for the hunger to hear their stories.

"I had no brothers or sisters. I went to school and learned to read and write." She looked at Nellie. "I saw Indian folks around here and there, but

I was forbidden to speak to them and warned to stay away." She trembled. "I yearned to go with them. I did not understand my curiosity."

"Once I met an Indian girl outside of town and Father told me if I ever played with her again that I would get a whipping. I never saw her again and never got a whipping." Her eyelids were heavy but she continued.

"My folks were good people. They never meant harm or ill feelings towards the Indians. Like most of the others, they simply didn't understand. And I expect they were afraid of the possibility of losing me, since they claimed to not know of my past."

Her face glowed in the lamplight. "I was married to an honest, strong man. I cannot say that he caused my heart to flutter, but he worked hard and always had a kind word. We had one son. Like the brother I never knew, his name was Benjamin." She managed a weak smile. "When he was thirteen, he took sick with the fever and died; my husband followed him to his grave a week later. That was a winter of great sorrow, for many people died in our small town."

She studied Nellie's face before continuin'. "Many summers ago, I met an elderly Indian woman who called herself White Flower. She was selling baskets near Lake Champlain. I talked to her for quite some time and she told me that I reminded her of Nanatasis – more like a sister than a friend."

Nellie sat up. "White Flower... "

"We both knew within moments that I was your daughter, the one who was thought to be dead. White Flower said that she never had another friend like you. She believed that your spirits could not be divided. You shared secrets and understood each other without having to speak. She said that most people were intent on getting you to talk, so they missed the meaning of your presence. She told me that words were not necessary to know and love Nanatasis." Isabelle seemed to gather strength from her own words.

"She told me that after your daughter died, you moved to New Hampshire and married a man named Elijah Baldwin. So, I set out to find the mother that I had always longed for, to make myself whole. I was prepared to find your grave; it would have sustained me. The road was dark and difficult, but I have your heart, which understands."

"After searching long and facing many challenges, I discovered a distant relative in Ossipee that carried the same name. Though he was unsure about you, he remembered an old story about Elijah working at a mill with his grandfather. I felt that I was getting closer, but this was yet another agonizing blow that brought me disheartened and weary to the inn. Had I not fallen ill, I would not have found you. My senses may be dim, but we are reunited with each other and with the spirit of love and truth. I always prayed for this gift, and it has been delivered. The men brought me here, to the end of this part of the journey."

She nestled into Nellie's shoulder and continued to speak. "The Great Spirit has been a mystery. I trusted a voice that I heard in the north wind. It provided wisdom and strength when mine had withered. It showed me how to blend courage with compassion, take rain as nourishment and to honor the good spirits that dwell in every part of Creation. I gazed upon countless stars, bringing the River Woman into my present awareness, bridging Father Sky to Our Mother. I remembered the way of cleansing in earth, air, and wild water. My heart danced in the fire. I was prepared to walk proudly and forever to find you. My ancestors heard my words and opened my eyes. Hail the Great Spirit, for I am humble before you. Life gives life."

Other than Joshua's cries and the risin' pitch of the wind, it was quiet. As my eyes rested on Brown's Ridge, my thoughts turned to my own mother and the bones of our farm buried somewhere deep in the woods. I tried to guess if I could see it.

Nellie interrupted the silence. "Abigail, we should drink water now."

"Of course." I gathered my skirt and scrambled to my feet.

I was turnin' to go when Nellie called, "Abigail?"

"Do you need tea?" I gulped.

"No, bring Hope with you," she whispered.

Such an odd request. I took the back way to the outhouse to avoid unwelcome conversation. Steppin' outside was like wakin' up. I took a deep breath of the cold, fresh air.

I filled the cup with water from the barrel in the kitchen and went back upstairs. Bella was standin' over Samuel. She smiled. "How is Nellie?"

I pulled Hope out from under my blanket. "Nellie is fine, as far as I can tell," I said. "I don't know about the other woman. Her name is Isabelle. She's quite ill."

"Oh." Bella hung her cape on the hook. "Go. All is well here."

I hesitated before crossin' the hall. "Here is the water, Nellie."

The two women were locked in an embrace with their foreheads touchin'. I stared at Nellie's chest. No movement. I fell to my knees and dropped Hope on the floor. The yellow leaf had finally let go.

CHAPTER 81

Silas – November 3, 1873

I WAS ABOUT to leave when I caught sight of the lamplight in the upstairs window. Abigail worked hard, too hard at times. I dropped the reins. I decided to check on 'em one more time. Since she took to talkin' with Sally, Jessie didn't complain as much when I got home late.

I hurried up the pathway, kickin' at the brittle, yellow grass and paperthin leaves. I opened the door and entered the kitchen. The women were busy scrubbin' and scourin' and didn't take notice of me. I dashed up the stairs and stopped when I heard the soft cries. The door was framed by a faint line of light. I pushed it open to see Abigail lyin' in a heap at the bottom of the bed.

She sat up. "She's gone."

"She's gone?" The two woman looked like they was asleep. Nellie's hair moved slightly in the icy draft that blew through the cracks in the wall.

"I went to fetch water and when I returned they were like this," she sobbed. "My Nellie is gone."

I gathered her into my arms and kissed her forehead. "You did all you could."

"That woman, Isabelle, is her daughter." She wiped her tears on the last threads of her sleeve.

"She is?" I studied the woman and she did resemble Nellie. "Well I'll be damned."

"Silas?"

"What?"

"What will I do without Nellie?" She buried her face in my shirt.

"You'll be fine. She's in a better place." I stroked her head.

"She was like a mother to me."

"I know. She was like a mother to most folks here." Her hair felt soft on my chin.

"I s'pose she'll be placed in one of them pine boxes stacked in the barn?"

"Yep. That's a fact."

"And have a numbered headstone?" She pulled away with her eyes fixed on Nellie.

"Yep."

"She should have her name on the stone."

"They don't have time or money for that here."

"No one will remember her if she's nothin' but a number."

"Well, I'm sure someone will remember her." Though I reckoned she was right.

"Who?" She continued starin' at the women.

"You'll remember. I'll remember. Lot of folks will remember Nellie."

"But what about after we're gone?"

"It won't matter much by then, will it?"

"I don't know." She held a curl over her eye and looked through it. "And Mamijôla?"

"Mami... what?"

"Mamijôla. That is Isabelle's real name. It means butterfly in Abenaki."

"Well... I'll be." I closed the door when folks down the hall started makin' a ruckus. "I recall hearin' Nellie talkin', but there was so much confusion."

"She told Mamijôla and me all about it... her life. She spent most of the day tellin' us of her fate. Then Mamijôla told us her story. They were separated when Mamijôla was a little girl. They fell into a river and Nellie thought her to be dead."

I barely heard her words as I watched her graceful features in the golden light.

"They finally found each other," she whispered.

I envisioned a woman and child swirlin' in a river. "We'll bury 'em together."

"And Nellie's real name, her Indian name, is Nanatasis," she said. "It means hummin'bird. She showed me last spring out by the lilac trees."

"She showed you?"

"Nellie had a way of communicatin' with me. I'll never forget that day," she said and laughed. She hugged her doll. "Did you know that she made her?"

"The doll?"

"Yes, Papa got her for me. Nellie actually created her." Her face lit up.

The door burst open and Polly marched in. "What's a doin'?"

Abigail stared straight ahead. I could find no words.

"How are they?" She craned her neck past us to get a look.

"Umm." Abigail swallowed. "Nellie and her daughter are dead."

"What?" Polly rushed past us and stood over the bed. "Well—"

"This isn't the time for cussin' or hatred," Abigail said. "If you have any knowledge of lady-like words, it would serve you well to use them."

Polly sighed and ran her hands through her hair. "We'll have to leave 'em here 'til mornin' when the men arrive. We can git 'em buried before the ground tightens up."

"I s'pose that's good," I said.

She pulled at the blanket. The women, still embraced, slid to the side.

"Wait." Abigail lunged forward.

"Wait what?" Polly yanked the corner of the blanket from Nellie's frozen grip.

"I'll take care of them," Abigail said.

"You'll do no such thing." Polly jabbed her finger into Abigail's chest. "You've done more than enough and should return to your place."

"Hold on, Polly." I clenched my fist. "She jest wants to help out."

"Never mind, Silas. I can handle this." With her cheeks ablaze, she faced Polly. "Nellie was like a mother to me. I will make the necessary preparations. There is nothin' left to say." Abigail clutched her doll.

Polly finally spoke. "Did you say her daughter?"

Abigail carefully pulled the blanket over the women's heads. "Yes, Isabelle here had been lookin' for Nellie for several years and poor Nellie thought her to be dead."

Polly studied the outline of the women under the gray blanket. "I s'pose I'm gonna' miss the ole Injun." Her voice softened and I detected a genuine tear in her eye. "She took good care of folks."

We stood in the shadows while the wind hollered and branches beat against the already cracked windowpane. It was impossible to think of the farm without Nellie.

Polly broke the silence. "We've had enough commotion around here. Tomorrow's a new day."

CHAPTER 82

Abigail – November 3, 1873

"YOU SHOULD GO to sleep now," Silas said after Polly left.

I stared at the lifeless gray blanket, certain that I wouldn't sleep. "I know."

"I best be goin' home."

"You'll be back first thing to take them?" My voice was childlike. I could not hide the desperation, the need that I had for him to stay and to never leave my side again.

"Ayuh. Billy, Charles, and me."

"Can you put them in together?" My thoughts turned to the pine boxes in the barn.

"Ayuh."

"Will the both of them fit in one box?"

"We'll make do."

"Will you bury them tomorrow as well?"

"I believe so."

"Well," I said. "There it is." My stronger self – the part of me who could walk away, did so.

He grabbed my arm. "Wait."

I kept my head down to avoid the urge to throw myself at him. "Good night." I wiggled my arm free and fled across the hall to my room. I stood beside Samuel's crate gaspin' for air.

I avoided lookin' at her empty bed when I went to her place in the floor. The week before, at the mention of Mahitable's death, Nellie showed me how to prepare the dead body with juniper oil and pine boughs, a sacred tradition that I would honor. I reached into the floor and rooted around with my fingers 'til I found the tiny bottle of oil. The boughs were brittle and orangey. I would go out for fresh ones.

I took the hall lamp with me to the other room. I stopped at the foot of the bed and got on my knees before the ominous gray blanket.

"Dear Lord in Heaven, guide me at this time as I prepare Nanatasis and Mamijôla for burial. Give me the strength to carry on without faintin' or be-comin' distraught. And Lord? Please bless their souls and make sure that they find their way to their people in the afterlife as is necessary to their beliefs. In the Lord's name I pray, A-men."

I don't know how much time passed after I prayed. An hour? I simply couldn't summon the courage to pull the blanket away from the two women. My back hurt from kneelin', and I feared that someone might catch a glimpse of me.

Forcin' myself to breathe, I finally leaned over and tugged at the blanket. With tremblin' fingers, I pulled Nellie's eyelids down over her eyes that gazed into nothingness. I was overcome with relief at the sight of Mamijôla's closed eyelids.

I crouched down and studied the two women. It seemed as though the lines on Nellie's face all but disappeared. The bright moon was slowly risin', castin' light upon one side of her. I reached out to touch her but yanked my hand back, rememberin' that she'd be cold.

I stared at Mamijôla – the outline of her face was the same as her mother's. Nellie was about a hundred years old, and Mamijôla more than eighty. I tried to imagine what it was like to lose your child in a river.

A man from down the hall, where folks weren't right in the head, started in hollerin', bringin' me to my senses. I had to get this task done.

Nellie showed me that the dead should face the west. When I tugged at Nellie's arm, she fell away from her daughter and slumped forward. I was re-lieved that she wasn't too stiff, as the piglets were when we found them dead that mornin' in the pen. Papa said that rigga' mortis had set in.

I looked out the window and thought about where the sun set each night on Brown's Ridge. I dragged Nellie around to face that direction. Then I went over to Mamijôla and brung her around to Nellie's side.

Even though it was gettin' a bit cold, I started to perspire. I rubbed my hands together before reachin' into my pocket for the bottle of juniper oil.

I tried not to take notice of the laughter that trickled down the hall. I squatted down beside Nellie and traced my fingers over the small, perfect shells on her beloved belt. "This is the last time I can take care of you, Nellie." I ignored the uprisin' in my chest.

I dabbed a small amount of the thick oil from the vial onto a corner of the cloth and gently rubbed it over her face, arms, legs, and feet.

When I got to Mamijôla's side, there wasn't much left. I held the bottle upside down and shook it. "A tad bit more. Please, Lord." I spread the last of the oil on her cool skin.

I collected the pine boughs from the floor. At first, I didn't know quite what to do. I decided to pluck the needles from the boughs and sprinkle them about on their clothin', hopin' that the thought would do and that Nellie would have approved.

I sat in silence as the lamp died down to a mere ember. I returned to our room across the hall. The circle of vines and feathers that hung by Nellie's bed made a shadow on the wall in the moonlight. I paused by her empty bed before takin' her sacred circle and returnin' back to where they lay.

I pressed Mamijôla's hand inside of Nellie's. It dropped to the floor. I got onto my knees and wrapped a corner of the blanket around their hands to hold them in place. I kissed Nellie's cold cheek before settin' the circle of bittersweet and feathers in between them. The moon seemed to watch over me when the lamp light vanished with a final burst.

I returned to my room and stood over my son. He sighed and nestled into the remains of his blue quilt. I almost reached for him, but thought better of it.

The dried cornhusks crackled when I climbed into Nellie's abandoned bed sack. I covered myself with her shawl, imprintin' its divine earthy scent, while holdin' Hope close to my breast. I fell into a deep, dreamless sleep.

CHAPTER 83

Silas – November 7, 1873

Mamma leaned forward in the rockin' chair and bleated jest like a goat. "Don't stack that wood in the barn, ya hear?" She started talkin' nonsense after Daddy passed away, seein' she didn't have nobody to look after.

The men stacked the wood in the shed off the back of the kitchen. I bolted into the house to spare the men from her peckin'. "Don't fret. We're puttin' it where we always do."

"I ain't got the strength to be haulin' it." She wrinkled her nose and looked out the window as if she didn't hear a word I said.

"You ain't got no worries." I smiled. "Besides, I'll be lookin' in on you." I stirred the ashes in the fireplace in hopes of findin' a few hot coals.

"Never mind, I'm used to bein' without the likes of a man. You was off workin' and gettin' married and bein' all fancy." She coughed. "I don't need a damn man around here. You know how Daddy was after the war. God rest his soul. I–"

"Mamma, it's cold in here. You let the fire go out." I had heard enough. "You should be usin' the stove; the fire lasts longer."

"Don't be scoldin' me." She wagged a long, gnarled finger in the air and glared at me with the dark eyes of a stranger. "There's a heap of kindlin' out in the barn. If you're cold now, what ya gonna' do when winter gets here?"

I stormed out to the barn. I couldn't stand that she quoted Daddy. He always had somethin' smart to say. I wailed on the door, which had become stubborn on the account of rusty hinges. The air rushed in behind me. It was odd walkin' into a quiet barn. Course, Mamma sold off the last of the animals before Daddy died.

I rummaged around in his old splintered box in case I found somethin' that I might fancy. Jest as I 'spected, there was nothin' worth takin'. On my way to collect kindlin', I passed by my old workshop. Everything was jest as I left it. I picked up my whittlin' knife from the table; the smooth wooden handle felt good in my hand. My eyes caught sight of all them things on the shelf that I made or attempted to make over the years, but didn't finish. I started fillin' my pockets. Pine burns hot and quick.

I gathered wood scraps from the kindlin' pile and made my way back to the house. Mamma stared out the window with heavy lidded eyes, not lookin' at anything in particular, like them old folks at the farm.

I emptied my pockets, pilin' the kindlin' jest so. I was about to toss in one last pine trinket. I couldn't do it. I tucked it back into the pocket of my sack coat and built a roarin' fire, wonderin' if she would even bother to stoke it later on.

After we filled the woodshed, the men and I returned to our farm duties. We spent the afternoon diggin' the grave and then continued with preparations for the long, hard winter to come.

CHAPTER 84

Abigail – November 10, 1873

THE DAYS SEEMED to be without order or significant value. It had been a week since the death of my beloved Nellie, a time filled with distress and anxiety. With a sinkin' heart, I wondered if I would ever recognize my good self again. I maintained my faith in the Lord and prayed earnestly for Him to shine away the darkness that prevailed. It became apparent that I must never give up.

It was no secret. Nellie taught me her ways of tendin' to the sick and the weak. I could not say that I understood all that she showed me, but in her honor, I was devoted to bein' the healer at the County Farm. It was no fault of hers that I didn't always know which plant was which. I knew enough to carry on. I learned to sit with the plants, to observe, honor, and embrace their powers.

She left a large assortment of oils and dried herbs – roots, seeds, leaves, flowers, and needles – all neatly stored in her special place in the floor. She showed me where they grew in the wild, when to harvest them, how to dry and store them, and how to prepare them for medicine.

The breakfast bell broke my concentration. The women milled about, gettin' dressed for breakfast and daily chores. I went over to the calendar that I made with a stubby pencil and old papers that I found in the barn. I had circled the date. "Everyone?"

"What?" Patience scrambled past me to fetch Joshua. "This child is too busy and he don't pay me no mind. I've had it!"

In spite of Patience's complaints, which had become endless and tirin', I remained pleased. "It's my birthday. I'm seventeen years of age."

"Happy Birthday," Bella said and gave a gentle embrace.

"What does it matter in here?" Patience mumbled as her son broke free from her grip.

"Well, we don't have to be miserable every day. Do we?" I could see my breath as we walked together down the hallway.

"I ain't never seen a reason to be happy here. Whether it's your birthday or not. It's hellish. One day I will leave," she said.

I walked from table to table to see to it that the old folks and those who weren't right in the head ate a good amount of gruel. I had no worries about Samuel. Bella had become a second mother to him, and he took to the tin bottle and cow's milk, makin' my work easier.

I went to the launderin' room singin' a song in my head. Things got a bit better since I asked God to give me the strength not to complain, which simply invited more misery. As difficult as it were, I started each day givin' thanks for whatever I could find worth mentionin'. It was a task at first, but required less effort with the passin' time.

"Abigail Hodgdon!" Polly shouted from across the room.

"Yes?" I rolled up my sleeves and took a deep breath.

"You won't be in here today." She fetched her stick.

"What?" I thought it might be a trick.

"You'll be in the sewin' room."

"Whatever for? This is my day to..."

"Are you gonna' take to questionin', or are you goin' to the sewin' room?" She didn't smile. She only smiled at of the misfortune of others.

"I'll go to the sewin' room." I resisted the urge to hug her, which could possibly bring on that stick of hers. She was such a miserable sot. However, I believed anyone at the farm was preferable to the wicked Miss Noyes. Sometimes I imagined that Polly had a hidden soft side.

Fearin' that she might change her mind, I quickly untied my apron and tossed it on the table. Samuel bounced on my hip as I rushed to the sewin' room, wonderin' about her possible motives.

I sat next to Betty and sewed bedticks for most of the day. Late in the afternoon, I spotted a movement outside the window. I tried to keep from lookin'. Hopin' to catch a glimpse of Silas offered no chance of focusin'.

I sensed someone watchin' and spotted the shadow that I had become accustomed to. I cleared my throat. "Excuse me."

I went to the window. Silas waved. My heart raced as I edged towards the door. I opened it a crack and peeked out. "What is it?"

"Go to the barn and visit Old Gray Mare," he whispered.

"Is she not well?" I opened the door a bit wider.

"She's fine. Jest go. You'll see." He hurried off.

"Abigail, it's cold. Close the door," Betty whined.

Amidst stacks of blue material, I returned to my station and started sewin' frantically. I licked a drop of dark red blood from my fingertip and then ripped the careless stitches out of the bed ticks that I hastily sewed together.

"He's a married man. Pay him no mind," Betty muttered.

"I have no idea what you mean. I am clumsy with a needle." I blushed, relieved when the bell signaled the end of the workday.

After a supper of meat stew with a half a potato, a turnip, and a piece of crusty bread, I sat on my bed sack and waited for folks to settle down. It seemed that Martha Smith had to go into lock-up because she had a scrape with Miss Noyes. Personally, I thought that Miss Noyes got what was comin' to her, seein' she chipped Martha's tooth in a fit of rage.

When it was quiet enough for me to fetch the lamp, I went to the barn to see about the fuss with Old Gray Mare. I pulled Nellie's shawl over me and headed for the back door.

The sky was clear, almost startlin'. A hazy ring embraced the partial moon, indicatin' rain or snow. At least that's what Papa told us. I stopped when I heard coughin' and chokin' comin' from the outhouse. After listenin' for a spell, I continued.

I hadn't been to the barn at night for some time, and in the past Nellie accompanied me. I stood in the open doorway. As expected, I was overwhelmed by the scent of hay mixed with fresh woodchips. It was like goin' home and almost better than Mother singin' a lullaby.

The animals, hushed and settled, snuggled close together to share warmth. After a few steps into the barn, I thought of the room with the pine coffins. I rejected the urge to look.

In traditional fashion, Miss Emily darted out from the darkness, causin' my heart to faint. I held the lamp high over my head and went to the horse stalls, leavin' the coffin room behind.

With Miss Emily weavin' in and around my feet, I approached Old Gray Mare. Too much time had passed since I had been to the barn.

"Hello, Old Gray." I rubbed her nose.

What was the purpose of this? My thoughts turned to Silas.

Miss Emily walked to the edge of the stall, purrin' and rubbin' her head the way that cats do. She knocked somethin' over. I wasn't sure what it was. "What are you doin' now, silly cat?" I crouched down.

There before the toe of my boot was a heart-shaped pine box of fine craftsmanship. I picked it up and marveled at the wood grain and tiny details. I read the neatly carved letters on the bottom. *A.E.H. + S.J.P. Nov 10 1872.*

1872? I leaned on the edge of the trough, shakin' unmercifully. Somethin' in the box rattled. The deep-rooted ache emerged.

I finally summoned the courage to lift the perfectly fitted cover from the box and cried out when my eyes rested upon a horseshoe nail made into a ring. I took it from the box and slipped it over my finger. I wept until I could weep no more. Finally, I heaved the wretchedness from the deepest part of myself onto the barn floor.

I awoke when the roosters started in crowin' and the animals in the barn fidgeted, gettin' ready for the new day. The barn took on a deep rose hue. I tried to ignore the pain that twisted viciously into my neck and shoulders when I tried to sit up. Through swollen eyes, I looked down at my hand. "Not now." I slipped the black ring off of my finger and dropped it into the box. I wedged the cover on, clutched it close to my chest, and ran.

CHAPTER 85

Abigail – June 22, 1878

"Mamma, look." His face was smeared with remnants of strawberries. When he laughed, he wrinkled his nose exactly the way his father did.

"Strawberries for me?" I smiled. "Mmm, they smell divine."

"I picked them myself. And there are more over there," he said, pointin' to a thick green patch.

"I don't have a basket. Wrap them in this." I pulled my handkerchief from my apron pocket.

He studied the handkerchief. "No, thank you. It'll get spoiled. I s'pose I'll have to eat them."

"But it's jest an old thing that I made a long time ago. It isn't so special." My son's good heart and disposition brought a smile to my lips and enabled me to keep him by my side at the farm.

"Nope. I like the butterfly, even with a hole in it." He returned to the berry patch.

The moss felt good on my feet. I ran my fingers over the smooth leaves of an evenin' primrose. On visitin' day, after we finished our chores, we stole away to the peaceful granite garden. I meandered through the rows of small numbered stones. *152, 153, 154... There it is.*

I wrapped my skirt around my legs and sat down on the prickly grass. I traced my finger over the number *155* that was etched in granite. "Oh, how I miss you." I closed my eyes to imagine the corner of her yellow dress flappin' in the wind.

I mean she wasn't perfect, but I could see it comin'. Every day became harder for her to get her chores done with Joshua runnin' about and gettin' into mischief. She couldn't keep him under her fingertips, but she loved him. Under the circumstances, she was a good mother, indeed.

My eyes followed the sweet sound of my son singin'. The sun radiated from behind him, creatin' an illusion of a halo around his head. "Thank you, Lord. I promise to keep him out of trouble. They won't take him away."

A woodpecker tapped on a nearby tree. With a full heart, I leaned against the thick granite stone where my beloved friend, known as 155, lay buried beneath the earth. They took her son. They took her life. And finally, they took her name. The sun warmed my face. I closed my eyes. The memory was fresh.

The wicked Miss Noyes stormed into the room as we all slept. *You're comin' with me now.*

Patience sat up. *What's a doin' Miss Noyes?*

There's a family that's gonna' give your boy a good home. She plucked Joshua out of a dead sleep and pinned him under her arm. He tried to wiggle free, and he hollered for his mamma.

Patience screamed, cried, and carried on like all the mothers did when their children were taken away. Old Miss Noyes jest walked away with her ears closed. She marched out to the cart that was waitin' in the yard, as if Patience wasn't worth the bother.

Patience followed behind Miss Noyes, beggin' and wailin'. I finally caught up with her and held her as tightly as I could. I knew it did no good to fight, but I would do the same if they came for Samuel. I may have even killed someone who tried to take my boy.

She broke away from me and ran after the cart, catchin' her foot against her skirt, takin' a wild spill, and hurtin' her leg.

Bella and I dragged her into the house and fixed her up. For several days, she sat in her bed without speakin' a word. I tried to get her to eat, but she wouldn't look at food. I brought healin' tea. It was no use. She had lost the will to live.

About a week passed. The sun shined brightly, and the bird chorus sang cheerfully. When I went to the outhouse, I saw somethin' out of the ordinary. I stopped and looked at what I believed to be the corner a yellow dress flutterin' in the wind. I ran past the barn to see Patience hangin' from the big oak tree with the clothesline tied around her neck. I screamed and reached for her, but it was simply too late.

·>═◉ ◉═<·

Samuel approached with his hands full of strawberries. I quickly wiped away my tears.

"Mamma, I'll take that handkerchief now." He took it from me and examined it closely. "How did you sew this?"

"I'll show you someday."

"I like that the best." He pointed to the butterfly.

"Me too." I dropped the berries into the handkerchief and folded the sides, makin' a small pouch.

"Come. We must visit Nellie." I stood up.

"I don't see anyone here, Mamma. Are they hidin'?"

"No, jest because we can't see them doesn't mean that they aren't with us." I took his small sticky hand in mine, and we walked down to the next row of granite stones.

He looked around with wide eyes.

"Don't be afraid. They went to heaven to live with God and the angels." We lingered by the fence that divided the County Farm folks from regular town folks.

"Why is there a fence in the middle?"

"That's where other folks are buried. In fact, that's where my mother and father, your grandparents, are buried."

"Why are they over there? Shouldn't they be here with us?" He ran his hand over the top of the fence.

"Someday I'll explain it." I started walkin' again. "In God's eyes, we are the same, no matter which side of the fence we are on." I stopped in front of number 140. The wind rustled the boughs of the tall pines that surrounded us in a protective circle.

"Do they see us?" He nibbled on a strawberry.

I smiled. "They know that we're here. We will always be together. Someone may get very sick or have an unfortunate accident and die, but love never dies."

I sat in front of the stone and fished around in my pocket for the pinch of tobacco that I took from Moses's pouch when he wasn't payin' attention. I overheard Asa say that it was customary for Indians to leave an offerin' of tobacco at their graves.

"Who lives in this stone?" Samuel asked.

"It's Nellie…" My eyes followed a crow that flew above our heads and rested on a nearby pine bough. "… and her daughter." I sprinkled the tobacco over their grave. "Their Abenaki names are Nanatasis and Mamijôla."

I paused. "Nellie and Isabelle, I am here rememberin' you with an abundance of love, and I pray that you are blessed in peace."

"Here." Samuel dropped two strawberries in front of the grave. "I hope you like them. I picked them myself." He nodded at the grave.

"That's very kind of you." I kissed him on the forehead. *Perhaps someday you will truly understand.* "We must get back to the farm. No one can see us comin' from here. Remember, it's our secret."

"I can't even tell Silas?"

I fidgeted. "Not even Silas." Appropriately, I remained vigilant. My head was crowded with fear that the truth would emerge. The two of them had become quite fond of each other.

"But he's nice. I don't want to keep secrets from him."

"Yes, he is nice, but there are some secrets that we must keep between us. Remember, he's a farm boss." I thought that the reminder might have been more for me. Although we saw each other most every day, there were times when the heated passion tried to seep into the moment. I would never permit it. We had learned to be friends.

"If you say so." He stuffed his hands in his pockets and headed down the path towards the farm, whistlin' a song I had never heard before.

CHAPTER 86

Silas – June 28, 1878

SAMUEL SAT QUIETLY on the steps. Since Jessie and I were childless, the time spent with my son was important to me. I took to showin' him things around the farm that any father would show his son. Moses got feisty now and then, tellin' me I oughtn't to show favoritism.

"Good mornin', Samuel." I ruffled his soft curls.

"Mornin'." He didn't look up.

"You don't seem so happy." I knelt down beside him. A young red rooster chased a hen, cluckin' and scurryin' by the bottom step.

"I ain't so happy, sir." His eyes followed the chickens.

"What's troublin' you?"

"Mamma." He shuffled his small feet inside a pair of oversized boots with curled-up toes.

"What's a doin'?" I studied him, tryin' to ignore the boots, yet thinkin' I would find a pair to fit.

"She's sick with the fever."

I felt an uprisin' in my chest at the thought of her runnin' about with steamin' hot potions, takin' care of the sick that up and died anyway. "Are you certain?"

"She ain't gettin' out of bed. She told me to get her some hot water so she could stir somethin' in it." His eyes watered.

"Did you?"

"Miss Noyes whisked me outta' the kitchen." He wiped his nose on his shirtsleeve.

Every kind of bad thought rushed in. "I'll get the water for her."

For the past few weeks, Abigail had been tendin' to the sick. The previous week alone we lost a half dozen old folks to the fever. She didn't stop to rest or eat much. She worked hard jest like Nellie did.

"What's a doin?" Polly came into the kitchen from the woodshed.

"Abigail has the fever?" I poked at the coals in the stove, and then I picked up the kettle, still hot from breakfast.

"I ain't heard that." She scratched her head.

"Samuel says it's so. She needs tendin'." I poured hot water into the cup. "She knows which kind of potion to make."

"Well that ain't good, so far ain't nobody lived to tell about it. Once they—"

"I know." I brushed past her and hurried upstairs.

"Wait." Samuel followed.

I burst into the room. She looked frail lyin' on her bed sack with her thick, dark hair fanned out on the soiled linen. Her cheeks was red, and her swollen lips cracked with fever blisters.

She winced when she tried to open her eyes. "Silas, is that you?"

"Yes, I'm here." I felt her forehead with the back of my hand. She was burnin' up.

"Can you fetch the white pine?" She tried to sit up. "Get it outside if you can't find the sack. And dried elderberries... yes, elderberries..."

"Where do I find these things?" I looked around the room. "I don't know what to look for."

"I'll show you." Samuel tugged on my hand.

I watched him lift the floorboard and reach inside. He pulled out one dried plant after another and several pouches and sacks, until he found a large sack tied with twine. He beamed. "Here's the pine."

He continued rootin' 'round in the dark space in the floor. "Here's the elderberries." He held up a small, weathered pouch. And you'll be needin' this." He got to his feet. "The stirrin' stick."

"Thank you." I patted him on the head and returned to Abigail.

"Break up the needles and stems and put them in the tea pouch. Then add three or four dried elderberries. Press the pouch in between your fingers for a spell to crush and blend it all, and place it into the water and give a good stir." She draped her arm over her eyes. "Let it steep…"

My hands shook while I stirred and watched the water turn a sort of amber color. The voices of bickerin' women drifted up from the launderin' room, and men shouted from out in the yard.

I think I waited long enough before I reached behind her and lifted her head. "Drink this."

She took the tea in tiny sips and looked at me with glassy eyes and her moist curls clingin' to her forehead. "Thank you." She spoke in a girlish voice. She took once more from the cup and flopped down.

"Wait. Shouldn't you be drinkin' it all up?" My head pounded.

"Yes, but I can't." She closed her eyes.

I sat beside her on the floor, supported her with one arm, and fed her the tea with my free hand. Samuel sat on her other side bitin' at his fingernails and watchin'.

Her eyes widened when she took the last of the potent drink. "Samuel must not be here. He should have fresh air, not catch the fever."

"I won't go, Mamma. I'll take care of you." He crossed his arms.

"Such a good boy, I'm blessed." She managed to smile. "But, you must go."

"Your mamma is right. Go out and see if Moses has some chores for you." My chest tightened at the thought of Samuel gettin' sick.

"Sarah is comin' back. She wrote and told me that she and her husband will be movin' to Ossipee no later than August." She coughed. "She is with child." She looked towards the window and closed her eyes. I thought she was asleep.

"That's splendid news." I caressed her blazin' hot forehead.

"She invited Samuel and me to live with them." She took a long, shaky breath. "I can help out with her child and the chores." She fought to keep her darkened eyelids opened.

"I will meet my aunt and uncle," Samuel said. "And have my very own cousin."

"And no longer live here workin' your precious little fingers to the bone with a mother sentenced to this yellow dress." Abigail attempted to smile and then whispered in a voice that I had to strain to hear. "You will live in a real home filled with love, dear heart."

CHAPTER 87

Abigail – June 28, 1878

THE SWEET, PEPPERY brew burned its way down my throat. The light pierced into my head with such a throbbin' that I thought it would surely break apart. Everything took on a tawny hue, as if I was lookin' through colored glass.

Samuel's lips felt cool on my cheek when he kissed me. "I'll be back, Mamma. Moses is gonna' let me collect eggs from the chicken coop." He sounded far away.

"I love you." I wasn't sure if I said it or was thinkin' of sayin' it.

I strained to see his silhouette in the doorway. My eyes became hot coals burnin' in the sockets. Warm air escaped from my lungs in short bursts, and I didn't have the strength to cough. But when I did, white lights flashed against the inside of my eyelids.

"Mother?" I thought I saw her standin' by the bottom of the bed. I closed my eyes, and when I opened them she was gone.

Silas kept on rubbin' my forehead. "Jest rest, sweet Abigail." He sounded far away too.

"Don't leave me." I shivered. "God… it is… it is cold… so cold."

He tucked the blanket around my shoulders. "I won't leave you."

"I'm a-afraid." I shook, my bones ached, my muscles ached, and even my hair ached. "It hurts. Everything hurts. Hurts bad…"

"Don't be afraid." He gathered me in his arms and began to cry.

"Take care of our son." My voice came from somewhere else.

He was gettin' farther and farther away, but I could still feel him. "I love you, Abigail. Please don't die." He squeezed me tightly and I wanted him to. I did not want to run or leave or be away from him. I needed his arms around me, where they were supposed to be.

Music came in the uncertain rustle of chickens, clinkin' chains, and a chorus of hollerin' folks, all accompanied by the howlin' wind. It swirled in my ears, reachin' a high pitch.

Heavenly Father, is this Your call for me? I fought the great cloud that threatened. *Samuel!* If necessary, I would have clawed my way back. I reached out into limitless darkness. I stopped at the edge of fallin' cold. The wind retreated. *The time has come for me to lie in an unknown grave amongst the others, where berries grow sweet, and a swell of yellow primroses bloom secretly in the night.*

I paused. *I have been dealt the harsh hand of fate. Forgive me, Father. Please shine Your light about me and restore my goodness.*

The perilously deep strains of the dense chorus were replaced by the sound of a gentle tricklin' stream. A brilliant white light emerged. I grasped a familiar, strong hand. The flames that scorched my insides were no more. The throbbin' pain in my head washed away. I raised my eyes to look into hers, brown eyes to brown eyes. She placed our doll in my hand. Hope. The struggle had reached an end.

CHAPTER 88

Samuel Josiah Hodgdon – June 30, 1878

MAMMA SAID SHE would never leave me. So I s'posed that she was jest asleep for a bit and would come back to fetch me when it was time to live with Aunt Sarah.

I sat in front of the hole in the floor takin' out twigs and dirt and makin' little piles. Mamma said that it was the place where secrets lie, secrets from the soul of the earth.

I wanted to be a big boy, but somethin' scared me, and I weren't so sure that Mamma would be back. I walked over to where she slept and stood over the bed.

I spotted the corner of her handkerchief stickin' out from under the quilt. I picked it up and held it to my nose. It smelled like her. I poked at the hole in the middle of the orange and black butterfly and fell on the bed. "Please, Mamma, come back! I promise to be good and take care of you." I cried 'til all my tears was gone.

When the men took her away on the burlap sack, I watched her yellow dress draggin' on the ground gettin' all dirty. She said that she didn't much like that awful dress, but she needed to keep it as nice as could be 'spected for her own good.

I chased after 'em thinkin' I might get her doll and keep it safe while she was away, but the men carried on and paid me no mind. It was jest as well. She probably needed Hope where she was goin'.

Silas cried and called out her name when they took her into the barn. Moses pulled him aside and gave him a talkin' to. Then Bella brought me back upstairs and sang songs 'til I pretended to be asleep.

After she left, I went to the secret place in the floor and dropped the twigs, one at a time, into the hole. I rubbed the soft pouch in between my fingers thinkin' it might be a good thing to keep with me.

Jest then I heard squeakin' comin' from the yard. I ran over to the window and looked down below at the cart with a long pine box set on the back. I had seen so many of them before.

I stuffed the pouch into my pocket and hurried downstairs. Mean ole Miss Noyes was causin' a rumpus with Mrs. Foster, who wouldn't go to the launderin' room. Polly was pokin' poor Mr. Hobbs with her stick.

I ducked behind the chairs and ran out into the back yard, hopin' that no one would see me. I followed our secret path through the lilac trees that were all dried up and brown. Mamma said if you take the time to smell them, you can detect their beauty long after they're gone.

After passin' through the apple orchard and field, I finally got to the woods. I started out slowly, but each step got quicker 'til I broke into the fastest run ever.

I reached the top of the hill and stopped at the edge of the trees to catch my breath. I looked down at the small stones, where Mamma visited her friends. There were a few strawberries left over from the birds and what I didn't pick the week before. I gobbled 'em up so fast that I didn't even taste 'em at first. I puckered up and spit the half-chewed berries onto the ground. Mamma said that you must pick them at the right time, or they'll leave a bitter taste in your mouth. She was right.

The squeaky cart got louder. I ran and hid behind a giant pine. The creakin' stopped. I peeked out from behind the tree, hangin' onto the bark to keep from fallin'. Silas was standin' beside Prince, the biggest brown draft horse on the farm, while he talked to Charles and Big Ben Wallace. He took off his hat and stood very still.

They talked a bit more and shook hands before partin' ways. Silas climbed onto the cart and drove it in between the stones. He stopped and sat without movin' at all, jest starin' straight ahead.

He took the shovel from beside the box and started diggin' a hole. I watched for some time before goin' to see if there might be one or two sweet berries. Then I heard somethin'. I stopped chewin' and tiptoed over to the edge of the woods. Silas was by the hole with his hands in his pockets, whistlin' a song I thought I knew.

He took and slid the box all by himself into that hole he dug. I leaned against the rough bark on the tree, finished eatin' a handful of berries, and watched him through the curl that fell over my eye.

A twig snapped under my foot.

Silas looked. "Who's there?"

I didn't move.

"I heard you. Come on out." He stood with his hands on his hips.

I walked slowly down the hill with my head down, waitin' to git in a heap of trouble for bein' away from the farm and all.

"Samuel?" He was soakin' wet and breathin' hard.

"Yes, sir." I kept my eyes fixed on the yellow buttercups by my feet.

"How did you get here?"

"I went on our secret path. Mamma and I come here to pick berries, and she visits with Nellie and Patience and the others, and she teaches me birdsongs…" I stared at the wooden box down in the hole.

He leaned against the shovel not sayin' nothin'.

"Is Mamma in there?"

"Well…" One big tear fell on his shirt.

"Mamma says that jest 'cause we can't see them don't mean that they ain't with us." I couldn't look away from the box. I secretly hoped that she would open it and climb out.

Silas picked me up. "That's right, son." He pressed my head into his chest. His shirt smelled like wood and sweat.

I patted his shoulder. "Don't be afraid. She went to heaven to live with God and Nellie, my grandmother and grandfather, and the angels." I swallowed hard and believed hard.

He set me down on the seat of the cart. I wiggled from one side to the other. I hadn't ever sat on a cart before. I wondered what it might be like to ride or even hold on to the reins. I simmered down and returned to watchin' him dig and cry and wipe his face and dig some more.

He tossed the last shovel of dirt over Mamma's box. "Samuel, come here."

I hopped down from the cart and stood next to him. The birds sang louder than I remembered and the sky turned all sorts of blazin' colors as the sun set over Brown's Ridge. Mamma told me it was a canvas, and all of those who were in heaven painted it every night to remind us that love never dies.

Silas cleared his throat. "Dear God in Heaven."

I bowed my head and waited for the rest of the prayer. I thought that maybe he choked on one of them mosquitoes. I kept my head down and watched him with one eye.

He rubbed his hands over his face and took a good breath. "I pray that you bless this dear woman, Abigail Hodgdon. May she rest in peace. A-men."

"A-men." I swatted at a mosquito.

"Are you ready to go home?"

"Yeah." I looked to where the path disappeared behind the trees. "I better hurry, I ain't never gone in the dark." I hopped off the cart thinkin' it better to cry alone in the woods.

"Samuel." Silas took a hold of my arm. "Where are you goin'?"

"Home... on our secret path... you can't tell."

He crouched down and looked all peculiar. "You have a new home."

"I do?" I wondered if Aunt Sarah had arrived early.

"Ayuh, you're comin' home with me." He set me on the seat of the cart again and climbed up and sat next to me.

"I am?" We rocked back and forth as we rode along the deep ruts in the granite garden.

"Ayuh, to a home filled with love, son." He put his arm around me.

I looked at where Mamma lay beneath the earth near her friends and then across to her mother and father on the other side of the fence. "Did you know that in God's eyes, we're the same, no matter which side of the fence we're on?"

I reached into my pocket and pulled out the red-stained, crumpled handkerchief and held it up to my nose. It smelled like her. I ran my finger over the hole that covered part of the butterfly. I liked that the best.

Glossary

Abenakis and English Translation

⋅⊱⊰⊙ ⊙⊱⊰⋅

Asepihtegw – Ossipee, New Hampshire
Bitawbagok – Lake Champlain, Vermont
Kasko – Heron
Kchi alakws – Morning or Evening Star
Kmitôgwes – Thy Father
Mamijôla – Butterfly
Nanatasis – Hummingbird
Nigawes – My Mother
Nmitôgwes – My Father
Nokahigas – The month of June
Wawôbadenik – White Mountains Region
Wiwininebesaki – Lake Winnipesaukee, New Hampshire
Wnegigw – Otter

Laurent, Joseph. *New Familiar Abenakis and English Dialogues*. Vancouver: Global Language Press, 2006.

A Partial List of Those Buried at the Carroll County Pauper Cemetery Ossipee, New Hampshire c.1870 –

⊷⧟⊙ ⊙⧟⊷

The number of paupers buried at this site diminished greatly after the 1930's. The highest number recorded was approximately 75 between 1870 – 1880.

Though there are 298 numbered gravestones in this cemetery, the exact number and names of everyone buried is not known, as often times the paupers were buried with more than one body per grave. Therefore, it is likely that there are many more anonymous and lost souls buried in the earth here, whose names I cannot include. The 268 names that I have listed were found after extensive research. This book is a tribute to all of them, lost or found.

William White ~ Judith Clarke ~ Polly Ferguson ~ Huldah Burley ~ Lewis Sanborn ~ Rachel Moulton ~ Lydia Copp ~ David Weed ~ Susan Moody ~ Mary Wentworth ~ Betsey Dame ~ Eunice Eldridge ~ Thomas Weeks ~ Rebecah Weeks ~ Hollis Weeks ~ Betsey Sceggell ~ Nettie Conner ~ Joseph Danforth ~ Nancy Edgely ~ Sarah How ~ Martha Nute ~ Eunice Allen ~ William Love ~ Clarinda Wallace ~ Lydia Thompson ~ Eri Keniston ~ David Campprennell ~ Moses Copp ~ Jeremiah Cook ~ Isaac

Farrah ~ Mary Farrah ~ Edward Weeden ~ Michael Burkley ~ Jeremiah
Nay ~ Richard Nichols ~ Hannah Smith ~ Mary Hearth ~ Dolly Rogers
~ Albert Merrow ~ Samuel Brennan ~ James Grant ~ Anny A Carlton ~
Joseph Copp ~ Ann Conley ~ Sally Blake ~ Rosa Rice ~ George Brackett
~ John Hill ~ Mary Hill ~ Mahitable Odway ~ Lewis Prime ~ John
Spencer ~ James Flanders ~ Sally Hodgedon ~ Harriet Cook ~ Martha
Haines ~ Jonathan Bryant ~ Deborah Piper ~ William Stiles ~ Mary
Willey ~ Daniel Chandler ~ Hannah Campnell ~ Clemantine Fairfield
~ Lettie Few ~ Sophia Copp ~ Timothy Eastman ~ Sarah Staples ~
William Copp ~ Jane Guptile ~ Henry Tuksbury ~ Sarah Perkins ~
Abizil Doe ~ Joseph Blake ~ Emma Williams ~ Lewis Ricker ~ Hannah
Meader ~ Hannah Foss ~ Harriet Perkins ~ John McArthur ~ Luch
Gannet ~ Emily Harris ~ Edward Anger ~ Almira Burbank ~ Daniel
Allen ~ John Maleham ~ Sally Maxfield ~ Alan Foss ~ Joshua Fallington
~ Mary Norton ~ William Goswick ~ Lidie Witham ~ Jeremiah Smith
~ Elijah Tibbetts ~ Sarah Dury ~ Lydia Welch ~ Elizer Mitter ~ Sally
Quimby ~ Mary Garland ~ Jonathan Trask ~ Joshua Peavey ~ Lillian
Foss ~ George Quimby, Jr. (Archie) ~ Cyrus Harriman ~ Josiah Merrill
~ Jane Drew ~ Benjamin Pray ~ Nancy Copp ~ Eliza Roberts ~ John
Hubbard ~ John A.H. Copp ~ James Chamberlain ~ Nathaniel Burbank
~ Samuel Blackey ~ Loring Danforth ~ Mary W. Blood ~ Baby Bagley
~ Baby Tibbetts ~ Alvin Bryant ~ Laura Hutchins ~ Ida M Wentworth
~ Jessie Keniston ~ Richard Hutchins ~ Nancy Woodhouse ~ Henry H.
Doe ~ James Murphy ~ Mrs. Lewis *Indian Woman* ~ Jonathan Jennes ~
Polly Allan ~ Johanas Huse ~ John McVey ~ Archie Quimby ~ John Allen
~ Sarah Worthen ~ Capt. Geo Quimby ~ Levi Hill ~ Rosie Edwards
~ James McLean ~ Sarah Whittier ~ Frank Bedell ~ Charles Durgin ~
John Ryan ~ Mary Hanson ~ Emmanueal Silas ~ William Dyer ~ Lillian
May Felch ~ Joseph A Stuart ~ Charles Bennett ~ Page Allard ~ Ellen
Quimby ~ Olive Anderson ~ Adelaide Walker ~ Lillian M Norton ~
Mary Wallace ~ John Evans ~ Mary Allen ~ Belinda Hubbard ~ Charles
Goldsmith ~ Fanny Peavey ~ Charles Graham ~ John Wallace ~ Kate
Jones ~ Charles Jenness ~ Nettie B Carter ~ Susan Brown ~ Andrew

Wentworth ~ Samuel Sargent ~ Nellie Dyer ~ James Hanson ~ Josiah Morrison ~ Roxanna Jackson ~ Hannah M. York ~ Daniel McGinnis ~ Ira E. Wentworth ~ Adah Tibbetts ~ Drusilla Wallace ~ James M. Bennett ~ Eleazer Thompson ~ Abbie Hill ~ Frank Wilkinson ~ Richard Dinzey ~ Unknown Baby ~ Mark George ~ Joel Perkins ~ Mattie Kimball ~ Mary Jane Emery ~ John Glidden ~ Albert Pennell ~ Augusta Thurley ~ Berthana Wallace ~ Luke Jenness ~ Andrew Sullivan ~ Julia Davis ~ Frank Heath ~ Charles Poisson ~ Julia Burleigh ~ Berry Leonard ~ Patrick McLaughlin ~ James Carter ~ Abbie Corson ~ James Tulley ~ James F. Horne ~ David Frye ~ Hiram Henderson ~ John Copp ~ Mary Ellen Foss ~ Patrick McCarty ~ George H. Floyd ~ John Dolloff ~ Phillip Crotte ~ Diantha Buckley ~ Emma Hill ~ Byron Copp ~ Charles Mehan ~ Roy Ludger ~ Michael Moran ~ James Cobb ~ Isaac Harriman ~ Georgia Haddock ~ Mary Green ~ Gilbert Goodblood ~ Bertha O'Hare ~ David Mason ~ Mary E. Drake ~ Abner Allard ~ Gaynor Child ~ George Hutchins ~ William Cloutman ~ Ebenezer Cook ~ Timothy S. Clifford ~ Sarah Kenison ~ James Gould ~ William Colby ~ Mabel F. Deland ~ James R Bryant ~ Emma Carter ~ Charles E. Corson ~ Frank Drew ~ Daniel Fitzgerald ~ Augusta A. Corson ~ Alonzo Carter ~ Frank Coleman ~ John Murphy ~ George Berry ~ Sarah J. Berry ~ Amelia McCloud ~ George Ballou ~ Peter Thibedau ~ Edgar M. Doe ~ Jonathan Colbath ~ Sewell Moody ~ Allen F. Larabee ~ George Eastman ~ Lafayette Hanson ~ Joseph H. Moulton ~ Ellen Brown ~ Weston A Johnson ~ Lettie Hanson ~ Joseph Mason ~ Dan Brown ~ George Allen ~ Bert Leavitt ~ Hattie Kenison ~ Jason M. Hannan ~ Dorothy Howard ~ Lawrence Stevens ~ Eddie E. Wade ~ Timothy Lee ~

About the Author

Mj Pettengill is an author, lecturer, and American historian. Her focus is on New England history, cultural and social narrative, and intergenerational studies.

As a freelance writer, she has contributed to numerous magazines and is a facilitator of writing and transformative arts workshops.

She is a cornetist and performs Civil War Era music and presents oral narratives throughout the Northeast.

Mj lives on a small farm in the White Mountains of New Hampshire, where she is also a wildcraft practitioner, aligned with her passion for nature and exploring the ancient healing traditions, customs, and folklore of her Abenaki ancestors.

She holds degrees in history, psychology, and an M.F.A. in creative writing.

⊷⊷⊷ ⊶⊶⊶

Made in the USA
Coppell, TX
15 July 2020